Sker House

By C.M. Saunders

Chapter 1:

Welcome to Sker

"What's the name of this place again?" Lucy asked.

"Sker House," replied Dale, giving her a sidewise glance as he drove. He loved the way the breeze ruffled her long, dark hair, causing a few rebellious strands to fall over her eyes which she expertly flicked away.

They took an exit off the M4 motorway, and continued toward their destination. The air was slightly chilly, but the weather clear and sunny. A perfect spring day. The sound of the car's wheels on the smooth tarmac mingled effortlessly with the muted strains of vintage Green Day issuing forth from the speakers of Dale's battered old Vauxhall Astra. One of his guilty pleasures. The sun streamed through the trees and glinted off the windscreen as they wound their way carefully through a maze-like sequence of narrow country lanes, Dale gripping the wheel tightly. He was used to driving in the city. Navigating lanes carved out of the earth for horses and carts half a millennia ago called for an entirely different skill set.

"Sker House. Right. How could I forget? And the place is a guest house now, right?"

"Right," Dale confirmed, applying a little nervous pressure on the brake as they approached yet another harsh bend. "I did a little digging around on the Internet. Apparently, it was first built as a monastery over nine hundred years ago. Then it was turned into a farmhouse for a couple of centuries and after that, you know, shit happens. It fell into 'disrepair,' as the website says. Which I guess means it went to shit. Some new owners bought it a couple of years ago, and turned it into a seaside inn. It's taken them this long to make the place liveable again."

"Is it even open for business? I mean, you did check that, didn't you? I don't wanna drive all this way if the place isn't open yet. And I don't fancy spending the night in the car."

"Technically you aren't driving, I am. Worst case scenario we'll just find another haunted hotel to stay in. There must be loads around here." Going back to the place he was born always stirred up a complex set of emotions in Dale. Childhood memories of a time when life was carefree and simple flooded back, and he was happy to bask in their glory for a while. But they were inexorably linked with all the bad stuff that followed, and he was powerless to stop his mind being pulled in that direction.

"You know what I mean," Lucy protested, unamused. "This little jaunt of yours is still taking up my valuable time and energy. I don't want to come all this way for nothing."

"Ours. This little jaunt of ours. This is as much for your benefit as mine, remember. You're the one obsessed with ghosts and stuff. But to answer your question yeah, it's open. I talked to the owner yesterday. He's very excited to have us stay."

"And why would he be so excited by the prospect of a couple of students?"

"Our money is as good as anyone else's. And lets just say I was a little economical with the truth..."

Lucy tutted and shook her head. "What did you tell him, moron?"

"Hey, there's no need for the abuse. I didn't tell him anything much. I just implied that we are journalists going there to write a feature for a big national magazine. I didn't specifically say those words. I mean, I just told him we wanted to do an article about Sker and let the guy's ego do the rest. I convinced him it would be good publicity. Something every new business needs. In the end, he even gave us a discount on the room."

"Dale! What is wrong with you? We do NOT work for a big national magazine! We're journalism students doing a write-up for a pissy campus rag nobody reads!"

"Hey! Solent News isn't a pissy campus rag. It's kind of a national publication. We could send copies anywhere. That makes it national. Hell, that makes us international. Intergalactic, even. We could smuggle a copy onto the next space shuttle and be the first magazine in space. How would that be for a PR stunt? There's a difference between lying and bending the truth. Like I said, I just wasn't entirely honest. It's what journo's do, Lucy. It gets results. In this case, it got us a discount on the room, didn't it?"

"S'pose so," Lucy relented. "And the place is supposed to be haunted, yeah?"

"It's about as haunted as haunted gets, baby! Haven't you ever heard about the poor Maid of Sker?"

"Can't say I have. Was she your last girlfriend?"

"Ha-ha, very funny. Actually, no. For your information, the Maid of Sker is the ghost that haunts the place."

"She has a name?"

"Of course she does. And this is actually a lot more than just a ghost story."

"Really?" suddenly interested, Lucy turned in her seat to face him, her seatbelt pulling tight against its constraint. "Okay, consider my curiosity piqued. How do you know so much about it?"

"When I was a kid my folks used to take me on holiday to Porthcawl, which is only a few miles down the road from. Superstitious bunch, the Welsh. The Maid of Sker is just one popular legend."

"So are you gonna share it with me or what?"

Dale hesitated. "Nope. Not yet. I don't really know all the details well enough. I couldn't do it justice. I'm pretty sure the people at Sker will do a much better job of, er, scaring the pants off you than me. Unfortunately. I'll leave it to them."

Lucy groaned. "Okay, have it your way. Tell me another story instead, if this part of the world has so many."

"Well, Kenfig Pool is nearby. It has an interesting legend associated with it. Not exactly a ghost story, but interesting all the same. Wanna hear it?"

"Sure, hit me."

"Once upon a time, long, long ago, there was a town where one day a peasant killed and robbed a local lord, to get money to impress this girl he fancied. He used his ill-gotten gains to pay for a lavish wedding ceremony. But at the reception, a strange booming voice came out of the sky and told all the guests that vengeance would come with the ninth generation of the victim's family."

"That hardly seems fair."

"Such is life. Time went by and when the ninth generation finally appeared, a huge torrent of water came from the sea and engulfed the whole town. Hundreds drowned. The pool is still there, and they say that at certain times you can still hear church bells ringing from under the water."

"That's more like a fairytale than a ghost story," Lucy said, unimpressed.

"Not exactly. Because under certain conditions, people say parts of the old submerged village are still visible beneath the surface of the water."

Dale neglected to mention the fact that when an investigation was carried out, nothing more was found in the lake than the remains of an old Victorian boat house. No sense shattering the illusion.

"They say most legends have a grain of truth in them," Lucy said. "However unlikely they might seem. Things like that happen all the time. Floods, tidal waves, underwater eruptions."

"Not in Wales," Dale said as he slowed the car to a crawl in order to take a particularly nasty bend.

"Maybe not recently. But the story could be based on much older events. Things that happened hundreds or even thousands of years ago, and then became woven into the local folklore. On the other hand, it could be metaphorical."

"Anything can be metaphorical if you want to go down that road. Maybe when we tie up this Sker house business we can launch an investigation into Kenfig Pool. Anyway, it'll be fun working together on this article, won't it? Me being the wordsmith and you the... the what?"

"Um... I'll be the Photographic Director, please."

"Is that even a real job?"

"It is now."

*

Sker House, tall and majestic, stood overlooking the dunes a few hundred yards from where the sea met the land. From a distance, it looked more like a stately home than a guesthouse. Served by a single narrow road that terminated in a tiny rectangular car park, it was the only building in sight apart from a few crumbling barns and outhouses scattered across the nearby fields. Looking at it, the main building called to mind a single rotting tooth sticking out of an ageing gum and if Lucy let her imagination run wild, which she was prone to doing, the shape of the cove in which the house was situated even had the rounded appearance of a mouth.

Sections of the imposing, grandiose structure had obviously recently been renovated, and though it wasn't the crumbling Victorian country pile she'd hoped for, it had somehow managed to maintain its character. Four stories high with masses of green ivy snaking up the walls like long, probing fingers, the only thing that looked like a new addition was the small reception porch protruding rudely from the main building which looked almost like an afterthought.

Dale parked in the empty car park, then they retrieved their luggage from the boot and made their way down the short cobbled path leading to the entrance. Once inside, they saw that the porch opened into what was, to all intents and purposes, an old fashioned-style pub with a hardwood floor and oak-panelled walls adorned with brooding oil paintings of stormy seas and old sailing ships. The maritime theme was hardly original, nor unexpected, but the place had a warm, homely atmosphere, reinforced by the smell of stale beer that hung in the air.

"Awesome!" exclaimed Dale, obviously delighted at the sight of a well-stocked bar after a two-hour drive.

There appeared to be no conventional check-in point, so they left their luggage at the door and headed for the bar, where a slightly overweight, jovial-looking man wearing jeans and a white t-shirt was grinning at them expectantly.

Must be the landlord, thought Lucy. She hoped so, because apart from him and an old man with long wispy hair and a thick white beard sitting at one of the tables nursing a pint glass and reading a newspaper, the place was completely deserted.

"Alright, but!" greeted the man behind the bar in a strong South Wales accent.

"But what?" asked Lucy, perplexed.

"It's just what local people say, means 'friend.' Like 'mate' or 'bruv,' up in Sarfampton, innit," Dale explained helpfully. She knew how excited he was to be home. Or at least, near home. She couldn't imagine what it must be like to leave everything behind, your family and friends, and move to what was effectively a different country.

"Right. Got it," said Lucy, as if trying to memorize some priceless nugget of information that could serve her well in the future.

"Do you 'ave a reservation, like?" the man behind the bar asked, wiping his hands on the front of his t-shirt and making a clear effort to look professional. The fact that he had to try so hard was slightly unnerving.

"Like?" asked Lucy. The landlord glared at her, a thick vein pulsing in his temple and little beads of sweat standing out on his forehead.

Dale stepped in and answered the question. "Erm, yes we have a reservation. Two people, two nights."

"Good, good! Well, I'm James Machen. The landlord around 'ere. You can just call me Machen. Or Mach for short, if 'ew like. Most people do. Let me just get the book out..." He ducked behind the counter for a few seconds and popped back up holding a large leather-bound notebook and ballpoint pen. The pen immediately tumbled from his grasp and he stooped to retrieve it, groaning as he did so.

"Not gone digital yet?" said Lucy with what she hoped was a sympathetic smile. The only time she had ever stayed in a hotel before was on holiday last summer in Crete, and it was nothing like this.

"Digital?" the landlord said, returning the smile. "Not entirely. There's a computer with Internet access in the games room for the guests to use, and I do the accounts on my little laptop in the office. Easier to keep records that way. But I'm old-school myself, like. This notebook is a lot easier to use than a computer. For me it is, anyway. Plus, whatever's in here doesn't get lost or stolen by... them people, you know, the geeky criminals you hear so much about on the news. What do they call them? Cyber wookies? Computer whackers?"

"Cyber crooks and computer hackers?" offered Lucy.

"Yes! Them ones. Clever buggers, they are. I'm better off keeping my records in my notebook. All in black n' white. Or blue sometimes, depending on what pen I have to hand." The landlord chuckled heartily, resting a hand on his ample stomach as he did so. "Hmm... let's see... Dale Morgan and Lucy Kerr?"

They nodded their heads in confirmation.

"So where're you folks from?"

"Lucy's a Southampton girl and I'm from Wales, originally. A village called New Tredegar in the Rhymney Valley. I left to go to uni," explained Dale.

"Oh aye, well you haven't lost your accent yet, boyo!"

"It's funny," he said. "Welsh people usually say I sound English, but English people always go on about how Welsh I sound. I guess I have an identity crisis going on."

"So who would you play rugby for then, Wales or England?" Machen the landlord's tone suddenly turned serious and his eyes narrowed. It seemed like an odd question. At least, not one of the first things you ask someone when you meet them. But Lucy understood. Dale had already filled her in on the Welsh obsession with rugby. Here, it wasn't just a game, it was more like a religion.

Lucy couldn't help smiling when Dale mischievously turned the tables on the landlord. "England, of course," he said.

Machen looked offended, placing his hands on his hips and puffing out his chest in exasperation, "And why's that, like?"

"Because I'd never get in the Welsh side, they are way too good! My mum could probably get a game for England."

It took a second or two to sink in, then realizing he had just been duped the landlord laughed uproariously, reached out and shoved Dale hard enough to push him off balance. Now seemingly at ease, his curiosity came to the fore. "So what's your business here? You're the journalists, right? So is it just work, or a little break you're after?"

"A bit of both," replied Dale. "My friend Lucy has never been to Wales before, and I thought she should visit God's Country at least once."

"I've always wanted to come, though," interjected Lucy, hopefully giving her credibility a boost. "I heard its beautiful here."

"We also want to do a story about Sker House," continued Dale. "I'm the writer, Lucy takes pictures."

"I see. Proper little double act, then. So tell me, did you do your research, like? What do you know about Sker?" Machen's eyes darted from Dale to Lucy and back again.

"We don't actually know that much," Dale said. "Just what we could find online. We decided to come with an open mind and were kinda hoping you could fill in the blanks for us. When you have time, of course."

"Be a pleasure. What kind of article are you doing? Is it about starting a small business? The inn-keeping trade? Restoration? This is a Grade One listed building, you know."

"Is it really? To be honest we don't actually know what direction the article will take yet," Dale lied, probably not wanting to show his hand too early. "When did you open for business, Mr Machen?"

"Like I said, you can call me Machen. 'Mister' is just for the tax man. I reckon he skims so much money off me every month he should call ME mister!" The landlord erupted with laughter again before making a visible effort to compose himself. "Well, let's see... I bought the place over two years ago. In a hell of a state it was then. Nobody had lived here since the sixties, see. We officially opened on St David's Day. The first of March."

The look he gave Lucy told her the last scrap of information was added just for the benefit of the English tourist. "So have you had much business yet?" she asked, struggling to keep her barbs under wraps.

"To tell you the truth, it's been quiet so far," the landlord said. "But we expected that. In this business you have to build up a reputation. That takes time, it does. What we need is a bit of publicity, you know?" He winked as if the three of them had just hatched a foolproof plan for world domination.

"Well, hopefully we can help with that mister... sorry, Machen." Dale corrected himself just in time. "We'll definitely try and turn a few heads this way."

"Cheers, I'd appreciate that. Most hotels and guesthouses are only busy from May through to October. But we wanted to open a couple of months early to get everything in working order. Iron out any wrinkles, like. The only other guest at the minute is Old Rolly over there..." the landlord nodded at the old man with the wispy white hair and beard, who still hadn't looked up from his newspaper. "Though he's not really a guest. Lives here, he does. Stays in his room or the bar most of the day, then walks on the beach mornings and evenings. He's harmless enough."

Lucy and Dale glanced over at the old man sitting at the table. Whenever someone was described as being 'harmless' the implication was that in actual fact, the opposite was true. Both heads snapped back when the landlord cleared his throat loudly to win back their attention.

"So yes, we've already had some bookings for the summer..." Machen continued. "In fact, we're booked solid for the last week of July and the first week of August. The old Miner's Holiday. The pits may be closed but people still need a holiday, don't they? Hikers, fishing parties and couples like yourselves mostly."

"Oh, we're not a couple," Lucy quickly interrupted.

"A couple of what? Miners?" The landlord laughed again. "Didn't think so. None left, see, after Thatcher had her way. Old cow."

"I mean we're not a couple. We're just friends and colleagues." Lucy was growing tired of this guy's performance and was feeling an increasing need for a quiet lie down.

"Really?" Machen exclaimed, eyes widening. He must have sensed the familiarity between them and assumed it was of an intimate nature. "In that case you'll be wanting a twin room, rather than the double, will you? Just let me know if you want to change it back at any point." He smirked at Dale, who blushed right on cue.

"So er, is this a family-run business? You and your wife?" Dale asked.

Lucy got the impression the question was designed more to change the subject and save what was left of his self-esteem than a genuine desire to know the answer.

Now it was Machen's turn to look awkward, and Lucy couldn't help but feel a small twinge of satisfaction. Those barbs. "Erm, not exactly. Not at the moment, anyway. My wife's... gone away for a while."

The ambiguous nature of the answer and the tone of his voice alerted both Lucy's journalistic instincts and her female intuition. Judging by the look that came over Dale's face, the response triggered red flags within him, too. There must be some kind of problem with the marriage. A serious one. Either that, or the happy-go-lucky landlord had murdered his spouse and buried her in the sand dunes. That would be a story.

"Most of the time it's just me and Champ," Machen continued. He motioned to a spot on the floor in the corner of the

13

room where a tired-looking German Shepherd lay. His coat so closely matched the colour of the wood floor that until then he had gone unnoticed. At the sound of his name, the dog raised his head questioningly, offering them a first look at his droopy, bloodshot eyes, before giving a limp swish of the tale and laying his head back down on his paws.

"He's the guard dog," said Machen proudly.

The poor thing looks washed out, Lucy thought. More of a couch potato than a guard dog. If an intruder broke in it was doubtful whether Champ would be able to muster enough energy to fart let alone raise the alarm.

The landlord must have read her thoughts. "He might not look like much, but if anyone so much as sets foot behind that there bar he'd bite a leg off, he would."

"No doubt," Lucy said, not at all convinced. "So you and Champ run the place by yourselves?"

"We can't do everything, so we have help. Mrs Watkins and her daughter Izzy drive in from Newton and are here from ten or eleven 'til eight most days. Between them they prepare lunch and dinner, take care of the cleaning, laundry, shopping, and anything else that needs doing, like. You'll see young Izzy behind the bar a lot. She likes bar duty cos she can just sit there and play with her bloody phone."

"Oh, you do food here too?" Dale was always thinking about his next meal.

"Have to, really. Being so far away from the nearest restaurants, our guests wouldn't eat unless they ate here or went onto the beach and caught their own grub. Most of our food is home-cooked by Mrs Watkins. The plan is to grow our own veg before too long. You know, orgasmically."   There was a pause while the landlord reconsidered what he had said. "Organically, I mean. Lunch is between twelve and two by the way, and dinner is five 'til seven. I do breakfast between seven and nine. Just bacon, sausage and eggs. Or you can have toast and cereal if you'd rather. There's some chocolate, crisps and nuts behind the bar if you just want a snack and if you have any special requests, let me know and I'll see what I can do."

"That won't be necessary. A fry up would be lovely. We're not vegetarian or anything."

"Glad to hear it," replied the landlord, "Young 'un's like you need the protein. Let me see... what else? Bar's open eleven 'til eleven and the games room's next door. In there you'll find a pool table, dartboard, jukebox, some books and a karaoke machine, if you like that sort of thing. If you don't, all the rooms have Sky telly. They have en suites, too, so you never have come out if you don't want to. We get the Times, the Independent, the Mirror, and Wales on Sunday delivered every week. Sundays, obviously. Have you ever tried buying a Wales on Sunday any other day of the week?"

"I'm pretty sure I can speak for us both and say no," Dale said.

"Well, you'd have a job, though you might be able to find a shop somewhere still selling last weeks!" Machen laughed again. "In peak season we'll probl'y get newspapers every day, but at the minute the only person that reads 'em is Old Rolly and it takes him all bloody week, any way."

The landlord handed them two keys. "I lock the front door at midnight. If you come in after that, you'll have to use the side entrance. That's the big key. Don't forget to lock the door behind you. It's quiet around here, but you never know. The other one's your room key. I'll put you in twenty-three, on the second floor. Like I said, let me know if you want to change to a double at any point."

"Okay, er, thanks. We'll go and get ourselves sorted out," said Dale as he and Lucy headed for the stairs.

"Oh, one more thing," the landlord called after them. "Welcome to Sker House!"

They each mumbled their thanks and made their getaway.

Newly renovated or not, the wooden staircase creaked like it was three-hundred years old under the combined weight of Dale, Lucy and their luggage. Maybe it was three-hundred years old. Or more. Who knew what 'renovations' actually meant? It would make sense to keep as much of the original building in place as possible to keep costs down.

At the top of the stairs a door opened into a corridor, and on the carpeted floor outside each room lay a little mat with a picture of a dragon on it. Beneath the dragon were the words, Croeso y Cymru.

"What does that mean?" asked Lucy.

15

"'Welcome to Wales.' In Welsh," replied Dale.

"Well I didn't think it was Chinese."

Dale, who must be used to her scathing wit by now, didn't register any reaction as he counted off the room numbers. "Twenty-one... twenty-two... here it is! Twenty-three."

"Oh, joy." That sarcastic streak again. She would have to work on that.

Dale used the key to open the door and flung it wide with an over-dramatic, "Ta-dah!"

The room was small, but nicely decorated and spotlessly clean. It boasted a large ornate dressing table set against a wall, complete with mirror, the sight of which made Lucy whoop with delight. A small desk and chair had been placed near the only window, and two neatly-made single beds were separated by a nightstand on which stood a reading lamp. A portable television was fixed to the wall opposite the beds, and an electric kettle was placed on the floor near a socket along with two white mugs full of various complimentary sachets. The walls were cream-coloured, and the carpet and curtains light brown. The smell of newness was so intense that Lucy could easily believe they were the first guests to ever use the room.

As promised, there was a tiny en-suite bathroom, just big enough for a toilet, washbasin and shower cubicle. Crisp fresh towels hung from a rail, and a selection of toiletries lined the only shelf; two disposable toothbrushes, a tiny tube of toothpaste, shower gel, shampoo, even moisturising lotion.

After a brief inspection, Lucy was more than impressed, "Seems like a decent choice, dude! I'm liking all the free stuff."

Ever the realist, Dale replied, "Well, it isn't technically free, is it? It's just all included with the price of the room."

"Yeah, yeah, okay Mr Rainy Day," Lucy said as she watched Dale unpack and start setting up his laptop at the desk near the window. "Hey, do you think we'll be able to get Wi-Fi this far from civilization?"

"I don't see why not. Anyway, didn't the man say there's a computer downstairs? Wouldn't be much point if it wasn't hooked up to the Internet."

"Oh yeah." She was looking forward to some time away from Southampton, but the thought of complete isolation filled

Lucy with dread. She needed human interaction, even if it was via a screen, and was accustomed to having her senses constantly bombarded with bright lights and white noise. Truth be told, she was already finding the stillness of the countryside a little disconcerting. Knowing she could still use Facebook and Twitter made her feel a lot better

Get a grip, she told herself. It wasn't like she was running away or hiding. She just wanted a break. Obviously, she was aware of how it would look if her now-ex boyfriend, Steve, found out where she was, or who she was with. He didn't believe in platonic relationships and would just think she'd bunked off for a dirty weekend at the seaside with some other guy. But that was his problem, and he was in no position to criticize anybody.

She lay her compact pink suitcase on the bed nearest the door and opened it wide. All the things she thought she would need that weekend were neatly packed inside. There was no evening wear, bikini or beach towel. It wasn't sunbathing weather and she had already been warned that there were no clubs or fancy restaurants nearby. This was supposed to be a working weekend, so she'd brought only practical clothing and camera gear.

Her and Steve's relationship wasn't officially over. But only because there had never been an official relationship. That much was obvious now. She had only been a trinket to him, and he probably had a dozen other trinkets to play with. At first she had been more attracted to sense of reckless abandon that seemed to radiate from him than his rugged good looks. It was exciting. But then she found out about his wife and kid. The dangerous, edgy facade was just that. A facade.
Well, that's what you get for getting involved with a married man. If she'd known, she wouldn't have gone near him. But he wasn't about to tell her, was he? The whole experience hurt Lucy deeply. How could she have been so stupid?

It also triggered some kind of existential crisis. What, exactly, did she want from life? Where was she going?

She didn't know the answers yet, but accepted the fact that she wasn't a teenager any more, and didn't have much time to waste. She had to get serious and apply herself to something, get on track, or she would end up forever floundering in a pit of obscurity. She had already wasted far too much time wallowing in

Steve's possessive clutches and missed too many other opportunities, not to mention lectures and seminars. In order to graduate she had to not only turn in her final assignment, of which this Sker House feature was a major component, but get a mark over ninety percent. The Head of Department told her in no uncertain terms that if the paper failed, so did she.

No pressure, then.

Chapter 2:

On the Scent

After much fussing around, Dale finally succeeded in establishing a Wi-Fi connection on his laptop. It was a weak signal, constantly flitting between a healthy four bars to a sickly one bar, but it was a connection just the same. He wasn't even sure how much he would actually need to use the Internet during their stay at Sker beyond periodically checking his email. He wasn't really one for social networking, that was Lucy's department. He was baffled by some people's fascination with constantly telling everyone else in the world what they were doing. As if anyone really gave a shit what you were having for lunch. It was the word processor he needed, and that didn't even require an internet connection. He opened up a blank Word document and quickly tapped out: Ghostly goings-on at Sker House.

He'd have to think of something better than that, but it would do as a working title. Then he retrieved a pencil and notebook from his rucksack. He preferred writing longhand when making notes, and even when interviewing people. He felt more connected that way, only using his digital Dictaphone as a safeguard. There were certainly advantages to using modern recording equipment. Not least that they looked a lot more professional and minimized the danger of misquoting someone. But Dale was old-school. He enjoyed the rustic feel of lead on paper. It felt more tangible and substantial. Plus, pencils never ran out battery. He wanted to get an early interview with Machen the landlord in the bag. Hopefully, he could fit in several separate sessions during their stay and splice together the best parts.

"I'm going to get the low-down from the landlord. Back soon," Dale said.

"Okay. Knock yourself out," a mildly-irritated Lucy replied as she fussed with her suitcase. "I'll follow you down later to get some snaps. Need to unpack first."

Dale didn't know what had gotten in to her lately. She seemed even more unapproachable than usual. It might just be her time of the month, but something told him it was more than that.

"Sure thing."

Dale went back downstairs to the bar. As he entered, Champ the German Shepherd lifted his head off the floor to see who the new arrival was and sniffed the air. Satisfied there was no imminent danger, he allowed his head to flop back down again onto the hard wood floor. Machen was still hovering behind the bar, and the old man was still sitting at his table hunched over the newspaper.

"Um, Mr Machen?" Dale asked tentatively.

"For the last time, it's just Machen."

"Oh right, sorry. If you aren't too busy, I was wondering if could I could get a quick interview for our, er, magazine?"

The little man's chest swelled almost visibly, "Interview? With me, like? Okay! Never done an interview before. This'll be my first one. After it gets printed, I'm going to frame it and stick it up in the bar."

"I'll send you a copy," Dale promised. "Do you mind if I take notes while we talk?"

"No, no. If that's what you do, go ahead. Who is it you work for again?"

"It's national publication called, er, Solent News..."

"Solent News?" Machen the landlord replied. "Never heard of it. What's that about, then?"

"It's about lots of things Mr. Machen. Sorry, Machen. Current affairs. Anything newsworthy. And you and Sker House are certainly that. We really like what you've done here." Dale had learned quite early that when interviewing someone, flattery can be a powerful tool.

"Er, ta very much, like. Solent News, is it? I get the news part, but what does Solent mean?"

"The Solent is the stretch of water off the south coast of England, between Southampton and the Isle of Wight," Dale said, laying his notebook and pencil out in preparation.

"Oh, right." Machen replied, as if he had known that all along.

"I have a digital recorder upstairs," Dale said, trying to put Machen at ease. "But I like to do things the old-fashioned way. A bit like you and your guest book. Must be a Welsh thing. Are you ready?"

The landlord took an over-dramatic deep breath and said, "I'm ready."

"So you've owned Sker House for over two years now. Is that right?"

"Yes. That's right."

"Have you ever experienced anything... out of the ordinary here? Anything that you would call supernatural or paranormal?"

The landlord's face immediately darkened. "What kind of bloody first question is that?"

Scrambling, Dale said, "Given what we already know about the history of the place, its a legitimate one."

"And what do you already know, exactly? What have you heard, like?"

Dale wasn't expecting such an angry reaction, nor was he expecting his question to be answered with another question, and was hopelessly unprepared. "I'm sorry if the question offends you, but the legend of the Maid of Sker is quite well-known. I was wondering if you'd come across her at all."

"The Maid of Sker? Is that what you came here to talk about? "The landlord's eyes narrowed still further as he looked Dale up and down. "You know, come to think of it, you look awful young to be a journalist. More like a student, I suspect." His eyes bored into Dale's, searching for an admission of guilt.

Dale tried to stonewall his facial expressions, but was powerless to prevent a red flush brightening his cheeks. Playing the percentages he stayed silent, allowing Machen time to continue, hoping that he would. Eventually, he did.

"I don't see what this has to do with your story, but if you must know, then yes. I don't know if you'd call them supernatural, or para.. para..."

"Paranormal?"

"Yeah, that. Thing is, strange things happen everywhere, like, don't they? Not just here. It's a funny old world we live in."

"It certainly is," Dale agreed. "But would you mind giving us a few examples of what you've experienced?"

"I suppose I could. Though I don't know whether I should or not. What if you print all this stuff in the, what you call it? Solent Newspaper."

"Solent News."

"Yeah, Solent Views, or whatever. What if you say something in there that scares away all the punters? There's me out of a job and owing a fortune to the creditors. This is a new business, you know. I can't have any negative publicity."

He wanted to ask what guests the landlord was referring to as the place was empty, but instead Dale smiled reassuringly and said, "That won't happen. It's true what they say. Any kind of publicity is good publicity. Even if we did publish stories about supernatural occurrences at Sker House, the place would be swarming with visitors in no time at all. Ghost hunting is big. People pay a fortune to stay at haunted locations hoping for some kind of experience."

"They do, do they?"

"Absolutely."

"But some of this stuff is... private. You know? We... I... wouldn't want it splashed all over the bloody papers, like. Whether it attracts visitors or not."

"I completely understand, but this isn't the Daily Mirror read by millions of people every day. It has a much lower circulation than that. Unfortunately. But if it makes you feel better, we'll let you have copy approval before we go to press. Fair?"

"What's that?"

"Copy approval means we'll let you read over what we write before it's published, and if there's anything you don't like, we'll change it."

The landlord considered this for a few moments, then said, "I suppose that's fair enough... You're going to think I'm mental, though. If I get into this, I mean."

"I can assure you, whatever you say, nobody is going to think you're mental." Dale tried to sound convincing, and resisted adding, 'because they probably already think you are.'

There was another long pause while the landlord composed himself. Finally, he continued, "Okay, okay. I'll tell you. It's not so much what you can see and touch, but what you can feel. You know what I mean?"

Dale didn't know what the man meant, but nodded encouragingly.

"At first I thought it was just the stress of everything. But after a while I came to realize there was more to it than that. Sker House seems to suck all the energy out of you and just puts you in a bad mood."

Dale almost groaned out loud. Nobody would be interested in an article about a place where the proprietor was in a bad mood.

Where was the story in that? He needed good, hard, meaty copy. Gruesome murders, restless spirits, witch trials, werewolves, vampires, or any combination of the above.

Machen must have sensed Dale's disappointment. "Look, I told you it's hard to explain, okay?"

"Sure, I understand," Dale lied. "So have you or the staff ever actually seen or heard anything out of the ordinary? Anything specific?"

"And how would you define ordinary? Is there any such thing? This world is anything but ordinary, lad."

That was a fair comment. Dale was beginning to feel that the fragile bond between interviewer and interviewee was in danger of being severed completely. Irreparably so. There was more. He could tell. And right now, the landlord was probably having an internal dialogue about how much he could safely say. Dale decided to stay calm and see what developed. The worst thing you can do is push interview subjects into a corner, because they always came out fighting.

"If you've done your research like you say you have, then you'd know there's a lot of history attached to this place."

"Yes, indeed."

"Over the years people have seen many, many strange things here and hereabouts. You say you're familiar with the Maid of Sker legend?"

"A little," replied Dale with a shrug. He actually knew more than a little, but needed Machen to tell him the story, not the other way around.

Right on cue, Lucy appeared, gliding silently through the door mouthing, "What did I miss?"

Machen appeared not to notice the new arrival. Instead, he slipped into an obviously well-rehearsed raconteur routine, one he probably used on any tourist or out of towner who expressed an interest, and undoubtedly a few who didn't. Over the years, he'd almost perfected the technique, his sing-song Welsh lilt bringing the classic tale to life.

"In the Eighteenth Century, Sker House belonged to a wealthy landowner by the name of Isaac Williams," Machen started. "He had a daughter named Elizabeth. A very beautiful girl, by all accounts. She fell in love with a local minstrel called

24

Thomas Evans, but her father was very strict. Fathers were in them days, see. He didn't approve of the romance and locked poor Elizabeth in her room, upstairs in this very house, until she agreed to marry someone her father picked out for her instead. A man by the name of Kirkhouse."

"He sounds like a nasty piece of work," Dale chipped in.

"Isaac Williams? Oh, yeah. Had a reputation, he did."

"A reputation for what?"

"Always getting his own way I s'pose is the simple way of putting it. He had friends in high places see, magistrates and that. That's how he got to be so powerful. The story goes that he kept an old plough on his land. If he had any kind of disagreement with a neighbour, he would arrange for that plough to 'disappear' and be found on the neighbour's property. Isaac would then have them charged with theft and his magistrate friends would do the rest. Sometimes, the poor neighbour ended up in jail. But more likely they would have to pay a fine, and be happy to do so in exchange for their freedom. Either way, Isaac got what he wanted, whatever that may have been, the magistrates got a lump of extra cash out of it, and the neighbour was very careful not to step out of line again."

"Tell me a bit more about his daughter and the guy she married," Dale asked, eager to get back to the story.

"It was a marriage of convenience, which wasn't unusual in those days. Although she put on a brave face, Elizabeth always pined for her true love, Thomas the minstrel. Not long after the sham wedding she fell ill and died young. Some say she died of a broken heart, others that she starved herself to death in protest. Some even say that her own father murdered her. We'll never know the truth."

Machen paused again, allowing Dale a few precious seconds to catch up as he scribbled furiously in his notebook. His wrist and fingers ached, but he didn't want to stop for fear it would interrupt his flow. It was one of the pitfalls of taking notes the old-fashioned way.

"And then the weirdness started."

"What kind of weirdness?"

"In the days following her death, passers-by on the road outside began making strange remarks," Machen continued. "Folk were very superstitious in them days. They said that they could see Elizabeth staring out of the window."

"After she died?" It was Lucy this time.

"Well, yes," said Machen, as if it were the most natural thing in the world. "And not just one or two people saw her, either. Dozens, there were. She was such a common sight up there that some locals didn't believe she was really dead, even though they'd all gone to her funeral. Thought it was some kind of trick Isaac was playing."

"What happened to Thomas? The one she was waiting for?"

"Nobody knows. It was assumed he just moved on. What more could he do? Whether she wanted to or not, the love of his life had married another man."

"So do people still see the ghost?"As he posed the question, Dale could have sworn he saw a nervous flicker in Machen's eye.

"There are no passers-by any more to see much of anything." Machen said, skilfully avoiding the crux of the question before ploughing on, seemingly determined to get through his well-practised spiel. "But after Elizabeth died, her father was never the same. Not long afterwards he died too, and the estate fell into ruin. All the farmland around the house turned barren, you see. Nothing would grow on it."

"Why not?"

"Superstitious locals claimed the land was tainted. Cursed, like. When the land turned bad, all the people left. The workers and servants all moved out and found other work, and people just stopped coming down here. No reason to any more, see. Isaac's surviving relatives even had the only road that runs down to the house blocked, cutting Sker House off from the rest of the world like a gangrenous limb."

"Why would they do that? It seems a bit drastic," Dale said.

"They just wanted to forget about the whole unsavoury episode, I s'pose. They were quite well off themselves and didn't need the money, so they left the house to rot. Just wanted to just forget about it, probl'y."

26

"Have you or any of the staff ever seen the Maid of Sker yourselves?" Lucy asked.

This time the landlord could not hide his emotion. "What's with all the Maid of Sker stuff?" he snapped. "I already told you the story, what else do you want?"

"I... we... would just like to know if there were any eye witnesses we could talk to."

"Personally, I never had the pleasure. Now if you don't mind, I have work to do."

With that the landlord abruptly turned and exited the bar through a door behind the counter, leaving Dale and Lucy staring after him. Evidently, the interview was over.

Chapter 3:

Behind Closed Doors

James Machen, landlord and proprietor of Sker House, closed the door of his tiny office firmly behind him, slumped into the chair at his desk, and buried his head in his hands. He stayed that way for quite a while, waiting for the spinning wheels of his mind to slow down, before reaching into a drawer to retrieve a half-empty bottle of Jack Daniels. Twisting off the cap, he took two generous swigs straight from the bottle, closing his eyes as he savoured the fiery liquid burning a path through his insides. As the heat spread through him, it brought with it a soothing sensation.

That's better.

Setting the bottle down on the desk, he fumbled around in his pockets until he found a crumpled pack of Benson & Hedges and a Sker House-branded lighter. He'd ordered two hundred of them as part of a marketing strategy, not realising until later that smoking was now about as cool as genocide.

Shaking a cigarette out of the pack he poked the filtered end into his mouth, lit the other, and inhaled deeply. It was probably illegal to smoke in his office now, with all the anti-smoking laws, but he didn't care. Sker House may be a workplace but it was also his home, and in his own home a man should be allowed to do whatever he bloody well wanted. He drew the line at smoking in the bar. That might upset the customers, assuming there were any, but he saw no problem with doing it here in his office. He was doing a lot more of it these days, since Sandra had left.

"Damn it!" He brought a fist down on the desk, immediately wincing at the sharp jolt of pain that shot up his arm. Every day he promised himself that he wouldn't think about that woman, and every day he broke his own promise at least a dozen times before lunch time. She'd been gone over five months now. It was about time he got used to it. But she'd been the only woman he'd ever loved, and life without her was just wasn't the same.

Sometimes, he thought the only thing keeping him functioning was the cheap buzz he got from the fags and booze. What was it Richard Burton said?

Show a Welshman a million exits and he'll always choose the path to self-destruction.

Or was it Anthony Hopkins?

Maybe they both said it.

Whatever.

It sounded about right.

Maybe it was part of a Welshman's genetic make-up. Work hard, play hard is something hammered into you at school.

Machen often thought about those grammar school rugby games he played. Brutal, they were. Second row forward was his position. A human battering ram. He got the ball and ran as far as he could with it before somebody thumped into him and dragged him to the ground. It's the job of the forwards to make yards, do the slog, and create a platform for the backs to work their magic and score the points that win games.

As tough as it was, that kind of education was good preparation for the future. Much more useful than the classroom kind of education. By the time boys grew up and went to work in the pits or steelworks, they were tough and hard, and knew the ways of the world.

But now most of the work has disappeared, resulting in a lot of angry, frustrated young people with no prospects and nothing to do. That was why Machen got into the pub business. He remembered reading somewhere that people who worked in the trade toed a thin line, fighting a constant battle against temptation. Publicans, hoteliers, club owners. It was the decadent lifestyle, and the constant close proximity to booze and the comfort it offered.

The occasional foray into drunkenness was tolerated by most. Expected, even. But it was easy to get lost in the wilderness and never find your way back. The way he felt most days, he wanted to be as far from sobriety as circumstances allowed, and welcomed the all-consuming blackness he eventually found at the bottom of a bottle. Obviously, by the time he arrived at that stage the guests were all safely in their rooms. Usually.

He wiped a stray bead of sweat from his brow with the back of a hand and played over the magazine 'interview' in his head. What did the kid say the name of the thing was? Soul Time? Soul News? Solent? Solent Views! That's it, isn't it?

His memory wasn't what it used to be, and seemed to be getting worse. If he didn't have the same thing every day, scrambled egg on toast, he'd probably forget what he had for breakfast in the morning. Concentrating on anything for longer than a few minutes without his mind wandering off on some unrelated tangent was impossible. He had trouble controlling his temper. Things just got on top of him. And apart from all that, there was always something unseen chewing at the fat of his mind, a constant nagging, tugging sensation, as if there was something important he should be seeing or doing, but wasn't. More often than not, a few slugs of JD was enough to quieten that particular beast.

Although he drank most days, he didn't class himself as an alcoholic. Who did? The very concept of being addicted to something, not in control, was embarrassing. But he was different. He could stop whenever he wanted.

That's what they all say!

The near-constant craving he endured wasn't for alcohol. All that did was numb the senses, take the edge off. Cigarettes served the same purpose, to a lesser degree. They calmed him down. He didn't even know what he craved most any more. It wasn't alcohol or nicotine, it was something less definable. He'd felt it since the moment he'd set foot inside Sker House, and it had been getting worse ever since. He was sure Sandra felt it too, before the end. Before she departed.

Departed. Yes, he liked that word. It was... adequate. It conveyed the sense of emptiness and longing he felt. And sounded much better than some of the other words you could use to describe what happened.

He could keep it together enough for the punters. On the surface, anyway. He could keep the drinking and smoking in check, stop himself rambling and talking rubbish, smile in all the right places and keep a lid on his temper. But inside, his mind was in turmoil. Sometimes it felt like a sponge that had soaked up all the liquid it could, but still there was more. So much more that eventually the saturated sponge ended up floating in the stuff.

And then it would get dragged under the surface.

Machen smiled as he sucked hungrily on his cigarette. That was what he had been reduced to. A saturated sponge.

That sounds like the name of a song, he thought. Or a punk band.

Here, for one night only, would you please put your middle fingers in the air for... the Saturated Sponges!

31

He struggled to reel his wandering mind back in. What had he been thinking about? What was the important thing?

What, what, what?

Oh yea, the kid and his interview. Who did he think he was, anyway? Swanning around like he was...What was the guy's name? The famous American writer? It was on the tip of his tongue.

Hunter S Thomas?

That sounded wrong, yet somehow right.

Who cares?

To say the interview could have gone better would be an understatement. Nerves had gotten the better of him. He didn't think he'd been rude. Well... not very. Not as rude as he could have been. He fulfilled his obligations as a landlord, tried to make Sker House sound mysterious and exciting to the public. Nothing more and nothing less. He had really thought the kid was going to talk about how he had built the business up from nothing to where it is now.

It's still nothing!

He would happily answer any amount of questions about being a small business. Rugby, even. He'd always fancied himself as a rugby columnist for one of the newspapers. One of the big ones. But he hadn't been expecting a barrage of questions about the Maid of Sker. Who even cares about something that happened hundreds of years ago? There was nothing else could he do but wheel out the old story. It should at least fill a few paragraphs for the kid.

Even so, he shouldn't have lost his rag like that. Journalist were smart. Even student journalists. They could sniff a lie a mile away.

Stupid, stupid!

Not that he had lied, in so many words. But he'd probably come across like a prized idiot. He should have been more prepared, and maybe a little less defensive. But landlord or not, he was entitled to his privacy, wasn't he? And his bloody opinion.

So have you or the staff ever actually seen or heard anything out of the ordinary? Anything that you would call supernatural or paranormal?

Blow it out of my arse, kid.

No, I mean blow it out of your arse!

That's the right way around, isn't it?

Your arse?

He should just have told the kid to go and talk to Mrs Watkins, the eyes and ears not just of Sker House but of the whole bloody area. She always had news, and wasn't afraid of sharing it. No doubt she could spin a good yarn, too. She could probably do all that kid's work for him. Though Machen tried to make sure he was never around long enough to hear one of her yarns in its entirety. Life was too short for that nonsense. He didn't want to hear about the weird things she claimed happened to her and Izzy, either. He knew they were just angling for more money. If they didn't like working here, they could just leave like Sandra did.

You know it's not more money they're after.

What did the kid expect? There was no way he could tell him, never mind the whole world (or the entire readership of The Solent View Newspaper, or whatever it was called) about the noises he heard when he was alone at night. The low rumbling and growling, the weird bumps, bangs and scrapes like someone was moving furniture around in empty rooms, or the awful scratching sounds as if some desperate animal was trapped inside the walls trying and dig itself out.

Neither did he want to mention the things he saw out of the corner of his eye. The leaping shadows, or the leering faces that came out of the ceiling as he lay in his bed treading the border between being asleep and awake, hovering above him, mocking him.

At first, he thought he was just dreaming. Then he hoped he was just dreaming. But as he cowered beneath the sheets, he swiftly came to realize that those awful faces, with their pained expressions and accusing eyes, were much more than just the product of his fevered imagination. They were as real as real can be.

That opened up a whole other set of questions. Who were they? Where did they come from? What did they want?

Above all, nobody, absolutely nobody, could know about the voices that spoke to him from the darkness, calling his name at night and begging him to go down to the cellar. Not the beer cellar behind the bar, but the original cellar deep beneath Sker House with its labyrinth of tunnels fashioned straight out of the earth. The cellar he didn't even know existed until the voices told him it was there. No, he couldn't tell anyone about that. People would think he was as mad as a March hare.

Come and stay at Sker House with the lunatic landlord who sees and hears things that aren't there! A good time to be had by all!

That wouldn't exactly have the punters banging down the door, would it? The only people banging down the door would be people in white coats. If he was honest, there were even times when he thought about calling the people with white coats on himself. None of what he was experiencing at Sker was normal.

Not at all.

Still, that's no excuse. He had been a bit abrupt with the journalist. Or student, whatever he was. He just wanted to hear the ghost story, that was all. That was all anyone ever wanted to hear about. They didn't know what it was like living here. The pressure of trying to build a business from scratch.

Besides, maybe the boy was right, maybe the publicity would be good. It might draw a bit of a strange crowd, but their money would be as good as anyone else's.

Taking another slug of JD from the bottle and stubbing out his cigarette in the overflowing ashtray, Machen resolved to make amends with his new guests before nightfall. Never let the sun set on an argument was something Sandra was fond of saying, not that it was enough to save them. He assumed it meant going to sleep after a difference of opinion was a bad idea, in case someone died during the night and you never had the chance to settle your differences. It seemed logical. Morbid, but logical and frighteningly true. He would treat the young couple that weren't a couple to a drink on the house by way of apology. It wouldn't do his profit margin any good, but it it might get him back in their good graces. He couldn't have them going off and writing nasty stuff about him, could he? That might be the final nail in his coffin.

Chapter 4:

Sensitive

Back in room twenty-three, Dale turned to Lucy and said, "Did you see that? What's with that guy?"

"Maybe your interviewing technique needs some work," Lucy said as she flopped onto her commandeered bed and picked up the copy of Empire magazine she'd been reading. "How about that Isaac dude, huh?"

"Yeah, Machen was right, he was a nasty piece of work."

"He basically put himself before his daughter's happiness. What kind of father does that?"

"Times were very different then," Dale said. "At least we've moved on from that. Mostly. Arranged marriages are still the norm in some places."

"That's no excuse," Lucy said dismissively. "How did the rest of the interview go? Did you get what you needed?"

Dale lay his crumpled notebook on the desk and flexed his still-throbbing wrist. "It went okay, I guess. Mr Machen is an... interesting character. Don't call him mister, by the way. He hates it."

"I didn't. It was you who insisted on doing that."

"To be honest, Lucy, I don't think the guy's all that comfortable being interviewed. I might not ask him again. I only got a few usable quotes. I was thinking we could get some back-story from the employees. Or maybe that old dude who hangs out in the bar. I bet he has a few tales."

"No doubt. You'll think of something. Writing is what you do. I'm going to grab a shower and get changed." With that, Lucy disappeared into the en suite bathroom and shut the door behind her.

Dale immediately made himself at home at the tiny desk he had converted into a work station, and began transcribing the interview into the Word document he's prepared. This was one of the most laborious and frustrating aspects of the entire interviewing process, which was why the job so often went to interns and work experience kids.

A lot of people are under the impression that being a journalist is a glamorous and exciting profession. Not quite up there with fighter pilot or spy, but close. Generally speaking, those people are deluded. No doubt it *can* be glamorous, with all those socialite parties, invitation-only events and expense accounts. But

Dale knew that kind of privileged existence is only true for the chosen few. Most journalism is nuts and bolts stuff. The endless struggle to make contact with people who didn't want to be contacted, and countless hours pouring over hazy computer screens trying to write something that someone somewhere might want to read.

As an unfortunate consequence of the human condition, most people tend to talk a lot of shit. You didn't really realize how much until you were charged with analysing a conversation and sorting out relevant, useful information from reams of meaningless drivel. People repeated themselves a lot, or said the same things in different words. It's almost as if the human brain can only comprehend a handful of central ideas at any one time, so we do our best to apply those few basic themes to everything and anything we do to bring a modicum of sensibility to our existence. Dale sighed as he listened to the shower running in the little en suite bathroom behind him. He would have to put all thoughts of seducing Lucy to one side, at least temporarily. He could still cling on to a thin thread of hope, but he wasn't going to force the issue. He didn't want to come on too strong and wreck their fragile friendship, not the way Lucy was acting lately. She was liable to stick one of his pencils through his eye.

He and Lucy had known each other for over two years, having enrolled on the same journalism course at uni. During the first year they shared most of the same classes and got to know each other pretty well, spending many weekday evenings at each other's digs, drinking cheap cider and watching reality television shows. It was there they discovered they shared the same slightly warped sense of humour and the same taste in music, though Lucy tended to veer more towards indie rock, which to Dale's mind was usually just a bunch of posh boys in cardigans singing about how jolly hard life was.

Several times their strictly platonic relationship even extended to sharing the same bed, usually when one of them was too drunk to stagger home. Dale often suspected this was some kind of test Lucy was putting him through. On the occasions she stayed over, he was sure she could have made it home if she'd really wanted to. Besides, either one of them could have slept on the floor or sofa. Having slept on a multitude of floors and sofa's in his time, he wouldn't have minded in the slightest. But no, Lucy insisted on sleeping in the same bed, only after pointing out that any 'wandering hands' would be snapped off. Fair enough. A guy who can be trusted to share your bed and not try any funny business must be a good guy, right?

True to his word, Dale ensured that his hands didn't wander, but instead he spent all night lying uncomfortably on his stomach trying to smother an erection. He winced at the memory. Whatever test he'd been put through he hoped he passed it, though recent evidence would indicate otherwise. Lucy had seemed increasingly distant and irritable these past few months, giving Dale the impression that whatever opportunity he might have once had was gone. Sometimes, he got the feeling that she actually wanted him to try it on, probably so she could turn around and shoot him down in flames. Show him who was boss. She wasn't a vindictive person, far from it. But in affairs of the heart, normal rules didn't apply. She knew how much he liked her. How could she not? He didn't try to hide it. He'd never grabbed her and tried sticking his tongue down her throat, he was more subtle than that, but surely she must have got the message by now.

What he didn't know was whether or not she felt the same way. Like most girls, she gave off mixed signals. Sometimes she flirted with him outrageously, other times she acted like she wouldn't have sex with him if he was the last man on earth. She wouldn't answer his calls, or reply to his texts or emails for days, and if they attended the same lectures, she would rather sit alone at the back of the hall than anywhere near him. She was also always keen to stress to everyone that they were 'just friends.'

Damn the Friend Zone. It's a place no self-respecting man wants to be. A horrible, uncertain neverland full of missed opportunities and shattered dreams. You get all the negative aspects of a relationship; trust issues, jealousy, deceit, and emotional baggage, without any of the good stuff. Like sex. And sex. And more sex. Guys who think the way into a girls pants is through the Friend Zone invariably set themselves up for a long, frustrating, ultimately fruitless slog.

He knew Lucy was damaged goods, but he got the impression that there were things he didn't know about her. She was a complex individual. It was one of the things that first attracted him. That and an arse you could bounce pennies off. She wasn't as transparent and superficial as most of the airhead girls he met at uni. All most of them cared about was cars and money, and not always their own, either. Lucy was different. She had more substance, which was revealed cautiously, one layer at a time.

Even so, despite knowing each other for over two years, he still had no idea where he stood in a romantic sense. The girl was a complete mystery. He remembered reading somewhere that the reason men didn't know what women wanted was because women didn't know what they wanted. That made perfect sense. He'd reluctantly come to the conclusion that he would be happy to just be friends. Anything more than that would be a bonus.

Right now, there were more important things on his mind than girls. Even girls of Lucy's calibre. He would be graduating soon, and a good, thoughtful and interesting article about Sker House would definitely help his final grade, not to mention help bulk up his portfolio. So, back to the interview.

*

A few minutes later, clean, invigorated and wearing a fresh Biffy Clyro t-shirt over a pair of faded jeans, Lucy stepped out of the shower. Dale was hunched over his computer at the desk, a look of concentration etched into his face. "Still working on the interview?"

"Yeah. The Maid of Sker stuff is pretty interesting, but apart from that we don't have much," Dale replied.

Lucy casually peered over his shoulder at the computer screen, where a line of text was highlighted.

It's not so much what you can see and touch, but what you can feel.

"The landlord guy said that? Very philosophical. What was he talking about?"

"Fucked if I know," Dale sighed. "He didn't make a whole lot of sense. And toward the end, just after you came, he lost his rag and stormed off."

"Well, that's what you need me for, right?"

"How so?"

39

"Because I'll take so many outstanding images there won't be any page space left for much of your deep, insightful scribblings," she grinned.

Dale smiled back, "Gauntlet accepted."

"In fact, I'm going on a quick expedition now, give you some time to finish what you're doing. Then maybe we can go for a walk on the beach before dinner."

"Sounds good."

Lucy carefully unpacked her Nikon from her suitcase, enjoying its comfortable weight in her hands, and turned it on to check the battery and settings. Everything seemed to be in working order. Flashing Dale a quick wave, she closed the door behind her.

Outside the room, she took a few shots of the corridor and staircase, but soon decided that wasn't very interesting and went down to the bar instead. To her surprise, it was empty except for Champ the Guard Dog, who was still lying prostrate on the floor. She didn't think he had moved an inch since they'd arrived.

Tiptoeing over to where he lay, she reached out and warily stroked the greying fur on his head. She half expected the dog to turn and bite her, but he didn't. In fact, the poor old thing seemed glad of the attention. As she tickled behind his ear he cocked his head to one side and studied her with wet, red-rimmed eyes. Lucy began firing off some shots, moving around to change the angle. She didn't think Solent News would want to use any doggy pics, so these would remain in her personal collection.

Human-canine relations cemented, she looked around for anything else in the bar she could shoot. There was an old-fashioned brass oil lamp sitting prominently behind the bar and little silver bell on the counter. She almost rang the bell for service before thinking better of it.

The landlord would probably be back soon enough.

She could wait.

Besides, it would give her a chance to work without any interruptions. When she was taking pictures she often got lost in the act. The real world melted away, her only association with it being the small distorted rectangle she saw through her viewfinder.

As she moved through the bar, her attention was drawn to a large framed picture hanging on the far wall. For some reason, this picture stood out from all the others. But when she got closer, it seemed unremarkable enough. It was a faded black-and-white still of a small group of men standing on a pebble beach in front of a small boat. If she looked carefully, she could just make out the name painted on the side.

Edward, Prince of Wales.

The inscription beneath the photograph said: Mumbles RNLI, 1947.

Something about the photograph made her vaguely uneasy, yet she couldn't tear her eyes away from it. Of all the pictures in the bar, this one was special, somehow. Different. She leaned in closer and used a tissue to rub away some of the brownish film clinging to the glass. As was the norm in photographs from that era and before, none of the men were smiling. Studying their faces, she noticed that although they ranged from young to old, they all shared the same air of steely camaraderie, like they were soldiers going into battle together. Their forlorn stares gazed back across the decades, filled not only with determination but also a grim sadness. Whoever they were, whatever they did, these were men who knew tragedy, hardship and loss. Furthermore, if the date in the inscription was correct most of them would be dead now, making the photograph even more poignant. There was always something deeply unsettling about looking at photos of dead people.

She adjusted the settings on her Nikon and reeled off a few close-quarter shots, and for the millionth time or more marvelled at the magic of photography. A simple push of a button, a flash of light, and a single fleeting moment in time captured forever. Immortalized. Lucy knew there was a science to it, but in her mind she still thought of it as a kind of magic. Like alchemy. There were times when she found herself shying away from the more technical aspects she learned about, not to burst the bubble of enchantment. She liked believing in magic.

Then, without warning, something changed.

She suddenly started feeling very exposed and the hairs on the nape of her neck stood up, as if someone was breathing on her. She whirled around, fully expecting to find either Mr Machen or the old gent from the bar looking over her shoulder.

But the room was still empty except for Champ, who looked directly at her and let out a low whimper as if to say, 'Yes, I feel it too.'

Goosebumps peppered her arms and the air around her seemed charged in some way, as if an electrical current was running through it. Her mind was dragged back to the snippet of Dale's interview she'd read upstairs.

It's not so much what you can see and touch, but what you can feel.

Now, all at once, Lucy understood.

She was reminded of her grandmother on her father's side, who died when Lucy was six leaving behind little more than a bunch of vague, jumbled memories of friendly brown eyes set in a mask of papery skin, near-white hair pulled back in a bun, skinny, liver-spotted arms, the sickly smell of scented Lavender water. Towards the end, as her mental state deteriorated and she eventually succumbed to dementia, she spent an increasing amount of time talking to people who weren't there. It was painful to watch, even for a child of Lucy's age with a limited understanding of death and the way the world worked.

But something her grandmother said stuck with Lucy. Now, more than fifteen years later, the words were once more brought to the forefront of her mind.

"You are a Sensitive, my dear. That's what we call ourselves. Other people may have other names for us. You are the latest in a long line. We can trace our history back to before the Conquests and the Witch Hunts that drove us underground. Your skills won't be as polished or finely honed as those that went before. We have less use for them in the modern age. But every so often, things will happen around you. To you. You may sense a presence, or hear an unfamiliar voice speaking. Sometimes, you'll see things that your brain will tell you aren't really there, or even catch a glimpse of the past or the future. Whatever happens little one, don't be scared. Embrace it."

At first, Lucy thought it was the dementia talking. But true enough, in the years since she had lost count of the times she was in a place she knew to be empty, yet sensed she was not alone. Other people, or things, prowled there, hiding out of sight. Perhaps just beyond her field of comprehension.

42

Sometimes, the presences wanted to communicate. They would whisper softly to her, or plant fragmented words and images in her mind that made little sense.

She could never lay claim to having an uneventful childhood. There were always people to play with, even when she was alone. There were a few visitors in particular that made a lasting impression. One was a boy about her own age called Tom who liked to play with a little blue ball. His favourite trick was to turn invisible, which Lucy had to admit was pretty impressive. He did every time somebody else came into Lucy's room. Sometimes he would move things around, too. Just little objects and ornaments in the house. Nobody knew it was him, so Lucy often got blamed. But she knew Tom didn't mean to be spiteful or troublesome. It was just his way of getting attention.

Some of Lucy's childhood visitors weren't altogether human. She knew that. One was a tall, thin man in a smart black suit with a giant strawberry for a head. He would appear in her room and dance, his arms and legs moving slowly and methodically at first, then gathering pace and purpose before building into a blurry crescendo. When that happened his arms and legs would move so fast that they practically disappeared, and all that would be visible of him would be a double-breasted jacket with a huge strawberry perched on top of it swaying hypnotically in the air.

When Strawberry did his dance, the young Lucy would squeal and clap her hands in delight. To her undeveloped mind, it didn't seem the least bit unusual. Only later when she looked back did she realise how strange these experiences were. But by then, she couldn't be sure if Strawberry was real or if she had imagined the whole thing.

If she ever mentioned them, her mother would roll her eyes dismissively. But Lucy couldn't forget the look on her father's face. It was a look of understanding. Though he never gave any explanation, probably in an effort to protect his daughter from the shadowy 'Otherworld' and its weird and wonderful occupants, her father's reaction alone was enough to assure Lucy that her assortment of misfit friends didn't just exist inside her head.

As Lucy grew up and passed into womanhood, she grew less attuned and Tim, Strawberry, and the multitude of 'others' that

43

filled her childhood, faded away. Occasionally, she still had what she called 'inklings,' usually in the form of strange sensations or thoughts that suddenly filled her head, almost as if they had been plucked out of someone else's mind and implanted into hers.
The intuition, if that's what it was, was impossible to control. Even though she tried every damn week, twice if she remembered the midweek draw, she never could guess those winning Lottery numbers. That made all the 'Sensitive' business pretty redundant. She wished grandma was still alive to answer some of the questions. Why was she a Sensitive? Assuming everything in nature had a purpose or else it wouldn't exist, what was her purpose? Were there others like her? Did they have social clubs? Support networks? Facebook groups?

Nobody else knew about her hidden talent, if you could call it that. People would think she was nuts. She often thought about talking to her father about it, him being the only one who might be able to understand. But she suspected that anything he might know about the topic, he would rather forget. Besides, Lucy didn't want to taint whatever memories he had of his dead mother. The 'sensitivity' was an ability only bestowed on the females of the family. This was something she just knew instinctively, the same way she knew you shouldn't play with fire. The menfolk of the family went about their daily lives blissfully unaware, or unwilling to acknowledge, that there were forces at work around them that went above and beyond the physical. She certainly couldn't tell Dale. He would just laugh and call her a flake. And maybe she was, her young, impressionable mind irreparably twisted by the musings of a sick old lady.

As quickly as it had come, the feeling that somebody was hovering over her dissipated. Lucy shuddered as the last remnants drained away, leaving her staring blankly at the old photograph hanging on the wall, mouth hanging open. Suddenly, the door to the bar opened and someone came in.

Lucy gasped and whirled round, almost dropping her precious Nikon in the process. She fumbled and caught it just in time. When she saw Dale standing in the doorway, relief washed over her like a cool wave.

"Hey, miss Photographic Director. How about that stroll on the beach?"

44

Chapter 5:

The Face in the Window

Directly outside Sker House's porch was a meandering, overgrown footpath bordered with little tufts of unkempt foliage. A few metres along it veered off sharply to the left and disappeared into the nearby sand dunes. "Is that the way to the beach?" Lucy asked.

"We live on an island, every way is the way to the beach," Dale replied sarcastically.

"You know what I mean."

"Yeah," Dale grinned. "Well, the sea is this way, just over those sand dunes. Unless things have changed radically since the last time I saw it, that the beach will be next to the sea."

"I don't know why you have to be so bloody condescending all the time. It's not funny."

"I guess I do it because being mean to others makes me feel better about myself. Classic schoolground bully mentality."

"Well, I suppose you need something in your life to give you a boost," Lucy giggled. They tussled playfully on the narrow path. Dale easily won due to his size advantage, but at least he did the gentlemanly thing and caught Lucy before she tumbled head-first into the undergrowth.

A few metres after the abrupt left turn, the path dipped sharply and the vegetation flanking both sides fell away to be replaced by huge mounds of sand caressed into gentle, rounded shapes by the wind and waves.

The dunes.

Dried seaweed and bits of rubbish, washed white by the elements, blew across their path like mini tumbleweeds. Dale did a neat 360-degree turn. "Man, this is more like the Gobi desert than the Welsh coast."

"No doubt there are similarities."

"Hey, is that a veiled attack on my heritage?"

"No. It wasn't veiled at all."

Dale feigned disgust. "Hey, how come in an advanced PC-friendly society, it's still okay to slate the Welsh? I mean, if I was black or Indian you wouldn't dare have a go then. That would be racist. But us Welsh, Irish and Scots just have to take your abuse."

"It's just banter. We all do it to each other, it's an intrinsic aspect of the complex and unique relationship us Home Nations have. Didn't you ever attend Social Studies class?"

"Yeah, but it was on a Wednesday morning so I was usually hungover. Anyway," Dale shrugged, "You're not in Kansas now, Dorothy."

"Ooh, what does that mean?"

"It means a bit of respect would be nice." Dale saw Lucy's eyes flicker the way they did when she thought of some witty, super-funny comeback. But to her credit, she didn't give voice to it.

A few minutes later, they reached the top of a gradual incline and the sand dunes melted away. The path terminated at the edge of the beach, and beyond that lay the vast expanse of the sea.

"Wales doesn't seem so bad with areas of natural beauty like this, does it?"

"You know, sometimes you sound like a walking tourism brochure."

"Oh, do I really?" Dale dug Lucy sharply in the ribs, and she swatted his hand away. "And sometimes, you act like a spoiled child."

"Yeah, I know," Lucy admitted. "And I also know you secretly love it. Anyway, this child wants to sit here for a while and watch the sea. You should be grateful she doesn't want an ice cream. I don't see an ice cream van around here so you'd have a bloody long walk."

"Yeah, right." Dale said plopping himself down next to Lucy where the foliage met the sand. They sat in silence for a while as dusk settled, watching the white-topped waves crash against the shore. From their viewpoint, the sea seemed to tower above them like a wall of water that could come crashing down at any moment. A solitary ship, lights ablaze, passed silently on the horizon. Set against the vast expanses of the sea and the sky, it could have been a toy.

"It's awesome, isn't it?" Dale said. "All that water in one place."

"It's... romantic." Lucy said, a hint of melancholy creeping into her voice.

Dale frowned. "How the hell can water be romantic? It's cold and wet, but not romantic."

"It just is, stupid. Everyone knows that. Haven't you seen Titanic?"

"I think everyone in the civilised world has seen Titanic. And most agree that the best part is when the ship sinks. Again, not romantic."

"That's a terrible thing to say. What's wrong with you?"

Dale held up his palms, "I'm just stating a fact. People love movie carnage. It's what passes for entertainment. That's why disaster movies are so popular. The more death and destruction, the better."

"Well, it depends who you ask, I suppose. But I think anyone with feelings would disagree."

"What's so romantic about it? Boy meets girl, boy falls in love with girl, boy dies in a freezing ocean. The end. That's not romantic, that's fucking tragic."

"But love is tragic, don't you get it? That's the whole concept of Romeo and Juliet."

Dale stood up. "Who says love should be tragic, Shakespeare? A posh drunken poet who died centuries ago? Why can't love be a wonderful adventure, full of happiness and joy? It doesn't have to be so bloody depressing. Call me old-fashioned, but I want a happy ending. What's so wrong with that?"

Lucy joined him on her feet, dusting stray grains of sand off her behind. "Nothing's wrong with happy endings. That's what everyone wants. But unfortunately, things never turn out like that. I mean, if two people manage to overcome all the odds and actually stay together for any length of time, death will separate them eventually leaving the other one lonely and heartbroken. That's the best any of us can hope for."

"Jesus, Lucy. You're so cynical." Dale said, shaking his head. "Come on, lets build up an appetite."

They walked for a few minutes, chatting and stopping at regular intervals so Lucy could take some panoramic pictures in the rapidly fading light. It was during one of these impromptu sessions that she suddenly said, "Why is that woman watching us like that?"

"What woman?"

"Up at the house. Third... no, fourth floor. The window on the far right."

Dale looked back at Sker house. From this distance he couldn't make out every detail, but he could plainly see each window facing them. There wasn't see anybody watching. "I don't see a woman," he said, puzzled. "Is this a wind-up?"

"Are you serious? She's right there. Look." Lucy pointed a finger.

"Nope. Sorry. Don't see her."

"Here look through this. I have the zoom on. The window on the far right. Quick."

Lucy handed Dale her Nikon. He held it to his eye, training the lens on the house. After a few seconds he said, "Lucy. Seriously, there's nobody watching us. From that window, or any other. You were either mistaken, or you've gone completely mad. I sincerely hope its the former. I don't want to spend the night in a haunted house in the middle of nowhere with a crazy person. It would be like the fucking Shining."

"Give that to me," Lucy said, snatching back the camera and training it on the house once more.

There were a few moments of silence, until Dale's impatience won out. "Well, do you still see her?"

"No, she's gone."

"I told you."

"That doesn't mean she was never there."

"Okay. So what did she look like?"

Lucy's brow creased and she gazed into middle distance as she struggled to remember the details. "She was wearing a dress, or an old fashioned nightdress. Light coloured. And she had long dark hair hanging down over her shoulders."

"Anything else? Was she young or old? Fat or thin?"

"Thin," Lucy replied. "How the hell should I know how old she is?"

"Well, whoever she is, she's gone now. Come on, let's go and investigate."

"Wait," said Lucy. "Didn't Machen say we were the only guests staying at the house tonight?"

"Yeah, but that doesn't prove anything. It could have been a visitor, or a cleaning lady or something. What's up? You think you saw the Maid of Sker?"

Lucy thought for a moment then said, "Nah, I doubt it. Probably more like some nosy old battleaxe hoping we were going to have sex in the sand dunes."

"Well in that case it would be a shame to disappoint the woman. After you..." said Dale, motioning towards the sand dunes behind them. Lucy tried to force a laugh, but what came out of her mouth was more of an uncertain splutter.

They finished their walk in troubled silence. Dale tried to lift Lucy's spirits by cracking jokes and generally acting the fool, but nothing seemed to work. She didn't even freak out when he picked up half a dead crab chased her with it. When they arrived back at Sker House, they were surprised to find that another car had joined Dale's old Astra in the tiny car park. An even older Nova. "See? Must be more guests after all!"

"Yeah, maybe," replied a still preoccupied Lucy.

They went directly to the bar to seek out Machen. Champ the guard dog still lay prone on the floor, but they were surprised to find that the landlord hadn't yet returned to his post. Instead, the bar was staffed by a pale-looking blonde girl of seventeen or eighteen wearing faded, ripped jeans and a black t-shirt. She was sitting on a bar stool furiously thumbing the buttons on her phone. When they walked in, she looked up and smiled weakly. "Hiya! You must be Mr Morgan and Miss Kerr, room twenty-three?"

"Er... that's right," said Lucy. "How do you know that?"

"Easy. You two are the only people staying here at the moment, apart from Old Rolly over there, who's a permanent fixture." The girl nodded in the direction of the old man with the white beard sitting at a table. If he heard his name being mentioned, he didn't acknowledge it.

"You can call me Dale. Mister is just for the tax man," Dale joked, hoping to get a laugh out of his dig at Machen. However, evidently neither Lucy nor the barmaid thought it was funny and his quip was met with a stony silence from both of them.

"Er, okay.... Dale. I won't call you mister," said the pale blonde girl. "My name is Isabel, but everyone calls me Izzy."

"Nice to meet you, Izzy," said Dale almost sheepishly.

"Nice to meet you, too. Can I get you a drink?"

Yes. That was what he needed. Beer. He ordered a pint for himself and a glass of lemonade for Lucy, who proclaimed that it was too early for her to start drinking. As the barmaid poured his pint, he leaned in closer and said, "Um, Izzy... Can I ask you something?"

"S'pose so. What's up?"

"Don't you think you're playing on this Maid of Sker thing a little too much? I mean, what do you do? Pay someone to stand up there looking out of the window all day? Who is it? Machen himself in a dress and a wig?"

"Machen in a dress and a wig? Whatever are you talking about, sir?" Izzy replied. She was either genuinely taken aback, or she was the most convincing amateur actress on the planet.

In a desperate bid to salvage some dignity, Dale backtracked and tried a different tactic. "Okay Izzy, forget the Machen comment. Just tell me, who's the woman in a white dress with long hair we saw watching us?"

The half-smile on the barmaid's face faltered, allowing something else, something darker, to momentarily creep into her expression, "Oh, it was probably just Old Rolly," she said with a dismissive flap of the hand.

Lucy bared her teeth in what Dale assumed was an attempted smile and shook her head slowly and deliberately. "No. We've already met Old Rolly. Seen him, anyway. He's sitting right there. This was definitely a woman. We were wondering if you or anyone else had maybe stood in the window overlooking the beach about twenty minutes ago?"

For a few seconds, a few seconds too long, Izzy and Lucy locked eyes. Then the barmaid's gaze dropped sharply to the left and she said, "Oh yes, I remember now, I had to change the bedding in that room."

"Which room?" pressed Lucy. Dale could hear the suspicion in her voice.

"The room where you say you saw somebody."

"But we didn't tell you which room it was. Plus, you have blonde hair. The lady I saw had dark hair. And a white dress. You're wearing black."

The young barmaid pursed her lips as if mentally cursing her own stupidity at being caught in a lie. "Well then, I don't know who you think you saw. Like I said, you're the only guests we have at the moment. I really don't know what else I can say."

Dale could feel the tension mounting. It was easy to make enemies instead of friends when chasing leads. He decided to step in before the two girls ended up in a cat fight. "Then maybe it was a cleaner?"

"Nope," Izzy replied. "There's no other cleaner. I'm here almost every day. Mam and me do all the cleaning, but neither of us have been upstairs tonight. We have a schedule. And besides, we only arrived about ten minutes ago. Machen didn't want us in until dinner time today, 'cos it's so quiet."

Izzy the barmaid finished pouring the drinks and set them on the bar. Dale paid for them, thanked her, then picked them up and followed Lucy who was already on her way to a secluded little table at the far window.

By the time he got there she was already perusing the laminated menu. "I forgot how hungry I was," she said. "There are only three choices of main meal, but they all sound gorgeous."

Food. The great leveller. It didn't matter what else was going on, or what differences people had, everyone had to eat eventually.

Dale snatched the menu out of Lucy's hands, who slumped back in her chair, folding her arms across her chest in a show of petulance. "You know, it's no wonder you're single. You have the manners of a Gorilla."

"It's better than having the ass of a Gorilla."

"Are you saying I have a big bum? Or that it's hairy or what? Anyway, how would you know?"

Despite his best efforts, Dale felt his face reddened. Damn it, she always knew exactly what buttons to press. He decided to give up on that particular verbal exchange and change the subject. He would live to fight another day. "So... anyway, I'm thinking steak and ale pie, chips and garden peas. What about you, Madam?"

"Oh, so I'm Madam now am I? In that case, Madam will have the vegetarian option. Home-made cheese and potato pie with baked beans. And bread and butter."

Dale was certain there was a joke there somewhere involving the vegetarian option, Lucy, and a lack of meat, but he didn't try too hard to think of it. He couldn't handle another put-down. Maybe later.

Rather than potentially evoking Izzy's wrath by waving her over, Dale went back to the bar to place their order. When he got there, the barmaid seemed to have had a personality check and was the picture of pleasantness. She took Dale's credit card with a polite smile, then as they waited for the transaction to go through the system said, "On which floor did you see someone at the window?"

The question took Dale by surprise. He thought that matter had been settled, or at least swept under a metaphorical carpet. He shot a glance back at Lucy, but she was too far away to hear.

"Er... I'd have to check with my friend but it was the fourth floor, I think."

"The fourth floor you say?"

"Yep. Think so," repeated Dale with as much conviction as he could muster.

"Well, that's impossible. The fourth floor is closed for refurbishments, and not open to staff or the public."

"You mean the renovation work isn't finished yet? I thought it was."

"Well, it would've been finished by now except there were issues with the builders."

Once again, Dale's journalistic instinct kicked into high gear. Machen hadn't mentioned anything about that. "What kind of issues?"

Izzy turned away and awkwardly began polishing a glass that was already clean with a length of blue kitchen roll. "Oh, you know. Boring legal stuff mostly, I think. Better ask Mach about it." She looked almost relieved when the hand-held credit card machine gave a little electronic burp to denote that it had finished devouring Dale's card. "Sign here, please.... thank you... I'll bring your meals over when they're ready. Was there anything else, sir?"

"Er, no, nothing else. Thanks, Izzy." Dale made his way back to their table wondering why Machen hadn't mentioned the fact that the building work at Sker House wasn't yet finished. But then again, why would he?

"Befriending the locals, I see? How did it go?" Lucy asked.

"Ooh, catty. Are you getting jealous?"

"Yeah, yeah. As we speak I'm consumed with burning envy. I'm just hiding it really well," Lucy replied with a poker face. And then, "You know she's lying, right? The girl couldn't even get her story straight."

"Don't worry," Dale grinned. "I think I've solved the mystery."

"Okay then, let's hear it. And before you start rubbishing my story, I know what I saw, okay?"

"I believe you really did see someone up there. Probably a woman, and probably watching us, just like you said."

"You do? Oh, that's a relief. I feel validated."

Ignoring the remark, Dale continued. "Don't you see? They're just perpetuating the myth."

"They're doing what to the what?"

"Perpetuating. It means to continue something."

"I know what perpetuating means, thanks."

"They're obviously just trying to capitalize on the whole Maid of Sker thing."

"How?"

"It wouldn't surprise me if they send someone up there a couple of times a day to stand in the window freaking people out. Like the Maid of Sker in the old legend. If people think they've seen a ghost, then they'll go back and tell all their friends about it. Word-of-mouth is the best kind of advertising there is. And it's free. Well, apart from the 'ghost.' And how much does a pretend ghost cost? They'd probably be available on minimum wage. Not much skill involved in just standing about looking moody."

Lucy sipped her lemonade and nodded, "Ah, I get it."

"And us being journalists... well, student journalists... If we go off and write in Solent News that we saw an actual ghost in this place, ghost hunters would flock here hoping for a glimpse, while sceptics would flock here hoping to prove us wrong. Quite a savvy move."

"That's such an underhanded thing to do."

"Underhanded?" Dale said. "The hotel industry is very competitive. They're just playing to their strengths, that's all. Nothing wrong with that. They have a bit of history, a selling point, so they're trying to capitalize."

"But deceiving people into believing they were seeing ghosts?" Lucy looked disgusted, as if she had just found out that the landlord was harvesting human body parts.

55

"Try not to take it personally. Maybe it's just a mannequin or a cardboard cut-out. Or maybe it really is Machen standing up there in a wig and a dress, who knows? The point is, that's all they're doing. Standing in the window. How you choose to interpret seeing someone standing in a window is entirely up to you. Some might not think anything of it. While others, who may be more familiar with the history of this place, especially after hearing it from the staff, might think they are seeing the Maid of Sker. It's the power of suggestion."

"But that's exactly what I did say! I did think it was a woman! You were the one who started talking about fucking ghosts!"

"So what do you think now?"

Lucy lowered her voice, "Call it women's intuition if you want, but I think the staff here aren't being entirely truthful."

It was too early for Dale to make any judgements, but he trusted Lucy. If she thought something was amiss, it probably was. Suddenly, he remembered something. "While we were walking you took pictures of the house, right?"

"That's what I do, Einstein."

"Do you think maybe you caught something in one of the frames?"

"I'm not sure. I'd have to upload them to your computer, maybe run them through some enhancing software. If there's anything there, I'll find it."

"Good," said Dale. "We'll do it later. At least then we'll know, one way or the other."

*

A short time later, Izzy brought two steaming plates of food over to the table. "Steak and ale pie and chips?"

Dale raised his arm high in the air like an over-excited schoolboy.

"Then you must be cheese and potato..." Izzy said, addressing Lucy.

Lucy wanted to point out that her name was, in fact, Lucy Kerr, not Cheese And Potato, but she supposed the poor girl heard lame jokes like that all the time and didn't want to burden her with

56

another one. Instead, she smiled politely and thanked the young barmaid who left with a cheery, "Enjoy your meal!"

The cheese and potato pie, one of Lucy's favourite dishes of all time, was absolutely delicious. With huge globs of browned cheddar seasoned with onion and a smattering of herbs, it seemed to melt in her mouth. As she ate, she looked around the room. The atmosphere in the bar was different now, not at all like it had been earlier when she'd been alone. The soft yellow glow of the ambient lighting made the place feel warm and homely, especially with the deepening darkness outside pressing against the window.

However, again and again she found her gaze pulled back to the framed photograph hanging on the wall. The dead men standing with the good ship Edward, Prince of Wales.

Dale must have caught her attention wavering, and managed to mumble, "Food good," in between giant mouthfuls.

Not knowing if it was a statement or a question, Lucy replied, "Mmmm... fantastic," as she piled some baked beans onto her fork.

"You know..." Dale said as they he neared the end of his meal, "... I really hope they get more guests soon. This place won't see the year out otherwise, and that would be a shame. They could make a lot of money here if they play it right."

"Here? But it's in the middle of nowhere."

Dale cocked his head slightly the way he did when he was about to impart some wisdom. "Because it's a captive market, see? You just said so yourself. When people come here they pay for the room to start with, but there's nowhere else to can eat, so then they end up buying two or three meals per person per day on top. Plus drinks and entertainment. The pool table and all that other stuff won't be free."

"But isn't the idea to come here and go out hiking or fishing?" Lucy asked. She wasn't comfortable with Dale's use of the word 'captive.' It inferred many things, none of them good.

"That's the pretext. But everyone knows the weather in Wales is atrocious. Especially along the coast. It probably rains two days out of three. Sure, when visitors come they'll brave the elements for a couple of hours a day, but they'll spend the majority of their time here."

"In that case, maybe the article really will help get the word out."

"I don't think it'll help that much, to be honest. Not unless Sker House is suddenly inundated with students from Solent University who, in case you hadn't noticed, are the only people who read our rag."

"Yeah, and even then it's debatable how much of it they actually read. If we dumbed-down any more we'd be writing pop-up books."

"We got into journalism at the wrong time," Dale grumbled. "Nobody's interested in reading anything unless it's on a computer screen. The media is more popular and accessible than it has ever been before. But traditional print is dying a slow, painful death. Circulation figures are down right across the board." As if to mourn the current plight of news stand publications, he drained his glass and wiped his mouth on the back of his hand.

"I think rumours of the industry's demise are greatly exaggerated," Lucy said. "The big media companies still make shit loads of money and most magazines and newspapers are still profitable, they just make seven million a year instead of ten million."

"Yeah, but what about the future? If the decline continues how many of them will still be profitable in ten years? Or even five?"

"Who's to say any of us will still be here in five years? The way the world is going we'll all be dust sooner rather than later."

Dale tutted. "We've been on the brink of another world war since the fifties. And they said the world was going to end in 1999, when the Millennium Bug was supposed to make all the planes drop out of the sky. And what about 2012 when the Mayan calendar ended? Nothing happened then, either."

"Now who's the cynical one?" said Lucy.

As they were finishing their meals, Machen the landlord appeared back behind the bar, a huge smile spread across his reddened face. He looked a little unsteady on his feet. If Lucy didn't know better, she'd say he'd been drinking. He said something unintelligible to young Izzy, who shot Lucy and Dale an inquisitive look as she scurried back into the kitchen. Lucy was about to comment on it when Dale jumped in first and asked her if she wanted another drink. The dinner had been so delicious that she hadn't even noticed she had also drained her glass. "Why not? Get me a Cardiac Breezer, please. Lemon if they have it."

When Dale came back from the bar he was smiling from ear to ear and walking with such a spring in his step that he struggled to keep from spilling his beer. "What's up with you?" she asked.

"You'll never guess what! Mist... Machen, the landlord..."

"Yeah I know who he is. What about him? Did he turn out to be your long lost uncle or something?"

"I don't know about that. I never thought to ask. Anyway, I went to the bar right, got the drinks, and then when I went to pay for them, he said he didn't want the money. Said he was sorry that the interview went so badly this afternoon, and that we could try again tomorrow when he's not so stressed out."

"When he's not so drunk, more like."

They both turned to look at the landlord, who was sitting in a bar stool across the room facing them. He smiled and waved.

"You think he's drunk? Can't the guy just be nice?"

"Well you changed your tune. Two hours ago he was just a bad interviewee. Now he's in line for a Nobel Prize. I can't believe you just allowed yourself to be swayed by one free drink."

"I didn't!" Dale looked offended. "It was two free drinks. I didn't pay for yours, either. And guess what? He said he had a special surprise for you. He just sent that barmaid out to get it."

"A surprise for me? What kind of surprise?"

"How the hell should I know? He didn't go into specifics. Just said you'd love it. Don't look a gift horse in the mouth. Isn't that what they say? Or is it the ear? Or the..."

"It's the mouth."

"Okay. It's the mouth. Well, it should be the..."

"No it shouldn't," scolded Lucy. She knew what he was going to say. When Dale got himself into this kind of excited state, especially after a drink, he reverted back to an eleven-year old boy. His child-like enthusiasm was infectious, and he had lifted her spirits more than anyone else. She supposed she should be grateful. That was why she'd agreed to come on this jaunt. Some escapism. Maybe an adventure.

Lucy and Dale were so busy arguing about horses anatomy that neither of them saw Izzy coming until she was virtually standing over them.

"Looks like your surprise has arrived..." said Dale, straining his neck to see what the barmaid was carrying.

"This is on the house," said the young barmaid as she collected their empty dinner plates and replaced them with two white bowls.

"Mmmmm! Strawberries! With cream and sugar!" squealed Dale. "Surprise!"

Lucy stared at the bowl of fruit in front of her, feeling like she had just seen a ghost.

Chapter 6:

Images

Dale made disgusting wet noises as he systematically devoured his desert, and didn't notice that Lucy hadn't even lifted her spoon until his bowl was almost empty.

"What's up?" he asked, dabbing at the corners of his mouth with a napkin to soak up any spare globs of cream. "I thought every girl loved strawberries."

"I guess I'm full," replied Lucy. Even to her, the remark sounded unconvincingly. Luckily, Dale was too busy stuffing his face to notice her discomfort. "I mean... I used to like strawberries a lot when I was a little girl," She added. "Just not tonight, that's all."

"Okay, fair enough. Your loss," said Dale as he reached over and grabbed Lucy's untouched bowl. "Waste not want not and all that. Do you mind?"

"Not at all," she said, standing up. "If it's all the same to you, I'm going to go upstairs to check through the images I got today. See if I really did get a shot of the woman in the window. Then I'm gonna grab an early night."

Dale nodded absently as Lucy swept the room key off the table and left. She made her way up the stairs and used the key to let herself into their room before she realized something. She had the only key, and Dale was still drinking downstairs.

Shit.

She contemplated taking it back down to the bar, but then she wouldn't be able to open the door when she came back up. There had to be an easier way. She lifted the corner of the mat outside their room, the one emblazoned with Croeso y Cymru, and tucked the room key under it.

It should be safe. Dale will be back in an hour or two.

That done, she stepped into the room, flicked on a luminous light switch (nice touch), and allowed the spring-loaded door to close softly behind her. Sitting on the edge of her bed, she took off her battered pair of Converse and flexed her toes. Her feet ached. That walk on the beach had wiped her out. Plus, there were a lot of things floating around her mind just now. Emotional baggage, you might call it. Things she had to try and make sense of sooner rather than later.

Try as she might, she couldn't get the image of the woman at the window out of her head. Furthermore, whenever she thought of the mystery woman she felt an overwhelming feeling of sadness. It could almost be an inkling, a prelude to something bigger.

And the strawberries the landlord served up as a 'surprise.' What was that about?

Surely he can't have known about Strawberry, the childhood companion who kept her entertained with his crazy dancing.

How could he know?

Yet it seemed too far-fetched to be a simple coincidence. Lucy couldn't remember the last time she had even thought about Strawberry before today. It was almost as if that by thinking of him she had summoned him, called on him to give her a sign. And Strawberry duly obliged.

Before she forgot, Lucy sent Dale a text message telling him where he could find the room key, then sat for a while mulling things over.

Eventually she got up, went over to the window and looked out. She wasn't expecting to see much. It was dark, and their room wasn't facing the sea so she wouldn't even be able to stare out at the passing ships. What she wasn't expecting was the sheer emptiness on the other side of the glass divide. Though she gazed out for a couple of minutes, mouth partially open and breath fogging the glass, all she was able to make out were gently rolling hills set against the night sky. There wasn't even the distant twinkle of stars.

Lucy didn't think she'd ever been so far from civilization in her life. The sense of isolation was both disconcerting and all-consuming. Cities were big, dirty, dangerous places, but they were never as silent and still as this. There was comfort to be had in all that activity. The traffic, sirens, street noise, and sodium lights banished shadows even in the dead of night. You were never really alone, even if you were.

Drawing the curtains against the oppressive darkness, she went to sit at the beautifully-carved wooden dressing table. The chair creaked under her weight, but Lucy didn't take it personally. It was an old chair. She looked at her reflection, examining her face for any new spots or blemishes. Thankfully, there were none. As she stared at herself in the mirror, she ran her fingers along the stained wood. It was cool to the touch, and the feel of it against her fingers together with the gentle rubbing motion was soothing. She wondered if every room at Sker House came equipped with antique furniture of this quality. She supposed so, it would make sense to have all the rooms decorated the same way. Unless Dale's trick of telling the proprietor that they were here to do an article really did have a bearing on their treatment as guests.

As she caressed the dressing table's delightful contours and curves, she felt herself drifting off into a pleasant, wide-eyed daydream. In the absence of any pressing social engagements, she allowed herself the luxury.

But as she slipped into the fugue, a heavy weight began pressing down on her.

It was grief.

Loss.

Pure, mournful sadness.

The kind of burrowing hopelessness that consumes you from the inside out.

Lucy moaned and clutched at her chest. She wanted to rip out her heart and hold it until it stopped beating.

What was wrong with her?

In her anguish she let out a soft, angst-ridden moan, and then another. The second moan was almost a complete word.

Forever

Inside her head, the awful depression was accompanied by a name, repeated over and over again in a hoarse whisper.

Thomas.

Who the heck was Thomas?

Then Lucy remembered the shambolic interview with Machen, and the story he'd told of the Maid of Sker. She was Elizabeth. And what was the name of her true love? The man she was forbidden from marrying?

Thomas. It was Thomas.

Maybe the name was just fresh in Lucy's mind, but it didn't change the fact that something was burrowing away inside her, taking advantage of her psychic sensitivity and sucking the energy right out of her.

Lucy was still fighting to rise above the crushing sense of despair when all at once, the awful weight was lifted and she was brought crashing back to the here and now. She blinked several times and ran her fingers through her hair as her heart thudded desperately in her chest.

What the hell just happened? Was her imagination playing tricks, or did she really just experience a visit from the Maid of Sker? It was almost as if the spirit of the lovelorn girl had entered her body. Occupied it.

There was another, even more disturbing possibility.

A sensitive had no control over who or what made contact with them. They were effectively open, and vulnerable to all comers. Any passing spirit could stop by. Even demons. Demons liked to lie. They knew what you were thinking, what you wanted, and wouldn't hesitate to use the knowledge to trick you.

Lucy shivered. Still shaky on her feet, she crossed the room and unpacked her camera from its case. Extracting the memory card, she inserted it into a card reader which she then attached to Dale's laptop. When the desired program responded, she called up the contents of the memory card and began clicking through the images.

The first few were old experimental shots taken when she first bought the camera; she and her friends hitting West Quay and Bargate Shopping Centres, Starbucks, St Mary's Stadium. Then there was a solitary picture of her ex Steve in his favourite YSL work suit. Lucy had forgotten all about that picture. Without giving herself time to think about it, she hit DELETE and Steve disappeared forever. "Rot in hell, you bastard," she muttered as she skipped through to the photographs of Sker House she had taken from the beach.

There were twenty-four in total, six of them showing at least a partial view of the window where she'd seen the figure of the woman. One-by-one, she blew the pictures up and carefully inspected each of them.

The images showed the exterior of the house in exquisite detail; the stonework, the ramparts, the creeping ivy, the ornate windowsill. But as much as she studied the images, she could find no discernible trace of the woman. There was some curious shadow play in a few shots, something that may or may not be a portion of extended arm or the profile of a face. But there was nothing that could be considered solid photographic evidence.

Disappointed, she began to close the programme, then changed her mind and decided to spring clean her memory card instead. She had taken a few pictures to test the camera before they left.

Delete, delete, delete.

Then it was on to the pictures she'd taken in the bar, mainly of Champ the poor tired guard dog. And there Lucy stopped, finger hovering over the keyboard.

What the heck?

There was something wrong with almost every picture. Most looked as if the exposure had been mistimed somehow, but that couldn't be true. Digital cameras made it virtually impossible to take a bad picture. You just pointed the damn thing and hit the button, everything else was done automatically. Yet none of the images from the bar were clear. All were blurred or out of focus, and in some you could make out nothing except a few random shapes and contrasting colours. They were unusable.

"How?" Lucy said to herself as she picked up her camera and examined it. Maybe something was stuck to the lens, or obstructing the mechanism. But when she checked everything appeared to be in working order. Besides, the exterior pictures were taken after the interior pictures and they were all crystal clear.

Putting the camera to her eye, she found the desk and laptop in the viewfinder and squeezed off a couple of test shots. Then she took pictures of both the beds and the en suite door. When she checked the results, there was no problem. The photographs were all just what you would expect.

Stranger and stranger.

Intrigued, Lucy leaned forward to look at the photographs from the bar again. On closer inspection, she noted that not all were blurred, but instead ruined by wispy white trails that looked almost like cigarette smoke. There were also littered with coloured balls of different sizes.

Several images in particular caught her attention. One was a close-up of Champ, lying prone on the floor. His reddened, downcast eyes looking straight at one of the wispy white trails that had seemingly wrapped itself around him, almost as if the sheer weight of it was pinning the dog to the floor. One of the protuberances had the sinewy appearance of a bare arm, and the tendrils of mist terminated in what could be interpreted as splayed fingers. The fact that the dog acknowledged their presence indicated that the weird lights and trails were not the result of a technical fault at all, but rather some kind of physical manifestation that only the dog was able to see with the naked eye.

Something had been in the room with them.

But if there had been any orbs of light or smoke-like substance floating around down there, she would surely have noticed. It would have been hard *not* to notice. She had been oblivious to them at the time, yet Champ obviously wasn't.

She suddenly realized how tired she was and checked her watch. Not yet midnight, but it had been a taxing day. Maybe it was the long drive, the sea air, or the lemon Baccardi Breezer she'd put away with dinner. Whatever the cause, it was getting more and more difficult to keep her eyes open. She collected all the pictures she had identified as being weird or abnormal together into a separate folder and saved them onto the computer's desktop to show Dale, then ejected the memory card and changed into her pyjamas. After brushing her teeth she decided to forego the rest of her nightly pre-bed ritual, opting instead to curl up beneath the covers where she could savour the silence and tranquillity of this haven by the sea and get an early night.

Chapter 7:

Another Round

Only after Lucy had gone back to their room did Dale realize how weird she had been acting. Even more weird than usual. He'd stopped trying to figure out what went on inside her head, or the head of any other female for that matter, a long time ago. But there was definitely something up with her tonight. Whoever said that men were from Mars and women were from Venus had a good point. He speculated that maybe it was Lucy's 'time of the month'. Or maybe it was just prior to her 'time of the month'. Or just after. Whichever the dangerous part was. Who could keep up? When you added up all the potentially sensitive times in the menstrual cycle, it didn't leave much of a safe window. Too many girls used it as an excuse to behave irrationally without fear of reprisals. It was nature's get-out clause.

Oh, you have to let me get away with it, its not my fault, I'm having my period, you should be more sympathetic.

Yeah, right.

Laying aside the second empty bowl of strawberries and cream, Dale took a deep breath. He didn't think there was any more room left in his stomach for another crumb. Even if it was free. But he wasn't ready to go to bed just yet. He seriously doubted Lucy's announcement that she was hitting the sack had been any kind of invitation. Why did he need a moody girl, anyway? There was a bar and an eccentric barman that kept giving him freebies. That was more than enough to keep him occupied. As a sign of goodwill, he picked up the dirty dishes from the table and took them back to the bar where a grinning Machen waited expectantly.

As Dale approached, he noticed Izzy working at a furious pace wiping down surfaces. She must have somewhere else to be tonight, he thought. Then again, didn't everybody have somewhere else to be when they were at work? "Any chance of another pint mist... I mean, Machen?" he asked, stepping carefully over Champ's extended paw.

The landlord nodded, plucked a clean glass from the shelf above his head, and began filling it, his face a picture of relief. Was business that bad he'd be so happy to sell just one more pint of beer? Surely not. No matter how bad business was, the four more quid he spent in the bar was unlikely to make much of a difference. The landlord wanted company. It soon became apparent that Lucy's assumption of Machen being 'a bit tipsy' was quite accurate. In fact, 'a bit tipsy' didn't even begin to cover it. If not quite the entire three sheets to the wind, he was at least two-and-a-bit.

As he waited for his beer, Dale's eyes drifted back to Izzy, who'd finished her manic bout of cleaning and was now washing her hands.

"Right, that's me finished 'ere," the barmaid announced. "I'll go and help mam finish off in the kitchen." Drying her hands on a towel, she disappeared through the door behind the bar.

Dale paid for his beer, collected his change, and turned to take his place back at the table in the corner. But then his eyes settled on the man they called Old Rolly. He was sitting in the same place as he had been when they first saw him, staring into space and nursing a half-empty pint of no-doubt warm dark ale, a well-read newspaper lying neatly folded on the table. The bloke had to be seventy-five years old. With his long white beard, he looked like a renegade Merlin.

The pubs of Great Britain are full of men like him. Their working careers over, their lives had no structure, and with nothing else to do with their time they became slaves to their own self-devised routines. As they approached their twilight years they still wanted to be sociable, a part of something, but all they were physically capable of doing was sitting around and reminiscing, doing crosswords and watching telly. So they became creatures of habit; sitting in the same place, drinking the same thing, bringing order to their lives the only way they knew how. Most of them were just lonely old men who craved a bit of interaction, even if they could only ever be on the periphery of things. It was sad to watch them while away their remaining hours alone in pubs because they had nothing better to do. But at least they were able to do what they wanted.

To help pay his tuition fees, Dale worked in a Southampton pub called the Saint. When he took the job he knew a Welshman working in a pub in an English port city would get his share of ribbing. It was one of the reasons he applied for the job in the first place. He wanted to see what it was like inside the lion's den. During the afternoons, the place was the domain of regulars like Old Rolly. Dale never had any problems with them. But it was a different story with some of the younger local lads who seemed to resent him being there came in when they finished work. They usually called him 'Taff,' which was tolerable. One of those affectionate insults, like calling a Scotsman 'Jock' or an Irishman 'Paddy.'

But some punters didn't stop there. They had to go the extra mile and wheel out the old 'sheepshagger' jokes. They were just boring. You would think that in all the years people have had to think up more imaginative insults, they would be able to come up with something more original by now. But no, every night the same brainless individuals, all Burberry shirts and baseball caps, saying the same brainless things.

Even the sheepshagger brigade were bearable. Usually. They were just trying to be funny. If a Welshman doesn't have his sense of humour, he doesn't have much. It was the vindictive ones that really made him angry. The ones who, on hearing his accent, openly berated him for being a bloody foreigner and told him to fuck off home and leave jobs in England to the English. Not that any of those people would have wanted his job.

Turning on his heels, Dale went back to the bar for a second pint, this one full of whatever Old Rolly was drinking. Luckily, Machen knew what it was. After a moment's thought, he reconsidered and told the landlord to pull one for himself too. Machen obliged, his face lighting up. Dale had the impression that the landlord's delight was about more than just the extra money going in the till. The transaction complete, Dale carried Old Rolly's drink over to where the old man was sitting and put it on the table in front of him. "This is for you, sir."

Old Rolly's nostrils flared and a pair of piercing blue eyes flicked up at Dale from beneath overgrown eyebrows, the same shade of speckled white as his long unkempt mane of hair and beard. For a moment he looked wary. Then, just as the silence was heading into uncomfortable territory, the old man's wrinkled, withered face crumpled into a wide smile. "Thank you, son."

Judging by how surprised and grateful he was, it must have been a long time since anyone had bought Old Rolly a drink. Not wanting to impose any further, Dale then did a slow walking tour of the bar, looking at the ornaments and various decorations that hung on the walls. He stopped at the dusty framed picture that he had seen Lucy looking at so intently. The photograph showed a group of men standing in front of a small boat. Dale peered closer. It was called Edward, Prince of Wales and the inscription beneath the photograph said: Mumbles RNLI, 1947.

RNLI? Royal Navy Lifeboat Institution? Dale didn't know how he knew that, but he did. One of those useless scraps of information your brain gets hold of and never gives up, storing it away in some deep, dark recess until such a time as it comes in useful.

"You like that photograph, son?" It was Old Rolly, speaking from his seat. Calm and deep, his voice resonated around the four walls.

Without turning around Dale replied, "I don't know about liking it, but its certainly interesting. Who are those men?"

There was a pause that lasted so long Dale began to think that Old Rolly had already grown bored of their budding conversation and nipped it in the bud. When the old man spoke again, he completely ignored the question and instead asked one of his own. "Do you read books, boy?"
Dale was taken aback, "Erm, yes."

"Which kind?"

Dale took a swig of his beer, "I read text books for uni, you know, books about journalistic theory, media models, public relations and all that stuff. And I when I have time I read novels. Contemporary fiction, mostly. I like Tony Parsons and Nick Hornby, 'man books' Lucy calls them. My favourite writer of all time is Stephen King. The Master."

"The horror writer?"

"That's what they call him but it's not entirely accurate. He writes in lots of genres; fantasy, crime, thriller, noir. Horror is just one of them." It crossed Dale's mind that he should return the question and ask Old Rolly what kind of books he liked to read, but he sensed that the old man didn't really want to have a conversation about books. This was leading somewhere else.

"Do you know what you are looking at there?"

"I know its an old picture of some men and a boat, but I don't know the significance of it if that's what you mean."

"There are more things in heaven and earth, Horatio, than dreamt of in your philosophy."

It took Dale a few moments to place the quote. English literature wasn't his strong point. "Is that from Hamlet?"

"Indeed it is. Top marks. Do you understand what the phrase means?"

"I think so. Truth is stranger than fiction, right?"

"Exactly. And not only stranger, but more terrifying than you could ever imagine. What you are looking at there is a painful reminder, a slice of real life horror. And I don't mean vampires and werewolves and all that other make-believe Hollywood stuff."

"Then what do you mean?"

"I mean, there have been enough real-life horrors around here without delving into the realms of fantasy and science fiction. Are you familiar with the Mumbles Lifeboat Disaster? I hear you and your friend are here to write a story. If you want to write a real story you should write one about the heroes that died that night."

Now Dale thought about it, the Mumbles Lifeboat Disaster did sound familiar, but he couldn't remember specifics. In the end, he was forced to concede ignorance. "What's the Mumbles Lifeboat Disaster?"

"It was April of 1947 when the Great Storm struck," Old Rolly began. "One of the worst we've ever had. The Samtampa was a Liberty ship left over from the war, heading through the Bristol Channel to Newport from Middlesbrough when she was blown onto rocks. The lifeboat in the photograph was launched on a rescue mission. But the waves were so big that they capsized the Samtampa causing it to fall onto the smaller lifeboat, smashing it to pieces. There wasn't a single survivor from either ship. Altogether, forty-seven people lost their lives. The picture you are looking at is of the very crew that died, taken only a few weeks before the disaster. If you look closely, you can see death in their eyes."

The old man's words echoing around his head, Dale found himself peering closer at the old framed photograph. "Where did it happen? Mumbles?"

"Mumbles? Christ, no. It's called the Mumbles Lifeboat Disaster because that was where the lifeboat came from. It happened on the Black Rocks of Sker Point. Just a few hundred yards froim where you're standing right now. You can see the rocks plain-as-day from out there on the beach. I remember that night as if it were yesterday."

"You were there?"

"Yes. I was just a boy, but I'll never forget what I saw. I remember standing out there on the beach, watching everything unfold. Not that you could see much. Pitch black, it was. You could only make things out in the lightning flashes. The rain was hitting so hard it stung your face. Most of the locals came out. In the days of the wreckers, they would have been waiting for cargo to get washed ashore so they could claim it for themselves. But on this night, people were just... watching. Wishing there was something more they could do. We watched as the boats were ripped apart and the men disappeared beneath the waves. The worst thing was feeling so helpless. Do you know what killed all those men?"

"I guess they drowned," Dale said. It seemed logical.

"Oh, they drowned alright. You see, the Samtampa was carrying a cargo of crude oil. When it struck the rocks the holding tanks ruptured, spilling it all out into the sea. By the time the lifeboat got there the water was thick with the stuff. It floats on the surface, you know. When the lifeboat went down, the water was too thick for the crew to swim in it and they choked to death."

There was a pause. Dale wondered if he should try to fill it, but then Old Rolly continued. "Looking back it seems kind of ghoulish to say we just stood there watching. Like when you see a car accident and deliberately slow down so you can get a closer look. Why do we do that?"

Dale shook his head. He'd thought about that himself. He used to think pure blood lust fed the compulsion to rubberneck, and maybe it's true of some people. They want to see severed limbs, mangled corpses, bodies and hot metal twisted together. Others genuinely want to help, but don't know how. But maybe the highest percentage of people are just thankful that it didn't happen to them.

"There was nothing else we could do," Old Rolly continued. "A few of us had boats, little dinghy's mostly, but if we had tried to use them, we would have perished too. A full-scale search and rescue was launched the next morning after the storm had passed, but by then it was too late and the beach was strewn with bodies and wreckage."

Dale sensed Old Rolly had been carrying this burden with him for a long time, and was glad of the opportunity to finally unload. He tore himself away from the photograph, suddenly feeling like a ghoul himself, took his beer and went to sit with his new friend. He noticed the newspaper on the table was almost a week old. Finally, he said, "You don't have anything to be sorry about. Like you say, there was nothing you could have done."

"But all those people. Their families. What it did to them. All that grief and sadness. It leaves a mark, you know. Not just on people, but on places."

"What do you mean?"

"I mean sometimes, death, sorrow, misery. It pollutes a place. Affects it."

"So you're saying Sker House is... polluted?"

Old Rolly tipped his head to one side. "For want of a better word, yes. And I don't just mean that the bloody sea is full of rubbish. Which it is, by the way. The Mumbles Lifeboat Disaster wasn't the first tragedy to befall this place."

Dale was suddenly excited. At last! This was exactly what he needed for his article. First-hand knowledge, real-life accounts, not just sanitised tourist stories that anyone could pull off the web. He suddenly wished he'd brought his Dictaphone with him, or at least his notebook and pencil. No matter. He would commit as much as he could to memory, and make notes later. "There have been other... disasters?"

"Many more, son. More than you can imagine. Not all as famous as the Mumbles Lifeboat, but a lot of terrible things have happened in and round these walls." Then, the old man said something that gave Dale chills. "In some places, evil lurks."

"It does?"

The old man sipped his pint and wiped froth from his moustache. "Absolutely. Did you stop to wonder what that ship was doing there? It was way off course. The seas around here are dangerous. Ships and boats have always taken care when traversing the shipping lanes. The Samtampa's course should have taken it well clear of the Black Rocks. But for some reason, it didn't. It was almost like it was drawn here."

"Maybe the wind, the current..."

"Yes, maybe. That's what I told myself, son. But the captain was no fool. He was an experienced seaman. I'm willing to wager that he had survived worse conditions. He'd probably travelled these same waters many times and came away unscathed. It's this place, Sker. I don't know whether it's tainted because of all the tragedy, or whether the tragedies happen because it is tainted. Which came first, the chicken or the egg? I don't bloody know. But I'll tell you something else. Something I haven't told anyone in a very long time."

"What?"

"I saw something else that night. I know I wasn't the only one, because it was the talk of the playground the next day."

"What did you see?" Dale prompted.

There was a long pause, then the man said, "Lights. We saw lights on the beach."

Dale frowned, unable to grasp the significance. Lights on the beach? What could that mean? He wanted to hear more. He wanted to hear everything. But the conversation was cut short when Old Rolly suddenly stood up, yawned, and without another word sauntered out of the room, leaving the fresh pint of dark ale untouched on the table next to his neatly-folded old newspaper. Dale watched him leave, wondering what to make of their exchange.

In some places, evil lurks...

Was he unhinged? Deliberately trying to scare the new guests? Or did he really believe that this little part of South Wales was some kind of breeding ground for bad luck and general nastiness? The old man had seemed so rational and sincere. Either he was an exceptional liar, or he really believed what he was saying.

Just then, Izzy appeared from the kitchen, accompanied by an older, stern-looking woman who was undoubtedly her mother. They both looked flustered and red-faced, and were still wiping their hands on paper towels even as they bustled around each other. "Right then, that's us done!" said the older woman.

"Okay ladies, drive safe." Replied Machen, but he was too late. The door had already closed.   Obviously, Izzy wasn't the only one in a hurry.

76

Dale took a large double swallow of beer and watched through the window as the two women practically ran to the little Nova in the car park and jumped inside. Mrs Watkins started the engine and pulled off so quickly that the passenger side door was still partially open forcing Izzy to reach out a skinny arm to wrench it closed.

He didn't know about evil, but paranoia and slightly bizarre behaviour definitely lurked in Sker House. Machen, Old Rolly, even Izzy and her mum were all on edge and permanently jumpy, as if just waiting for something terrible to happen. Every smile seemed forced, worn just to keep up appearances, yet beneath the façade everyone was falling to pieces.

But Dale had never met any of these people before. Maybe this was normal behaviour for them, and him being an outsider and not attuned to their living habits and mannerisms was causing him to misinterpret the whole situation. Perhaps he was the flaky one. It crossed his mind that he was making everyone nervous by asking too many questions. He should tone it down and not make his intentions so obvious. But isn't that what people do, ask questions? Isn't that how normal conversations start and relationships develop?

"I wouldn't take too much notice about whatever Old Rolly says." Machen had evidently finished his work behind the bar and taken a seat right next to Dale. "He's a nice fella, really. But he's not playing with a full deck, that one. If you know what I mean, like. Don't let anything he says worry you."

"I'm not worried," Dale said, taking another large gulp of beer. "If he doesn't like Stephen King, that's his lookout."

"Who?"

"Nothing," Dale said. "What's the story with him, anyway?" Damn. There he goes asking questions again. It was a hard habit to break.

Machen seemed happy to answer that particular query. "A bit of a mystery is Old Rolly," he said. "The guy will just sit in here reading old newspapers and supping his ale, not speaking a word to anyone. We just leave him to it. He pays his bills on time and spends a fair bit in the bar. Can't ask for much more that that."

"No, I s'pose not. It's just a bit sad to see. Does he have any family around here?"

"I reckon with you being from the Valley's and that, you know all about what small towns are like for gossip."

Dale nodded. He knew.

"Rolly comes from money, he does. So they say. Though you'd never think it to look at him. I don't know about any family. He never talks about them. But I know they've lived in the area for donkey's years. The day after we opened, he turned up on the doorstep with a suitcase and asked if he could stay here. Long term. Now me, I like the idea of live-in guests, I do. Even if it's only one. Gives you some regular income you can work into the budget, see. We offered him a discount, but the silly sod wouldn't have any of it. Said he'd always paid his way in life and wasn't going to stop now. I think he was a bit embarrassed 'cos we might have thought he was a charity case. Fair enough. Pay full price if it makes you feel better, I thought. We wasn't going to argue with him about it."

"Who's we? You, Izzy and her mum?"

"No, me and the wife, Sandra. She was here then. Izzy and Mrs Watkins came later, after we advertised in the paper for staff. Had a hell of a problem finding people to work here, we did. Don't know why. Must be 'cos it's a bit out of the way. The wife was worried Old Rolly was going to come here and get sick. He's knocking on a bit, like. She didn't want the responsibility of looking after him. Said the place would turn into a nursing home if many more like him turned up, and she wasn't a nurse."

The landlord thirstily drained his glass.

Dale wanted to ask where Machen's wife was, but stopped himself. Hadn't he mentioned something about her earlier? Something about her being... away? But where could she be? Surely she wasn't away on business, her business was here. On holiday, perhaps? He didn't want to jump to conclusions. The absent wife could be anywhere. But something about the landlord's demeanour and downcast eyes suggested that wherever she was, she wouldn't be coming back any time soon.

"More beer, is it?" Asked Machen as he lumbered off toward the bar.

"I shouldn't. Lucy's on her own upstairs"

"We're all on our own, son. Don't worry, she'll be fast asleep by now, I reckon. Go on, one for the road, eh? Or the stairs. One for the stairs? It's my round."

That was the clincher. Nobody in their right mind ever walked away when it was someone else's round. It was also a subtle indication that the landlord didn't find Dale quite as annoying as he'd first feared. Realizing that it could be in his best interests, Dale agreed to stay.

Even on Saturday nights at the Saint when things got rowdy, with the football crowd either celebrating or drowning their sorrows, Dale had never seen anyone drink so much in such a short space of time as Machen did that night. When he poured Dale's pint of beer he poured himself two, and finished them both before Dale could finish even half of his.

When his two pints of beer were dispensed with, the landlord went behind the bar and helped himself to a bottle of Jack Daniels and two shot glasses. That was Dale's cue to leave. Whisky didn't agree with him. He fished his phone out of his pocket and saw Lucy had sent him a message.

TURNING IN. THE ROOM KEY IS UNDER THE WELCOME MAT. SEE YOU IN THE MORNING X

The text was time-stamped over forty minutes ago. She would be fast asleep by now.

Dale couldn't help but feel a slight sinking sensation. Although he'd all-but given up on ever hooking up with Lucy there was always a faint glimmer of hope, which had just been extinguished for another night. That, on top of the imminent threat of whiskey was enough to curtail his evening.

As he said good night and slipped quietly out of the bar, he noticed the landlord was already busy pouring himself another drink.

Chapter 8:

All The Eggs in One Basket

Sandra, Sandra, Sandra.

The name of his absent wife repeated in Machen's head over and over again, as if caught on some broken tape loop. Scowling, he threw back his head and drained the last of the JD from his glass, then coughed and winced as he swallowed back the sour-tasting bile that filled his mouth.

She's gone. Get over it.

But it wasn't that easy. The sense of loss he felt was an almost physical yearning, a huge dimensionless void deep inside him. Every moment was a struggle to keep from being drawn in. He would give anything to go back to the way things were, before they came to Sker House, knowing all the while that it was impossible.

They'd first met back in 1976, the year Wales won the Grand Slam with the group of players known as the 'Entertainers,' who would become the benchmark for all future Welsh national rugby teams. By the time Wales won their next Grand Slam two years later (which would be their last for a while) Machen and Sandra were married and living in a two-bedroom terraced house in Bridgend. In those days they had a happy and stable life, with barely a crossed word. After a short stint down the coal mines, Machen worked for a succession of breweries that sent him to different pubs all over South Wales, never staying in any one place longer than two or three years. This was the lifestyle they enjoyed for the next thirty-odd years.

But then people started buying their booze in supermarkets rather than the pub, and Machen was astute enough to realize that their days in the publican trade were numbered. He and Sandra discussed their next move at length, and decided to finally put their dream of running their own guesthouse into motion. After that, it was simply a case of consolidating their savings and waiting for the right opportunity.

Not long afterwards, Sker House went on the market and Machen and Sandra bought it at auction. There wasn't much in the way of rival bidders, which should have been a red flag, and they ended up with a fairly good deal. Even then it was a huge financial undertaking, but between their savings, a council grant, and a small business loan, they could just about scrape together enough. However, having put all their eggs in one basket, Sker House then represented the entire sum of their wealth. It was the embodiment of their dreams. They had no idea at that early stage that those dreams would soon turned to nightmares.

Things changed the moment they moved in. Though 'moved in' wasn't exactly the right term. Sker House was in such a decrepit state that they lived in a tiny two-berth caravan on the grounds for the first six months, while various contractors worked on the roof and structure in order to make the place liveable again. In those early days, there was a lot of stress. At the same time, however, Machen felt empowered with a sense of freedom he'd never known before. In a roundabout way, he was finally fulfilling his childhood fantasy of becoming a gypsy, even if he didn't travel very far. Thinking about it later, he realised that he'd been a gypsy all his life. Never settling in one place, always restless, and dragging poor Sandra along for the ride. The only thing missing until then had been the caravan.

It's a cliché, but the moment they took the plunge, whatever could go wrong did go wrong. First, there was all the unforeseen legal stuff that Machen didn't fully understand, but paid blood-sucking solicitors ridiculous amounts of money to deal with on his behalf. On top of that, or maybe because of that, he and Sandra's relationship began to disintegrate and they started arguing over the smallest things. Their money was being frittered away, yet so much work still needed to be done.

To save a few quid, Machen shopped around for the cheapest building firm, eventually settling on a group largely comprised of Eastern European immigrants and fronted by an unpleasant cockney geezer called Dave.

He should have known something was off with Dave from the start. He could talk his way out of a paper bag, that one.

Was that the right saying?

Talk his way out of a...

Anyway, hindsight is a wonderful thing, and being in the pub game for so long had taught Machen that you don't have to like someone to do business with them. The two parties agreed on a price and Dave put his crew to work, though he disappeared back to Essex the minute the cheque cleared leaving a foreman in charge who could barely speak English. Despite lacking communication skills (and possibly work visas) the crew threw themselves into the job. At first, anyway. They opted to live on site, sleeping in what was now the bar area on the ground floor, which meant that early each morning Machen and Sandra were rudely awoken by the sounds of men at work. Not that it mattered. It was the sound of progress.

Not having much else to do, Machen and Sandra would regularly drop in on the workmen. Trying to decipher their broken English was a challenge Sandra relished, and the visits allowed Machen to oversee the work. Or at least give that impression. The motley crew of workers actually seemed like a decent bunch of blokes when you got to know them. Not the kind you would want to meet in a dark alley, mind. In between ripping up floorboards and smashing down walls, they would smile and show off pictures of their families.

In the first few weeks, they were actually running ahead of schedule. But then, something changed. Almost overnight, the smiling bunch of friendly ruffians turned into solemn caricatures of themselves. They stopped talking and laughing, instead going about their work methodically and without any measure of enthusiasm. The only verbal indication that something was amiss came when one of them once mumbled something about not being able to get enough sleep at night. At the time, Machen didn't pay it much thought but soon after, things really degenerated. Either because the men were overworked, inexperienced, or simply because they fell into some weird malaise, they started having accidents. One of the younger lads fell off a ladder on the fourth floor and broke his leg. Nasty fracture it was, too, the shin bone coming right out through the skin. Another worker came out on the losing end after a run-in with a nail gun.

Then there was the guy that disappeared.

Machen didn't believe a word of it himself. How could someone just fall off the face of the earth like that? But that was what his friends insisted. He went to inspect the sub-cellar, the old disused cellar beneath the actual cellar, and never came back out.

When they told him, the crew acted like it was his fault. As if! Even if one of their number did go missing, it was nothing to do with Machen. He had an idea they were angling for cash. Hush money or compensation. Good luck with that, he remembered thinking. Even if he had a surplus of cash, which he didn't, he wasn't about to start giving it away.

The final straw came just a day or two later when Machen paid his usual morning visit (unaccompanied by Sandra, thankfully, who had opted for a lie-in that morning) only to find one of the four remaining workmen walking round and round in circles, clutching a hammer and mumbling away to himself in some language Machen didn't understand. The bloke had quite obviously gone around the twist. When his colleagues woke up they promptly packed up their personal belongings and walked off the job en mass, taking the poor crazy sod with them. Pity. He was one of the blokes Machen had built up a relationship with. The last time Machen saw him he was sitting in the back of their truck, still clutching the hammer and talking gibberish. In that instant, Machen wasn't too upset to see him leave. He didn't care for the look in the man's eyes. It was an empty, vacant expression, as if something had reached down inside him and yanked everything out.

In the aftermath of that sequence of events, Machen must have called Dave a hundred times or more. At first, the absent foreman was apologetic and vowed to get the men back down. Then, evidently giving up on that idea, he said he would hire a new crew. But the new crew never materialized, and after a while Dave stopped taking his calls. Then he changed his phone number. Bloody cowboy. The whole thing was now in the hands of the solicitors, the latest news being that Dave had declared his contracting company bankrupt. The way the legal system worked, it would be a long time before Machen would be able to get back any of the money he paid out, if at all, and without that he was unable to hire anybody else to finish the job. He was stuffed. Out of desperation, he took it upon himself to finish up whatever he could manage. Plastering, painting, tiling, and so forth. Fortunately, Dave's cowboys left a load of materials behind and had done most of the larger jobs before they left. The roof, foundations and shell had all been patched-up and declared sound. But work on the top floor had barely began, cutting the capacity of Sker House by almost half. The place couldn't even pay for its own upkeep until it was functioning at a higher occupancy rate, and that was assuming the guests would come. Advertising might help, but he couldn't arrange any until he had funds. Everything cost money.

"What a bloody mess," said Machen to no one in particular. Champ the lethargic guard dog was in his usual place at Machen's feet. At the sound of his master's voice, an ear twitched and with great effort he raised his head off his paws. "You're not gonna run off and leave me as well, are you?" Machen asked the dog, who whined a response then promptly went back to sleep. Taking that as a sign that he was now even boring dumb animals with his luckless tragi-drama of a life, Machen stood up, tottering unsteadily on his feet as the world around him spun wildly in and out of focus before zooming back to clarity.

Satisfied he wasn't going to fall over, not this time anyway, he snapped off the lights, locked the bar door behind him, and made his way up the stairs to his living quarters, a half-empty bottle of JD nestling under his arm. He didn't bother with a mixer.

Chapter 9:

Drowning

Dale knew it couldn't be real. But just knowing that wasn't enough to stop the terror spreading through him like a cancer.

The dream started innocuously enough. He was a sailor on a cargo ship. He knew this the way you just know things in dreams, the knowledge instilled rather than acquired. It was dusk and he was standing on the slippery deck, gripping the guardrail and gazing out over a calm sea as the last of the light faded into black, salt air in his nostrils and sea breeze on his face. Overhead, gulls swooped and dived around the ship's bulging sails, cawing as they went about their business.

A tiny speck of land in the distance had been growing steadily larger, and was now so close Dale thought he could almost reach out and touch it. It had been a long, perilous journey, but thankfully it was almost at an end.

The men, his comrades, were in good spirits. The excitement was palpable, bordering on euphoria. The sea bonded men as tightly as the battlefield. They were brothers in arms, their massed ranks fighting an eternal battle against nature. Soon the ship would be docking, and then they would see their loved ones for the first time in months. Wives, sweethearts, parents, children, brothers, sisters, all eagerly awaited their return.

For Dale, it had been an especially momentous journey. His very first. He hoped he had impressed enough to be given a second chance. The work was fraught with difficulty and danger, but a young man could make a good living on the ships. The wage was attractive, and the adventurous lifestyle far outweighed the risks.

Suddenly, the mood changed. The sky clouded over, at once blocking out the dying sun, the pleasant sea breeze turned into a howling wind, and rain drops the size of pennies began to fall. At first just a few, then more and more. The sense of euphoria shared by the crew dissipated to be replaced by a sense of workman-like urgency. As close to home as they were, there was still much to be done. Orders and instructions rang out, men raising their voices to be heard over the brewing storm as each slipped effortlessly into his assigned role. Dale busied himself lashing loose containers to the deck with metal chains and lengths of frayed rope. Beneath his feet, he felt the ship's body creak and groan.

With the wind came the waves, some so big they were like sheer walls of black water topped with angry white froth, towering over the ship before crashing down on the deck with terrifying force. This was the great lawless beast of the sea at its most vengeful and unforgiving. Dale was exhausted, and had to fight for every breath as the wind tried to suck it from his lungs. His clothes were sodden and stuck to his body, and his hair plastered across his face. He couldn't feel his fingers any more, but he had almost finished his task. Soon he would be able to go below deck to wait out the storm. They were close to their destination. So close. Any minute now they would be able to see the harbour lights.

There they were! Tiny orange orbs twinkling in the middle distance. The inviting sight of boats safely at anchor in the harbour. They must have been closer to port than he'd thought. Either that, or the storm had propelled them along their designated course much quicker than anyone had anticipated. Whatever, it didn't matter. Despite the peril they were in, there were triumphant shouts and whoops of joy as word spread amongst the men. The ship lurched unsteadily to one side as it endeavoured to change its course, and then followed an eerie moment of tranquillity. The howling wind died, the pounding rain eased off, and the great swells that threatened to engulf the ship subsided. For a few precious seconds, it was like being held in suspended animation. This must be the fabled eye of the storm.

Amazingly, miraculously, Dale was able to see through the darkness, across the vast expanse of water, straight into the heart of their destination. And what he saw there chilled him to the bone. There was no safe harbour. The lights flickered and winked out to reveal only a desolate, deserted beach, painted grey in the fading light. Worse than that, between the beach and the ship, ranks of jagged black rocks jutted up out of the treacherous water like murderous teeth.

The ship was heading straight toward them.

He felt a surge of panic run through his body. Could nobody else see what he was seeing? Why didn't someone sound the alarm?

He had to warn someone, get them to change course. It would be a hopeless task, the conditions were against them, but he had to do something. He screamed and hoped somebody would hear, but no sound came out of his mouth. He was struck dumb. That awful feeling of helplessness and vulnerability so prevalent in dreams washed over him as he resigned himself to his fate. They had been deceived, either by God or man, and there would be a heavy price to pay for such naivety.

There was a horrific, splintering crunch as the ship hit something unseen, and Dale knew that it was already too late. The vessel was jolted violently, sending those unfortunates still working top-side slipping and sliding across the deck, striking various immovable objects with sickening force as they went, snapping bones and ripping flesh.

Dale was thrown against some hand rails so hard he felt his ribs break. What little wind he had left in him leaked out slowly, he guessed through a punctured lung. One man cleared the rails completely, and was thrown head-first over the side into the thankless water below. He screamed as he fell.

At that moment, a gigantic wave rose over the ship, lifting it out of the water on its swell and throwing it onto the waiting black rocks, and it was then Dale knew they were doomed. There would be no welcome kisses, no glorious homecoming. The ominous sounds of wood being shredded mingled with the screams of the frightened and dying as the ship was mercilessly battered and smashed against the unyielding rock.

Then, there was water.

Only water. As cold and black as the night.

He tried to swim, frantically kicking and thrashing his limbs in desperation, but his ribs hurt and the swirling currents were too strong to resist. The water kept sucking him under, almost as if a demonic hand had a grip of his legs. He was twisting and turning in the depths so much that he didn't even know which way was up any more.

He tried to find a purchase, something solid that would keep him still, but his flailing arms found nothing. As his lungs filled with freezing, salty, vile liquid, the will to survive ebbed from his body.

In the end, he welcomed the silent tranquillity.

*

Dale opened his eyes. At first his befuddled mind couldn't make sense of what had happened, what was still happening.

He was suffocating!

He wanted to scream for help, but he there wasn't enough air in his lungs. Instead he lay on his back gasping and sucking grateful mouthfuls of oxygen into his body.

It was just a dream.

He lay still for a few moments, collecting his thoughts and waiting for his eyes to adjust to the darkness. The luminous face on his watch told him it was just after three in the morning.

Instinctively, he looked across at Lucy's sleeping form in the adjacent bed. He blinked once, twice.

Something was wrong.

It took him a few seconds to realize what was different. Then, his confused mind put the pieces together and he realized that the bed was empty, and all he was looking at was a bunched-up duvet.

He sat bolt-upright, heart thumping like a drum in his chest.

Where the fuck was Lucy?

He flicked on the bedside lamp and quickly scanned the room.

Nope.

No Lucy.

Furthermore, there was no light on in the en suite bathroom and no sound of running water, which meant she wasn't in there, either.

"Lucy?" he called tentatively.

No answer.

He called her name again as he fumbled around for his jeans and hoody. Where the hell could she even go? Worst case scenarios ranging from the banal to the extremely unlikely ran through Dale's mind; the landlord and Old Rolly were part of an international syndicate that drugged female guests and sold them into the sex trade, she had been abducted by aliens, or fallen down the unfamiliar staircase and now lay unconscious at the bottom. As unlikely as every explanation seemed, the fact of the matter was that Lucy was missing.

Then something struck him. Lucy wasn't in the room, that much was evident, but maybe she'd gone outside voluntarily. Yes, that must be it. You never know with creative types, they were

90

liable to do some damned unusual things in the name of art. Sneaking out after dark to take night scape pictures was pretty tame in comparison to some of the stories he heard.

He should call her. Yes, that's what he would do. If she'd gone out for a walk or something, surely she would have taken her phone. It would be stupid not to.

Dale quickly located his own phone, scrolled through his contacts list until he found Lucy, and pressed CALL.

Something stirred in the room, and a sudden noise fractured the stillness. Dale whirled around, unsure of what to expect. His heart sank a few notches when he realized that the noise he heard was just Lucy's phone, which had been left on her pillow. It vibrated softly, before breaking into the opening chords of the 21 Pilots track she used as her ringtone. He didn't know which one, they all sounded the same to him.

Shit. So she didn't take her phone with her. She must have taken their room key, though. They only had one key between them, so if she had gone somewhere and intended to get back in, she surely would have taken it. A quick scan of the room revealed the key still lying on the desk next to his notebook exactly where they had left it.

This was bad. Very bad.

Swearing under his breath, Dale swept the key up in his hand and thrust it into his pocket whilst simultaneously squeezing a pair of Vans onto sock-less feet. After a last look around the room, he quietly opened the door and slipped into the corridor.

The soft yellow lighting couldn't disguise how chilly it was. His breath left his mouth in plumes as Dale looked from left to right and back again. Every visible door was closed, and everything seemed just the way it should be.

He stood and listened for a few seconds. Nothing stirred. Heart thudding in his chest, he tip-toed toward the staircase at the far end. His feet sank into the lush blue carpet as he made his way down the corridor. When he reached the staircase he gripped the bannister, fingers curling around the icy cold wood.

Descending the staircase it felt like every nerve in his body was being pulled taught, every sense heightened. The faint smell of fresh paint hung in the air. At the bottom of the stairs were two doors. Knowing one led to the bar, he tried it. Locked. The other door, he guessed, was the 'after hours' entrance and exit Machen briefed them about.

He double checked that he still had the key to get back in.

Yes, it was in his pocket.

In his mind's eye he saw Lucy waking up during the night, coming down to get some air, and forgetting to take it with her. Right now she was probably standing outside, shivering. Dale, primed for a knight in shining armour cameo, unlocked the door and flung it open.

No Lucy.

He stuck his head outside and peered into the darkness. In the sky overhead, stars blinked intermittently through clouds racing across the sky. His car was still there, he could see its silhouette. At least Lucy hadn't stolen it to go joyriding. He wondered if he should risk calling out to make sure she hadn't taken shelter somewhere within earshot. But that would probably wake up everyone within a mile radius. He settled for calling her name in a hoarse whisper a few times instead.

No response.

Standing on the doorstep, he scratched his head.

What should he do now?

What could he do?

Raise the alarm?

When would be the appropriate time to push the red panic button?

Away to the left, the path he and Lucy had walked together just hours earlier stretched out into the darkness beyond and a gentle breeze ruffled the foliage. If Dale listened carefully, he could hear the constant restless murmur of the sea. He thought about venturing down to the beach, but knew it would be a pointless exercise. It would be so dark down there Lucy could be right under his nose and he wouldn't be able to see her. He whispered her name once more, as loudly as he dared, waited and listened.

As if in response to his voice, this time there was a noise. Something unidentifiable and foreign, yet unmistakeably manufactured. It came from somewhere on or near the path. His head snapped in that direction. Holding his breath, he scrutinized the dark expanse stretching out before him.

Something was moving.

He looked for recognisable shapes and outlines, but could distinguish nothing amongst the perpetually crawling shadows.

"Lucy?" he said cautiously, "Is that you?"

Suddenly, a strange feeling settled over him. No, not a feeling, more a conviction. An awful certainty that whatever lurked a little way up that path was something inhuman, something terrible.   Dale struggled to slow his racing heart and stay calm. Without even realizing it, he retreated warily back over the threshold of Sker House hoping its bricks and mortar would provide refuge. He thought about calling out again, but decided against it. Maybe a cat or a dog made the noise, a hedgehog or field mouse, even a werewolf or a zombie.

Whatever, it wasn't Lucy.

He decided to check their room again to see if she'd returned. If not, he would rouse the landlord and find out what the usual procedure was when one of his guests went missing. With no small sense of relief, he closed the self-locking door behind him and retraced his steps back up the stairs, cursing himself for getting spooked so easily. Some knight in shining armour he was turning out to be. He was halfway back to their room when he noticed the second flight of stairs leading to the upper floors.

Of course! How could he have been so stupid? Knowing Lucy, she was off trying to get pictures of the Maid of Sker in action. The fourth floor, where she'd seen the figure at the window.

He didn't bother checking their room again. Instead, he bounded up the staircase two at a time. As he neared the top he slowed and became more cautious. Here, the smell of paint was stronger. Didn't Machen say this part of the house was still being renovated? Who knew what he would think if he found Dale or Lucy roaming around up here at night unsupervised.

He carefully opened a door leading to another corridor. A large hand-drawn sign hanging on the door reading PRIVATE: NO ADMITTANCE was enough to make Dale pause for no more than a second.

Find Lucy, get the hell out.

The corridor was as black as the night outside. And why wouldn't it be? Nobody was even supposed to be up here. Hot on the heels of that thought came another, this one even more disturbing.

Was it safe?

There could be any number of unforeseen, life-threatening hazards laying in wait. The darkness seemed to ooze out onto the landing like an ink spill as Dale swiftly closed the door again to buy some time to think.

He was way out of his depth. Dale wanted to go and find Machen. He probably wouldn't be best pleased to be woken up at this hour, but at least he would know what to do.

On the other hand, he couldn't turn back now. If it hadn't been for him, Lucy wouldn't even have come to Sker. Now he was here, it wouldn't hurt to have a quick look around. Taking a deep breath, he opened the door again. It immediately tried to close itself, so Dale looked around for something to brace it open with. There was a large red fire extinguisher on the floor, which he shunted over and leaned against the door. The light from the landing would provide at least a little illumination, but more importantly, would stop him becoming disoriented. That done, he moved quietly into the corridor, squinting to see better.

The floor in this part of the house was littered with debris and yet to benefit from the luxury of a carpet. Even though he wore trainers and tried to tread carefully, the sound of his footsteps announced Dale's presence.

As he made his way down the corridor he kept imagining long, skeletal arms with rotting skin and flesh hanging off in strips reaching out and grabbing for him. He found himself moving quicker, the rectangle of light behind him diminishing with every step.

Around half way down, he realized he wasn't alone. There was a figure up ahead.

Dale stopped dead in his tracks and stared, his breath coming in short gasps.

It was definitely a human form, wearing something white, standing motionless at the dark end of the corridor. Judging by the shapely contours, he guessed it was a female.

The Maid of Sker?

Was he looking at a ghost? All the strength in his legs was sucked out and he leaned against the cracked, blistered wall to stop himself sinking to the floor. At any other time (preferably with a TV crew in tow) he would be happy to catch a glimpse of a famous apparition. But not tonight. Not now.

His first instinct was to run. Get away. Go and get Machen. But what would Dale say to him?

I was just trespassing upstairs, you know, the part of the house currently closed to the public, whilst looking for my friend, who's missing, by the way, when your ghost jumped out and scared the shit out of me.

That didn't sound very plausible, and Dale couldn't think of a way to make it sound any better.

Eyes glued to the apparition floating in front of him, he summoned every ounce of courage he had and pushed himself off the wall.

This is why you came here, he told himself. You came looking for ghosts and you found one. You should feel lucky, not scared. How many fishermen go fishing then run away at the sight of a fish?

Forcing his legs to do what they didn't want to do, he took a few hesitant paces forward. He wanted to try and make contact with the spirit, find out why it was here. At least he would get to see what a ghost looked like close up.

Eyes fixed on the eerie sight in front of him, he edged closer.

The figure hadn't moved an inch, and he began to wonder whether it could be a mannequin, liberated from some High Street shop and left to rot here in the upper reaches of Sker House. Optimistic, maybe. But as the old saying went, 'Hope for the best, plan for the worst'. Applying the maxim he found himself hoping for a mannequin, planning for a supernatural entity, and getting ready to run just in case.

Suddenly, the figure swayed slightly, like a blade of grass bending in a gentle breeze. It was no mannequin. It was a girl, standing outside a door and facing away from him.

Dale stopped dead. Self-consciously, he cleared his throat, "Er... miss?" At the sound of his voice the girl's head twitched, then slowly began to turn. He quickly checked behind him to make sure the exit was still clear and visible, the dependable, ever-shrinking rectangle of light waiting to act as a guide.

95

Curiosity drove him on, and he took another step forward. Hardly any light could penetrate this far, it was virtually pitch black. The girl faced him now, but he still couldn't make out any features.

Then, she shuffled forward a few steps and reached out a hand. "Dale, is that you? What happened?"

He'd found Lucy.

Chapter 10:

Alone with the Horrors

Machen lay motionless in his too-big bed, bathed in light from the lamp on his bedside table. It was switched on most of the time these days, its 60-watt bulb blazing defiantly on through the night. He may have lapsed into a couple of hours of fevered dozing after he polished off the latest bottle of JD, but he knew that was his lot for the night. Sleep was a luxury, and some nights were better than others. Once, a couple of weeks ago, he managed a full four hours. Or at least, he thought he did. Looking back he wasn't so sure. He may only have dreamt he was asleep all that time.

Is that even possible?

What little sleep he did manage to get was rarely restful. The wheels of his mind never stopped turning, and awful things stalked his dreams. As much as he was loathe to admit it, he sympathised with the workmen who complained about being unable to sleep at Sker House.

Now he understood. But as usual, it was too late.

And what good was understanding, anyway? Understanding something didn't magically grant you the ability to change it.

Like most children, in his early years Machen had been afflicted with a profound fear of the dark. He remembered watching the sun go down through his bedroom window with a sense of building trepidation, because he knew another night was coming.

But as he grew into a man, the fear left him to be replaced by more mundane preoccupations like love and work, and was largely forgotten. When he matured, he came to realise that the root of his anxiety was a simple fear of the unknown, rather than a fear of the dark itself. Darkness renders you blind, depriving you of the most essential of the five senses, and you fear what could be there rather than what is there, which was usually a big fat nothing. As soon as he accepted this fact, the nights became easier. As he grew older he learned to savour the serenity, and welcomed its silent embrace. Nights were quiet and peaceful, a time for rest and reflection.

But now in his twilight years that irrational childhood fear was back, and he had grown to despise the night more than ever. As daylight faded, he found himself getting more and more agitated. He dreaded the onset of darkness almost as much as he

98

dreaded counting his bar takings at the end of the day. That was when he usually reached for the bottle of whisky, telling himself it would soothe his shattered nerves and help him sleep.

It never did. In fact, many times it seemed to have the opposite effect and he would lie awake, head spinning violently as he tried not to throw up. Darkness made him feel inconsequential, like he didn't even exist. The knowledge that all his adult life had been spent in denial didn't sit well with him. All that time spent fooling himself, wrapping himself in a thick cloak of ignorance. Sker House had taught him that all those terrible things he imagined when he was a child, like salivating monsters with yellow eyes and long, sharp teeth and claws ready to tear the flesh from his bones, were more than just figments of an over-fertile imagination. They were real.

To his detriment, he also knew that even worse prowled the nocturnal landscape in those fateful hours before dawn. He had seen things. And not just in dreams. Nothing as graphic as a salivating monster with yellow eyes and long, sharp teeth and claws. Not yet, anyway. Thank God. But things every bit as disturbing. Once, he caught a glimpse of what looked like a long, tapering tail flicking in a shaft of moonlight in the corner of his bedroom. He would routinely turn off the bedside lamp and watch the shadows in his room converge and became one with the darkness, then morph and twist into monstrous shapes right before his very eyes. There were things in there. Figures. Some hunched and distorted, others towering over him, long and slender.

At that point he would snap the light back on, feeling a small spark of elation as the darkness and all that dwelt in it immediately receded. Sometimes he played the game all night, revelling in the small sense of control it provided. He could invite the monsters into his world, then banish them at the touch of a button. If needed, there was a handful of spare bulbs in one of the drawers of his bedside table, right next to his torch and the supply of candles, matches, and cigarette lighters he kept close at hand.

The light kept the crawling, creeping shadow figures at bay, but did nothing to curtail the strange cacophony of sounds, which were always more noticeable at night. He suspected the noises were there in the background all the time, going unnoticed beneath the din of daily life. But when the night settled there was no camouflage, and the muffled knocks and scrapes were plainly audible.   He worried about the guests more than himself. If he saw and heard these things, maybe they did, too. He didn't want to have to answer any awkward questions at breakfast. He had enough on his plate.

Enough on his plate at breakfast! Ha-ha!

Machen wondered if Old Rolly saw and heard things.

That was a lie. He knew the old man saw and heard things. He must.

What he really wondered was what Old Rolly *thought* when he saw and heard things. Despite his outward appearance, he was a shrewd character. He'd lived a life, and often gave the impression that he knew far more than he was letting on. He was a man of secrets.

What brought him to Sker House? Why here? Why now?

Machen knew there was a reason. But on the other hand, why should he care? As long as the old guy paid his keep.

When the noises first began to be a problem Machen tried listening to Classic FM on his clock/radio to block them out. But the noises would only rise in volume, seemingly in direct correlation with how loudly the music was being played. Occasionally, he was tempted to crank the volume switch as high as it would go, just to see how far he could push things. Being on a different level to the guest rooms meant he wouldn't disturb anyone. Especially with walls and floors this thick. But he feared the experiment would end badly. Through a process of trial and error, he discovered that as long as he didn't try to fight them, the noises usually remained at an acceptable level.

However, tonight was different.

Tonight, the knocks and scrapes seemed somehow different. They had risen above their normal volume and were more deliberate and agitated. Almost as if they were reacting to something.

But what? He hadn't done anything wrong. He'd lived up to his end of the uneasy amnesty he thought he'd reached with the entities with which he shared Sker House. No more Billy Joel at ridiculous volume, he got it. No problem.

If not him, something else must be troubling them. Upsetting the status quo.

No prizes for guessing what that must be.

Chapter 11:

A Midnight Adventure

Lucy's first thought was that she was no longer tucked up in bed. The cold seeped through her skin and into her bones, making her teeth chatter.

With dawning horror, she realized that she wasn't even in their room. Strangely however, once she had fought off the initial waves of panic and disorientation, she was surprised to find another emotion lurking beneath. A faint sense of belonging. Wherever she was, whatever she was doing, she knew that in some way it was the right thing to be doing.

As she began to assess her whereabouts, she became aware of someone or something behind her. Heart racing, she slowly turned around.

The sight of Dale standing in the corridor broke whatever spell she was under. It was the look on his face that did it; stark terror mixed with relief and bewilderment. Forgetting about her own predicament, she started to ask him what was wrong, then realized she was the object of his concern.

Now things made a little more sense.

She immediately felt safer knowing that Dale was with her, even if he had temporarily been struck mute. His mouth opened and closed like a goldfish as she moved toward him.

"I had a crazy dream about being on a sinking ship," Dale was saying. "Then I woke up and you were gone. I thought someone had taken you. I looked everywhere."

They were embracing now. Or, more accurately, Dale was holding her upright. They were so close, and for one fleeting moment Lucy had an overwhelming desire to raise her head and kiss his lips. Then, faced with the imminent prospect of playing tongue tennis with Dale, she suddenly came to her senses and at the last moment pushed him away.

What the hell was that?

Dale had some decent qualities, and she had even considered pulling him once or twice after a few too many vodkas in the student bars, but until that moment Lucy hadn't really thought he was her type. Obviously, she could read the signs and knew he liked her. But she was afraid such a development would change things between them. If it didn't work out romantically, there was a good chance their friendship would be destroyed forever. She knew it was a cliché, but that was something she valued too highly to put at risk.

"Where am I?" Lucy said again.

This time, Dale answered. "You're in Wales. In a haunted guest house near Porthcawl, to be precise."

"How did I get here?"

"I drove you. Yesterday."

"Be serious for a minute, will you?" She was in no mood for sarcasm. Dale's way of dealing with problems was to mask them with humour, but on this occasion it wasn't appreciated. She was scared. "I mean... here. How did I get HERE. What the hell happened to me?"

"Like I said. I woke up and you weren't in your bed. I looked everywhere for you and was just about to deduce that you had ran off with that Old Rolly geezer, when I stumbled across you hanging out up here. Presumably, you sleepwalked your arse here all by yourself with your eyes closed. Clever girl."

"Sleepwalked?" Lucy said the word as if it came from a foreign language.

"Yeah, sleepwalked. I can't think of a better explanation, can you?" Lucy shook her head slowly, while Dale looked her up and down to presumably check for injuries. "Erm... Have you ever done anything like this before?"

"No, never. At least, I don't think so." Lucy replied solemnly. She racked her brain for a precedent, but drew a blank. Surely, if she had a history of sleepwalking somebody would have alerted her to it by now; her parents, various room mates, friends, one of the lucky few she had invited into her bed.

"Well, I guess you wouldn't know, would you? I mean, you'd still be asleep."

"Guess so."

"That's freaky, Lucy."

"Yeah, tell me about it. Thanks for that. Now I feel a lot better. So... what was I doing when you found me?"

"You were just standing there."

"Standing where?"

"Right there." Dale nodded at a spot a few paces behind her. She turned around and looked. The stillness of her surroundings was oppressive, and she folded her arms across her chest against the chill. Goosebumps peppered the bare skin of her arms and legs. "Which floor are we on?"

"Four. The one that's not fit for human inhabitation yet."

She glanced up and down the silent corridor to get her bearings as Dale continued with his safety lecture. "You're damn lucky you didn't fall over something and break something, you know. There's loads of dangerous shit lying about. How did you do it, anyway? Navigate your way here, I mean. You had your eyes closed, for fuck's sake."

"I don't know how I did it, but I do know something."

"What's that?"

"I know that this floor is the same floor that I saw the woman watching us through the window earlier. She must have been in one of these rooms."

Dale's eyes widened. "Are you sure?"

"Yeah, pretty sure."

"Are you thinking what I'm thinking?"

"Maybe."

"Now we're here, we should check these rooms out."

"Makes sense..." Most of the rooms were without doors, but the one closest to them was ajar. Lucy clung to his arm as Dale pushed it gently. It swung inwards, revealing an impenetrable wall of darkness. "Did you bring a torch?" Lucy asked.

"No. Did you?"

"Nope. I wasn't planning on coming up here, Dale."

"Right. Well that makes this a pretty pointless exercise then, doesn't it? We can't see a thing."

"Did you bring your phone?"

"Sure," Dale replied.

"Good. Give it to me."

Dale handed over his device and Lucy swiped to open it, then turned on the torch function, flooding the corridor with bright light. It wasn't too difficult to read the expression on Dale's face.

Why didn't I think of that?

"Let's try one more door," she said. "That one..."

It was the strangest thing, but Lucy felt drawn to another door on the opposite side of the corridor. She couldn't be certain, but she sensed this was the room where she'd seen the figure in the window.

But it was more than that.

The room was special.

She couldn't explain how she knew that, so she didn't even try. Instead, she swallowed hard and put a hand on the cold wooden door. Summoning all her courage, she gently pushed.

It didn't move.

She pushed again, harder. Still, the door stayed firm.

"It must be locked," Dale whispered. "Do you want to try the rest?"

Lucy definitely didn't want to try the rest. She wanted to go back to their room, lock the door, get warm and try to wrap her head around the events of the evening. "It's useless. I don't think it's the right time to be exploring."

"Yeah, right," Dale agreed. "No bother, we can come back another time. It's not like any of these rooms are going anywhere."

"You know, I could just be going crazy."

"I've been telling you that for years, Lucy. So what are we going to do about it?"

"What can we do?" replied Lucy, her frustration growing. This whole experience, this whole place, was beginning to freak her out.

"We can start by getting you back in your bed, miss Midnight Adventurer. You must be freezing."

Dale put an arm around her shoulders and guided her in the direction of a door at the end of the corridor. A sliver of light shone through it.

For once, Lucy was more than happy to be led. As they walked, she looked at Dale and said, "You won't tell anyone about this, will you?"

"Of course not," Dale replied. "Your secret is safe with me. And besides, who is there to tell? We're in the middle of nowhere."

Chapter 12:

The Message

Dale was still too spooked to be able to sleep. Instead, he sat upright with his fingers laced behind his head, staring over at the other bed where Lucy snored softly. She didn't seem to be adversely affected by her sleepwalking experience, but he certainly was. It had been his responsibility to look after her, keep her safe, and he had failed in his duty. It felt like he had just flunked an important exam.

After the short trip down the stairs, Lucy had simply crawled back under the covers and pulled them over her head without so much as another word. She still didn't seem completely 'with it.' As they had talked upstairs in the corridor, she'd looked dazed, as if operating at half speed.

It would be light soon. Through the window, he could see the first rays of the morning sun peeking over the distant mountain tops. This working weekend break was supposed to be fun, but had taken a distinctly sinister turn. Several in fact, and they'd been at Sker House less than twenty-four hours. The challenge now lay in extracting some kind of narrative from his and Lucy's misadventures and weaving it into a decent story. While it had certainly been interesting, Dale doubted they had enough thus far to warrant the four-page spread in the Solent News he had promised the editor.

Giving up on catching any more sleep, he climbed out of bed, tip-toed into the en suite and took a rare early-morning shower. As the warm water cascaded over his body and steam began to impair his vision, his mind was cast back to the drowning dream. The details were already beginning to fade, but he still remembered the emotion and intensity. The feeling of hopelessness, and the eventual surrender.

He tried not to read much into it. His subconscious mind had obviously been influenced by his surroundings, not to mention the alcohol he had put away before going to bed. But it was undeniable that he now felt much more of an affinity with the ocean, and those who chose to spend their lives trying to survive it.

He also thought about the awful sensation of panic he had felt at the door leading to the seafront path while he was conducting his search for Lucy. The sudden conviction that he was almost within touching distance of something so evil that it gave off putrid rays of corrupted energy, stirring his most primitive instincts and imploring him to run. He shuddered at the thought and reached for a towel to dry himself. It all seemed silly now in broad daylight, as most nocturnal escapades did.

You just got caught up in the moment, he told himself. Blew everything out of proportion. The thing you heard was probably just a startled animal scampering for cover.

Yeah, right.

Still deep in thought, he brushed his teeth, dressed, and went back into the bedroom. Positioning himself at the desk where he could watch the sunrise through the window, he switched on his laptop. It immediately buzzed into life. The first thing he noticed was the new, unlabelled folder on the desktop. Lucy must have put it there. He opened it to examine the contents, feeling a momentary pang of guilt as if he were about to read his friend's diary. But whatever was contained in the folder couldn't be that sensitive, or she wouldn't have left it where he would be certain to find it, would she? On his own computer, no less.

Unless she hadn't meant to do it.

That possibility made things exciting, but the excitement quickly turned to disappointment when he saw that the folder was just full of pictures she had taken the day before. No bikini shots there, then. Even worse, they appeared to be very bad pictures. Virtually every one was foggy, blurred, or out of focus. Not what you expected from a twelve-year old, let alone somebody with two years training and aspirations of becoming a professional photographer.

Assuming Lucy was either having some kind of experimental phase or had simply invested in a shitty camera, Dale closed the folder. Since it didn't look like Lucy would be getting up for a while, he decided to get to grips with the transcribing exercise he'd started. Picking up his notebook, he began leafing through it to the part where the interview with Machen was recorded. There, he froze.

"What the actual fuck?"

He loved writing on the facing page much more than the first page. It was new, fresh, and unspoiled, except for a few faint ballpoint indentations. He and Lucy had talked about this before, and she had immediately deduced symptoms of Obsessive Compulsive Disorder. He wasn't sure about that, but he was sure

Lucy knew that deliberately disfiguring one of his facing pages would bring her a world of hurt.

That was how he knew that what was written there, beneath his own writing, wasn't written by her. She would never dare. He also knew he didn't do it. Though his handwriting may be unintelligible to almost everyone else, it was a thousand times better than this abomination.

So if not he nor Lucy, who?

The worst thing about it was that whoever had disfigured his notebook had done so with extreme prejudice, pushing down on the writing instrument (undoubtedly the nearby 2B pencil, to add insult to injury) with such force that they had probably marked the next fifteen pages.

The rotten bastards.

In some cases, the pencil had torn straight through the paper, making it seem more like a frenzied attack than a genuine attempt at communication.

Dale stared at the display of random scratches, lines, scrawls and semi-formed letters, trying to make sense of them all. The first letter was most likely a 'C', followed by what could be a capital 'E' or a very badly drawn lower case 'A.' Then there were two figures that looked the same. But beyond that, it was impossible to decipher. Yet, the more he stared at the notebook, the more the letters seemed to make sense. If he let his imagination run wild, he thought he could even make out actual words.

But Dale suspected this was the same kind of mental trickery that made you see animals in cloud formations.

Matrixing.

If you look hard enough, your mind will ensure that you see something. Usually, just what you wanted to see.

After those first few barely-legible forms, the writing descended into indiscriminate lines and scrawls, growing steadily fainter as they stretched across the page as if whoever was writing it was running out of strength or vitriol.

Taken as an individual incident, the mysterious message, if that was what it was, didn't set off too many alarm bells. It was a crazy world, shit happened, and most of the time you don't know how or why. If Dale scrutinized every mini-mystery he encountered there wouldn't be any time left for anything else.

But the discovery of the message came right after Lucy's sleepwalking adventure, and her insistence on seeing the figure at the window. You could take one strange occurrence in your stride, but three in less than a day? It was too much to be coincidence.

Maybe there's a story here after all, Dale thought as he began to type.

Chapter 13:

Daybreak

Lying in his bed, Machen was also watching the sun rise through a very deliberate gap in his curtains, basking in the blessed sense of relief it brought. The birth of a new day was an almost divine event, as if God himself was sending his vanquishing angels to quell the dark rebellion. He revelled in the euphoria of surviving another battle, though lurking beneath it was the grim certainty that there would be many more battles to face in a war that he could ultimately never win. In the end, the darkness would get him.

He lived on the third floor of Sker House, directly above the guest rooms. He and Sandra's original plan had been to convert the fourth floor into a small apartment for themselves and maybe a Honeymoon Suite. But that idea had evaporated the minute those foreign cowboys walked off the job leaving it half-finished. These days, Machen utilized one of the few finished guest rooms instead. Temporarily, he hoped.

Reaching for the bottle of JD on the bedside table, he was disappointed to find it empty. Nothing got him in the mood to face the day better than a quick slug of whiskey. Unscrewing the cap, he lifted the bottle to his lips regardless, hopeful that enough of the noxious brown liquid remained to sustain him. Indeed, a few drops did remain. But not for long.

Satisfied the bottle was completely drained, Machen kicked off his filthy sheets, sat on the edge of his bed and stretched, groaning aloud as his spine popped and crackled. Then he crossed the litter-strewn floor to the window, opened the curtains wider to let the sunshine stream into the room, and took a few moments to drink in the scene. This window overlooked the sea. At this early hour, the water was still a seething deep blue mass broken by occasional slivers of white froth and topped by a swirling sea mist through which gulls swooped in search of breakfast. Glancing at his watch, he realized it was time to go downstairs.

Why? A voice in his head demanded. Are you expecting a sudden rush of customers? Perhaps a passing circus troupe?

The voice had a point. There were no new arrivals booked in today, and it was unlikely there would be much in the way of passing trade. The two new guests he did have, those journalist kids, didn't look the kind of people to get up early so he doubted breakfast would be required for a while. But what else could he do? Sit up here and hide from the shadows all day?

Not likely.

If he was going down, he was going down fighting. It's amazing the amount of positive energy one can draw from daybreak.

Besides, he needed a drink.

On his way out of his room, Machen snapped off the lamp on his bedside table. He had to minimize the electricity bill. Every little helps. Then he paused and turned it back on. He hated coming back to a dark room.

Decisions, decisions.

Even something as simple as turning off or on a light was beyond him some mornings. It was just typical of the bewildering array of conflicting interests that blighted every facet of his life since Sandra left. She was the glue that held all the strands of his existence together, and without her things had a habit of unravelling. Although some would say that outwardly Sandra lacked confidence, the reality was very different. Behind closed doors she was always the strong one, the adept mind that worked so well in tandem with his business connections and work ethic. She did all the banking, bill-paying, financial records and what-not, leaving Machen to concentrate on front of house. That was why he so often struggled when she wasn't there to guide him through life's numerical minefields. She'd even taught herself how to use a computer, doing a course at the local college. In her absence, it took Machen a whole morning just to figure out how to log on to the damned Internet. Even when he managed it, he didn't know what the hell to do.

"You can do everything on the Internet!" Sandra would say. The problem was, 'everything' was too much. It was overwhelming, like walking into the biggest library in the world, where the answers to every question you could ever ask were kept.

Everything reminded him of Sandra. This was still their life, the one they had planned and executed together. It was a life made for two, yet here he was alone. It just didn't feel right. Even the anger he harboured for so long, the sense of injustice that drove him forward, was starting to fade. All the bad things floated at the top of his mind like shit in a septic tank, and he had to dig through the festering layers before reaching the happier memories that offered a more balanced assessment of their marriage. They were there, bright and vivid. All he had to do was wipe off the shit.

He remembered one afternoon when, while Machen busied himself around the house, Sandra went for a walk by herself. She was gone a couple of hours, and when she came back Machen hadn't seen her so happy in years. She was beaming from ear to ear, and took on the manner of an over-excited schoolgirl as she related her adventures to her astonished husband whilst doing a little jig of joy right there in front of the caravan.

She'd found a secret garden, she said. An old forgotten place hidden behind high walls accessible only through a rusted metal gate. She even described the pond, a fountain, and various plants and flowers.

It sounded lovely. The problem was, Machen knew no such place existed. Not within walking distance of Sker House. He had explored every inch of it, as well as the grounds that radiated out in all directions a dozen times or more, and spent endless hours examining detailed plans and maps of the area. If the grounds contained any kind of garden, secret or otherwise, he would know about it. Yet, when she described it, Sandra was so convincing he had a hard time disbelieving her. Her enthusiasm and sheer exuberance was infectious.

The next day, they awoke to the sounds of builders at work as usual, and Sandra suggested visiting the garden together. Intrigued, Machen agreed and off they went. But Sandra couldn't remember where the garden was. Her excitement gave way to confusion, and then despair when she realized that things weren't what she thought they were. It was heartbreaking to watch, and it was then Machen started worrying. She wasn't an old woman by any means, but even in middle age, things like early-onset Alzheimer's were a risk.

After that day, Sandra became fixated with that bloody garden, and spent long hours roaming the surrounding fields, moors and sand dunes looking for it. Each day when she came home she would be a little more disappointed, a little more defeated. Machen soon began to wonder if he was witnessing the gradual mental deterioration of the only woman he had ever loved. Was this how it started?

115

As if to prove his wife's sanity, or his own insanity, since Sandra's departure Machen had taken on the mantle of finding the secret garden himself. Armed with a walking stick he went out searching a couple of times a week, when time permitted. It became like a sacred quest. If nothing else, the exercise and fresh air was good for him. But so far, he hadn't found anything remotely resembling what Sandra had described.

With all these thoughts and more tumbling around his head, Machen made his way downstairs to begin work, leaving the lamp burning brightly on the bedside table to keep the shadows at bay.

Chapter 14:

Barren Soil

A few miles away from Sker House, Ruth Watkins opened her back door and filled her lungs with crisp, clean air. She loved early mornings. It was a special time of day, ripe with promise and possibilities. There was just enough time to do a few chores before she and Izzy, who was right then doing her make-up assuming she'd managed to extradite herself from her bed, had to leave for work. Machen wouldn't be best pleased if they were late.

Slipping on her gardening gloves and clutching a trowel, Ruth stepped out into the sunshine. She'd always been blessed with green fingers. There was something magical about planting a seed, watching it take root in the earth, and nurturing it as it matured and flowered. Her obsession with growing things began when she was given a little potted cactus by her uncle as a teenager, and ever since then her life had been filled with greenery. Or brownery, depending on the season. She and her husband Dennis moved into their little detached house in the tiny village of Nottage soon after their wedding in '87, where they waited patiently for little Izzy to come along. Setting the pattern for the rest of her life Izzy was in no hurry, and they ended up waiting almost a decade. Still, she was worth the wait.

In the early days, while her husband worked shifts at Port Talbot steelworks, Ruth filled the empty void in her life by ploughing all her time and resources into the tiny garden at the back of their cottage. Single-handedly, she transformed it from the overgrown dump it had once been, to the lush showcase it was today.

At first she grew all the usual things; roses, violets, petunias. Before moving on to what she considered altogether more constructive endeavours. In a bid to become more self-sufficient in case the people Dennis referred to as 'Bloody Towel Heads' finally succeeded in bringing Western civilization to its knees, she began growing a selection of seasonal vegetables and fruit. Within two years, she was hauling in small crops of potatoes, turnips, carrots, runner beans, rhubarb, apples and various other foodstuffs which she regularly used in her cooking. Nothing could be as satisfying as growing something from scratch, eating it, then planting more in its place.

Birth, life, death, rebirth.

It was the circle of life, the cycle of the universe, played out on a miniature scale before your very eyes.

Ruth's appreciation of the circle of life was further underlined when Dennis dropped dead of a massive heart attack at work in '09. He was just fifty-four. That came as a shock. The death of a loved one always does, no matter how well prepared you think you are. Even if you have to watch someone waste away in a hospital bed for months on end as cancer eats them from the inside out, their death still comes as a shock. A small part of you always clings to some shred of hope. A miracle cure, or some Lazarus-like recovery. It hurts when that hope is finally, irrevocably extinguished.

What bothered her most was that she never had the chance to say goodbye. One day Dennis was there and everything was normal, and the next he was gone and everything changed. It often occurred to her that the fortunate ones are taken first, leaving the luckless behind to pick up the pieces and rebuild their lives as best they could.

In those dark times, Ruth had to be strong for Izzy's sake. She had to set an example, show her daughter that when the people around her died, it wasn't an excuse to shrivel up and hide behind the pain. Death was a fact of life, and as unpleasant as the thought might be, Izzy had to be ready for the time when Ruth herself would be snatched away. If she wasn't married by then, she would be left on her own.

After Dennis died, Ruth had wanted to die too. But she could never allow her tattered and shredded emotions to get the better of her. After a brief mourning period, she set about rebuilding. It was what Dennis would have wanted. She went back to the garden, and even went back to work. Despite the life insurance payout, most of which went to cover the funeral costs and other expenses, funds were low so it made financial sense. Not only that, but it gave her something else to think about. She carried the grief around like a rotting egg in her pocket, trying to compensate for the sadness by seeking out things that either challenged her or made her happy. Sometimes, both at the same time.

Cooking was her other love, and her other main pastime. To her, it comprised the same basic elements of creation and destruction as displayed by her gardening. The same dance played out on a different stage. She was fortunate that her hobbies dovetailed together so smoothly, at first saving money and even, recently, *generating* money. Ordinarily, she would have considered herself lucky to find a job not too far from home that allowed her to indulge her two main passions, even if the pay wasn't great (Machen promised to review the pay structure at the end of the season when the business had stabilized).

But the feelings of dread she experienced each time she set foot inside the creepy old house by the sea tempered her enthusiasm. It was more than a simple case of lethargy. This was something she felt deep in her bones, like the rumblings of some innate early-warning system.

Of course, she knew the place was supposed to be haunted. You couldn't live in and around the area all your life and not hear the stories.

So what?

Depending on who you listened to, lots of places were haunted. Especially centuries-old buildings in superstitious places like Wales. If every ghost story you heard was true, you'd constantly be rubbing shoulders with the earthbound spirits of the wronged and restless. Still, she pondered, maybe the stories had an effect on her subconscious. It was true the prospect of coming face-to-face with the supernatural filled her with trepidation. Doesn't it everyone? But she was more inclined to believe in some higher, or at least unseen, power since Dennis passed away. It comforted her to think that there was some other plain of existence after what we call life. The alternative, that all that ever was and ever will be was just a result of atoms randomly clashing together with no rhyme nor reason, was too bleak a prospect.

Crouching down in the garden, Ruth buried her trowel in the soft earth and delicately turned it over. It was almost seeding time. When her tasks were complete, she would get the bag of vegetables she'd put aside and leave. Today, if there was time (and there should be, considering that there were only two guests this weekend – three if you included Old Rolly) she would do some work in the tiny allotment Machen had given her in the grounds. Wiley as he was, the landlord made out that he had given her the patch out of the goodness of his heart. But Ruth wasn't stupid. She knew the real reason was that Machen thought by growing their own vegetables to serve up in the kitchen he could cut overheads a little.

She'd been tending the patch for a couple of months now. But despite her best efforts, hadn't managed to grow so much as a single shoot. That bothered her. It bothered her a lot. There was no practical reason for it. It was just earth. But the soil around Sker House was dry and lifeless. Nothing grew there except the most stubborn weeds. She'd tried everything, using fertilizer from her own supplies and turning the top layer periodically so the sun's rays could work their wondrous magic. But whatever she did, the soil remained stubbornly barren. Several times, she even carefully transplanted bulbs and fledglings from her own garden, where they'd been growing happily. But each time, the plants mysteriously withered and died within days. If Ruth didn't know better, she would say the earth there had somehow been poisoned. She didn't know how it could happen, but there could be no other explanation.

But she wasn't going to give up just yet. She sensed a breakthrough. Each day, except her day off, Ruth spent every spare minute at the allotment tending and willing those plants to grow. In many ways, it became symbolic of her fight to build a new life. It was a struggle at first. Oh yes. But she never let tragedy beat her, and there was no way she was going to be beaten by a patch of bloody soil.

Standing up defiantly, she brushed her gloved hands off on her gardening apron and took one last, lingering look at her bountiful garden before going back inside. It was time to go to work.

*

As her mother lovingly tended the garden, Izzy was getting ready in her room. Glancing at her radio alarm clock, which was playing some cheesy old eighties tune, she saw it was already after nine. Almost time to leave.

She let out a sigh. She planned to go to college in September, and had allowed herself to be persuaded that it would be a good idea get a job to save some money before she went. Her mother was very big on teaching her the 'true value' of things. Especially money. She thought that if Izzy earned it herself, she'd be more independent and sensible. Less likely to spend it all on clothes or books. That was why when mam found the job at Sker House, she'd managed to get Izzy in there too.

Things worked out quite well most of the time. They both worked the same hours, which meant Izzy got a lift there and back, and she didn't exactly have to do a lot. The only problem was, she hated working there.

It's only temporary, she constantly told herself. Deal with it.

It wasn't like she was adverse to working for a living. In fact, she couldn't wait to save up enough money to pass her driving test and buy a car of her own so she wouldn't have to rely on her mother and public transport. Then she'd be able to drive herself to college, a different job, or even right out of Wales if she wanted to.

At first she thought working in a bar near the beach and having a steady flow of new and interesting people introduced into her life would be fun. Living in Nottage village was like living in a goldfish bowl. She thought she might even meet a nice guy there. A cool surfer dude or something.

In the beginning, it *had* been fun. It was all fresh and exciting, and it felt good to be earning her own money. She couldn't help but feel proud of herself.

But that was then and this is now, as they say. Reality soon kicked in. The place was practically deserted most of the time, so she never met anyone cool. There was no energy. No vibe. Plus, all the ghost stories about Sker House the local kids told must have made her paranoid. Now, she couldn't relax there. Not even for a minute. And she hated being by herself. The place gave her the creeps, plain and simple.

She tried not to think about the weird stuff that happened. Lights and taps turning off and on when no one was in the room, things disappearing then reappearing. The shadows that seemed to crawl along the walls by themselves without anyone there to cast them.

One night, when she and mam had been cleaning the kitchen, they both realised there were three shadows on the wall when there should only have been two. There was something standing between mother and daughter, something tall and slender. Something that didn't belong. Then there was the time...

Don't think about it.

"Isabel! Are you ready yet?" Mam's shrill voice called up the stairs.

Shit! When she stopped being 'Izzy' and became 'Isabel' it meant there was a rush on. Either that, or she was in serious trouble. One of mam's little traits. "Yeah, just coming!"

Mam always tried her best, fair play. Especially since dad passed away. Right now, she was trying her best not to show her true feelings, but Izzy knew her too well. Her mother was just as reluctant to go to work as she was, which wasn't like her. When they first started the job she'd been so excited. 'Everyday is a happy challenge!' She would say.

But somewhere along the line, the days stopped being happy challenges and became arduous tests of the human spirit. Not many people could actually lay claim to enjoying their work, but you should at least derive a little satisfaction from it. Otherwise, what was the point? You may as well go out and do something else instead. Which was exactly what Izzy intended to do just as soon as she passed her driving test.

For the time being, however, she would just have to bite the bullet. As weird as the stuff that happened in Sker was, she knew her mother wouldn't let anything bad happen to her.

Stuffing her phone and some mints (you never know when that cool surfer dude might show up) into her bag, she slung it over her shoulder and took one last lingering look at herself in the full-length mirror covering one wall of her bedroom. Then she clicked her heels together three times, a ritual she'd undertaken every morning since she'd seen the wizard of Oz as a kid, and made for the door.

Chapter 15:

Secret History

Lucy awoke to a strange sound.

A tapping?

She lay motionless for a few seconds, giving herself time to shake off the shackles of sleep and come back to her senses. It was almost as if unseen hands were pulling a veil from over her face.

She listened.

The sound was familiar, even comforting. It ebbed and flowed with a soothing rhythm, and she was sure that if she listened to it long enough it would send her tumbling back into the abyss of sleep.

What could it be?

All at once she identified the source of the noise, and instantly cursed herself for taking so long to do so.

It was the sound of somebody hitting keys.

Typing.

Dale.

Just to be sure, Lucy opened her eyes a fraction and peeked out from under the covers.

Sure enough, her friend was sitting at the little desk furiously tapping away on his laptop, no doubt working on the Sker House article. It seemed to be going well; his brow was creased in concentration and his lips moved silently as he mouthed the words he wrote, fingers gliding across the keyboard with practised precision. He must have found an angle, some kind of hook on which to pin the feature. Good. She had a little experience of writing articles and knew that could be the most difficult part. Try as you might, the right words just wouldn't come in the right order. Then something just clicked, the pieces fell into place, and you were away.

From the looks of things Dale had made the breakthrough, and that was not only good news for the article but good news for her. Dale could be a proper little bitch when he couldn't crack a story.

She sat up and stretched.

Dale immediately stopped writing and turned to her. "Ah, sleeping beauty arises. I was wondering how long it would be before we could get some brekkie."

"Is that all you think about? Food?"

"Pretty much," replied Dale. Then his smile faded and a peculiar expression took its place; something like a mixture of curiosity, concern and wariness. Cocking his head to one side he asked,   "How are you feeling now?"

"Fine, I guess. No worse than I usually feel when I wake up. You know I'm not a morning person."

"Who is?"

"You, obviously. I can see you're busy over there. Working on the Sker feature? How's it going?"

"Pretty good. But there's stuff we should talk about later. We need to compare notes."

"Sure thing, but lets get you fed and watered first." Lucy started getting out of bed, then stopped and added, "What do you mean by, 'How are you feeling now?'"

"What?"

"You just asked me how I was feeling now. Implying I wasn't feeling good before."

"Yeah, well. That's one of the things we need to discuss. After I'm fed and watered..." Dale turned back to the computer and started typing again, showing Lucy his back.

The urge to remove the yucky film of fur coating the inside of her mouth and a literally burning desire to pee cut short her contemplation time and Lucy bounded for the en suite. Inside, she did her business, brushed her teeth and took a quick shower, all the while turning Dale's words over in her mind. What did he want to discuss? Maybe she'd had a coughing fit or something during the night. He could be a proper worrier.

But there was something else. Some nugget of information hovering tantalizingly just beyond her reach. Was it a memory? She made a mental grab for it, missing by fractions, and was left with nothing more than vague abstract images of being alone and walking in dark hallways. The memory, if that's what it was, had the same wafer-thin translucent texture as a dream.

When Lucy exited the bathroom Dale was still tapping away at his laptop, but with less urgency now. Lucy sensed that his creative spurt was beginning to subside, at least for the time being. He must really have been hungry because he was waiting at the door even before Lucy had finished putting her trainers on.

"So do you remember anything about last night?" He asked, almost bashfully.

Lucy stopped midway through the act of doing up her left shoelace. That was a good question. Did she?

Again, that chunk of orbiting knowledge loomed into reach. Again she grasped at it, and again she missed.

"Er, I remember leaving you in the bar, coming up here and going to sleep, if that's what you mean."

"Anything else?"

It was a gentle prod. Whatever it was, Dale was cautious of going there.

"Oh God. We didn't have sex did we?" Asked Lucy, feigning alarm. She wanted to lighten the mood a little. No matter how tired she got, sex was something she always remembered.

"Sadly not."

"Who's sad about it?" Lucy couldn't resist a little giggle at her own joke.

Dale shook his head. "One day you will regret your cruelty, woman. Mark my words."

"Yeah, yeah, and this time next year Rodney, we'll be millionaires..."

As they left the room, Lucy happened to glance back at the desk and noticed that Dale had laid out one of his notebooks, opened to a blank page, and left one of his pencils lying across it. Nothing strange about that. He was always scribbling in notebooks. But the way the notepad and pencil were positioned just so seemed too precise and deliberate. There was also something about the look he gave the carefully positioned stationary before he closed the door, almost as if he were checking the notebook and pencil were still there. Odd.

They made their way down the stairs to the bar where they hoped to find 'Don't call me mister' Machen. However, en route they found the front door hung wide open allowing a fresh salty sea breeze and the harsh squawk of seagulls to circulate around the lower reaches of the building.   They paused for a few moments to fill their lungs, gazing out across the distant hills and listening to the gentle murmur of the sea. Later, when Lucy looked back upon her time at Sker, those precious few moments stood out against the horrors that came later like sparkling diamonds in a wall of granite.

The spell was broken when Machen suddenly appeared next to them like some goofy cartoon character. "Up early, I see!"

Lucy wasn't sure if it was meant as an observation or an announcement. The landlord was wearing the same clothes as the day before, and a patchy white stubble covered his cheeks and lower face. The lines around his watery, deep-set eyes seemed deeper and more pronounced. There were no two ways about it, the guy was a mess.

"We thought we'd get an early start," Dale said.

The landlord smiled broadly. "Early start, is it? And what have you young 'uns got planned for today, then?"

Lucy noticed for the first time how meandering clusters of broken blood vessels littered the landlord's red cheeks and nose, and a nervous twitch tugged at one eyelid. Trying not to stare, she said, "We want to get some work done on the article. Perhaps learn a little more about the history of Sker. You know, try to capture the mood of the place."

"Oh that's right, I forgot about the article you're writing." Machen managed to look both thrilled and apprehensive at the same time. He paused, then added, "Listen, I think I know what you're after now. You want something, right?"

"We just want to know the truth," replied Dale. "It doesn't have to be salacious gossip. Solent News is a long way from being the Daily Star. With a history this long, I don't think there'll be any need to over-dramatize anything."

The landlord's brow furrowed further. "Yeah, you could be right there. Look, I'll tell you some stories about the place later, when I've done my chores. Okay?"

"Sure thing," said Dale. "Maybe we'll take a walk on the beach, give you some time to do what you have to do. After we've had a bit of breakfast, that is."

Machen stared at them for a few seconds, his eyes going from Dale to Lucy and back to Dale again as he processed the information. Finally the penny dropped with an almost audible chink and his whole face lit up. "You want breakfast? Now, like?"

"If it's not too much trouble."

"Too much trouble? No, no trouble at all. Right this way!" Machen beamed as he led them into the bar. When they entered, Champ the guard dog gave a limp wag of his tail in greeting.

"So what would you like?" asked the landlord. "I can knock up a continental if you want, but I recommend the traditional Welsh breakfast."

"Which is?" asked Lucy.

"Sausage, baked beans, egg, bacon, black pudding, tomato and fried bread."

Dale shot Lucy a look that said don't say it! But it came too late. Lucy was too busy playing with Champ's ear to notice. "Sounds more like a traditional English breakfast to me..."

Machen chortled contemptuously. "You think you invented the fry-up, like?"

Though she was slowly adjusting to the landlord's fiercely patriotic disposition, Lucy was taken aback by anger in his voice. "No, I... Erm, was just wondering what makes it Welsh..."

"Local produce! Sorry, we're all out of laverbread and cockles at the moment, luv. And you can probably blame over-fishing by your lot or them bloody Spaniards for that."

"Overfishing?" said Lucy, perplexed. And then, "What's laverbread?"

Dale stepped in to save her. "It's a kind of food made from sea weed. Baked in an oven."

"You eat seaweed for breakfast?"

Machen huffed and disappeared into the kitchen, no doubt to prepare their traditional Welsh English breakfast, so Dale answered the question for him, lowering his voice slightly so the landlord wouldn't be able to hear. "Laverbread is a traditional Welsh food. I don't think many people eat it these days, not when there are McDonald's and KFC's on every street corner, but it's still popular with tourists. Lots of restaurants and guesthouses do it."

"Mmmm... sounds delicious!" replied Lucy in the sarcastic tone she knew Dale detested. Mind spoken, she went back to playing with the dog.

The breakfast was just what she thought it would be. English. Not a sliver of seaweed in sight. Thank God. You'd have to be pretty hungry to chow down on floating plankton, baked or otherwise.

During the meal, Lucy and Dale made small talk about the weather and reality shows the way British people are supposed to. It was comforting. However, there was a dark undercurrent running beneath their trivial ramblings that they both knew would have to be faced eventually. They were just delaying the inevitable, and would work their way around to this mysterious something sooner rather than later. So she laughed in all the right places until eventually curiosity got the better of her.

During a lull in the conversation she took an extra-long sip of coffee, set the mug back down and said, "Okay Dale, what's this important thing you wanted to discuss with me? Is this the part where you confess your undying love?"

To her mild disappointment, Dale didn't. Instead, he pursed his lips and said,"Did you know you sleepwalk?"

Lucy guffawed so hard a half-chewed piece of bacon flew out of her mouth and landed on the table between them. Belatedly covering her mouth with the back of a hand she said, "I so do not! Where did you get that idea?"

But Dale wasn't laughing. Reading his expression, she saw nothing but concern. He quickly related the events of the night before; his waking up from a bad dream to find her gone, the search, and her eventual discovery on the out-of-bounds fourth floor of Sker House. To her horror, the story he told matched the snippets of memories she recollected and had misinterpreted as fragments of dreams. As he talked, Lucy felt a peculiar sinking feeling.

"Why the fourth floor?" she asked when he'd finished. "What's up there?"

"Dunno," Dale shrugged. "You were standing outside one of the rooms. Do you know you could have gotten hurt?"

She looked up to see Machen ambling over, dirty cleaning cloth in hand, almost as if he had been watching and waiting for them to finish breakfast. Not wanting to spurn the opportunity to engage the landlord in conversation, Dale said, "Machen... I was wondering, is there any reason why the refurbishments haven't been finished yet? We were talking to Izzy yesterday and she said there were some legal issues?"

The landlord rolled his eyes as he picked up the empty plates and wiped the table with his cloth. "I wish that girl would stop being so bloody dramatic, aye. There are no legal issues as such. It was more a case of cowboys passing themselves off as professionals. I have to take them to court to get back the money they owe me. How can it be my fault if a guy falls off a ladder and breaks his leg? I wasn't even here."

"So there was an accident? Here at Sker?"

"Yes. Up on the fourth floor. Workmen all walked off the job and refused to come and finish it. Well, the guy with the broken leg didn't walk off, obviously, ha! Bloody foreigners. I didn't want to hire them in the first place, but they were half the price of anybody else. And now I know why. They only did half the bloody job. Can you believe they actually tried to blame the working conditions? Unless something was lost in translation. I mean, what did they expect? The Ritz? If the place was all pucker I wouldn't even have needed them, would I? Workmen are responsible for their own safety, everyone knows that."

"All because one of them fell off a ladder? Surely, that's par for the course when you're a builder?" Dale said, obviously trying to align himself with the landlord.

"Yeah, you would think so, wouldn't you? Other things happened as well as the ladder episode. They're a superstitious lot, the Polish. And the Romanians are even worse. They were living here, see. Gave me a discount on the work if I let them stay until the job was finished. I'm sure half of them were illegal and had nowhere else to go. Anyway, it was more convenient for them, and no skin off my nose, like. At first they seemed like a decent bunch. Good workers. But then they changed, they did."

"Why?" asked Dale.

"How the hell should I know? If you ever get the chance, ask them for me, would you?"

"There must be something you can do," Lucy said.

"Well yeah, the solicitors are working on it. We'll just have to wait and see what happens.   But you don't want to hear about that, do you? There's not much of an article in a bunch of cowboy builders. It's not exactly news."

"Not really," Dale said, "Though it certainly helps give us more of an idea about Sker. We'd like to know as much of what goes on here as possible. It all helps build a picture for the reader."

Machen's tone dropped conspiratorially. "Would you like me to tell you the real story of Sker?"

"Of course, if you feel like sharing," said Dale, ever the diplomat. He seemed pleasantly surprised that the landlord had suddenly decided to willingly impart some knowledge.

Pulling up an empty chair from a nearby table, setting it down and sitting on it, he said, "I'll tell you what I know, and you can pick the bones out of it yourselves."

"No problem," Dale agreed.

The landlord's voice dropped a few more octaves. "Well, you know Sker House used to belong to a man called Isaac Williams?"

"Yes, you said yesterday. The Maid of Sker's father, right?"

"Yes, that's right. Forced his daughter to marry someone else and all that. Well, by all accounts that wasn't the only bad thing he did in his life."

"Yeah, I remember. He used his connections to fit people up, too," Dale said.

"He did. But I'm not talking about that."

"Then what else did he do?" asked Lucy and Dale in unison.

Machen ran a hand through his thinning hair, then continued on what seemed like a different tangent. "You know in every country's history there are parts that modern people would rather forget? Sometimes when you look back on things, they look bad. People have a habit of modifying history to suit themselves, dressing it up, like."

"Selective teaching is the government's way of instilling national pride. You know, make people less likely to start a revolution or something," Lucy said, eager to contribute to the conversation.

"That's as may be," Machen continued, rubbing his stubbled chin. "Anyway, point is... For the most part Wales is working class, always has been and always will be."

The landlord gave Lucy a look that suggested she might not know what 'working class' meant. She wanted to set him straight, but was reluctant to interrupt his train of thought for fear that he may never get it back on course again.

"Have you ever heard of something called wrecking?"

Lucy looked at Dale and thought she saw a flicker of recognition on his face. She thought the word sounded familiar, but in that ambiguous way that words often did. It definitely sounded like a real word, but she didn't want to guess at its meaning. Instead, she shook her head.

"Wrecking is part of Wales' secret history," Machen said. "Imagine how heartbreaking it must have been a couple of hundred years ago for poor locals to watch ships packed with bounty and precious cargo sail around the coast. Never stopping here, never bringing anything to Wales, just passing by on the way to somewhere else. All the ships were sailing between England and the continent, see. Some folk 'round here barely had enough food to feed their children, yet watched the wildest riches pass within a mile or two. Eventually, the underclasses decided to strike back."

"How?" asked Lucy.

"They started hanging banks of lanterns and lighting fires on the beach at night. Sometimes, they would tie lights to grazing cattle. In the dark passing ships, most of which came from Europe and were unfamiliar with the area, would mistake the lanterns and fires for the lights of ships safely anchored in the harbour. Thinking it was a safe passage, they would be lured onto rocks."

"What? That's awful!" Lucy couldn't help herself. She deplored any kind of cruelty or social injustice.

Machen pulled back a little. "No more awful than some of the things your ancestors did, miss. Like I said, every country has a secret history. And when your belly's empty, there's no limit to the things you would do to fill it. It was law in them days that landowners could claim Right of the Wreck, meaning they could keep anything that washed up on their land."

"What about the sailors, the crew? Didn't they just tell the authorities what the local people were doing?"

"Most of the sailors drowned when their ships went down. The few that were left, well, they also met a sticky end. The locals didn't want any witnesses, see."

"You mean, they killed them?" Lucy was both horrified and disgusted.

"This was the eighteenth century, miss. Seafaring was a dangerous business. Ships went down all the time, so when they did nobody asked too many questions."

"But what does all this have to do with Sker House?" asked Dale.

"Isaac Williams was a notorious wrecker. And a very powerful man. Story goes that when he lived in this house, he was on the verge of bankruptcy. He owned lots of land, but his farms were failing. He also owned Sker beach, and realized he could claim Right of the Wreck on anything that washed up there, so he would send his workers down whenever they saw a ship passing in the distance. They were usually too late, either that or the captains on those ships weren't stupid. But sometimes, especially in bad weather, they would succeed in luring ships on to the Black Rocks where they were smashed to pieces."

"Oh God." Lucy said.

"You haven't heard the half of it yet, miss." Machen said with a knowing wink. "Isaac Williams had a son called James," he continued. "His first-born. The apple of his eye, he was. Isaac was a well-to-to landowner and local magistrate, so he could afford to send his son to Italy to study. James would make the journey home at the beginning of each summer. One year, he decided to come over for Christmas, but didn't tell his family. He wanted to surprise them, see. In those days, before airplanes and Eurostar, the only way to travel to the continent was by sea. It wasn't uncommon for the captains of merchant ships to take the odd passenger for a cash fee, their names and details never recorded."

"He didn't..." began Lucy, then stopped before she could articulate what she was thinking.

"Nobody is really certain," Machen said, apparently guessing what Lucy had been about to ask. "James Williams was never seen again, alive nor dead. In December 1753 a French vessel called Le Vainqueur went down in a storm off Sker Point with the loss of all hands. It was rumoured James had hitched a ride on that very ship, unbeknownst to his father, who sank it out of greed. Of course, there were other variations on the story. Other folk said that Isaac murdered James during a family row after he arrived."

134

"Doing it accidentally is one thing, but why would he murder his own son?" asked Dale, engrossed in the story. "Not exactly in contention for the father of the Year award, was he?"

"Because of pride. He was a wealthy, powerful man, but his influence was waning. Some said he could no longer afford to keep James in school but didn't want to lose face by pulling him out. It might have been better if the son just... disappeared. Even worse, at the time relations between France and Britain were pretty tense, and the sinking of Le Vainqueur caused an almighty stink. Almost started a war, it did."

"What happened next?" Lucy urged.

"Well, the authorities had to be seen to be doing something. Too many ships were being lost in the area. So, they had a formal investigation. They questioned Isaac Williams and his workers, who of course all denied having anything to do with the wrecking. But when they searched Sker House they found some of the ship's cargo hidden in the cellar. Isaac Williams was arrested and charged, along with sixteen others. Faced the hangman's noose, he did. But like I said, he was a very powerful man."

It was easy to see where this one was going. "He got away with it, right?" said Lucy.

"Bloody right." Machen confirmed. "He got away with it. Another of the sixteen wasn't so lucky. They made an example of him and had him executed. Afterwards, the Right of the Wreck law was changed, pretty much ending the reign of the wreckers."

"And what happened to Isaac Williams?" asked Lucy.

"Well, he may have escaped the noose but it's said that the episode ruined him, and he died not long afterwards of natural causes. Right here at Sker House, as it happens."

"Oh great," said Lucy. "When were you going to tell us that?"

"Chill out," piped up Dale. "This is an old house, of course people are going to snuff it here. It's the same with the big hotels, people die in them all the time. Afterwards they just clean the room, and the next day its business as usual. Actually there's a place not too far from here called Skirrid Inn. It used to be a courthouse and place of execution, now its a pub. They say

135

hundreds were hung there, some for just petty crimes that wouldn't even get you a slap on the wrist these days."

"Is that place haunted?"

"Obviously."

"What is it with you two and ghosts, anyway?" asked Machen.

Lucy felt herself instinctively pull away. She didn't want to explain to the landlord about her unhealthy interest in the paranormal and how it all began. He would only laugh. So instead, she said, "This is just a great story. It has everything people like. History, tragedy, love, controversy. The supernatural element adds another layer."

That seemed enough to placate the landlord, who raised his eyebrows slightly and regarded Lucy for a few seconds before saying, "So do you... believe in all that stuff?"

"In the supernatural?" Lucy asked. "Of course. Its a bit naïve of people to think that this is all there is, don't you think? Same as it's ridiculous, and a bit arrogant, to think that all the intelligent life in the universe lives on one planet."

"P'raps." the landlord conceded. From his position at the table he gazed at a spot on the floor. His eyes looked haunted, pained, and full of secrets. In that moment, it wasn't too difficult for Lucy to imagine that she was staring into the troubled eyes of Isaac Williams himself.

Chapter 16:

Watching

Old Rolly watched Machen talking to the two young ones from his usual place across the room. Not having slept very well, he was feeling even more unsociable than usual this morning. He didn't like to interact with people too much at the best of times. Talking was overrated. The world was full of people who talked and talked when they had nothing to say. It just made more noise. When will people learn how valuable words were? And the more they were thrown around, the more they were devalued until they became worthless.

There wasn't much that went on at Sker that escaped his notice.

It was his business to know.

So he studied the staff, the guests, everyone who came and went. He listened to conversations, assessed body language and facial expressions, and right now he could make a fairly accurate guess as to what the group was talking about. The kids were reporters writing some kind of article. He didn't know what it would be about exactly, but if it involved Sker it could only end badly. The last thing anyone needed, except Machen, was lots of people crawling around asking questions and digging up the past. That would just be inviting trouble. Some things should stay buried.

Machen was too materialistic for his own good. All he wanted was as much free publicity as he could get in the hope that it would somehow be magically converted into cash. Who knows what the misguided fool might tell those kids? It wasn't as if he had no idea what was going on here. He didn't know everything, but he knew enough. How could he not? If he chose not to heed the warnings, then he deserved whatever happened to him.

It was about time Machen realised that he was just a tiny cog in a much bigger machine. There was more at stake here than the financial security of one man. As present owner of Sker House, he had a role to play. Just like every owner had before him. But it was a role often elevated far above its true station. Owners came and owners went. They always had, and always will.

In his years on earth, Rolly had learned exactly how to deal with such self-important people. The secret was to humour them, indulge them, let them feast on their own perceived value and assume you knew appreciated how important they were, when the opposite was actually true. You appreciated how unimportant they were.

It was generally much easier to make friends than enemies. Though for Rolly, most people inhabited that netherworld between the two extremes. For them, one can only feel indifference. There was only so much energy in the universe, and you could barely afford to waste yours on tears for strangers.

That wasn't to say he was totally insensitive to the needs of others. He simply worked to a different agenda. What was hidden here at Sker had to be protected at all costs, and if that meant keeping Machen in the dark about certain things, so be it. The silly man would potter around until he eventually realized that Sker was no place for him then, bankrupt and deflated, he would sell up and move on like all the others had before him. Sker House might stand derelict for a while. A few years, maybe. Then some other budding hot shot, blinded by the lure of pound signs, would see a business opportunity and the dance would begin all over again.

Rolly sighed as he idly fingered a corner of the newspaper page he was reading. Something about a Premier League footballer he'd never heard of being caught playing away from home. He'd read the same story piece at least three times. He couldn't absorb the words. They were unimportant. Right now, there were more immediate concerns.

Having lived in and around Sker all his life, Rolly had become attuned to it. He could feel the evil that resided here stirring, flexing, undulating beneath and around him, radiating out toward Sker Point and polluting the atmosphere with its wickedness.

It was a worry.

A storm was coming.

A big one.

And he could do nothing but wait.

And watch.

Chapter 17:

Communicating with the Dead

Damn! This was a lot to remember. Names, dates, events, both real and assumed, all tumbled around Dale's head as he struggled to put everything he'd learned in the last twenty-four hours into some kind of logical order. He yearned for his notebook and pen, and had already decided that the moment he could, he was going to rush upstairs and commit as many of Machen's words as he could remember to paper. Thank God for Lucy being there. She could help fill in the blanks. Between them, and with a little independent research, they should be able to develop something approaching a linear time-line of Sker House's gruesome past. Combined with some nice quotes, it should form the basis of a good article. Finally, it was taking shape. If he could weave legend together with historical fact, compare past and present events, and bookend the whole thing with a progressive theme of rebirth and revitalization, they might have something. If he used the right terminology and wordplay, he might even be able to use Sker House as an analogy for the development of Wales as a country. The flourish, then the slow decline. The editor of Solent News was a big advocate of profound, multi-layered stuff.

Dale and Lucy made awkward conversation with the landlord for a little while longer, but as soon as they were politely able to do so, stood up and excused themselves.

"What'd you pair say you were doing today?" asked Machen, looking surprised and a little disappointed to see them leave.

"I need to get to work on this article before my deadline catches up with me," answered Dale.

"Oh aye, gonna try an' grab that mouse by the balls, eh?" Machen said, and smacked Dale on the shoulder with a pale, meaty fist. The gesture was probably intended to be friendly, but came across as awkward and over-blown.

"Mouse? You mean muse? Erm, I hope so," replied Dale whilst trying to regain his balance. Later, he was thankful that the landlord didn't get him in a headlock and ruffle his hair.

He couldn't help but feel relieved when Machen's attention turned to Lucy. "And you, miss?"

She hesitated. "Me? I'm not sure. I might go for a walk. Take my camera and leave Mr. Writer here in peace for a while."

"Good idea," agreed Dale with a grin.

141

"A walk, you say? Well, do me a favour and keep an eye out for a secret garden for me, will you?"

Lucy raised her eyebrows in surprise and looked at Dale for reassurance. He quickly shot a look back that he hoped said, how the fuck should I know what he's talking about?

"Erm, sure thing," she stammered, eager to be gone. "I always keep my eyes open for secret gardens."

"Glad to hear that. Because you never know when you might find one, see."

"That's right, you don't," agreed Lucy, looking increasingly mystified. "I need to nip back to the room to pick up my camera." A gentle shove with a bony elbow was Dale's cue to leave.

As they left the bar, the landlord called after them, "Do you's two have plans for dinner? I meant to ask."

"Erm, no. Not yet." replied Dale over his shoulder. "We'll probably just have something here, if that's okay?"

"Oh, good! Then I'll 'ave a word with Ruth, then. Maybe between us we can rustle up something special for you. One more thing..." he called. "When you go out you might want to take a coat, and don't go too far. Old Rolly says there's a storm coming. And he's been around long enough to take at his word."

"Okay, thanks!" Dale shouted. As he followed Lucy out of the bar, he noticed the man himself had appeared.

Speak of the devil.

Wondering whether the act of buying someone a pint still held any sway in drinking culture,   Dale shouted a polite "Good morning!"

Whether he heard the greeting or not, Old Rolly didn't even glance up from his newspaper. He looked like he had the weight of the world on his shoulders.

*

The first thing Dale did after swinging open the door to their room was rush over to the desk to check his notebook for more phantom messages. That was the real reason he wanted to get back so quickly.

The first thing he noticed was that the notepad and pencil appeared to be in the same position as he left them. But underneath the pencil, partially hidden, he could see fresh scribbles on the virgin-white paper.

Yes!

Snatching up the notepad, he saw that the same level of fury seemed to be there, but this time the message was slightly more legible. Again, it appeared to be just one word. There was a jagged R which slipped straight into an E, then a C, then an unmistakeable O, the circle not fully closing before veering off prematurely to form another letter. Was that an R? Then another O, this one much fainter and so loose that it could easily be a C or even a Q. Finally, there was another downward stroke, this last one firmer than all the others, almost as if the writer summoned their last reserves of energy for one last titanic effort. What could the downward stroke be? The makings of an I? a T? Another R?

It appeared to be gibberish. There were at least a million possibilities as to what the message could be trying to spell out.

Sitting in the chair at the desk, Dale leaned over and compared the two pieces of mystery writing.

Could they be two parts of the same message?

Both appeared to have been written by the same hand, and they could safely rule out Machen who had spent virtually the entire morning with them. Furthermore, Izzy and Ruth hadn't yet arrived, leaving Old Rolly the only likely suspect. It seemed to be stretching things a bit far. Dale could place the old man downstairs for at least part of the morning, leaving him a very small window of opportunity for him to sneak in their room. Could the old dude move that fast? Dale doubted it. How would he know when he and Lucy vacated their room? And how did he get in through the locked door?

But as the famed fictional detective Sherlock Holmes was fond of saying; when the impossible had been eliminated, what was left must be the answer, however improbable.

That settled it.

They had a prime suspect.

The next step was to establish a motive. Why was Old Rolly doing this? What could he possibly have to gain? Maybe he and Machen were in cahoots together, working in tandem perpetrate a host of supposedly ghostly occurrences in an attempt to drum up trade.

But that solution didn't quite ring true. If part of their plot included leaving a message, why be so bloody vague about it? Why not leave something more direct, even threatening? That would be much more effective than a few barely-distinguishable letters.

Having already tried and failed to extract any meaning from the first message, Dale decided to concentrate on the second for a while.

R

E

C

O...

He looked around the room for inspiration, and caught the eye of Lucy, who had been watching him from the bed. "What'cha got there?"

"I'm not sure," he replied. "You saw me leave this notepad here before we went to breakfast. It was open on a new page, right?"

"Right, I remember. You were very fussy about it. Why?"

"Because it's not a new page any more."

"What do you mean?"

"I think somebody's leaving us messages."

Lucy rolled her eyes. "Who the hell would leave us a message? We don't know anybody else here. And besides, the door was locked and we had the key."

"Maybe we don't have the only key. This is a guest house; there must be spare copies for the maids, and in case any keys get lost."

"Who would have access to any copies? Our friend Don't Call Me Mister Machen?"

"Undoubtedly. But he was with us virtually the entire time. In fact, didn't you think he almost made a point of being with us?"

Lucy whistled between her teeth and looked Dale squarely in the eye, making his heart rate quicken even more. "Are you stoned?" she asked. "Or are you suffering from residual paranoia or something?"

"What? No. Is that even a real thing or did you just make it up?"

"Dunno. I think I just made it up. But it sounds plausible, doesn't it. Residual Paranoia. Like it. Sounds like a Manic Street Preachers B-side." Then her brow furrowed. "Wait a minute, what do you mean 'messages' plural?' There's been others?"

"Yeah, this is the second time its happened. The second time I know of, anyway. Every notebook I have might be full of random bits of hidden writing by now for all I know." Dale hadn't thought of that before, and instantly set about checking.

As he rifled through the pages, Lucy commented, "There's nothing hidden about that last message. It was left there on the desk, so whoever wrote it wanted you to find it. What did the last one say? Was it the same?"

"No. Here." Dale showed her the first message. Not wanting to influence her opinion he asked, "What do you think it says?"

She leaned in closer, squinting her eyes. "Hard to tell. The writing's even worse than yours. I can only make out a couple of letters; a C, maybe an O, an L? And even they would be questionable. Could it be Welsh?"

"I don't know. I don't speak it."

"Why?"

"I'm from the south. My family settled there during the Industrial Revolution like most people did. They came from other parts of Britain, mostly. That's why English is so common there. Welsh is more prevalent in the North. They call themselves 'True Welsh' like the rest of us are some kind of sub-species."

"Oh, I see. That second message though... That's more clear. There's an R, and E, a C, an O? Record? Is it asking you to play a record?"

"Doubt it," said Dale. "Nobody plays records any more. Not even ghosts."

"Then maybe it's telling you to record something. With your Dictaphone."

"Record what?"

"How should I know? Just hit record and see what happens. Have you heard of EVP?"

"Electronic Voice Phenomena? It's when disembodied voices are caught on recording equipment, right? A TV ghost hunter's favourite."

Lucy whistled between her teeth. "Wow, I'm impressed. How come you suddenly know so much?"

"I saw the movie White Noise with Michael Keaton years ago. Not as good as Batman, or even Mr Mom, but watch-able. It was all about EVP's."

"Oh, right. Well, in real life the voices are usually only audio on tape when you play them back. One theory is that they operate on a different frequency to what our ears can pick up, but somehow electronic equipment enables us to hear them."

"Where are they supposed to come from?"

Lucy shrugged her slender shoulders. "Different people believe different things. Some say they come from heaven or hell, or some place in between, like purgatory. Other people claim they come from lingering spirits, or a different dimension, while some believe aliens are trying to communicate with us. Another theory is that the atmosphere somehow captures recordings, then replays them. Sceptics maintain they are just misplaced radio signals."

The part that disturbed Dale most was that if intelligent earthbound spirits existed and were able to communicate, then it probably meant they were around all the time. Hovering, lurking, hidden in plain sight. Watching you sleep, watching you eat, watching you... do everything else.

"What's up?" Lucy asked, evidently reading the discomfort on his face. "This is exciting! It's why we came here."

"I know that," Dale conceded. "But I didn't expect some kind of paranormal entity to just pop up and introduce itself. I don't think stuff like this happens much, Lucy. If EVP's were commonplace we'd be reading about it everywhere. There'd be books, investigations, TV shows about them."

"There are," Lucy said. "It's just a bit niche, isn't it? Maybe they need a certain set of conditions in order to make themselves known. Look at the history of this place, all the horrible things that have happened here. There has to be a reason for it. What if this thing really wants us to record it? Maybe it has something to say and thinks it can communicate with us easier that way. It obviously can't write for shit. Let's try it, we don't have anything to lose."

Dale was reluctant, but what were the alternatives? It certainly seemed as if something was trying to communicate with them and Lucy was right, they didn't have anything to lose. A reporter's career hinged on taking risks. Recording in an empty room didn't seem like the most constructive use of his time and resources, but much stranger things had been done in the name of a good story.   "Okay," he said finally. "How do we go about it? Just hit the button and wait for the voices?"

"Well yeah, basically. We can say 'hello' and tell it we're recording, in case it doesn't realize. Maybe ask it a few direct questions. I don't think there is an official protocol we have to follow. We'll try a few different techniques and see what works."

"How confident are you? Of getting some EVP action, I mean?"

"The voices are there, that's for sure. There are literally thousands of recordings on file. Just surf the net. You can see for yourself. Or listen for yourself. The debate is not over whether they exist or not, but where they come from."

"It's like you're trying to turn an ordinary piece of reporter's kit into a modern-day Ouija board," Dale said, dubious.

"There's nothing wrong with being resourceful. You of all people should know there are a million uses for paper. You can write on it, or you can make a fire."

"But aren't Ouija boards... dangerous? Isn't it like opening a doorway to the spirit world and inviting something in or whatever? I don't want to end up with a haunted Dictaphone."

"But this isn't a Ouija board, Dale. You're a sceptic, right? How can you be scared of something you don't even believe in? And besides, if you ended up with a haunted Dictaphone you could write one hell of a follow-up article about it."

Dale sighed. When Lucy was in this mood it was sometimes easier to just let her have her own way. "Okay. Let's go."

Lucy immediately sprang into action. "How much recording time do you have left?"

"Just over three hours."

"That 's more than enough. We'll record for fifteen minutes or so, then play it back and see what we find."

Lucy hit the RECORD button on the device, and said, "Test, test, test."

Then she stopped the recording and played it back. Her voice was repeated at them, slightly softer and more distant, but unmistakably hers."

"It's working," she said, satisfied.

Some multi-faceted emotion Dale couldn't quite identify stirred within him. Something sank a little, while something else sprang to life. There was a chance, however remote, that in the next few hours they might capture something that could change his whole outlook on life.

"You stay here and monitor the recording," Lucy said, getting up. "I'm going to nip out to get some snaps in case there really is a storm later."

"Excuse me?" Dale said, stunned.

"What's up? Not scared, are you?"

"Of course not," Dale replied, trying not to sound as offended as he was. "It's not like I have anything better to do, is it? You go off and have some fun on the beach, while I stay here and try to communicate with the dead. Sounds like a great plan to me."

"You'll have a great time," Lucy winked at him and strolled out, leaving Dale sitting at the desk clutching his Dictaphone.

He cleared his throat a little louder than he needed to, checked the machine was recording, and said, "Hello? Is there anybody here?"

Chapter 18:

A Storm is Coming

Ruth and Izzy Watkins drove on the narrow cobbled roads winding through quaint little Nottage village, past the solitary Gothic-style church with its tiny graveyard and wrought iron fence, and past the dozens of tiny detached cottages with thatched roofs. Soon, they joined the dual carriageway that took them towards the coast. Throughout the entire journey, they encountered only a handful of other vehicles.

As small and secluded as Nottage was, Ruth remembered that not so long ago it had been a jolly and vibrant place, especially on Saturday mornings. Market day. She didn't appreciate them at the time, but she missed the collection of unglamorous pitches selling fresh meat, vegetables, dairy, and the odd case of beer or bottle of spirits 'straight off the back of a lorry' as her Dennis used to say. Her pillar of strength, he was still a source of comfort even this long after his death. Together they often lamented the passing of the small village business as modern shoppers migrated towards the more convenient and cheaper supermarkets with car parks the size of football fields.

Ruth was perceptive enough to realize this was a wider trend not confined to Nottage, but it still sent a stab of regret through her heart.

Where would it all end?

Some rebel spirit within told her to fight, not to let the big faceless corporations win, but every weekend she still did her weekly shopping at ASDA. She just couldn't buy everything she needed in the village. And, truth be told, it was not only more convenient but cheaper, too. Who could blame people for going there instead of shopping locally?

As she drove, Ruth craned her neck and looked anxiously up at the dark clouds gliding in from the sea. The weather forecast didn't say anything about rain, but the weather forecasts were wrong at least half the time. At best it was educated guesswork. She trusted her own forecasting abilities much more implicitly than those of some sparkly perma-tanned minor celebrity on Sky News, and today she predicted that although the day had started brightly those clouds, some of them an ominous dull grey, would soon be upon them.

She increased her speed slightly, nudging up towards forty-five, looking forward to getting some work done at the allotment before rain stopped play.

It rains a lot in this part of the world Ruthy, and you better just get used to it, she heard her dead husband's voice like a refrain from somewhere deep in her memory bank. Dennis had a saying for most occasions, and Ruth was able to call on them as and when she needed. It was his legacy. A head full of words and a heart full of sentiment. Like her, Dennis was a product of a simpler time. Post-war babies, they were brought up grateful for peace, freedom and the little things. The hardships they endured in their early lives as war-torn Europe recovered from the war instilled in them both a steadfast resolve and unshakeable sense of duty, which seemed strangely out of synch with the modern world view. Now, everybody wanted everything, and cried foul when they couldn't get it.

She glanced at Izzy in the passenger seat. Her daughter's face was a picture of discontent. "Alright, love?"

Without even turning to face her mother, Izzy answered in the affirmative, retrieved her phone from her handbag and proceeded to punch buttons, her thumbs moving over the keys at a furious pace.

She was miserable.

Not just today, but in general.

Ruth felt bad for her daughter. Unless she left the village and went away to college or university, she would never have a fulfilling life. Nobody aspired to a career washing linen and pulling pints at Sker House. It was hard for kids these days to find direction, something that really interested them. In Ruth's world you had fewer options. If something needed to be done, you did it and persevered, staying strong for the people you cared about.

Like the rest of her generation Izzy faced an uncertain future. There were no such things as 'jobs for life' any more and most struggled just to climb on the career ladder, masking the resultant anxiety with a belligerent attitude and resigned indifference.

But something else was troubling Izzy.

Something more profound than boys or a rubbish job. Something more even, than having her father taken from her at such a young age.

A mother knows.

Since taking the job at Sker House, Izzy had become increasingly sullen and withdrawn. It was as if something were systematically sucking the energy and enthusiasm out of her. Whatever influence she was under was also having a physical effect. Her appetite was non-existent, she always looked tired and strained, she used concealer to cover the acne that plastered her cheeks and forehead, and the weight was falling off her.

A small part of Ruth actually wanted to believe that her daughter was into drugs. At least that was a problem you could face, understand and overcome. This, she felt, was more subversive.

Just before ten, they pulled up outside Sker House and parked in their usual spot. Ruth was still waiting for the time when she would have to park on the road because of all the customer's cars.

Fat chance.

Through the dirty windscreen the old structure, with its one remaining tower reaching up toward the sky like a fist of defiance, looked more intimidating than ever. Something indefinable squirmed in the pit of Ruth's stomach and she tightened her grip on the steering wheel as she fought the familiar urge to slip the car back into gear and go straight back home. She was aware that she always left the engine running a few seconds longer than was necessary while she and Izzy sat uncomfortably together.

Was the money really worth it?

No. The money couldn't even be described as 'good.' But this was about more than money. This was about showing Izzy how to flourish in the face of adversity. It was a life lesson for them both. She would never admit it, but too often that sense of duty was the only thing preventing Ruth from following her instinct and driving back home. Now, even that most noble of causes was beginning to lose its allure.

"C'mon, miss. Another day, another dollar!" Ruth urged, as much to motivate herself as her daughter.

Izzy let out a deep breath, exited the vehicle without a word, and sauntered off ahead still engrossed in her phone, disappearing into Sker House and leaving Ruth to collect her tray of shrubs and saplings from the back seat.

As she locked the door behind her and hurried up the path, she risked one more glance at the sky. A storm was definitely coming. Foregoing the main entrance, she took the path that led around to the allotment hoping to get fifteen minutes gardening time in while Izzy made a start on the housework. Machen wouldn't mind. Technically, she was still working.

The allotment, or more accurately, the little patch of waste land at the side of the house sectioned off with rope, was just as she left it. Nothing had changed. It was still as barren and lifeless as ever, despite the generous helping of fertilizer she'd spread yesterday to hopefully encourage the newest additions to the garden, some runner beans, to take root.

Nothing had sprouted yet.

Ruth didn't know what she'd been expecting. Miracles didn't happen overnight. But the disappointment compounded the uneasiness that filled her.

Wait.

What was that?

There was something new, after all!

But it was no cause for celebration. Lying on its side in the middle of the enclosure, exposing its pristine white belly, was a tiny animal. A vole or a field mouse.

It was dead.

Frowning, Ruth prodded the animal gingerly with a gloved finger. It was still soft, meaning that it had been dead only a few hours, and unmarked, ruling out an attack by a predator. It appeared to have found it's way into Ruth's garden, then simply keeled over and died.

"What happened to you, little fella?"

Grimacing, she picked it up by the tail and debated what to do with it. It seemed disrespectful to just throw it away, but she didn't want to go through the trouble of burying it only to inadvertently dig it up again at some point.

Holding the dead animal in her rubber-clad hand, she peered into its glassy, unseeing eye. Suddenly, a feeling of revulsion came over her as if she suddenly remembered what she was doing, and she decided to throw it after all. Get it as far away from her as possible.

The tiny carcass arced through the air to land with a soft plop a few metres away, and Ruth whispered a silent apology.

*

As the demoralized duo of Ruth and Izzy were pulling up in the car park, Lucy was beginning her walk, idly picking her way along the overgrown little path that wound away from Sker House down toward the beach and enjoying the feel of the sea breeze on her face.

After a few minutes lost in thought, she became aware of a strange sensation settling over her, its approach so stealthy that it barely registered it until it was too late.

There were eyes on her.

Like she was being followed, or watched.

What she felt was a combination of both those things and more, similar to the sensation she had felt whilst taking pictures in the bar. It was the feeling you got when someone was standing directly behind you, so close you could feel their breath on the nape of your neck.

Or is it just the breeze?

She stopped dead and whirled around, convinced somebody was sneaking up on her.

The path was empty. Behind her lay only Sker House.

Yet she couldn't quite overcome that awful creeping sensation and icy fingers continued to trail down her spine.

For a moment, it seemed that the house itself possessed the power of sight, that its eyes were at that moment burrowing deep into Lucy's soul. Her eyes flicked to the window where she saw the woman's figure the previous evening, but the window was now empty, a revelation which left her feeling strangely deflated.

She still had no proof that she hadn't hallucinated the whole thing. Between that and last night's alleged sleepwalking episode, it was a wonder Dale wasn't already running for the hills. He must think she was a psycho, if he didn't think so before. At first she thought he must have been winding her up about the sleepwalking, but then she began to see images in her mind. Grainy visual representations of what she'd first assumed were remnants of a dream, but could just as easily be hazy snatches of memory. She saw herself in a dark, unfamiliar corridor. Dale was there and they were talking. The thing that impacted upon her most was an overriding sense of urgency, of looking for something. Desperately seeking... what?

There was more.

Now she remembered the biting cold seeping through her flesh, and the terrible moment of realization when she came to her senses for just the briefest of moments before retreating back into her twilight world somewhere between asleep and awake. The place where everything is possible and everything makes sense.

During that moment of clarity, even as the panic and bewilderment began to engulf her, she remembered a doorway.

A doorway to a very special room.

She inched forward, heart swelling with anticipation, and then...

Nothing.

Just a bottomless black abyss. She couldn't remember anything else.

It was as if what occurred the night before was so traumatic, so damaging, that her subconscious actively sought to block it out.

She shuddered as a gust of wind stronger than those preceding it tried to blow her over. To her left, separated from where she stood by only a thin strip of sand, the sea was beginning to churn and bubble, while to her right stood a scraggly, hip-high steel-mesh fence. Beyond that lay a few acres of dry, barren land interspersed with receding sand dunes eventually giving way to lush green hills.

As she gazed across the fields, she noticed a bird of prey circling overhead, and stopped to fire off a few snaps. It was a challenge trying to get good action shots of wildlife in its natural environment. Nature played by its own rules and didn't adhere to anyone's whims, least of all those of a student with a camera.

But the challenge was not without reward, as the industry recognized how difficult the task was and paid accordingly. It was rumoured that Maggie Tilburn from her media law class at uni once helped herself to an opportunistic picture of a couple of dolphins doing some cute dolphin thing on holiday somewhere, and sold it to a specialist magazine for five hundred quid. Later, she won some big award or other and basically launched her career on the back of it.

It was that easy.

All you had to do was be in the right place at the right time and take the chance when it came.

A bit like life, really.

Lucy watched the bird swoop down into a field of long, swaying grass a short distance away, and noticed for the first time an almost perceptible line cut clean across the countryside. On one side, the vegetation grew freely as you would expect in a largely unspoiled area like this. But on the other side, where Sker House was situated, there were only scattered patches of withered greenery strewn over coarse brown earth.

She put the effect down to the actions of an over-zealous farmer armed with weed killer, but felt compelled to investigate further. She didn't have anything better to do.

What did Machen say about a secret garden?

She looked around again. If there was a secret garden it was pretty damn well hidden. She had virtually unobstructed views for miles around and there was no sign of any garden. The wind was picking up now, and the sky darkening. She was torn between curtailing her walk and heading back to the sanctuary of Sker House, and allowing herself to be lured away by the prospect of capturing a bird of prey on the hunt.

After the briefest moment of consideration, she hopped over the steel-mesh fence and set off across the open field.

Chapter 19:

Skeletons

Once he accepted the fact he was having a conversation with himself in an otherwise empty room, Dale threw himself into the task of trying to interact with the ghost, if there was one. The first few questions he asked were hesitant, his voice sounding strange and self-conscious, but he persevered and kept the recorder rolling. Soon he was firing off questions on a whim, sometimes repeating the same one several times in different tones in an effort to provoke a response, mimicking the ghost hunters he saw on TV.

Alone with his thoughts, he couldn't help but be dragged back to the past, where the real ghosts were.

He'd started frequenting the local pubs when still in the last year of comprehensive school. Some of the landlords used to let him and his two best friends, Simon and Barry, play pool in the afternoons, even if they were wearing school uniforms. As long as one of you bought a glass of coke or two between you, there was never any problem. There they would talk about girls and sport, catching the balls before they went down the pockets to make their lunch money stretch further.

Having grown up within three streets of each other, the three boys were bound together most of their lives, but couldn't be more different. Simon was the studious one and destined for a life on the council, a feat he duly achieved around the same time Dale started work in a local factory the summer they left school. Barry, on the other hand, was always a bit 'dodgy,' as Dale's parents put it. And they weren't wrong. It wasn't that he lacked intelligence. Far from it. Barry was smart enough to turn his back on the rat race early-doors and explore alternative ways of making a living. He had his plump little fingers in all sorts of pies. It didn't make him a bad person, he just chose a different path. Unfortunately, it was a path fraught with danger that frequently landed him in trouble with the police.

Dale's mind was wrenched back to the present when, after precisely nine minutes, the Dictaphone's red RECORD light abruptly winked out.

No battery. Shit.

Like any good pro, Dale always carried a supply. There was a new pack in his rucksack, and he was almost positive there were one or two loose ones kicking around, too. As he crossed the room to retrieve them, he suddenly became aware of how cold it was getting.

Damn skinflint landlord, turn the heating on!

On checking, he was surprised to find that the heating already was on. The large wall-mounted radiator was almost too hot to touch.

The temperature must be dropping outside, he thought, glancing out of the window at the rapidly deteriorating weather.

Just then, he noticed something lying on the floor beneath the radiator and stooped to pick it up.

It was a long-barrelled iron key. The rust and level of discolouration told him it was very old.

Puzzled, Dale looked around the room. It didn't seem to fit any of the locks, and how could it have found its way underneath the radiator? Just another mini-mystery to add to the rest he thought, laying it down on the bedside table.

After replacing the batteries in the Dictaphone, he hit the RECORD button again. The machine's red light lit up, and the timer obediently started ticking over.

Each brush with the law had been another kick in the teeth for Barry, and another black mark on his record. He was still living at home and arguing with his parents a lot, who were naturally concerned about the direction in which his life seemed to be heading.

One morning just before his eighteenth birthday, Barry got up and told his mother he was going for a walk. He seemed normal, she said. If anything he looked a little happier than usual. It was giro day, she remembered. Barry always got up early on giro day to get to the post office before they closed for lunch.

However, this time, instead of going to the post office, he went into the woods and hung himself from a tree. An old man out walking his dog found him a few hours later. It was a 'teen tragedy,' the local newspaper said.

Looking back from this distance, it almost seemed like another life. For the first few months after it happened it was all Dale could think about, and it was all anyone wanted to talk about around the village until the next catastrophe came along and brightened up their existence. The worst part about it was he hadn't spoken to Barry for a couple of weeks before he died, and the last

159

time they did talk they had a mini-falling out over something so trivial Dale couldn't even remember what it was. He'd wanted to text Barry to sort things out. But always thought he'd do it tomorrow.

Always tomorrow.

In his darkest moments, he wondered how much he was to blame. Could he have changed anything? What was going through Barry's mind when he tied that knot and slipped the rope around his neck?

Dale had a dream once. In the dream, he saw Barry walking out to the woods in the rain. The light was failing, so it was either dusk or dawn. He was carrying a length of rope. Dale watched as his friend sat under an oak tree with the rope in his lap, caressing it with his fingers. He called out, but his friend didn't hear.

When Dale awoke, he was left with the unwavering knowledge that the dream was a vision of a journey Barry made many times. Always to the same spot, and always alone. Every time he found a reason to walk back.

Except that day.

The least Dale could have done was pay more attention. If his friend was in pain, he should have realized and done something about it. That's what friends are supposed to do, isn't it?

But people get too caught up in their own lives to notice what's going on in other people's.

Coulda, shoulda.

Didn't.

If only Barry had said something. Told someone, anyone, how much he was suffering. Maybe then he could have got some help and things would have turned out differently.

But that's not what men do. Especially strong men in small communities where public image and reputation is everything, and the smallest sign of weakness can be used against you. These men suffer in silence, their minds in turmoil, unable to process or even confront emotions they had no experience in dealing with.

What Dale felt was shame. Pure and simple. He felt like a coward. After the initial shock came the bitterness and anger, which had largely dissipated, but the guilt and remorse remained.

He shook his head vigorously, hoping to dislodge the bad memories that lingered there. It felt almost as if the crushing regret that constantly vilified him for not doing more to prevent the death of his friend had grown into a seperate entity that would never fade.

But over time, it did.

To an extent.

But there were still days like today when, for some reason, Barry imposed himself at the forefront of Dale's mind and refused to move. Almost as if he was trying to convey a message from the other side.

The little red light blinked out again.

Huh?

Dale gave the machine a little shake, then hit the RECORD button again.

Nothing. The Dictaphone was lifeless.

He took the 'new' batteries back out and examined them. They looked fine, but unless visibly corroded, a battery just looked like a battery.

With a shrug he threw the apparently faulty batteries in the waste paper basket and replaced them with the last two in the pack. Then he paused with his finger over the RECORD button. He was right. It certainly had gotten colder in the room. He could almost see his breath, and his fingers trembled. For a few long moments he couldn't find it within himself to depress the button.

He glanced around nervously.

He was still alone.

Or at least appeared to be.

All this supernatural mumbo jumbo must be getting to him, fraying his nerves.

Summoning every ounce of willpower, he finally hit the button again. He was so anxious that for a few seconds he forgot what he was doing before resuming the one-sided verbal exchange.

But this time, his heart wasn't in it. Whereas before the activity had a kind of surreal excitement, now he just felt ridiculous. He actually breathed a sigh of relief when the timer indicated the fifteen minutes allocated time was up.

He stopped the machine and held it for a while. It looked just like any other Dictaphone. But now, for a while at least, it was imbued with power, the power to change his whole way of thinking. What it might contain could potentially alter his entire belief system.

This was some heavy shit.

Needing something else to think about, he made himself a cup of instant coffee using the kettle and complimentary sachets in the room and peered out of the window again. Dark storm clouds were gathering, seemingly being drawn from all four corners of the globe simultaneously, as they often did along the Welsh coast. Violent storms could erupt suddenly and then disperse without leaving so much as a trace.

Lucy should be back soon.

The thought was quickly followed by a hot pang of guilt.

How could he be so stupid?

Letting let her go walking out there alone, in a strange area, after what happened last night?   What if she had another... blackout? Or worse, a fit or some kind of seizure?

Shit.

Something the philosopher George Santayana entered his head:

Those who do not learn history are doomed to repeat it.

Was he overreacting? Basing his uneasiness on what had happened to Barry?

Or did he have a real cause for concern?

Setting his coffee cup down Dale picked up his phone, scrolled through the numbers until he found Lucy's, and pressed CALL.

Chapter 20:

Secret Garden

Lucy's feet sank into the boggy earth as she made her way across the field. She hadn't seen the bird of prey, or anything else worth photographing, for a while now.

At least I'm not lost, she thought defiantly.

How could she be lost? Sker House, the only visible landmark for miles, may be getting steadily smaller but it was still there, silhouetted against the greying sky behind her.

However, something wasn't right.

She would walk for a while, then turn to get her bearings only to find that Sker House, all those hundreds or thousands of tons of limestone, concrete, and timber, had moved slightly. Logic told her that it was simply a result of her not walking in a straight line, but more than once the whole thing seemed to disappear altogether. Just for a split second, there was nothing but open sky. Once, she even saw it shimmer if it were a mirage. Then it took form and solidified before her very eyes.

When that happened, she was suddenly torn between wanting to get as far away from the place as she could and being drawn back there, where some indefinable part of her was beginning to feel she belonged. The whole weird episode was accompanied by a swoony dizziness. At one point, it crossed her mind that she may have somehow inadvertently ingested some of those magic mushrooms that grew wild here, and the thought made her giggle.

Her pace slowed until eventually, she stopped walking altogether.

She was in a field, both Sker House and the ocean somewhere behind her. She checked to make sure the house was still there.

This time, thankfully, it was.

The field was bordered with a spindly-looking hedge that was more brown than green, and the yellowing grass was completely absent in places exposing the raw, uncultivated earth beneath. She kicked at the soil. It was of a light brown, sandy consistency, and came up easily. No doubt all the sand and salt blowing in from the beach made farming this particular patch of land particularly difficult. Judging by the state of the place, it had been a long time since anyone had even tried.

She didn't see an entrance.

Then how did she get in?

Must've have climbed a sty, she thought, though she had no recollection of doing so. Climbing a sty in the country was one of those banal things you do without even thinking about, like crossing a road in the city. Moments like that were easily lost. Weren't they?

Shrugging, she decided to head back to the house to see how Dale was getting on with his assignment. She just needed to find that sty again.

As she began to retrace her steps, her eyes were drawn to an unkempt corner of the field in the shadow of a large oak tree with withered, twisted limbs.

There was something behind the tree, partially hidden by its great gnarled trunk.

As she neared it, she noticed that the hedge in that corner had been allowed to grow taller than anywhere else in the field, and what she'd spied from afar was some kind of gate.

It wasn't until she was within touching distance that she realized there was no hedge to speak of. What she'd mistaken for a privet was actually creeper vines attached to, and covering, a stone wall, the kind painstakingly erected by carefully slotting bricks together without the aid of cement or adhesive like a giant jigsaw puzzle. The vines twisted and turned all over the uneven surface, tangled up and growing into in each other, serving the dual purpose of concealimng and strengtheining the construction.

What the hell? Did she really just walk past all this?

It wouldn't be impossible. The creeper vines camouflaged the wall against the background, and unless you were at just the right angle, you would never even know it was there.

Beth reached out and ran her fingers along the cold stones. It was probably just a boundary marker or something. Stepping back to take a look at the gate, she realized there was a doorway cut out of the stone wall. The door it housed was a sturdy-looking wooden affair, built at chest height and reinforced with what looked like rusted iron or steel cladding. In one corner was a comically oversized padlock.

Lucy stared at the door, willing it to magically open. It didn't, so she stepped back and put her hands on her hips. The stone wall she had mistaken for a hedge was so tall she couldn't see over the top of it, even if she stood on tiptoe and craned her neck.

She looked around for something to stand on, but the field was devoid of anything helpful.

Unless...

She tentatively regarded the oak tree.

Could it support her weight?

At first glance, she thought not. But it's spindly arms were held out almost invitingly. She gave the trunk a little knock. It sounded hollow, which probably wasn't a good thing, and tiny flecks of bark flew off in all directions. She'd never climbed a tree before. She'd never needed to, or wanted to, for that matter. But how hard could it be?

She had a fleeting vision of falling off, shattering her leg in a dozen places, and being forced to endure the agony of dragging herself back to Sker House across all that rough terrain inch by agonising inch.

Still...

The tree looked climbable. Dozens of brittle-looking branches jutted out of the trunk, some ends splintered to expose flesh turned grey by the elements. Yet paradoxically, the upper reaches of the tree were in full spring mode. Lush green branches, resplendent with bright leaves, canopied over her head. That proved the tree was still healthy and strong, at least. If she was extra careful, surely she would be able to scale high enough to peek over the top of the wall.

Without any more pause for thought, she started climbing.

Three or four feet off the ground now, and still going. An unforeseen problem was that as she ascended, the tree the branches became thinner and more flexible meaning there were less hand and footholds she trusted.

Come on girl, you can do it! Don't quit now!

She manoeuvred herself adjacent to the wall. Just a little higher...

The moment she reached the summit, a lot of things happened at once. Afterwards, she would spend a long time dissecting events and their relevance. The thing she remembered most profoundly was the sun as it broke through the dark clouds, bathing her with angled rays of warmth and light. The moment was so dazzling it seemed to come from a divine source.

Lucy stopped for a split second to savour the experience, lifting her face to the heavens to feel the full effect. But even as she basked in the spontaneous sun shower, she looked down over the wall, and into...

A garden.

Though her eyes had precious little time to drink in the sight, and when she recalled it later she could never be sure how much of what she saw in her mind's eye was real and how much blank space had been filled in by her imagination, what she did see would stay with her forever.

The centrepiece was an ornate little pond and a beautiful marble fountain surrounded by a rock garden. A path led to the pond from the locked wooden door, lined by ranks of flowers of all different sizes, varieties and colours, and a small wooden bench had been placed in one corner in the shade of a willow tree. In addition to the flowers, various other plants were on display, every one of them lush and well-nourished, though Lucy couldn't identify any of them. Botany was never her strong point.

Skirting the perimeter were immaculately maintained hedges, trimmed into shapes which her mind would later twist into various animals. A rabbit, a miniature giraffe, maybe a lion. The garden was bursting with life and vitality, providing a welcome contrast to the bleak countryside around it like an oasis in a desert.

Unbeknownst to her, the secret garden would come back to haunt both her dreams and her nightmares. It became a place she could retreat when the world got too much, and on those occasions the garden was always sunny and warm, the gate hanging open to receive her, negating the need to climb petrified trees just to get a look. It was safe, serene.

But how different the same place could be.

Sometimes, she found herself in the other secret garden. This time it was dark and cold. Things slithered and writhed in the shadows, and something hidden in the far corner made a low, guttural growl.

In this version, Lucy would walk up the path toward the little pond, where she stopped and stared deep into the murky black water, hypnotized by its soft lapping sound. Then she would

167

notice something beneath the ripples, something white and translucent.

Curious, she would lean in closer to get a better look. Then the hand would break the surface. Paralysed with terror she could only watch as it extended into a bloated, fish belly-white arm, reaching for her.

On some fundamental level she understood the message the nightmare was trying to convey. The secret garden was a place between worlds, of equal light and dark, where anything is possible. Your wildest dreams, or your darkest nightmares.

But that level of understanding came later.

Right then, at the moment of discovery, all Lucy felt was wonder. She couldn't believe her eyes. How could a garden like this, so lush and healthy, exist unnoticed in the middle of a wasteland?

She was reaching around to unhook her camera so she could get some pictures when the third thing happened.

Something touched her.

It felt more like an animal than a person. Or a bird, fluttering its wings against her upper thigh.

In that moment, whatever illusion she was under shattered. She instantly lost her grip on the branch, and then she was falling. The journey to the topsoil seemed to take a very long time. Had she really been that high?

Then she hit the ground with a bone-jarring thud, and the wind was pushed out of her with a loud oosh!

There was a sharp pain in her side, and the world went grey around the edges before the darkness swallowed her whole.

She had no idea how long she was unconscious. Or even if she was. There was the sensation of drifting on clouds, although that could have been because that was all she could see from where she lay.

It was the weird fluttering against her leg that brought her back to reality. She could feel it, like leathery wings beating against her leg. When she tried to move her head to investigate, the pain hit like a blinding flash. She'd landed on her face, as ungainly and unladylike as you could get. Her jaw throbbed, she could feel the left side of her face swelling, and the coppery taste of blood filled her mouth. Her tongue flicked around, checking for new cavities or chipped teeth. Thankfully, there didn't seem to be any. She touched a finger to her nose and it came away bloody.

Great, gonna look like the Elephant Man in the morning.

It was proving a day of new experiences. The first time she'd ever climbed a tree, the first time she'd ever fallen off one, and the first time she'd ever managed to give herself a nose bleed. Quite the hattrick.

Struggling to her feet she hunched over, holding her ribs with trembling arms. There seemed to be less pain that way. When she stood, the world swam in and out of focus a couple of times before finally settling on a slightly skewed, off-kilter view. She saw Sker House roughly where it was supposed to be, and made an unsteady beeline for it, putting the oak tree and the the secret garden behind her.

But still that damn annoying thing on her leg!

She swatted at it impatiently, and felt something hard and bulky. It was moving, vibrating urgently.

Her phone.

Of course!

There was no animal.

She fished the device out of her pocket, pressed RECEIVE, and in her best telephone manner said, "Hello?"

"Lucy!" It was Dale. "Where've you been? I've been calling you for ages. Kept going to voicemail?"

"Sorry, didn't hear it," Lucy replied, the fog beginning to clear.

"I thought you'd... never mind. Is everything okay? You sound half asleep."

"I'm okay," she slurred. "I fell off a tree."

"Sorry, I thought you said you'd fallen out of a tree."

"I did."

"What were you doing up a fucking tree?"

"I found a garden. But the gate was locked. I couldn't get in, so I had to climb a tree. And, well, you know what happened next."

"And that's when you fell?"

"Yeah."

"Are you hurt?"

"I don't think so," Lucy still wasn't sure, and used her other hand to touch various parts of her body in search of pain or open wounds.

"Maybe you should come in for a check-up."

"I was just on my way. How did the EVP experiment go?"

"Status unknown. I haven't played the recording back yet. Thought I'd wait for you so you can offer some expert analysis."

"Very gentlemanly of you. And probably wise. So why did you call?"

"Just to see where you were, and to see whether or not we needed to send out another search party?"

"Nope. Not at all. Be there soon."

"Well, okay. If you get lost or something, call me."

"Lost? Dale, I can see Sker from here. I won't be long."

Not wanting anyone to see her dishevelled state, when she arrived back at Sker House Lucy elected to use the side entrance. Her route took her past a tiny enclosed patch of land adjacent to the house being tended to by the woman she'd seen earlier. Ruth? Was that her name?

The side entrance was open. She was about to sneak up the stairs to their room, when something made her stop.

Raised voices.

Raised voices always commanded attention, that was why people raised their voices in the first place, wasn't it?

It was two men.

Dale?

Lucy stopped and listened.

No, not Dale.

Both talkers had strong Welsh accents, whereas Dale's had become far less pronounced since he'd moved away. Besides, she would recognize his voice anywhere. If it wasn't dale, it must be Machen and... Old Rolly? She couldn't remember hearing the old man talk before, but while one sounded like the landlord, the other was deeper and more weathered. They appeared to be midway through a heated discussion.

"Sandra understood the way things are around here," the older man was saying, an accusatory note ringing in his voice.

"That's why she bloody left!" came the terse reply.

They must be talking about Machen's absent wife. So he didn't murder her and bury her in the garden, after all! The fact that Lucy felt more relief than disappointment suggested that her moral compass still pointed in the right direction, and hadn't been totally distorted by almost three years of journalism training. Not too much, anyway.

Cautiously, she put an ear to the door.

"Listen to yourself, will you? You're like a big kid. Its always somebody else's fault, isn't it? Don't forget you're the one she was married to, nobody else."

"How can I forget it? I love that woman!" Machen's voice trembled with emotion. "It was all that rubbish you told her about this place that did it. Got her believing all sorts of stuff, you did. By the end, she was like a different person."

The two men were in full throttle now, and didn't sound a million miles away from firing pistols at dawn.

"Maybe you were the one that changed, not her. I only told her what she needed to know. Don't you think people should understand the dangers of living in Sker?"

Dangers? Did he say dangers of living in Sker? Lucy swallowed hard. The voices suddenly grew hushed as if, mindful of being heard, both men were making an effort to contain themselves.

"There's no danger here. I wouldn't stay if there was, would I? And I certainly wouldn't bring my wife here."

"You just can't see it. Your judgement has been clouded by the lure of the almighty dollar, just like every other owner Sker's had."

"And you've been driven senile by old age, mun! What makes you such an expert, anyway?"

"My family has been here or hereabouts for generations."

"And you think that gives you the right to have a say in what goes on? It doesn't work like that. Don't forget that the only reason you're tolerated around here is because you're a paying customer."

"See! It all comes back to money with you."

"I have to make a living, same as everyone else, don't I? And what have you ever done for Sker? I didn't see you step up to save it when the place was going to ruin."

"As you said, I'm a paying customer. I do my bit. When all things are considered, my family has done more for Sker than you are ever likely to do."

"But I brought it back to life!" Machen was almost shouting. "This is my dream, not yours. Your dream is something else, and you're welcome to it. Without me, Sker House would still be a crumbling wreck."

"Maybe that's how it should have stayed. Kicked a hornets nest, you have. Some things are better left alone. One day you'll see that. I just hope it won't be too late. Sker has suffered enough tragedy."

After that, the conversation petered out. Or carried on at a more respectable volume that Lucy couldn't hear. Lost in thought, she continued on her journey.

Arriving at their room, she found the door open and Dale sitting on the edge of the bed holding his Dictaphone.

"There you are," he said. "Oh my God! You look like you've just fought for the heavyweight title." Catching her glare he quickly corrected himself, "Sorry, I mean featherweight title, or pubeweight title, whichever's the lightest. You know, 'cos you're so slim and everything..."

"Good boy. Is there such a thing as a pubeweight title?"

"I don't know. But if there isn't, there should be. And you'd probably win it. So what happened?"

"I told you, I fell off a tree. I'm fine, really." Before Dale could object she made for the en suite bathroom and hurriedly shut the door behind her.

"What were you saying about finding a garden?" Dale shouted through the door.

"I'll tell you about it later," Lucy answered.

Already her recollection of events had become hazy and she was beginning to wonder if she had knocked herself unconscious and dreamed the whole thing.

On seeing her reflection in the bathroom mirror, she was relieved to find that she wasn't too badly beaten up. There was a little graze on her chin, and maybe the beginning of a bruise high on her right cheekbone. Some blood from her nose had run down to her lip and been smeared everywhere, making her condition look far more serious then it actually was.

She cleaned herself up as best she could using warm water from the tap and cotton swabs then tied her hair into a ponytail. As she studied her reflection in the mirror, the glass began to cloud over, misting up like a car windscreen on a frosty morning.

Strange, while the hot water tap was running there was no condensation, but now...

A part of her mind said; it's the misty stuff from the photographs! It's here!

Whatever it was, the greyness encroached from all sides until it perfectly framed Lucy's face in the centre of the mirror.

Then, the first tendril of mist crawled across her cheek, closely followed by another, this one thicker and faster than its predecessor, and then another. The wispy forms twisted and contorted into one big swirling mass and her features melted away into nothing. Lucy was transfixed by what was unfolding before her. She couldn't tear her eyes away, and as much as she squinted and peered into the grey swirls, she could no longer see herself.

Then how do you know you're still here?

Of course I'm still here, where else would I be? You can't simply vanish into thin air before your own eyes.

Then the greyness slowly began to disperse. Amidst the thinning grey swirls she could make out the outline of a head, framed just as before. But...

What's wrong with this picture?

The face in the mirror looking back didn't belong to her.

It was someone else.

There were similarities. They were both girls, and around the same age. But this face was narrower than hers, the features sharp and well-defined, and the eyes smaller and darker with dark bags beneath them. This new face was pale, drawn and haggard. A mask of tragedy.

Instinctively, Lucy swung around, fully expecting to find someone standing behind here. But she was alone in the tiny bathroom.

As she struggled to comprehend what she was seeing, staring hard at the person in the mirror. The sad, defeated eyes seemed to call to her, implore her.

What do you want me to do?

Lucy felt dizzy, and gripped the wash basin for support. Whatever was going on, she would like it to end now, please. Enough of this weird shit.

Stop the world, I wanna get off!

Before she could stop herself, she bent over the basin and vomited, the hot noxious fluid burning her mouth and throat as it came up.

It's shock.

You're in shock.

You had a fall, and this is ome weird delayed reaction.

Her mind scrambled for an explanation.

A trick mirror? A dream? Was she still lying unconscious under the tree? Or was she having a brain embolism or something?

She pinched the skin of her forearm between her thumb and forefinger, making herself wince. She knew she winced because she felt the muscles in her face contract and her lips pull back over her teeth, but the face in the mirror didn't flinch.

That was when she started screaming.

Chapter 21:

Changing Destiny

Whilst Lucy did her thing in the bathroom, Dale took the opportunity to change into his good jeans (good in the sense that they were worn-in enough to be comfortable, but still new enough to be considered smart) and a black shirt. His options were limited in that department, as it was the only shirt he owned. His social activities didn't often call for formal wear.

As he carefully gelled his hair into spikes and groomed himself in the dressing table mirror, he thought about how excited he used to be when he first discovered the forbidden world of pubs and clubs. In those halcyon days he would start getting ready at least three hours before he had to leave, then endure an anxious extended wait either sitting in his room or standing on a street corner somewhere waiting for his friends. He'd since learned the art of restraint, and though the mere prospect of getting drunk still thrilled him, it no longer sent the same waves of anticipation through his body.

Nothing ever felt as good as it did when you are young and every experience was fresh, new and exciting.

It was as if his senses had been deadened by Barry's suicide. Dale was pretty sure that if it hadn't been for that, he wouldn't even be here now. He would never have made it to university. Either directly or indirectly, Barry was the reason Dale decided to leave Wales and see what else the world had to offer. His friend's death was the catalyst, the one momentous event that changed everything. The thing that made him get up and do something. He didn't want to end up swinging from a tree.

Working at the factory, he could see his life stretching out before him like a long, featureless road. Doomed to a life of mediocrity, putting things in boxes day after day. If he was lucky and kept his job for ten or twenty years there was a chance he might make supervisor or even floor manager, but that was as far as he would go. There was more chance of career advancement at MacDonald's.   If he was lucky, he'd meet a nice girl along the way and fall in love. A job and a girl, that was enough for most people. But Dale knew it would never be enough for him. That kind of simplified existence would drive him crazy. Too many people in the world made do with a job they hated and a partner they clung to for fear of never being able to find anyone else. He saw it happen on a regular basis; the factory was an endless procession of life's victims. People who now did things becaause they had to, not because they wanted to.

Sometimes you saw the light in their eyes simply wink out. *Click.*

The fire inside that kept them going, kept them hungry, suddenly died. It was like seeing them give up. It couldn't be that far removed from the look of a Death Row inmate en route to the execution chamber.

Given enough time, factory life can crush anyone, cruelly snuffing out any last vestiges of hope that lingered after you were spat out by the state education system. There were times when Dale thought Barry had the right idea. Opting out seemed like a viable alternative to slaving away lining other people's pockets for half your life.

But suicide was the easy way out.

Selfish.

And tough on the family.

Not long after Barry's suicide, his mother and father separated and his little brother was taken into foster care. The village gossip-mongers said they blamed each other for what happened.

Barry's death had galvanised Dale's thoughts and ambitions, made him more focused and determined to follow his dreams. Giving him the gift of appreciation was the greatest thing Barry had ever done for him. Since then, he'd come to find solace in the fact that his friend's last act on this earth, his parting gift, was to teach him a valuable lesson; live life to the fullest. Treat each day like it was your last. Because one day, it will be. The days run out, and the clock is ticking for all of us.

You can't just sit around hoping for a lucky break. That's not enough. You have to make it happen. Everyone is responsible for their own happiness. You have the power to either succeed or fail, and you can't always rely on other people to help you out.

Why should they?

Nobody owes you anything. Everyone is too wrapped up in their own lives. You have to formulate a plan for yourself, then find the skills, courage and belief to make it work.

Writing was Dale's avenue. He wasn't fooling himself into thinking he could be a famous novelist (though that remained a distant ambition) but a job on a newspaper or magazine wasn't beyond him. He was still learning the trade, and knew that writing was a skill you never stopped learning. The main thing was he'd discovered something he enjoyed, was reasonably good at, and could make a decent living from. He was lucky. And he wasn't like most of the pretentious snobs at his university who deluded themselves into believing they could change the world when most of them couldn't even change their own underpants. They would write a paragraph, or a single sentence, then sit back admiring it.

Not that it mattered too much. Upon graduating, most of them would be absorbed into daddy's company where they probably wouldn't even have to change their own underpants.

Suddenly, there was a scream and Dale's attention snapped back to the here and now.

Heart thudding furiously in his chest he bounded over to the bathroom door and hammered on it. "Lucy? Lucy!"

No answer.

Shit!

Dale was preparing to kick the lock off when the door opened and Lucy casually strolled out.

"What's wrong? Why all the screaming?"

"What? Oh, nothing. There was a spider."

"Haven't you seen a spider before?"

"Yeah, but this one was BIG."

"Okay. Where is it? I'll throw it out of the window." Dale said, striding purposefully into the bathroom.

"Too late, his ass is grass. He went down the toilet."

Dale was sceptical. He couldn't believe a spider caused all that fuss. It wouldn't be the first time in history an impromptu encounter with an insect had made a girl scream, but he had the impression Lucy was lying. He knew her too well. There was something else going on. And what about her allegedly falling out of a tree on top of last night's escapades?

Why all these things together?

Why now?

Was Lucy going nuts?

She hadn't been herself for a while. Dale had an idea it must be something to do with Steve, the guy she'd been seeing. It usually was. Lucy had terrible taste in men. That was well documented. If she had any taste at all, she would be on his arm by now instead of going off with idiots who just wanted to use her.

But it was her life. All Dale could do was stick around and pick up the pieces when she fell apart. Which, by all indications, was right now.

A quick inspection of the bathroom proved that there was no spider loitering in the toilet bowl. If the toilet had been flushed as Lucy claimed, he would certainly have heard it, which proved beyond doubt she was lying.

But why?

Chapter 22:

Talking to the Dead

Lucy needed a lie down. That was all. It had been a long, trying day. How often do you wake up in a haunted house and fall out of a tree whilst trying to gain access to a secret garden?

Sitting on the edge of her bed, she slipped off her shoes and flexed her toes. As she did so, she noticed something lying on the bedside table. Something that hadn't been there before. It seemed so foreign, so alien, that it demanded attention.

"Dale? what's that?"

"What's what?" Dale said, emerging from the bathroom. He was looking at her in a way she didn't much care for, as if he was angry or disappointed. Like all this craziness was her fault. She pointed at the object on the table.

"Oh that," he said dismissively. "It's a key."

"Yeah, I can see that. I mean, where did you get it?"

"I found it," Dale replied proudly. "Over there behind the radiator. I don't think it fits anything in the room, so I'm going to hand it in it to Machen later. Maybe the last guests left it here or something. Why?"

"Just wondering." She picked the key up and examined it. It was heavy. Placing it back on the table, she saw that it left a brown residue on her fingers which she wiped on her jeans. "Ew, dirty."

"Dirty key, yes. Are we going to listen to this tape, or what?"

"Oh, I forgot all about your little experiment."

"My little experiment? Can I just remind you that this whole recording ghost voices thing was your idea?"

"But it's your machine. Hence, whatever happens is your fault."

"Oh, right. Like that, is it?"

Lucy sat on the bed next to him, and Dale hit the PLAY button. She noticed his hands were shaking ever-so-slightly. There were a few seconds of empty static, then the sound of his voice.

Can you hear me?
Who are you?
What do you want?

After every question there was a short, almost hopeful pause.

"Very professional." Lucy said. "You sound like a TV reporter doing his off-air warm-up."

"Is that a compliment?"

"If you like."

"Oh, then ta very much!"

"Welcome. Is this as clear as you can make it?"

"'Fraid so."

"No offence Dale, but I think your equipment needs to be updated. When are you going to invest in a new Dictaphone?"

"Do you know how much these things cost? I'm an impoverished student, remember."

"Is there any audio enhancing software we can download from the internet to clean it up?"

"Probably. But I don't have any. Not right now. I can have a scout around later."

"Helpful."

"Yeah, well. A good craftsmen works with the tools he is given. You should be thankful I brought the Dictaphone at all. I was going to just bring the notepad and pencil. Without which, I might add, we wouldn't even be on our way to solving this mystery. Now, just listen, will you?"

Did you write in my notebook?

Recorded Dale asked.

Pause.

Hello? Did you write in my notebook?

Pause.

And then...

Yes.

Lucy's jaw dropped open. Dale stopped the recorder, rewound it a fraction, and played the section again. It only said one word, but there was a voice. Very faint, but unmistakable. It was the small voice of a woman or girl, weak and desperate. It sounded as if it was coming from a long way away, drifting in and out of clarity like a distorted radio signal. There was a pained, breathless tone to it, as if the speaker was expending a lot of energy.

But it was answering his question. That made it intelligent.

Dale stopped the tape and looked at Lucy, eyebrows raised and mouth open. The colour drained from his face.

Lucy was too shocked to speak. Yes, the experiment had been her idea, but she never expected results like this! She knew they mustn't get carried away. They had to stay objective, and debunk the obvious first.

"Was there anyone else here, Dale? If not in the room then maybe outside in the corridor? Maybe you just got a snatch of a conversation between Isabel and her mother?"

"Do you think I'm that stupid?" Dale scoffed. "I was alone in here. The door was closed, and I didn't see or hear anyone else the whole time I was recording."

Lucy believed him, knowing he would have much preferred to have made a recording of him asking unanswered questions of an empty room just to prove her wrong.

"Then it could be that we have a recording of an intelligent spirit voice. You communicated with the undead, Dale. Congratulations!"

"The undead?" Dale sneered. "Do you have to say that? It's very George A. Romero-sounding. Like we're on the verge of a zombie apocalypse."

"I wonder if there's more," Lucy said.

"Let's see," Dale replied as he hit PLAY again.

As before, Recorded Dale was asking questions, leaving the obligatory gap before the next one. Except now, each gap wasn't filled with empty static, but with echoes of that same weak, timid voice struggling to be heard above the raging silence.

Dale and Lucy both huddled closer to the device.

Can you hear me?

Yes...

Who are you?

Liz

What do you want?

Rest.

Hello, is anybody there?

Leave us.

Lucy was numb. Dale was having a conversation with... a ghost. And it was all on tape.   "Play that bit again," she asked. When he did, the voice was still there. On second and third listen, the words were even more plainly audible. "Oh my God, Dale. She says her name is Liz..."

"I know," Dale said. "So?"

"So isn't Liz short for Elizabeth?"

"As in Elizabeth. Maid of Sker."

Lucy shook her head, "No, it can't be."

This was all getting too much.

"Look, you wanted to try and capture spirit voices, right? Well, you got your wish. You know, the funny thing is, all this stuff happened between the ninth and twelfth minutes of recording."

"So?"

"So that was exactly when the batteries in my Dictaphone died. I had to replace them. Twice. I remember."

Lucy thought about this for a moment then said, "You know, some people believe spirits need to draw energy from some kind of power source in order to manifest."

"Well, nicking the power out of all my batteries is a bit of a liberty."

"Never mind, I'll buy you some shiny new ones, okay?" Lucy cooed. "I'm more concerned about the last thing she said."

"The 'leave us' part?"

"Yes. Didn't that bother you at all? She doesn't want us here, Dale. She basically told us to get out."

Dale thought for a moment, then said, "Yeah, it bothers me. But no more than the fact that we just made contact with a fucking ghost. I'm still trying to get my head around that part. What she was talking about is kinda irrelevant. There's still a few minutes of tape to listen to. You wanna go for it?"

"Sure, why not?"

Recorded Dale asked more questions, but this time there were no answers. Once, in the hollow silence, a far-away animalistic growl could be heard. They rewound the tape several times to try to make sense of it but were unable to draw any conclusions. In the end, Dale tried to make light of the situation.

"And what the fuck is that? The ghost of a guy snoring?"

But the sound sent shivers down Lucy's spine and she could tell that despite his joviality, it had a similar effect on Dale. The noise was inhuman. Demonic, even.

After that, it was just Dale. As the recording wore on, Lucy could tell by the tone of his voice that he was beginning to lose

184

interest, as if knowing subconsciously the climax of the operation had already been reached.

When they had finally listened to everything, they both sat in silence for a while. Eventually, Dale said, "So what do you think?"

It took a moment for Lucy to differentiate Real Dale from Recorded Dale.

Was that question directed at her?

She turned to see he was looking at her expectantly.

Yes, he was talking to her. "What do I think?" she said. "I think we have one hell of a story, Dale."

A short time later, as Lucy was going back over the Dictaphone recording for anything they may have missed, there was a sharp rap at the door. It opened to reveal Machen's reddened grinning face. For one awful second, he looked like Jack Nicholson in The Shining.

Here's Johnny!

Judging by his slightly unsteady demeanour, the landlord must have sneaked another couple of drinks in since the last time they saw him. "What are you kids doing?" he asked. "Hope I'm not interrupting anything, like."

"No, not at all," said Lucy, picking up on the implication and ruthlessly putting it to rest.

"Good, good. I just wanted to come and tell you that dinner will be ready for six. Would you prefer to choose something from the set menu, or would you like to try Mrs Watkins' special? I think that'd be the way to go, myself. The woman's been cooking half the day. I'm not quite sure what it is, but it smells bloody lovely. Pardon my French, like."

"I guess we'll take your recommendation and order the special, then. Okay with you, Lucy?"

"Fine."

"Okey dokey. Two specials." The landlord hovered uncertainly in the doorway, his eyes flitting around the room. "Anything else I can do you for before I go?"

"No, everything's fine, thanks." Dale replied, a little too abruptly. "I guess Madam here will be wanting to make herself beautiful for dinner, so we'll see you a bit later."

"Fair enough." The door began to close slowly.

"Oh, Machen? Wait a moment."

"Yes? What is it?" The door swung open again with vigour.

"We found an old key and just wanted to return it." Dale hopped out of his chair at the desk and grabbed the key from the bedside table.

"Found an old key, you say?"

"Yep, under the radiator." Dale said, suddenly looking like a child about to receive praise. Then he caught Lucy's eye. She was giving him her best 'what the fuck have you done?' look. But it was too late.

He handed the rusted lump of metal over to the landlord, who raised an eyebrow at it.

"Hmm, I don't recognize it. Where did you get it?"

"I just said, under the radiator?"

"Oh yeah, you did. Get forgetful, I do. Must be old age creeping up on me. It does that, you know. Creeps up."

"No worries."

"Nah, I don't know this key at all," the landlord continued. "But I'll keep it in a safe place and maybe one day its lock will turn up. Its other half, you could say. Wouldn't that be nice? Send this lil' fella 'ome, like. Reunite two pieces in this world that were truly made for each other. Things have a funny way of doing that, you know."

"Doing what? Finding each other?"

"Sometimes. You know, just turning up in the right place, like. Well then, anyway, cheers. Bye now. Bye."

As he left the room, Machen put the rusty key in his inside jacket pocket and closed the door behind him.

Lucy waited until the sound of footsteps retreated down the corridor before landing a hefty right hook on Dale's upper arm.

"Ow! What did you do that for?"

"You gave him the key, you prick! That was... evidence. A clue, whatever."

"Evidence of what? That there's a lock somewhere that nobody can open because we have the key?"

"Evidence of something. It's all connected. I just know it is."

"The key didn't belong to us, so we had no right to keep it."

"It's nice to know you are a good person, Dale. But that key meant something. Didn't you see the look on Machen's face? He was stuttering all over the place."

"That's because the poor bloke has a speech impediment or something, and he's probably a bit drunk."

"But don't you think it's getting worse? What if it isn't a speech impediment at all, but a symptom of something else?"

"Like what?"

"I don't know, I'm not an expert. It wasn't just the way he spoke, it was the way he was acting. We usually can't shut him up, but as soon as you gave him that key he couldn't get out of here fast enough. And didn't it cross your mind that he might wonder what you were doing snooping around under radiators in the first place? It's not exactly normal behaviour, Dale."

"Hang on, what constitutes normal behaviour, anyway? In a haunted hotel, of all places? With a landlord straight out of the Shining and ghosts leaving us messages? And I'll tell you something else. From what else, from what Old Rolly was telling me last night, its hardly surprising the place is haunted."

"How? Have you been holding out on me?"

"No. I just didn't get a chance to tell you everything."

"So tell me now, damn it!"

Dale quickly brought Lucy up to speed about the Mumbles Lifeboat Disaster, and she reciprocated by telling him about the argument she'd overheard between Machen and Rolly on her way back from her walk.

"Kicked a hornet's nest, huh?" Dale said when she finished. "What does that even mean?"

"Who knows. But it doesn't sound good. If this keeps up, before long we'll have enough material for a whole book never mind one measly article."

"No shit."

"I don't know what it is exactly, but doesn't the place make you feel a little strange? It has a really weird vibe."

"Don't let your imagination run away with you. I get a weird vibe wherever I am."

"Let my imagination run away with me? Are you mad? We have an actual recording, and a written message from the other side."

"The other side?" Dale guffawed. "You make it sound so melodramatic."

"Well, how do you want it to sound? And there's something else."

"Oh wonderful. Well, I'm all ears."

"In the bathroom a few minutes ago, I didn't scream because I saw a spider. I screamed because I was looking at my face in the mirror and... it changed, Dale!"

"Changed how?"

"The mirror clouded over. Then when it cleared, it wasn't me any more. I was looking at the reflection of somebody else."

"Who?"

"How should I know? A young woman, long brown hair."

"The same woman you saw in the window?"

Lucy's jaw dropped open. "It was hard to tell. But now you mention it, yes. It must be the same person."

"And the same voice on the recording?"

"More than likely."

"It's still possible that the old boys downstairs are orchestrating this whole thing to drum up business, you know."

"And how the hell are they going to change my reflection in the mirror?"

"Stage magicians have been using mirrors in their performances for centuries. The eye is easily deceived. And with modern technology, it wouldn't be too difficult to rig a mirror."

Lucy was adamant. "It wasn't a trick, Dale. My face changed!" She took a deep breath. "And from what I could gather from the argument I heard, Old Rolly doesn't want lots of people coming here for some reason. That kind of blows your theory about them doing it all for publicity out of the water."

"Unless that's just what he wanted you to think. Reverse psychology."

"But he didn't know I was listening."

"Are you sure?"

"Damn Dale, how paranoid are you? Have you been smoking weed all afternoon or something?"

"Absolutely not!" Dale said, offended. "I forgot to bring any."

"Well, I'm going to confront our dear landlord about the key and a few other things at dinner."

"Are you sure that's wise?"

"What's he going to do? Throw us out?"

"Throw a wobbly, more like. Like he did the first time I tried to interview him."

"well, let him. Things have to be said."

"Great," Dale said sarcastically. "I'm looking forward to it already."

Chapter 23:

Lights Out

Machen and Rolly were right about the impending storm. The light gradually faded until by five o'clock, there were so many grey clouds obscuring the sun that outside was more like a winter's evening than a spring afternoon. The wind became an incessant low moan, rising and falling in pitch and intensity.

Soon afterwards the rain hit, pelting the window with water droplets the size of small coins.   "Wow! Look at that!" Lucy exclaimed, leaping off the bed where she'd been engrossed in a magazine and dashing over for a closer look.

"That's the price you pay for living on the beach," Dale said as he joined her. "It looks nice, but you get all the lousy weather blowing in from the sea."

"Sunbathing is out, then." Lucy said whimsically.

"Yep. Sure looks that way." Dale replied as if sunbathing really had been an option.

"Hey, how would you feel about doing it again before we go down for dinner?"

"Doing what again?"

"The EVP experiment."

Dale couldn't prevent a small tut escaping his lips. "Why? What's the point?" He asked, a little too defensively. "I did it once, we made contact and got the evidence. What more can we do?"

"Get more evidence. You could do an interview. A proper interview. Ask her what it's like... over there."

"Fuck that," Dale said. "Are you crazy? Interview a ghost? She's not on holiday, she's dead!"

"Whatever. Look, you're a professional. Or at least you WANT to be a professional. Look at this as a challenge! You got intelligent responses last time. "

"Yeah, a couple of times, amongst a shower of shit."

"Even if it was just one, it would still make everything worthwhile. That's evidence we can document. There might be clues, and at the very least you'll be able to use it in the article."

"Yeah, I guess so," Dale said with a resigned sigh. "When do you want to do it?"

"We? The last time you were alone, and you made some kind of connection. We should try to replicate the conditions as best we can."

"You're going to leave me on my own again?" He looked at Lucy for a sympathetic reaction.   Suddenly, her face went momentarily blank. There was no emotion at all. A deep shadow cast by a rolling cloud fell across it, and Dale watched as the blankness was replaced by an expression of anguish. "Lucy?"

She appeared not to hear him. Dale watched, horrified, as her face contorted into a vile sneer. She turned to look at him, and he could see the hate boiling within. "You're an evil little man," she spat.

Dale was shocked. "Bit harsh. How come I'm evil? I said I'd..."

"You can't force me to love another!"

The words were so venomous and so full of rage that Dale took a stuttering step backwards.   That word again; evil. It was fast becoming Word of the Day, and that didn't exactly fill him with confidence.

He took a few seconds to regroup before he tentatively asked, "Lucy? What are you talking about?"

But already, the moment was gone. The disdain melted away from Lucy's face to be replaced with bewilderment. "What?" she asked.

Dale gripped her by the shoulders, ready to shake her if necessary, "Lucy, what do you mean, I can't force you to love another?"

She looked as confused as he felt. "What are you talking about?"

"That's what you said. Just now."

"I said nothing of the sort. Unhand me, you ruffian."

Dale did as he was told, scratching his head in exasperation. "Are you kidding me? This is some kind of wind-up, right?"

The most confusing thing of all from Dale's point of view was that he could tell Lucy really had no idea what he was talking about. This was Adamant Lucy. Adamant Lucy didn't make jokes or mess around. Adamant Lucy was abrupt, businesslike, and efficient. And when Adamant Lucy said something was true, you'd better believe it was true. Why would she lie about something like that, anyway? What could she possibly hope to achieve from play-acting?

Then, Dale remembered what she'd said earlier about seeing her face change into the face of someone else in the bathroom mirror. And here she was apparently speaking someone else's words.

For a fraction of a second, he wondered whether he had misheard. Maybe he was the one going mad.

But no.

He'd heard the words as plain as day, and no amount of kidology on his part would change the fact. The only explanation was that Lucy had indeed spoken the words, but didn't know she'd done it. And what could that mean? Was she going crazy or did she get momentarily possessed? Taken over by a spirit?

"How do you feel?" he asked warily, not knowing what else to say.

"Fine. Why? How do I look?"

"Better than fine," Dale replied with a wink to relieve the tension.

At last, Lucy cracked a smile. "Why thank you, kind sir. But we're still sleeping in twin beds tonight."

"Wouldn't have it any other way."

"As long as that's settled. Now, are we gonna get started on experiment numero dos or what?"

"I guess so. But let's do it after dinner, okay? I'm starving. And besides, Mr Machen and company are expecting us."

The truth was, Dale was reluctant to stir things up any more. Not right now. Whatever was going on with Lucy was serious and couldn't be resolved in a few minutes. Most of all, he didn't want to leave her alone again. Bad things seemed to happen when Lucy was left alone.

"Okay, fair enough."

"So, are you ready?"

"Ready."

"Good. The sooner we have dinner, the sooner I can come back here to put myself in mortal danger while you keep the brood busy downstairs with your delightful post-dinner conversation. And if that doesn't work you could always..."

The sentence was cut short when the room was suddenly plunged into pitch blackness. As one, Dale and Lucy gasped.

193

Chapter 24:

The Custodian

"So does this happen often?" Lucy asked. "You're obviously well prepared."

"And lucky for you we were, isn't it?" Machen replied. "I know how disoren... disin... confusing a strange place can be in a power cut. If I hadn't come up to get you with the torch I bet you'd still be up in your room now, fumbling 'round in the dark. Bloody thing's thirsty on batteries, though. Use loads of 'em, I do. None left now."

As if to prove the point he picked up a torch from the table and turned it on. The lens remained dark. Lucy and Dale looked at each other, and she knew they were both thinking the same thing. The Dictaphone battery-draining incident wasn't a one-off. Something in Sker House was draining the power from every available source.

"Yes, you're our hero," Lucy said. It sounded sarcastic, but she actually meant it. "And Champ, too." She leaned over to nuzzle the dog who looked up at her and yawned, filling the air in the immediate vicinity with doggy breath.

However lazy and smelly they might be, all girls loved a pooch.

Lucy and Dale sat opposite the landlord on two tables that had been pushed together in a corner of the bar. They were awaiting the arrival of Old Rolly who, unfazed by the power cut, steadfastly remained in his usual chair. "He'll be over when the food arrives," Machen told them by way of explanation.

Several tall, white candles had been placed on the tables and strategically around the bar to keep the crawling shadows at bay, and two more boxes were perched on the table next to a box of Sker House-branded disposable cigarette lighters.

Outside it was pitch black, and the storm was gradually rising in intensity. The wind had given up moaning and instead howled and whistled banshee-like, throwing raindrops against the glass with increasing force.

The oppressive atmosphere wasn't helped by Machen's erratic behaviour. He kept fidgeting with the almost-empty whisky glass he held, picking it up and putting it down, and insisted on moving the candles around. At one point, he glanced over Lucy's left shoulder and almost jumped back in his seat. Grabbing the nearest candle and thrusting it toward her, Lucy recoiled from the flame then whirled around to see what was behind her only to find nothing there. When she turned back she almost burned her chin on a candle Machen had placed a little too close for comfort.

"Just seeing where we can get the most light. From the candle, I mean. No point otherwise, is there? No point at all."

"Er, no." Lucy agreed, bewildered.

"Oh my! What happened to your face?" The landlord asked suddenly. He obviously hadn't noticed Lucy's pretty collection of bumps and bruises before, even though he'd seen her upstairs not an hour earlier.

She almost told him she'd burned it on a candle just to see what he might say, but instead said, "I fell off a tree."

She briefly considered lying and claiming she 'tripped over' or 'walked into a cupboard,' or something equally lame. But both fabrications were only slightly less plausible and besides, she might get some comedy value out of the truth. She definitely would when she got home and told her friends.

If he was shocked or surprised it didn't show. Instead Machen said, "Why would a girl like you be climbing trees?"

This time, Lucy did lie. She didn't want to tell Machen about the secret garden. Not because she was afraid of ridicule. Of all people, she knew he would believe her.

No, she was afraid of the deluge of questions that would surely follow. Questions she wouldn't be able to answer. Besides, the secret garden was hers now, and she didn't want to share it.

"I wanted to get a view of the sea from a different angle, to get better pictures."

"Oh, gotcha," Machen looked resigned, before springing back to life. "You know us Welsh used to worship trees, back in the day."

Sensing an opportunity for ribbing, Lucy turned to Dale. "Tree worship? Really?"

"It wasn't just us," Dale explained. "It was a Celtic thing. They believed trees were a representation of life or something. The trunk is the earth, or the world as we know it. The top corresponds to the afterlife, or heaven. And the roots represent hell, or the Underworld, as the Celts called it."

"That's neat," Lucy conceded. "And it actually makes some sort of sense."

197

"The more you think about it, the more sense it makes," Dale said. "We need trees to produce oxygen, right? Without trees we'd all die. They couldn't have known that then, but somehow they knew that trees were essential to our survival. I think that's what it boils down to."

Machen was nodding in agreement. "I see they haven't beaten all the Welsh out of you yet, lad! You still have a good dose of logic in you, you do."

"That's debatable. But thanks."

"Interesting that other people had hard-on's for trees and it wasn't just in this neck of the woods," Lucy said.

Dale's eyes widened in surprise and Machen spluttered and coughed. Lucy made a mental note to check the settings on her filter. Must remember she wasn't in some dive in Bedford Place where it was socially acceptable to make dick jokes.

Any repercussions were averted when Izzy appeared carrying a steaming plate in each hand.   "Lucky we have gas stoves!" she said, setting the plates down on the table.

"Mmmm! What do we have?" Dale asked, rubbing his hands together eagerly.

"Mam's famous roast lamb and fresh garden veg," Izzy answered with as much enthusiasm as a weather man talking about a cold snap.

"Looks and smells fantastic! Thank your mother. Are you going to eat with us?" Lucy said. Hoping it sounded like a friendly invitation.

"Dunno. Doubt it. Prob'ly go home."

"Where do you live?"

"Nottage Village. Not far away. Mam drives."

"Maybe you should both stay here tonight in one of the empty rooms," Machen said. "Very dangerous out there on the road now. You know, dangerous? With the weather and that. I won't charge you for the room. I'll just deduct it from your wages at the end of the month, ha-ha!"

"I don't think that will be necessary. Thanks all the same though," Izzy said, a bit too hastily. She obviously had no desire to stay overnight in Sker House.

"And where will you be having your dinner, Rolly?" Machen asked. "You gonna stay over there on your lonesome or are you gonna be sociable for a change?"

"When you put it like that I s'pose I'd better come over, hadn't I?" Old Rolly answered in a gruff, beer-soaked voice as he reluctantly stood up and made his way over to the corner where everyone else had congregated.

For the first time, Lucy noticed that the old man's back was slightly hunched, yet he moved almost gracefully. Like a weary old tom cat whose body may be failing but any physical shortcomings were offset by the value of hard-fought battle experience.

Old Rolly plopped down into the chair next to Machen, who moved to the side to accommodate him. Lucy detected an uneasy air between the two men, probably a residue of the heated conversation she had overheard.

Beneath the table, Champ whined mournfully. "Aye, the dog knows," the old man said.

"Knows what?" asked Lucy, reaching between her legs to scratch behind Champ's ear. The dog whined again.

"Knows the thunder and lightning is coming. Animals don't like it. Dog's taken to hiding."

"I think this poor guy was already hiding, bless him."

"Thunder and lightning? Do you think?" Dale leaned forward and squinted through the window.

"Oh aye. Definitely." Even as the words passed Old Rolly's lips, there was a low grumble in the distance.

At the sound of it, Izzy went scurrying back off in the direction of the kitchen.

"Izzy! Izzy, love? Be a darling and pass a bottle of the hard stuff before you go," Machen called.

The girl paused mid-step, and for a moment Lucy wondered if she was going to carry on regardless. Then, evidently deciding it was too late in the day to argue, Izzy said, "Sure. Be right there."

She noted that Izzy didn't need to verify what 'the hard stuff' actually meant. Either it was a kind of code for a preferred brand of whisky, or it was a euphemism for 'any strong alcohol.'

Seconds later, she returned with a fresh bottle of Jack Daniels and put it on the table next to her boss. "Ah, my friend JD," Machen said, twisting off the cap.

Out of the corner of her eye, Lucy saw Izzy make her second getaway attempt. This time, it was Rolly who called after her. "Not much time left now, love. Better get moving if you're not planning on stopping here with us."

And move Izzy did.

"So what do you do, Rolly?" Lucy said to kick-start the conversation as she scooped a steaming fork full of garden peas into her mouth. "I don't think we've had a chance to talk before. Are you retired?"

"You don't retire from my line of work, miss," the old man replied sagely.

"And what kind of work is that?"

"I'm a custodian. Of sorts."

"Oh, I see," Lucy nodded. "A custodian of what?"

Before the old man could answer, there was a crash of thunder so loud it rattled the glass in the window frame. Rolly barely flinched, but Machen's hand jerked so violently that some of the freshly-poured Jack Daniels leapt out of his glass onto the table. He quickly covered the mess with a beer mat and repositioned two of the candles.

Lucy and Dale exchanged puzzled looks, why did he keep doing that? It was almost as if he were afraid of the shadows. Lucy noticed Rolly was also watching, a grimace of distaste etched onto his face.

Just then, Izzy and her mother appeared with two more dinner plates and set them down on the table. They were both wearing their coats. "Okay if we get going?" Ruth asked. "Before the weather gets any worse?"

"I told Izzy you're both welcome to stay tonight. Said I'd take the money out of your salary, I did. But I was joking. I did say that though, didn't I, Iz?"

"Yep, you did say that," corroborated Izzy, who had taken a position at her mother's shoulder.

"She mentioned it. But we should really get going, if its all the same to you. We'll clean all the plates and everything in the morning. Just leave them where they are."

"Righty ho. You drive careful, then."

"We will. Thanks, and good night all," Ruth gave a parting wave to the group, the smile on her face more relief than cheer. "If you need anything from the village, Mach, just call us before we set off tomorrow morning," she said as she trooped out, closely followed by her daughter.

"Heard you talking about trees earlier," Rolly said as the door closed behind them.

Lucy immediately thought he was going to start asking questions about her tree-climbing escapade and blushed, not that anyone would notice in the dim light.

"Trees, yes," Machen agreed, as if eager to resume any kind of conversation.

Lucy was getting the impression the landlord was the kind of person who liked to be at the centre of everything.

"We were talking about trees. How us Welsh used to worship them and everything."

"That right?" Old Rolly said. "Then it might help the young people's understanding of such things if they knew about the trinity of oak, ash and thorn."

"The what?" Dale asked, leaning forward on his chair. This must be new to him, too.

"They were considered very special trees," Old Rolly said. "Other trees were special, too. In different ways. But oak, ash and thorn were the most powerful. It would have taken a brave man indeed to chop one down."

"Why?" asked Lucy, her head filled with images of people dressed in white gowns and offering praise and gifts to trees. In her mind's eye, the scene looked like something from one of her dad's Monty Python videos. "What would happen if you did?"

"Certain trees were used in Pagan rituals."

"You mean devil worship?" Fittingly, as the words passed Lucy's lips, there was another loud crack of thunder.

"No, I mean Paganism," Old Rolly continued patiently, as if he were a professor explaining a complex theory to particularly dim student. "Paganism is an entirely different concept to Christianity. Nothing to do with the devil, which is a Christian construct. The Christians demonized paganism, and everything else that didn't fit into their neat little belief system. Tarred it all with the same brush."

"So what did the the Pagans do? Was it a kind of magic?"

"That depends what you call magic," old Rolly continued. "The Druids certainly conducted various rituals and sacred ceremonies. Still do, the few that are left. The few real ones, I mean. There are lots of pretenders. Some would call what they do a kind of magic, I s'pose. The main idea is that they worship the world around them and forge a harmonious existence with nature. Trees were central to all that. It was said that anyone who wilfully destroyed one of the trinity of special trees would be cursed with bad luck for the rest of their days. For that reason, people tended to stay away from oaks, especially. Parents would forbid their children to play around them, but of course some naughty children would climb them anyway. Up they would go, higher and higher, up amongst the top branches and out of sight."

"And then?" Lucy prompted, remembering her own surreal adventure that afternoon.

"And then, they would never be seen again."

"Sounds like a story a mother would make up to stop her kids climbing trees."

"Maybe. But the oak has a long association with fairy lore."

It was unusual to hear a grown man man talking openly about fairies and magic. Lucy waited for the sniggers, but they didn't come.

"The fairies lived in or around them, you see," Old Rolly continued. "So if you chopped one down, they would be left homeless and they would come after you seeking revenge."

"Wow, people really believed that vengeful, homeless, tree-dwelling dwarves would come to get them?"

"Not dwarves. Fairies. Dwarved are just little people. Fairies are supernatural entities. Of course, it sounds ridiculous to our ears, but it doesn't matter whether you or I believe it. People in the olden days certainly did, and maybe that was all it took to make it true."

"So what kind of... beings were they?" Dale asked. "These fairies."

"Were?" Old Rolly raised one bushy eyebrow in Dale's direction. "Or are?"

"Whichever," Dale replied.

"Most fairy folk were the mischievous sort, but some were more harmful. One of their favourite tricks was to lure people to the Otherworld. To you it would seem like you'd been gone just a few minutes, but when you returned home to your family you would discover that many years had passed. You still looked the same as you did the day you were taken, but your family and friends would have grown old without you. More often than not, the realisation drove people insane."

"Not that different from modern alien abduction, when you think about it." Dale offered. "Perhaps the phenomena – people being taken and returned – is the same, but how we perceive it has changed."

"Smart thinking," Lucy said as another crash of thunder shook the house. This time, the thunder was accompanied by a startling white flash which illuminated the entire room for a fraction of a second, catching everyone in freeze-frame. Beneath the table, Champ whined again. "Either way, we can safely assume that fairies or aliens, or whatever they are, are bad news."

"That would be fair," Rolly said. "To be respected, not abused. They represent nature, and that is a powerful force indeed. This storm we are currently experiencing is just one example. But do you know the most worrying part?" Dale and Lucy shook their heads. "The most worrying part is that... if we can use the tree as another analogy... you never know how deep the roots go. Or how widely they spread. They are hidden under the ground, you see. The same can be said of true evil. It's subversive, doing most of its work unseen. That is what I meant when I told you it lurks, lad." Old Rolly stared at Dale, his leathery skin looking even more pallid than usual in the flickering candlelight.

"So what does it mean when you fall off one? A tree, I mean?" Lucy asked.

"That, my dear, means that you should stop climbing trees." The table erupted with laughter. But the laughter soon faded into uncomfortable silence. "Just out of interest, do you know what kind of tree it was that you fell off?"

"Sure." Lucy said. "It was an oak." All at once she realized what that meant, and her jaw dropped open.

"What a coincidence," Dale offered tentatively.

"Or not," Old Rolly said, smoothing his beard with a wrinkled hand covered with skin like old parchment. "It's probably lucky that you did fall off. And luckier still that you found your way back to Sker. Who knows what might have happened to you otherwise."

Chapter 25:

Car Trouble

"You stop here, Iz," Ruth said as she and her daughter approached Sker House's main entrance. "I'll run up and get the car started. No sense in both of us getting soaked, is there?"

"No mum." Izzy shifted nervously on her feet, and Ruth read the pleading expression in her eyes.

Hurry up and get me outta here!

Ruth felt it too. Sker House was never the most pleasant place to be, what with the seclusion, the history, and the weird goings on. But it was especially bad tonight. A thick cloak of despondency seemed to have descended upon the place. Maybe it was something to do with the storm. All that electrical energy in the air puts people on edge.

As she hurried up the path toward the waiting vehicle, there was a huge crash of thunder.   The storm must be right on top of them. The thunder was quickly followed by a flash of forked lightning directly above, so bright it lit up the nearby sand dunes like an incendiary device.   For a split second Ruth felt as if she were running for her life through a battlefield, whilst all around her her comrades were being cut to pieces by bullets and flying shrapnel. In some faraway place there was an ominous low rumble that sounded too much like distant gunfire. Ruth gritted her teeth and pulled her jacket over her head.

When she reached the car, she stopped. The rain lashed against the side of her face as she fumbled the key into the lock, opened the driver's side door, and slid in behind the wheel. Needing no second invitation, Izzy started running down the path as Ruth slipped the key into the ignition and turned it. The dashboard lights flicked on and the engine purred into life. Depressing the clutch, Ruth slipped the car into gear, checked her mirrors, more out of habit than any real possibility of smashing into another vehicle, and prepared to release the handbrake.

And then, it died.

Not just the engine, but also the dashboard.

Inexplicably, horrifyingly, everything cut out at once.

"Shit!" Ruth rarely cursed, but felt that in this situation it was justified. She turned the key again.

Nothing happened.

Nothing at all.

She couldn't even muster a wheezy whimper.

Izzy arrived and plopped down in the passenger seat, her face a picture of anxiety as she wiped her face in her sleeve. "What's wrong, mum?"

"Damned if I know. Bloody thing won't start."

"Did you put petrol in?"

"'Course I did," Ruth said with a roll of the eyes. "Yesterday. You were there, remember?" Seeing her daughter's discomfort, Ruth's maternal instincts immediately took over. "It probably just needs a couple of turns, that's all. P'raps the engine got wet or something. It's proper chucking it down. It'll be fine in a minute."

But even though she turned the key several times, the engine still refused to start. Eventually she was forced to concede that there was something seriously wrong with their ticket home. "You stay here, Iz," she said with a sigh. "I'll nip back in and get us some help."

"Who in there's going to help us? Did a qualified mechanic check in while I was getting changed?"

"Well, what else can we do?" Ruth sighed. "You want to stay here in the car park all night? Or do you want to walk home?"

"Neither, really," Izzy replied. "I was thinking we could just leave the car here and get a taxi. Sod it."

"There'll be no chance of getting a cab this time of night. Not on a Saturday, and definitely not in the rain. They'll all be busy running around taking drunk people home from the pubs."

"Yeah, but we can try." Izzy was already scrambling in her bag for her phone. It was never very far away. She found it and flipped open the cover. It was one of those Hi-Tech Beam-Me-Up-Scottie Phones, as Dennis used to call them. She dialled a number from memory and Ruth heard it ringing the other end, but nobody was picking up. "What kind of bloody taxi service is this?"

"A busy one," Ruth said.

"Okay, then. We'll walk it, and get a taxi back in the morning."

"Walk home? Are you mad? The village is miles away. And have you seen the weather out there, my girl? We'll both drown before we get home!"

As if to emphasise Ruth's point, there was another crash of thunder and a jagged fork of lightning split the sky in two.

"I don't care. I'd rather drown than stay here. Or there," Izzy jerked her head in the direction of Sker House, as if she couldn't even bring herself to look at it.

"Yeah, well, lets see if any of those gentlemen in there know anything about cars before either of us does anything stupid, shall we?"

Suddenly Izzy grabbed her arm. "Wait!" she said. "The RAC! We could call them, and then just wait it out. Don't they give women on their own priority or something?"

"But I'm not on my own, am I? You're with me."

"We'll just tell them you're alone. I'll go hide in the bushes while they fix it if it makes you feel better." Izzy was pushing buttons on her phone again. "I'll get the number off the internet. Give me a minute." Then she frowned.

"What's wrong, love?"

"Bloody battery's dead. I must have forgotten to charge it. Weird though, it was okay a minute ago. And I thought it had a full charge when we left the bar."

"No worries. Use mine," Ruth offered as she hunted through the contents of her bag until she found her own phone. It was easily twice the size of Izzy's flash little model and as thick as a sandwich. The sheer size of the thing was actually one of the reasons she didn't want to upgrade. There was a reassuring heaviness about it, and its bulk meant it was easily located in a crisis such as this.

She pressed the ON button and waited. Nothing happened. "That's funny. My battery seems to be flat as well."

"Both our phones, AND the car?" Izzy said in a you cannot be serious tone. "How can that happen? This is like a bad horror film. Maybe one of us can run back in the house and put some charge in one of the phones. Just enough to make a call. I brought my charger with me."

"There's a power cut, remember? " Ruth said, stuffing her useless phone back into her bag. "So that's plan A out of the window, then. I'll go put plan B into action. And if that doesn't work there's always plan C."

Ruth opened the car door, pulling her hood up over her head.

"What's plan C?"

"I don't know yet. Let's just hope we don't need a one, shall we? Lock the door behind me." Ruth slammed the car door shut and turned to face the hulking mass that was Sker House. Lock the door behind me? Why had she said that? They were alone out here. It didn't matter too much, as Izzy didn't question the advice. Ruth heard the whir of the central locking even above the deafening cacophony of noise as she stepped out into the storm.

Chapter 26:

Into the Dark

"So did you find a home for the key?" Lucy asked.

The landlord visibly flinched, as if the words were physical blows. "What? What did you say?"

"The key Dale found in our room today. The one he gave to you earlier."

At the mention of his name, or more likely at the reminder of the bollock he had dropped, Dale shifted nervously in his seat.

"Oh, that key. No, not yet. But I'm sure I will." Machen flashed a smile and returned to his dinner.

"You know, I was thinking," Lucy started hesitantly. "Maybe it fits one of the doors on the top floor. You know, one of the locked rooms." She suppressed a shiver as she was reminded of the night before and the incident in the corridor. The key had been playing on her mind, and she was certain it had a role to play.

Machen stopped chewing and looked puzzled. "Locked doors on the top floor? That's impossible, you must've dreamed that part."

"How come?"

"Because unfortunately, locks are usually the last things to go on doors, so none of them on that floor got fitted with any before them lazy bloody foreigners up and left me in the lurch, did they? Most of them rooms don't even have doors, let alone locks."

Suddenly the moment of realization dawned on the landlord, happening so slowly it was almost painful to watch. "Hang on," he said. "When did you go up there?"

Damn it.

Lucy knew she should have kept her mouth shut about the key. Almost got away with it as well. Now she was in danger of digging a hole for herself she would never be able to climb out of. Good job the landlord was more than a touch forgetful and half-way crazy. Still, she needed a plausible excuse, and quick. "Last night. I got... lost," she scrambled. "Went up there by mistake while I was trying to find our room."

"Weren't looking for my room, were you miss?" Old Rolly interjected, a playful smile tugging at the corners of his mouth. So there was life in the dirty old dog yet.

"Maybe if I were a couple of decades older," Lucy winked, glad of the opportunity to deflect Machen's question.

Unfortunately, it didn't work.

"Hang on. You got lost? How could you get lost? This isn't the Heaton. Hilton, rather. Bit of a liability you are turning out to be, aren't you? L..."

"Lucy," she finished the sentence for him.

Could the man really still not remember her name? It wasn't like there were a hundred guests to keep track of.

"Right okay, Lucy." The landlord nodded firmly, making an obvious effort to lock the name in place. "Liability, yes. Liability Lucy, we should call you. Falling out of trees, getting lost. You should be more careful around the place. You might get yourself hurt one of these days, like."

If this was a bad movie Liability Lucy may have construed the warning as some kind of veiled threat. But the statement seemed more likely a genuine attempt to preserve her welfare on health and safety grounds. The last thing a struggling business needs is a potentially expensive compensation claim.

"Yeah, I suppose I am coming across as a bit scatty," she smiled. "I'm usually more on the ball than this, honestly. I don't know what's wrong with me this weekend."

"A bit out of sorts, are you? How so?" asked Old Rolly, leaning across and placing his leathery, liver-spotted hands on the table.

Lucy risked a glance at Dale. How much information should she divulge? Something told her not to mention making contact with spirits using Dale's Dictaphone. At least not until the lights came back on. "Well, apart from the getting lost and falling out of trees, I could have sworn I saw a woman watching us from an upstairs window yesterday afternoon while we were walking on the beach. Plus, I haven't been feeling too well. I feel... I don't know, drained. I just haven't been feeling myself."

That last comment, of all things, got Old Rolly's attention. "What do you mean by that?" he asked. "You feel like you're somebody else?"

"Almost, yes." Now Lucy thought about it, that was exactly what it felt like at times. She watched the old man's reaction closely. He remained as stony-faced as always, his skin paper white in the candle-light. Something stirred in his eyes, but he said nothing.

"Well don't worry about it too much, is it?" Machen chipped in. "Even the best of us make mistakes, don't we?"

"Oh, I'm sure I'm not mistaken about the room upstairs," Lucy said assertively. "It was definitely locked. Wasn't it, Dale?"

"I can't really remember," Dale said, in a transparent effort to sit on the fence and not upset either side. "It was dark and I had other things on my mind. Everything happened so fast. But there's an easy way to settle this."

"And what might that be?"

"A field trip," Dale continued. "It would only take a few minutes for us to nip up there and find out what the score is."

"You mean you want to go upstairs, like? In the dark?" The landlord looked absolutely terrified.

"Yeah, why not? There's not going to be much else to do tonight by the looks of things."

"No. Absolutely not." Machen said firmly. "What if someone trips over something and decides to sue me? It's dangerous up there, you know. Especially at night." He was still shaking his head when he drained the last of the Jack Daniels from his glass and refilled it.

"Why is it more dangerous at night?" asked Dale.

"Because it's dark, isn't it? Einstein."

Maybe it had more to do with nerves than anything else, but Lucy couldn't help but laugh out loud at Machen's brutal put-down.

For a moment Dale was shocked into silence. Finally he said, "We'll be careful, don't worry. You don't even have to come if you don't want to."

"The answer's still no, I'm afraid. I don't want any old Tom, Dick or Larry traipsing around up there in a power cut, do I? Anything might happen. There's no hospital ward here, you know. Haven't got around to putting one in yet. It's on the list though, right after swimming pool and helicopter landing pad thingy. You know, to land helicopters on."

"A heliport? Why would you want one of those?" Lucy couldn't resist a shot.

"I don't, do I?" Machen looked like he was confusing himself. He picked up his glass then, realizing it was empty, grabbed the bottle. "That's the point. I mean, the point is, no one goes upstairs."

"What, are we under house arrest?" Dale asked. "I could write a different article about that. What's the charge?"

"How about impersonating journalists?"

"We're not impersonating anybody. We're journalists, we just haven't graduated yet."

"So you're students?" Said Rolly, his tone more curious than accusatory. He turned to Machen, who was busily finishing his meal. "Is that a crime, Mach? Impersonating journalists? I mean, it's not like impersonating an FBI agent, is it?"

"If it's not already a crime, it bloody well should be. Obtaining favours through false… false pretences or something?"

"Favours?" Dale exclaimed. "What favours?"

"I been good to you, I have!"

"You have indeed, and we really appreciate it," Dale said. He was using his most persuasive tactics; lowering his voice, maintaining eye contact, giving the impression of sincerity. "It would only take a few minutes. We could just try the key I found in the locks, if there are any, and see if it fits any doors up there. Then the matter will be over and done with, and we'll know Lucy here isn't going nutty. Or we might find she is going nutty. You think me and her could be an item? I don't want to go out with her if she's mental. You wouldn't want to be responsible for that, would you?"

"They're all bloody mental, butt." Machen said, taking another slug of whisky. "The stories I could tell you about my Sandra!"

Dale's plan was working!

The landlord was beginning to crumble before their very eyes. He was approaching the stage where he would do anything to be left alone, and if he kept drinking at this pace before long he would be too drunk to even notice what they did.

Lucy almost felt a pang of sympathy. But another, harder side of her quickly suppressed it. The side of her that got things done, and wasn't held back by little things like compassion.

The vixen saw the wounded prey and went in for the kill. "We won't damage or steal anything, we promise. It would really mean a lot to me." She fluttered her eyelashes, not knowing if that

214

would work, or even what it looked like, just that it felt tickly. People always wrote about fluttering eyelashes in romance books, and like most girls Lucy wasn't adverse to exploiting her feminine charms when the situation called for it.

Machen let out a defeated sigh. "Okay, have it your way. Let's go up and see. Put your little minds at rest, is it? Then maybe a man'll get some peace around here, like."

At that moment the door opened, sending a ripple of harsh wind circulating around the bar, and Ruth entered looking wet, red-cheeked and flustered.

Everyone turned to stare, but it was Old Rolly who said what they were all thinking. "What the hell brings you back? Forget something, did you?"

"Not exactly." Ruth answered, pulling her hood down. "Bloody car won't start, will it? I know its raining. But I was wondering if any of you kind gentlemen would care to look at it for us?"

Lucy silently thanked Ruth for calling out the 'gentlemen' and leaving her out of it. Most people automatically assumed girls didn't know anything about cars, and in Lucy's case those people would be absolutely right. She often wondered how good it must feel to be able to stand up and prove those people wrong, but on nights like this, the men were welcome to the dirty car-fixing jobs.

She watched as Dale, Machen and Old Rolly all silently evaluated each other. The latter was too old. It would be a surprise if he could make it across the room without falling over and breaking a hip. Machen seemed like the kind of bloke who would fiddle about and ultimately make thinghs worse. Bersides that, he was half drunk and frightened of his own shadow.

That left only...

"Sure, I'll pop out and take a look." Dale said. "I'm not sure how much help I'll be, but I should check my car while I'm out there." He patted his pocket to make sure he had the keys. "Have you phoned a garage yet?"

"Can't. The battery in my phone is dead, and so is Izzy's. We can't understand it."

Lucy instinctively reached into her pocket to check her own phone, and saw Dale doing the same. She wasn't at all surprised to find that the battery was completely flat, and the look on Dale's face told her his device had suffered the same fate.

"Did you try the land line?" he asked.

"No, didn't think of that! I'll go check," Ruth said as she plucked a candle off a table and hurried off.

"Wouldn't worry too much. 'Appens all the time, it does," said Machen. "Power stays off a coupla hours then comes back on and we can charge everything up off the mains. I got jump leads somewhere, and re-chargeable batteries are a God-send. Used to have a generator out the back, but that packed up the other week."

"Didn't say that in the brochure," said Lucy.

"What brochure?" Machen replied, in all seriousness.

"It's the storm," explained Old Rolly. "I told you it was coming."

"How can a storm drain a car battery?"

"A storm can do many things. And in this case it's not the cause of our problems, more of a catalyst. Now hadn't you best run along and help that poor damsel in distress?"

As Dale passed he mouthed the words 'won't be long' at Lucy, who was left in no doubt as to his sincerity. He probably knew even less about cars than she did.

Chapter 27:

Shadow People

The wind blew the rain in sheets. Dale didn't bring his jacket. He contemplated running upstairs to get it, but figured that would be more trouble than what it was worth. Plus, though he didn't want to admit as much, he really didn't want to make that journey alone. He would wait until they all went up together and take a quick detour to his room to get changed. Even if he did have his jacket with him, the rain would probably necessitate a change of jeans anyway.

What are you scared of?

The question hit him like a punch in the stomach. And the answer was; fucking plenty of things. The ghostly voices and hand-written messages were only a part of it. He was actually more excited about that, now the initial shock and disbelief had worn off. There was trepidation, yes. But he wasn't in fear of his safety. When was the last time somebody got physically attacked by a ghost? Whatever they were, they'd undoubtedly been around longer than he had. In that sense he and Lucy weren't on the brink of a discovery, but a re-connection.

No, he wasn't scared of ghosts. It was something else. Something deeper, bigger. The longer he spent at Sker House the more he became convinced that this was the cause of it all. He didn't normally consider himself insecure. Quite the opposite, in fact. But the old house seemed to accentuate every negative emotion he was capable of. It was a breeding ground for mistrust and resentment, and whilst bencased in its walls he found himself questioning everything.

Ruth suddenly appeared behind him, using an arm to shield her face from the rain. "I tried the land line. That's dead, too."

Dale should have expected as much. "Right then. Let's see what we can do with this automobile of yours."

"Listen," Ruth put a hand on Dale's arm to stop him. "I just wanted to thank you. I really appreciate you doing this. Izzy does, too."

"You'd better save your thanks until later. I can check the oil and plugs and stuff like that for you. Basic things. But that's pretty much it."

"I know, dear. Just do your best, will you? Maybe you could give us a push to get it started?"

"If the battery's completely dead, Mrs Watkins, I don't think bump starting it will work. Also, you might break down again miles from anywhere with no phone."

"Let's go see what you can do. Come on," Ruth said, grabbing Dale by the arm and leading him into the storm. She held one half of her coat over him to keep off the worst of the torrential downpour.

"Pop the boot, I'll be over in a minute!" Dale yelled over the howling wind, as he jogged over and opened his own car door. Sitting in the driver's seat, he slammed the door shut behind him. The car rocked on its wheels as a huge gust of wind hit it head-on, and the rain cascaded down the windscreen in rivulets.

He turned the key in the ignition and pumped a fist in the air when the dashboard lights sprang to life.

That wasn't so hard.

But his joy was short-lived as the dashboard immediately died. After that, the engine wouldn't turn over at all.

He wasn't really surprised. If everything else was out of order, from torches to telephones, there was no practical reason why his Astra should be left unscathed. The idea that they were trapped in a secluded bubble in a raging storm miles from civilization didn't occur to him until later. Right then, all he could think about was how much money it would cost to get the damn car fixed. If the situation called for a visit to a local garage, it would mean spending another night at Sker. There might not even be electricity, and he and Lucy would both miss a days classes.

Fantastic.

Still, at least there was a bar.

He tried starting the Astra's engine one more time.

Still nothing.

Wiping condensation off the side window with his sleeve, he looked over to see Ruth and Izzy both peering anxiously at him through the window of their little Nova as it was buffeted by the storm. He made an exaggerated shrug and showed them his palms to indicate he was stumped. The expedition was off to a cracking start.

Taking a deep breath, he got out of his car and jogged over to the other vehicle. Lifting up the hood, he secured it in place and moved to the side so he was shielded slightly from the elements.

He wasn't quite sure what he should be looking for, but everything in the engine seemed to be in it's place. There were no visibly loose cables or plugs, and no obvious fluid leaks. Never-the-less, he jiggled all the connections to make sure they were sound then went over to the driver's side window.

Before he could get there, the door flung open and Ruth stepped out. Tipping back the driver's seat, she ushered him into the back. After he got in Ruth sat back in the driver's seat, slammed the door shut, and handed him a towel. One from a Sker House en suite, he noted with amusement.

As he dried his face and hair he said, "The engine looks fine to me. Try starting it again."

Ruth did. Several times. On each turn of the key there was a collective hopeful pause with Ruth, Izzy and Dale all willing the engine to start. But the battery was so lifeless all the willing in the world wasn't going to make a bit of difference.

"Has anything like this happened before?" asked Dale.

"Nope. She's been a pretty good runner til now, hasn't she, Iz?" Ruth said.

Her daughter nodded agreement.

"And what about everything else? This... situation," Dale struggled to find the words. "With all the energy being sucked out of everything, including people and dogs, is that unusual?"

Ruth gave a humourless cackle. "There are a lot of unusual things about Sker House. You don't get used to it exactly, but you learn to take it in your stride. But this... with all the power gone, I don't know. It's a new one on me."

Dale's mind flashed back to something Machen said when they first met, during the botched interview.

Mrs Watkins is the eyes and ears of this place.

What better time to put the theory to the test? Especially now that Mrs Watkins was indebted to him for coming out here in the rain to try and fix her car. "What kind of unusual things are you talking about? Would you mind elaborating?"

Ruth and Izzy glanced at each other, as if silently debating the question via some strange mother-daughter psychic bond. Eventually, it was Izzy who answered. "Shadow People, mostly."

"Shadow People?"

220

"Yup," Izzy confirmed. "Shadow People. And before you start thinking we're both mental, I'll have you know that we aren't the only people to see the things, whatever they are. Do a Google search, if ya like. You'll see. There's loads online about them."

"I'd love to do a Google search. And I will. Just as soon as the power comes back on," Dale pledged. "Until then, enlighten me. What the hell are Shadow People?"

This time, Ruth answered on behalf of her daughter. "Things move in the shadows. When it's dark, mostly. You catch a glimpse out of the corner of your eye. Usually it looks like somebody ducking through a doorway, or peeping around a corner. The shadow of a person, but no person attached to it."

"Or sometimes, you'll just see an arm or leg, or even a head or the shape of a face," interjected Izzy. "Or something that moves so quick, like, you don't know what the fuck it is. Sorry mum."

"You're forgiven, dear. We see different things. Just shapes sometimes, movement. Like the shadows are coming to life. Then when you turn to look, there's nothing there."

Dale was fascinated. For two people, even a mother and daughter, to be so convinced there must be some truth in what they were saying. Unless, of course, they really were both losing the plot. Perhaps everybody in this place had been driven around the twist, and he was the only sane one.

There's those negative thoughts again.

"And that," concluded Izzy, "Is why I'm NOT staying in the place tonight. I'll walk home first."

"Come on, love," Ruth said. "It won't come to that. I'm sure."

"So you've both seen these things? More than once?"

"Oh yeah," they both agreed. "Not every day," Ruth clarified, "But a few times a week, I would say. Usually around dusk, just as its getting dark. Did you notice how jumpy Machen was tonight?"

Dale nodded. He had noticed. And he'd also noticed how much Jack Daniels the landlord was getting through with dinner. "Is he always like that?"

"Pretty much. Izzy and I come and go, but he's here all the time, see. Living with them. Him and Old Rolly. He's changed since he's been here, has Machen. If you ask him, he'll probably just tell you it's just down to stress, but there's more to it than that. Why do you think his wife Sandra left?"

"I don't know," Dale shrugged. "Why did she leave?"

"We think it was too much for her, living here with those things. Machen, he has no choice but to stay. They invested all their money in it, see. He has nowhere else to go, and he's too stubborn to leave anyways."

"Have you ever talked about the Shadow People things with him?"

"Oh no," Ruth shook her head firmly. "Why would we? Some things don't need to be talked about, Dale. We all know they're there, and talking about them won't make them go away. It is Dale, isn't it?"

He nodded.

"I don't suppose either of you have any pictures of them? The Shadow People?"

"Never tried taking one," Izzy said. "I know they're there. Don't need no proof."

"Besides, taking pictures would be difficult, seeing as they're made out of the dark," Ruth added.

"Guess so," agreed Dale. "Do either of you see them anywhere else?"

Mother and daughter exchanged another of those now-familiar looks. "Once..." Ruth began.   "Izzy thought one of them followed us home."

"I saw it!" the teenager said in exasperation. "In my bedroom after we got home. This black... shape, moving across my wall. Like a figure with a hood."

Dale was gob-smacked. This was bad. If Izzy was correct, it proved that whatever creepiness was at large at Sker house wasn't localized, and had the potential to move somewhere else. "Did you see it again after that?"

"No. Thank God. But I didn't ask that thing to come home with me. That's why I hate workin' there so much. That and the fact that the money's shit. Sorry mum."

"You're forgiven, dear," Ruth said again.

Dale didn't know what to make of this latest revelation. Recently, he couldn't keep up with all the revelations. It must all be connected, somehow. In true Celtic tradition; everything had a purpose and there was a purpose for everything. What he needed to find out was how it all tied together. There must be a common thread, or some kind of root cause for all the weird occurrences.

Possibly the biggest mystery was why Sker House hadn't attracted more national attention. It could be as relevant in British paranormal circles as Borley Rectory or the Enfield Poltergeist. Maybe he and Lucy could be the ones credited with uncovering, or even better, solving, the mystery.

Imagine it. There would be feature articles, TV interviews, book deals. They could forge whole careers from it, if they could live with the stigma that would surely follow.

But they needed evidence. And right now all they had was a collection of spooky stories, some frightened people in a power outage, and a few of garbled words on tape that could be construed in any number of ways. None of it was hard proof of anything.

"So has anything like that ever happened to you, Ruth?" Dale pressed.

There was a pause. Dale was beginning to wonder if the woman had heard him.

Then, without turning around, Ruth said, "Not exactly. I don't think anything's ever followed me home. I've had different experiences."

"Like what?"

"Too many to mention. Things have a tendency to go missing a lot. Then they turn up days or weeks later in the most unexpected places."

Like old rusty keys.

"The thing that sticks out most would be the time I was in the kitchen making dinner. I was fussing around getting things ready, and I went to the fridge to get some eggs. While my back was turned I heard a noise, like something moved. I was on my own in the kitchen that day, everybody else was busy doing other things. So I turn around, and I see the spoon I just used hanging in mid air."

"What? Levitating?"

"By itself. Yes, just hanging there," Ruth confirmed in a business-like tone before continuing her story. "It was almost as if it was just waiting there for me to see. Showing off."

"What did you do?"

"To tell the truth I didn't know what to do. I was in shock, I suppose. I wanted to shout or scream. Not because I was afraid. I mean, who could be afraid of a spoon? But because I wanted someone else to come in and see what I was seeing."

"What happened then?"

"When the spoon was satisfied I had seen it, it swooped down to the bowl and started going 'round and 'round in circles. Like it was stirring something invisible. Slowly at first, then faster and faster, until it was spinning so fast it was just a blur. When it touched the sides of the bowl it wasn't the odd tink like when a person stirs something, it was a constant hum. Kind of like music."

"How long did this go on for?"

"The whole thing lasted less than a minute, I suppose. Probably more like thirty seconds. I just think its a shame that I can't ask spoons and things to work on demand. That'd be good, wouldn't it, Iz?"

"Yes mum, that would be fantastic."

Dale looked through the steamy car window at the house. If he couldn't accomplish anything here, he was eager to get back inside to the heart of the mystery. "So what's the plan?" he asked. "The car isn't starting. Are we going to stay out here all night?"

"I'm walking home," announced Izzy defiantly. "I don't care how long it takes or how wet I get."

"Don't be silly, Iz," Ruth scolded. "What kind of mother would I be if I let you do that? We'll just have to wait it out, that's all. The storm'll blow itself out soon enough. The power'll come back on. Then we can charge our phones and call Ghostbusters or the RAC or whatever."

Izzy looked crushed. She checked her phone again, shaking it in frustration. Evidently, it still wasn't working.

"Well, at least inside we have food, warmth, shelter and beer. Scary house or not," Dale reasoned.

"He's right, Iz," agreed Ruth. "I don't like the idea any more than you do, but our options are limited. We'll stay together the whole night, I promise. I won't let you out of my sight. Then we'll get out of there as soon as we can."

"Okay, okay," Izzy looked resigned. "But we leave THE MINUTE we can. Deal?"

"Deal," confirmed Ruth.

Chapter 28:

Last Resort

Left alone with Machen and Old Rolly, Lucy knew things would get weird. She just didn't know how weird, or how quickly. It all started innocuously enough, with the two older men talking about rugby. Again.

Come on and save me, Dale, Lucy thought to herself. What the hell are you doing out there?

"So is it true this place used to be a monastery?" she asked in an attempt to sway the conversation back to something more interesting.

"The first structures erected on this site were made by monks, yes," Old Rolly cut in. "And it's true they may have functioned as a monastery for a time. But this building we find ourselves in at the moment bears little relation to those buildings of old. It wouldn't be too much of a stretch, however, to suppose that some of the masonry and stonework used in the construction of Sker House came from the original monastic buildings. So in a sense, those old buildings are still here. During the Dissolution of the Monasteries, many of the monks were driven into hiding. This was one of their secret hideouts."

"But why did they have to do that?" Lucy asked. History was never her strongpoint. If her phone was working she would have a sneaky Google search, but unfortunately that wasn't an option tonight.

"The dissolution of the Monastries was a monumental event," Rolly explained patiently. "It occurred between 1536 and 1541, when Henry VIII decided to disband all the religious houses in the country, including monastries, nunneries, and the like, sell off the assetts and reappropriate them to the Crown to fund military campaigns. As there were claimed to be over 4,000 monks at the time from a total male population of around half a million, it meant a lot of those people suddenly had to find other ways to sustain themselves. Some, obviously, were reluctant to do so."

"Surely the king can't do that!" Lucy said, her inner social justice warrior already beginning to rage.

"He could do whatever he wanted," Machen said. "He was the king. Much like I'm the king of Sker, so I'll do what I want around here."

Lucy caught something pass between the two men. The last thing she wanted was to witness another shouting match. The atmosphere was tense enough as it was. "What did they do here? Just hang out?" she asked, hoping to break the tension.

"There was a lot of anger and resentment," Old Rolly continued. "Some of them felt betrayed. And not just by the king, but by God and the church. They believed God would step in and save them, and there were rumours that when He didn't, as a last resort, some of the monks showed their disapproval by turning to the dark arts."

"Devil worship?" Lucy said. The words tasted bad, and seemed to hang in the air long after she uttered them like a bad stench.

"I suppose that's one name for it," Rolly conceded. "You know, it never ceases to amaze me how people feel the constant need to put labels on things, classify them, make them fit neatly into boxes."

"Classification is how we rationalize the world around us," Lucy said, remembering something she'd learned in a social studies class.

"Through fear and intimidation, the Church instilled in everyone the notion that any form of religion that didn't recognize the Lord as the Supreme Being must be evil. But the Druids were practising Paganism in Britain thousands of years before Christianity was even a concept."

"By worshipping trees?"

"I don't think the details of what they did and why are significant. Not to us, anyway. Odds are we wouldn't understand. The point is when Christianity came along, it was too big to fight. Most people just gave in and switched faiths for an easy life, while others simply gave the outward impression they had and continued practising their true faith in private. Same thing happened during the enforced conversion from Catholic to Protestant. It was either get with the programme or face persecution. In fact, at the end of the sixteenth century, then-owner of Sker, a Roman Catholic called Jenkin Turberville, was tortured to death after being accused of hiding monks and promoting the 'Old Religion.'"

"Wow. Things like that actually happened here?"

"Oh yes," Rolly said. "Probably the most famous case is that of the martyr Saint Philip Evans. In 1679 he was discovered here at Sker House by the authorities, who sent him to Cardiff for trail. He was found guilty, of course, so he was hung, drawn and quartered. A terrible fate if ever there was one. Do you know what that entails, little miss?"

"I'm not sure," Lucy admitted.

"Well, it's when they hang you. But not until you're dead. Just for you to suffer. Then they put you on the rack and use it to stretch your limbs until muscles rip and bones break, and finally they chop you into four pieces."

"Oh God," Lucy said, as her stomach did a queasy flip.

"It doesn't end there," Rolly said.

"But surely they'd be dead by now?"

"Indeed. But then the four parts of the body would be sent to four different places, in the north, east, south, and west."

"But why?"

"Simple," Rolly said. "Because then, with your earthly body in pieces scattered far and wide, your spirit would never be able to find peace. For that reason, it was known as the the eternal punishment."

This was getting dark. Too dark for a haunted house in a power cut. "So going back to paganism," Lucy said, "is it related to witchcraft, magic and all that Harry Potter stuff?"

"Harry who?" Machen interjected.

"You should read the newspaper more," Rolly told him. Lucy stifled a giggle. "And to answer your question, miss, I suppose you could say some of the old methods were incorporated into witches covens and circles, yes."

"Wait a minute, there were witches around here, too?" Given her family history, Lucy felt a special kind of affinity with witches.

"Oh yes. Obviously most of that Witch Trial nonsense was just that. Nonsense. Lots of mass hysteria and miscarriages of justice, but genuine witches certainly did exist. Anything that didn't adhere to the strict rules laid down in the Bible was considered witchcraft. Belief in the Lord was strong, and so was belief in the devil. You can't have one without the other. Besides, when something goes wrong it's easier to have someone else to blame, isn't it? Then you don't have to accept responsibility yourself. How many people in history have claimed they did whatever terrible things they did because the devil made them do it?"

"A lot, probably," agreed Lucy. "And the flip side of it is, just as many people have killed in the name of God."

"Not as many," Rolly corrected. "More. Far more. Nothing has started more wars, and led to more bloodshed, than religion."

"What about women?" Machen interrupted with a dry cackle. "They've caused a fair bit of bloodshed down the years, I reckon!"

Both Rolly and Lucy glanced at the landlord. Lucy wanted to tell him how narrow-minded, chauvinistic and plain wrong he was. But she really couldn't be bothered and decided to continue chatting to Rolly instead.

"So you think there's no such thing as real, demonic evil? It's just misguided people looking to pin blame on something?"

"I didn't say that," Rolly's tone suddenly turned serious. "There's real evil in the world, and plenty of it. What I mean is, it would be wrong to lay the fault for all the evil in the world on the shoulders of some Christian creation called Satan. It's too convenient. What about all the famine, earthquakes and tsunamis? Then we have accidents, murder, corruption, disease, all that other good stuff. Is it all the work of the Evil One? Whatever hell is, surely it can't be any worse than that. You know, some say that evil can attach itself to a place, a geographical area, afflicting all who dwell there."

"Evil lurks, huh, Rolly?" Above the raging storm Lucy didn't even hear Dale come in and walk right up to the table, just in time to catch the end of the conversation.

"Yes indeed, my boy. Yes indeed." Rolly didn't seem at all surprised by Dale's sudden intervention. Maybe he'd been around so long nothing could surprise him any more.

Dale was accompanied by a red-faced Ruth and a dejected-looking Izzy. "No luck with the car, then?"

"Nope. Damn thing's stone dead. Have to get a garage out in the morning."

"What about yours, Dale?"

"That's dead, too."

"Just what is going on around here?" Lucy threw her hands up in exasperation as Ruth and Izzy sheepishly took seats at the adjoining table.

"Well," Dale said, "I have a theory. What if the thing in this house – and I think we're all agreed that there's something unnatural here, right?"

There was a muted round of acknowledgements.

"Right. Then what if whatever is present here is using all the power to manifest somehow. Including the house's electricity supply, our cars and phones, and the storm? It could even be sapping our physical energy. Have you noticed how tired and drained we all are? And look at Champ, he's a wreck."

At the mention of his name the dog, who had lain forgotten at Lucy's feet, raised his head and looked around. Then yawned and put his head back on his paws.

"All things considered, we're talking about a lot more power than your Dictaphone batteries," observed Lucy.

"Damn right, and if that was enough to enable it to manifest enough for us to hear it, who knows what it might be capable of doing with all the power it has access to now."

"You have a voice on tape?" Rolly asked, suddenly animated. "What did it say?"

"A woman said her name was Liz, and told us to leave."
"What else?"

"Nothing much, I don't think. Lucy?"

Lucy thought for a moment, replaying the brief recorded conversation in her memory. It was difficult. Even though only a few hours had passed, a lot seemed to have happened since then.

"I don't think so," she said. "Wait, there was something else. You asked her if she wrote in your notebook and she said yes, she did."

"Oh yeah. But I can't think of anything else. Nothing substantial. We were getting ready to do another recording session when the power went out."

Old Rolly leaned forward in his chair. "What did the message written in your notebook say?"

"I couldn't make it out," replied Dale. "Not all of it, anyway."

"Think!" Rolly said, spittle shooting out of his mouth.

"It was just a bunch of scribbles, with a few loops and things that kinda looked like they could be letters. We thought we could make out a couple of words, but we could've been wrong."

"What words? Try to remember. It could be important."

"We're not entirely sure. We think they may be written in Welsh. Neither me nor Lucy speak it."

"I do," Rolly was excited now. "Let me see the notebook."

"How about we give you full disclosure in return for yours."

Lucy knew Dale's slightly formal choice of words was meant to be taken lightly, but Rolly appeared to be seriously considering it making her think the old man had a lot of things he could potentially 'disclose.' Finally, he agreed and, in true machismo fashion, they shook on it.

"When can I see the messages?"

"Right now, if you want. I have to go upstairs to get changed out of these wet clothes. You could tag along. There's also the small matter of ending the earlier dispute about the locked room upstairs, isn't there Machen?"

The landlord, who until then had been sitting quietly nursing his glass, grunted acknowledgement.

"We could make it a group event. Entertainment is limited tonight, folks," said Lucy.

"well, I don't wanna go," replied Izzy immediately. She was well on her way to being Britain's sulkiest teenager, but Lucy couldn't resent her too much for it. The girl reminded her of herself four or five years earlier.

"I'll stay, too. Keep her company," said Ruth.

"I'll let you keep Champ down here. He'll look after 'ew, he will," said Machen. "Besides, he 'ates going up n' down them stairs, he does."

Lucy looked at the dog lying prostrate at her feet under the table and couldn't disagree. He wasn't going anywhere.

"Well, I need to get changed before I catch pneumonia," Dale said. With that he picked up the nearest candle, shielding the flame with the palm of his hand, and headed for the door. Rolly jumped into line behind him, quickly followed by Lucy. A lethargic, slightly wobbly and somewhat reluctant Machen brought up the rear.

Chapter 29:

Revelations

Dale's only smart shirt was sticking to him like wet tissue paper.

So much for the evening wear, he thought.

He couldn't wait to put his hoody back on. As he led the quartet up the first flight of stairs, shadows leapt across walls and ceilings and darkness retreated from the flickering light cast by their four candles. The atmosphere was dense, stifling, and he suddenly felt very vulnerable. He was reminded of what Ruth and Izzy talked about in the car.

Shadow People.

The logical part of his mind wanted to think the mother and daughter must be mistaken, that what they experienced was some kind of natural phenomena.

But surely they must be accustomed enough to the world around them to not be literally frightened of their own shadows. In view of recent events, Dale found he was getting more receptive to the idea of supernatural phenomena. Perhaps Ruth and Izzy's shadow people were connected in some way to the experiences he and Lucy had been having. All these small mysteries had to be components of some larger tapestry.

As he made his way carefully up the staircase, he felt compelled to do everything quicker, more efficiently, so events could reach their natural conclusion in as little time as possible. It was this sense of urgency that prompted him to suggest the group split up. He would go to get changed and show Rolly the messages, while Lucy and Machen would go to the fourth floor to settle their dispute about the locked door. Everyone was in agreement, which suggested that Dale wasn't the only one who wanted to move things along. Nobody wanted to be up here in the upper reaches of Sker House a moment longer than was necessary.

After a quick inventory to ensure both parties had sufficient lighters and candles, at the top of the stairs Dale and Rolly bade a temporary farewell to Lucy and Machen, and turned down the corridor. They proceeded with caution, half expecting something to leap out at them any second. But apart from the muffled howl of the wind outside and the occasional creak, the house was eerily still.

On unlocking the door to their room, the first thing Dale did was hurry over to the desk. From a distance, the pencil seemed to be in exactly the same position as he had left it. But as he drew nearer and the arc of light cast by his candle fell over it, he saw that beneath the pencil the clean, untouched paper wasn't clean and untouched any more. He snatched up the notebook and studied it by the light of the candle. Just like before, it had been defaced with deep, angry-looking scribbles. This time, the message was clear.

GET OUT

"What is it?" Rolly asked. "Another message? What does it say?"

"See for yourself," Dale said, handing the old man his notebook.

Rolly hunched over the scribblings, holding the notebook in one hand and his candle in the other. "Well," he said, "This one doesn't need to be translated. Show me the others."

Dale did, and watched as the old man's eyes widened. "I think this one says 'CELLAR?' It's hard to tell, and we should be wary of reading anything into it. But that one word is pretty clear to me. Some of these other markings look more like symbols than letters."

"What kind of symbols?"

The old man swallowed hard. "The kind used in ancient rituals, maybe? I'm no expert, but that's what a lot of them remind me of. The combination of those and that one word in English would seem to indicate what whoever or whatever left this message wants us to do."

"What?"

"It wants us to go to the cellar."

"Why?" Dale gulped. He didn't know what could be down there, he just knew that the thought of going down to Sker's cellar didn't fill him with joy.

"Who knows? Maybe we'll find the answer when we get there. I want to get to the bottom of this as much as you do. But before we go will you answer me a question?"

Dale felt himself nod.

"Apart from these messages, what else has happened to you both? Full disclosure, remember?"

Dale quickly ran through the list of strange events thus far; Lucy seeing the figure in the window, her sleepwalking, the time she told him that he couldn't force her to love another, the messages in the notebook, the voice on the tape, and the discovery

236

of the key. Even in relating the condensed version, there was a lot to tell.

When Dale finished, Rolly ran his fingers through his silver beard, sharpening it to a point. "Well, you've certainly had an action-packed weekend so far, haven't you?"

"Yeah, you could say that."

"It seems much of the activity is centred on your friend. Have you any idea why?"

"No. Do you?"

"It appears something wants her," old Rolly said ominously.

"What for?"

"Who knows? I wish I could wave a magic wand and conjure up all the answers for you, I really do, but not even I am capable of such feats."

"Come on, Rolly. You know more about this whole thing than you are letting on," Dale prodded. "The deal was full disclosure. And that works both ways."

The old man sighed deeply. "Yes, that was the arrangement, wasn't it? Okay. Mind if I sit?" he asked, even as he lowered his spindly frame onto the edge of Lucy's bed.

"Go for it," Dale said as he sat next to him. At this range Rolly smelled vaguely of wet wool. A fractious breeze made both candles flicker, and Dale felt around for the reassuring firmness of the cigarette lighter in his pocket.

"Earlier tonight," Rolly began, "I told the girl I was a retired custodian. That wasn't strictly true."

"So what's the truth?"

"The truth is I'm not retired. I'm still a custodian. A guardian. A keeper of knowledge."

"A custodian of what?"

"Sker House."

There were a few moments silence as Dale grasped the implications of what the old man was telling him. "So that's why you stay here? To guard it?"

Rolly nodded. "I'm not duty bound to live here, but it helps. Especially now the place is open to the public. The more people pass through those doors, the more chance there is of something... serious happening."

"Something like what?" Dale got the feeling Rolly would only live up to his half of the disclosure agreement only if asked the right questions. The wily old man was too shrewd to surrender information needlessly.

"Something like what's been happening to you and your... companion. Or Machen. And as for poor Ruth and Izzy, they're both scared half to death. There are strong forces at work in Sker House. That's what I meant when I told you that evil lurks. It's a reasonable assumption that whatever force here is drawing power from the cars and phones and everything else in order to help it manifest and communicate. But there is another possibility."

"What's that?"

"Perhaps whatever this thing is wants to keep us here. It doesn't want us to leave. Maybe you should have left when you had the chance."

A small part of Dale had been thinking exactly that. Now it was too late. They was stuck here.

"How or why does evil lurk here?"

Surely, that was the million dollar question.

Rolly sighed and tapped his cane on the floor. "It's a long story."

"I think we have time," Dale said encouragingly. "Mind if I change my shirt while we talk? It's soaked."

"Go ahead, lad. You'll catch your death. Well, it was the monks who did it."

"Did what?"

"When they went into hiding following the Dissolution of the Monastries they conjured up a presence, some kind of supernatural force or entity, which now happily resides at Sker alongside the living inhabitants. Or, more accurately, they may have somehow succeeded in creating a kind of vortex or doorway. It's this that allows beings from other realms to access to our world, and vice versa. Think of it as being like a back door that's been left wide open in a bad neighbourhood. If we don't close it, there'll be more and more spirits, demons or whatever else populates the Otherworld, slithering through and playing havoc. And that may only be the start of it. When the place stood empty there was little risk of anyone getting hurt. But the minute people came back here, things started getting out of hand. There is the potential for real damage to be done."

"How do we close the vortex thingy?"

"If I knew that, the task would be simple," Rolly said. "Nobody knows where it is or what it looks like. We might not even be capable of seeing it. Maybe this message we have is a clue pointing us in the right direction. The cellar would be as good a place to start as any. It's certainly the oldest part of the house. The underground sections were the very first to be laid and when they built foundations in those days, they built them to last. The story goes that the early construction was linked to ley lines, and worked by the same principles as other ancient sites like Stonehenge.

"There used to be a network of underground tunnels connecting all the different buildings on the property, and rumour has it that there are also tunnels linking the house directly with the caves down there on the beach. That was originally an escape route for the monks to use should they ever need to, and was probably utilised later by Isaac Williams in his wrecking days. Of course, in the hundreds of years since they were built, most of the tunnels have probably collapsed in on themselves. But who's to say for sure? Anything could be hidden down there."

"Or trapped," said Dale. "Wait, why would we get messages telling us to go the cellar? I mean, if that's where the vortex thing is. Wouldn't the spirits or demons want to keep us away?"

"Some. The evil ones. But I imagine these entities, or spirits, are much the same as people. There'll be some good and some bad. If not individually, there may be several different competing factions at work all with different agendas. It could even be as simple as good versus evil."

"Lucy and I think the spirit of Elizabeth, the Maid of Sker, is trying to make contact with us. The one trying to send us to the cellar. The voice we heard on the Dictaphone recording was definitely female, and Lucy says she saw her in the window. I have a feeling it may also be her who keeps scribbling all over my notepad."

"Elizabeth could very well be one of the good spirits," Old Rolly said. "It was her father Isaac who was the bad egg. All the accounts show that Elizabeth was just an innocent victim. Maybe in death, she wants to do the right thing and close the door. Put an end to the misery once and for all. She probably feels an attachment to Sker House, seeing as this is where she lived and died."

"How did you get landed with the honour of being custodian of Sker, anyway?"

"It's a bloodline. One of my ancestors was a member of the original group of monks that settled here. He was assigned the role of guardian of the property, keeper of knowledge, though over the centuries much of that knowledge has been lost. After my ancestor's death, the so-called honour has passed to the first-born male of the family. For generations, we've been trying to keep people away. For safety's sake. But now things have accelerated to such a degree I fear the only solution is to close the vortex for good."

"Why hasn't anyone tried before?"

"It's too dangerous. Nobody is sure exactly what we may be dealing with. When Sker House stood abandoned, we could just keep and eye on it from a safe distance. But now…"

"Now it's a hotel."

"Exactly."

"What happened to the monks who opened the vortex in the first place?" asked Dale, still trying to wrap his head around the whole thing.

"The six responsible for the ritual are said to have been driven insane by what they uncovered. The story goes they were ripped to pieces by one of the creatures they invited into our world. Their comrades discovered their mangled remains and buried them in a mass grave somewhere on the grounds. It had to be a mass grave because their bodies had been reduced to a pile of flesh and bone. Nobody could tell which parts belonged to who. Their penance was that their energy would be trapped here forever. But because they lack physical form, they appear as dark masses."

The Shadow People.

"Damn devil-worshipping monks," Dale grumbled. "I'm beginning to understand now. But what does this have to do with Isaac Williams or the Maid of Sker?"

"As soon as the vortex was opened, a terrible darkness descended. Those that lived here endured the most horrendous bad

240

luck. People got ill and had accidents, crops failed, investments turned bad, relationships crumbled, misery triumphed. Some believe that whatever force resides here brings the worst out in people. Have you found yourself to be more short tempered since you've been here? More, irritable, more prone to... outbursts?"

Dale thought for a moment. "Not really. At least, I don't think so. I'm not the violent type."

"We're all violent types lad, given the right persuasion. And your friend?"

"Lucy? She's always irritable and prone to outbursts, so its hard to tell if there's anything different about her. Apart from the zoning out she's been doing lately. That's new."

"Well, it works quicker on some than others. If people are especially susceptible, the effect can be almost instantaneous. Some people, like Machen's wife Sandra, sense it and just leave. After too much exposure the spirits will attach themselves to you. Follow you. Other times they can get inside you."

Dale thought about what Ruth and Izzy had told him outside, then his mind flashed back to the earlier incident with Lucy.

You can't force me to love another!

Not only was it totally irrelevant to what they had been talking about, it was something Lucy would never say. On reflection, the voice didn't even sound like hers. And those memory-lapses and sleep-walks? For some reason, the Maid of Sker was trying to exert her influence by controlling her, or at least using her as a conduit.

"Wow, my friend is being possessed," Dale said, disbelievingly. Suddenly the implications were dawning on him. Talk about a social stigma.

"Apparently so," Rolly agreed. "But it's not the Maid of Sker you need to worry about. She seems to be trying to help us. Yet if she's finding it so easy to inhabit your friend, other, less friendly spirits will find it easy, too. Your friend might be like an open vessel, just as susceptible to both good and evil. I fear it can only be a matter of time before she is possessed by someone, or something else."

"Dear God," Dale said, the gravity of the situation suddenly dawning on him. "Come on, we have to get moving."

Chapter 30:

The Locked Room

Lucy led Machen up the stairs all the way to the fourth floor. The closer to the top they got, the more the landlord lagged behind. Several times, Lucy had to wait for him to catch up. They didn't speak, so the only noises to be heard were their own shuffling footsteps, laboured breathing, and the sounds of the storm. Finally they reached their destination, and paused at the door with the PRIVATE: NO ADMITTANCE sign to catch their breath.

For a moment, Lucy swooned on the brink of understanding. Then the feeling retreated leaving her with nothing more than a vague recollection of being there before. "This is the place," she said, more to herself than her unwilling companion.

"Well, you just be careful," Machen wheezed, trying to be stern and authoritative and managing to sound anything but. "There's a reason we don't let the public assess, I mean *access* this part of the building."

"Yes, sir," replied Lucy. She couldn't resist doing a sarcastic little salute, and the guy was damned lucky it wasn't a salute of the two-fingered variety. "This way," she said, heading off into the pitch-black corridor, hoping that her bullishness made a statement of intent.

The corridor smelled musty, and strong drafts posed a constant threat to the candle she shielded with her free hand. Several times, hot droplets of wax fell between her fingers causing her to snap her hand back in pain.

As she tread carefully down the corridor past the unfinished rooms, she noticed that Machen was right, damn him. Most of the rooms didn't even have doors. Beyond each opening lay a yawning black chasm which she had no desire to investigate too closely.

They were approaching the half-way point in the corridor when the first noise stopped her dead in her tracks. It was somewhere between a thud and a scratch, and seemed to be coming from the wall itself. "Did you hear that?"

"Hear what?" Machen replied. "I hear an old house is what I hear."

"You didn't hear that... thud?"

"I hear things all the time. Thuds, bangs, crashes, even the odd wallop. Like I said, it's an old house, isn't it?"

Lucy couldn't believe a man as edgy and nervous as Machen could be possibly be so nonchalant about hearing disembodied noises, unless he was trying to make light of it to deflect her attention.

She stood still and listened.

Another soft thump.

Now her senses were becoming more attuned, she could hear a succession of sounds camouflaged by the noise of the storm outside. It sounded like a combination of cushioned fists battering walls and fingernails scraping wood, as if something was trapped inside the walls and was trying to claw it's way out. A few times, she could have sworn she could even discern low whispers and grumbles, snatches of distant conversations, fragments of words left to float on the wind.

"Might be rats," Machen said, shifting his weight awkwardly from foot to foot.

"Do rats talk?"

Machen shrugged. He was terrified, but more terrified of showing it. Noticing Lucy staring at him, he snapped, "So where's this locked door of yours?"

"At the other end of the corridor, I think. A bit farther up."

"Come on then, lets get this over with." Machen took the lead now, pushing past Lucy in his haste to prove her wrong.

On this occasion, Lucy was happy to fall behind. "Hope you remembered to bring that key with you," she said as he passed.

The landlord didn't rise to the bait, but instead marched directly to the end of the corridor and stood there with his arms out-stretched, flickering candle in hand. In the subtle yellow glow, his pose had an almost religious flavour. "See!" the landlord said triumphantly. "No door here. Just like I said. I'd hate to say I told you so, but I did. I did tell you so. Didn't I?"

Shit. He was right. There was a doorway, but no door. Never mind a locked one.

Unless she and Dale were the victims of an elaborate hoax and Machen had somehow fit a door up here then sneakily removed it without them knowing, the only alternative was that she must have dreamed or hallucinated the whole thing.

Even so, the memory she had of standing in this very spot trying to gain entry into a locked room was almost overwhelming.

Could she be sure this was the same room? They all looked the same in the dark.

Yes, she was sure. This was the room. She couldn't prove it, but she felt it. Except it was different now. Without a door, the dark, chilly space beyond the threshold was more like a walk-in tomb than a guest room. Before, she could think only of getting inside, convinced it held the key to the mystery. Now the promise was about to be realized, she wasn't so sure she wanted to go in there.

"Go on, then," Machen urged. "Have a good look if you want."

Lucy took a solitary step inside, still shielding her candle with her palm, and peered around the room. It was completely bare.

What did you expect?

Wait a moment.

No.

The room wasn't empty.

There was movement in the far corner, quick and fleeting. Something dark and fluid. On the wall.

The realization came just as Lucy was shoved rudely from behind and sent sprawling forward. She staggered a few feet into the room then fell, landing roughly on her hands and knees.   As she hit the ground for the second time that day, the candle flew from her grasp and darkness descended.

*

Machen stood in the doorway, horrified at what he had just done. In all his life, he'd never laid a hand on a woman before. Not even when his marriage was falling to pieces. He'd been brought up believing only cowards hit women. The shock of his own actions made his thought process deteriorate into a rapid-fire question and answer session with his own conscience.

What did you do?

Shut that hoity-toity bitch up, that's what.

Pushed her from behind.

Fuck off. She's lucky I didn't put the boot in.

That's assault.

So tell someone who gives a crap.

Why did you do it?

Because she was driving me mad, that's why. All her smarty-pants shenanigans.

Not good enough.

The girl's been getting right under my skin since the moment she walked through the door.

Eventually, the internal argument subsided and the red mist retreated. However annoying the girl was, it wasn't legitimate grounds to push her over. Machen's rational part, which was slowly wrestling back control, knew that. Putting up with annoying people was a life skill he'd had ample opportunity to learn. He never had a problem with his temper before moving to Sker. People used to call him placid.

This power cut wasn't helping his nerves any, and those fucking wall-bangers were especially loud tonight. He couldn't concentrate, couldn't get a moment's peace. It was overwhelming. Everything combined to make him forget his responsibilities, just for a split second. But that was all the time it took for someone to get hurt.

Oh well. What's done is done. Can't change the past...

No, but mistakes can be rectified and you should never let the past ruin your future. All that really mattered now was what he did next.

Swallowing his pride, Machen stepped into the room and knelt beside Lucy, who was now sitting up on the floor looking dazed. By the light of his candle, he could see that hair had fallen over her face, and she either didn't know or didn't care enough to brush it away. "Luv?"

What was her name?

He had it just a minute ago, he held it tight, then it was gone again.

At the sound of his voice the girl's head snapped around and she said, "If you make me stay here, I'll starve myself to death. I swear to God I will. I'll die right here in this room. And let that be on your conscience!"

Machen recoiled, blinking several times.

"Starve to death?"

Of all the abusive things he had been expecting her to say, that would have been near the bottom of the list.

"What on earth are you talking about?" he asked. "Starve to death? We had dinner not two hours ago. Not much chance of you starving to death with Mrs Watkins around, is there?"

"It's not you doing these evil things, father. I know that. It's this house. The things that come out of the cellar."

Father? Did she just call him father?

Machen was nonplussed. "Don't tell me you want to go down the cellar next. I'm not a bloody tour guide, you know."

The girl stared at him with wide, pleading eyes. "Can't we get out of this house? Can't we just leave, father? Please?"

There it was again.

Father.

Just what was this girl playing at. "Look luv, I know the 'lectric's off and I apologize for that, but I'm sure it'll come back on again soon. Until then, can't you find your own entertainment? You can still play pool, probably. I'll open the coin slot so you can play for free. How's that?"

She didn't answer. If the promise of free pool didn't appease the girl, then he didn't know what would. He should leave her here, on the floor in the dark, while he went to find her boyfriend. Maybe he'd know what to do with her.

But then, she got unsteadily to her feet.

Oh, relief! Not hurt after all.

She looked stupefied, as if waking from a dream. "Are you okay?" he asked, now more concerned than ever.

"What happened?" the girl asked, her voice slow and thick. "What was I doing on the floor?"

Machen located her candle and relit it, handing it to her like a peace offering. "I'm not sure," he lied. "I think you tripped over something. I told you it was dangerous up here, didn't I? Didn't I tell you that?"

"Was I just... speaking?"

Seeing how panicked and confused the girl was, all Machen could feel was pity. "You said a few things, like. None of it made much sense, to be honest. Mumbling, you were."

"What was I talking about?"

That almost struck Machen as funny. What a ridiculous thing to say. If the situation hadn't been so desperate, and the girl so frightened, he might have laughed right out loud. How could she not remember what she said not a minute earlier? As it was, there was nothing he could do but answer the question.

"The cellar," he said. "You were talking about the cellar."

The girl didn't look surprised. "Well, do you have one?"

"Of course." Another stupid question. Many more like that and she might be falling over again.

Stop that! Behave yourself.

"Then I guess that's where we're going next," the girl said as she set off marching down the corridor.

Before Machen could lodge a protest, a shrill scream cut through the night.

The girl stopped dead in her tracks, and Machen felt his own blood turn to ice in his veins. A long time as a publican had taught him screams were never good. The only good thing about this particular scream was that it trailed off after the climax because it was allowed to, and not cut short.   Even before the scream ended, the barking and howling started.

Champ!

Something had the dog in a right state. He rarely got himself worked up these days. Most of the time he barely even moved.

The sound of Champ's barking had an even more profound effect on Machen than the scream. He grabbed the girl by the arm and yanked her. "Come on! Something's going on in the bar!"

Chapter 31:

The Cellar

Lucy was still reeling from the shock of hitting the floor when the sensation of being taken over came upon her.

She could still see and hear everything around her, but suddenly had no control. It was as if everything that made her Lucy was being subdued, and another more forceful character was exerting its will on her. She knew Machen was standing over her, and could see the fear etched onto his face, but it was like seeing it through somebody else's eyes. More alarming than that was the sense of despair that swept through her like a black flood. She felt ruined, destroyed. As if her whole world had just come crashing down around her. She wanted to give up, lie down and die.

Then she was talking. She could hear her voice. But the words sounded too far away, and she had no idea what she was talking about.

Keep it together, she thought. Ride it out.

And then she was back.

Just like that.

The invading presence simply left, allowing Lucy's true self to return. Machen was telling her she'd been saying something about the cellar, but she didn't trust him. There was something about his demeanour.

He looked guilty.

That was when the scream sounded, followed by the dog's howl. She'd never seen the landlord move so quickly as he did when he thought there was something wrong with Champ.

Before she could even properly identify the doggy-in-distress sounds above the cacophony of other sounds, Machen was dragging her down the corridor.

By the time they arrived downstairs, the shouting and commotion had subsided. Dale and Old Rolly were already there, having evidently just arrived on the scene. It seemed as though Izzy was the screamer. No surprise there. She was now whimpering and clinging to Ruth, who held her in a motherly grasp as they both huddled over a solitary flickering candle. The rest of the candles had been extinguished.

The biggest immediate concern was Champ, who alternated between running around in circles and getting down on his haunches as if preparing to attack, barking and growling at some invisible adversary. He seemed confused, as if he didn't

251

know which direction posed the most threat. There was fury in his eyes and spittle sprayed from his mouth as he bared his incisors and snapped at the empty air in front of his face.

"What's up with you, boy? Calm down, is it?" Machen said.

Lucy's first thought was that there must be an intruder. But that didn't appear to be the case. All the doors and windows were still secured and apart from two frightened women and a dog, the bar was deserted. She went over to where the girl sat weeping with her hands over her face and asked what had happened.

Izzy glanced at her with teary eyes and instantly looked away.

It was her Ruth who did the talking. Judging by the tone of her voice she was just as shaken as her daughter, but probably had more experience at keeping her emotions under wraps. Voice trembling, she said, "A bloody wine glass came flying at us from outta nowhere, it did! Smashed right there on the floor by our Izzy's feet. Didn't it, Iz?"

The traumatized teenager nodded emphatically.

"Did it hurt you?" Asked Lucy.

Again Ruth answered on behalf of her daughter. "No, but frightened us all half to death, it did. Champ, too. Lookit him..."

Lucy did. Machen was now having more luck restraining his guard dog. Champ had stopped barking and was instead looking up at their faces almost apologetically.

"Where did the glass come from?" It was Rolly who posed the question.

Ruth shrugged, "Dunno. From somewhere over by the bar, I think. Couldn't tell for sure, it's too dark. And neither of us were looking over there, were we, Iz?"

This time Izzy shook her head.

Lucy looked over in the direction of the bar. "There's nobody there," she said, more to herself than to the group.

Dale stepped forward and put a hand on her arm. "Someone could be hiding under the counter. Are you sure nobody else came in here while we were upstairs?" he asked Ruth and Izzy.   This time they both nodded their heads at the same time. Unanimous, then.

"Somebody should go look, just in case." Even as she spoke Lucy found herself edging forward, the candle she held casting a small semi-circle of light in her path. Her heart was thudding in her chest loud enough to be audible. To her, anyway. Either realizing her actions were in the group's best interests or recognizing the fact that this was something she had to do by herself, nobody tried to stop her.

Arriving at the bar, she stood on tip-toe to provide enough elevation for her five-feet four frame to peek over the counter.

As suspected, there was nobody hiding there.

She quickly scanned the racks of wine glasses on display above her eye-line, and noticed one missing. None of the others seemed to be dislodged, indicating that some external force had acted selectively and exclusively upon the one glass that was thrown.

Weird.

If not a human being, then what? Lucy asked herself.

Suddenly, some inner part of her reached up and slapped her hard across the face.

Look, it's a ghost, okay? A fucking ghost did it. There are ghosts here. Why are you even still questioning it? The quicker you accept it, the quicker we can all move toward some kind of resolution.

It suddenly occurred to her that with all the far-out things that had happened to her already that weekend, a flying wine glass shouldn't really strike her as very unusual.

"All clear over here," she called. "Where do you keep the dust pan and brush? Someone should clean that glass up before Champ sticks his paw in it or something."

"Yeah, good idea, luv. It's right there under the counter," answered Machen.

Lucy saw the dust pan and brush and reached for it, when suddenly she caught movement out of the corner of her eye. Something skittered in the dark, murky corner. Similar to the thing she had seen upstairs, before she fell over.

She instinctively flinched and pulled her hand back. Whatever it was moved with such speed it looked almost like a cat, but it was half way up the wall! However, by the time she registered it the shape had already slunked away into the shadows, leaving nothing but an empty void where it used to be. She contemplated going behind the bar to look, but that would just be inviting trouble. Half the people watching already thought she was batshit crazy.

"What's wrong?" Dale asked, apprehension creeping into his voice.

"Nothing," Lucy called back over her shoulder. "Just coming." She took the dustpan and brush over to where the others were gathered, bent over and started sweeping up the debris. She wouldn't be able to get all the pieces by candlelight, but she could at least get the worst of it. The wine glass had been thrown with such force it didn't just break, but was obliterated. A short, splintered length of stem protruded rudely from the wreckage, most of which was little more than powder.

As she swept, the silence was broken only by the tinkle of glass, Izzy's child-like whimpers, Champ's yowls, and the muted strains of the storm raging outside.

Eventually, Old Rolly said, "If we're going, the sooner the better."

Lucy stopped sweeping. "Going where?"

"Down to the cellar," Dale replied. "Rolly thinks that's where the message we had is telling us to go. We were just on our way there when we got sidetracked by all this fuss."

Lucy gasped. Another coincidence? Surely not.

"I'm coming with you," she spluttered. "When Machen and I were upstairs I had one of those... I don't know... episodes. I blacked out, and apparently started talking about the cellar."

"What did you say about it?"

"How the heck would I know? I blacked out, Dale."

"Oh. Right. So what did she say about the cellar?" Dale asked, looking at the landlord.

All eyes turned to Machen, who threw his arms up in exasperation. "How the hell should I know? Rubbish, it was. Gobbledegunk. Gook."

"Can't you remember anything? It might be important."

Machen was quiet for a moment. Lucy noticed that his attention kept flicking towards the bar. Was he perhaps looking for that shape she had seen? Or was he just eyeing up his next tipple?

Eventually he said, "Let's see... Thought I was her father, she did. As if! And there was something about starving to death. She said she'd starve herself to death if I made her stay. That was it."

"Was she talking to you?"

"I s'pose so," the landlord shrugged. "I was the only person there. It was in the room up on the fourth floor. The room that wasn't locked after all, I'd like to add. Didn't even have a door. And I'm still waiting for an apology of some kind. Dragging me all the way up there for nothing."

"You have no memory of this?" Rolly asked Lucy, who shook her head. "It sounds to me like someone was coming through you. Using you to communicate."

"Who?" Lucy asked, even though she already knew the answer, she needed to hear someone else say it.

"Perhaps Elizabeth, the original Maid of Sker?" the old man said. "She's the only person I know of who starved to death here. And it would fit in with her chastising her father. What else did she say?"

Machen's brow creased and his eyebrows pulled together as he concentrated. "After that she said something about those things from the cellar making him do it."

"So there's something in the cellar, Lucy?"

"I don't know," she replied. "What are you asking me for?"

"Well, the excitement here seems to be pretty much over with now," Dale said, surveying the scene around them. "So let's get going. Lead the way, Mach."

To Lucy's surprise the landlord didn't protest, probably knowing it would be useless. Even more surprising was Izzy being the first to get up.

"What?" the teenager said upon noticing Lucy's quizzical stare. "I'm not bloody staying in here on my own, am I? Not now. Might get a pint glass in the face next time."

There was a steeliness about Izzy's manner that hadn't been there before. Ruth was also on her feet, and even Champ was hopping around in anticipation of adventure. It all indicated that in times of crisis, most people preferred to be proactive, rather than just waiting to see what fate would deal them.

"Wait," Rolly said. "We don't know what we are going up against down there. Maybe we should go equipped."

"Equipped with what?" Lucy asked. "Shall we take knives or something?"

That was the Southampton girl coming out in her again.

"That's just the thing. I don't know. It doesn't seem as though this is a physical creature we are facing, so conventional weapons won't be much good."

"How about a crucifix?" Izzy offered, suddenly looking as though she were getting a feel for the investigation.

"I don't think that would work either, Iz. Whatever powers or forces we're dealing with were probably around long before Jesus. We may as well wave coloured ribbons in its face. If it has a face. Tonight, I think darkness itself is the enemy, or whatever resides inside it, so we need as much light-making equipment as we can get. Torches are useless with this power drain going on, so grab anything else you can. Candles, lighters, matches. Does that brass oil lamp above the bar still work?"

"Think so," replied the landlord. "Has a wick and everything. We can probably use oil from the kitchen. We always have plenty'a candles, and there's a box of Sker House cigarette lighters. Pound each, normally. But I s'pose, under the circumstances, I can see my way clear to giving a couple out for free, like. One good thing about running a pub."

"Good enough," Rolly said.

"I'll go get the lamp and lighters," Izzy volunteered, and headed off into the crawling shadows with only a candle for comfort. Her transformation from helpless want-away victim to strong independent woman was almost complete, and Lucy couldn't help but feel a swell of pride. Maybe something good would come from this whole shared experience, after all.

"Good girl," Rolly said after her. "Now, apart from light, I have a feeling this might be our most effective weapon. Or more precisely, what's in it."

Rolly waved something in the air. It took a few seconds for Lucy to work out that the mystery object was one of Dale's notebooks. Did the old man know something?

When Izzy came back with the brass oil lamp Machen lit it and took the lead, Champ jogging alongside him as he directed the group through a door leading off the bar.

"This thing about darkness versus light," Lucy said, "Isn't it from the Bible, though?"

Dale shrugged. "Yeah, I guess. The Bible uses darkness and light as metaphors for good and evil, but maybe the connection between the two is much older than Christianity. That just came along and put a new spin on old ideas. Like one of your indie bands covering a Beatles song. It's natural to be afraid of the dark, bad shit happens when you can't see anything. Imagine what life must have been like in the days before electricity."

"We don't have to imagine any more," Lucy said. "We're getting quite an insight tonight."

"Well maybe that's why people naturally connect fear and danger with darkness and night. We are hard-wired that way."

"Maybe," Lucy agreed, then fell in line and concentrated on preparing herself for the next challenge this weekend from hell threw at her. She was sure she wouldn't have to wait long.

As they slowly continued on to their destination, Machen started telling them about the cellar. Sensing the information might be important, Dale, along with everyone else within earshot, listened intently.

"There's a sub-cellar, see. In the room we keep the kegs. Them builders, if that's what they call themselves, didn't know what to do with it. Couldn't decide whether to fill it in, seal it off, or incorporate it into the new plans. They asked me what I thought they should do and I didn't know either, so I just told them to go for the cheapest option. That happened to be to leave it alone."

"Is it sound?" Dale asked. "Structurally, I mean?"

"Far as I know," Machen answered without much conviction. "The guy they sent down there never came back out. Not long after that, his mates all up n' pissed off."

"What do you mean never came back out?"

"What I mean is, I assume he came back out somehow. He must've done. He can't still be down there, can he? I just never saw him."

"Did any of his friends see him again?" Lucy asked.

"How should I know?" Machen was sounding defensive again. "His mates weren't here much longer themselves. I bet he turned up somewhere else later on, like."

Dale looked shocked. "Didn't you think to tell anyone about this?"

"What for? It's hardly my fault if the man walks off the job. Who am I going to tell? The building police?"

"But he went missing!" Lucy said, exasperated.

"Says who?"

"You did! You just said!"

"Not my problem, is it?" Machen said, throwing up his hands in frustration.

"Look, just open the door, will you?" Dale said.

Machen stepped forward, used a key on his chain to open a door, and they all filed inside a narrow room which stank of stale beer. It was chilly, draughty, and bare except for stacks of barrels.

By the yellowish gleam of the oil lamp and half-a-dozen naked flames, a large trapdoor was visible in the middle of the floor. It had a bulky padlock held in place by reams of thick rusty chains.

Dale plucked the oil lamp out of Machen's hands and walked over for a closer look. Picking up the heavy metal chains he shook them to rattle the lock.

It was secure.

Dale's gaze wandered from the padlock to the door they had just entered through. Someone had gone to great lengths to keep this part of Sker House off-limits. The builders, or someone before them. Maybe it really was dangerous down there. Declared technically safe perhaps, but in need of urgent work. Or maybe there was another reason altogether.

"Where's the key for the lock?"

"I don't know, do I?" Machen answered. "S'pose them bloody builders took it with them."

"Wait..." Lucy said. "Dale, look at the shape of the lock. Isn't it like the key you found in our room today?"

Dale studied the lock more closely. "You know, you might be right! Machen, show me that key, Sir."

"Oh, I'm 'sir' now, am I. Now you bloody want something, like," Machen said as he reluctantly reached into his pocket, pulled out the old rusted key, and handed it over.

The group watched as Dale inserted the key into the lock and turned it. An expectant hush fell over the room, then there was a collective gasp as the lock fell open.

"It fits!" he said excitedly as he unravelled the rusty iron chains holding the trapdoor closed.   Then, gripping the handle with both hands, he took a deep breath and pulled. The trapdoor came up with a stubborn croak of the hinges and fell open with a loud thump.

Everyone instinctively took a couple of steps back and waited for something to emerge.   Nothing did, except a rush of stale air that reeked of neglect and salt water.

"Everyone okay?" Dale asked.

There was a round of muffled grunts and mumbled affirmations as the rag-tag group edged forward and peered down through the trapdoor into the inky darkness below. It was almost like looking over the edge of a precipice. A wooden ladder reached down into the black void beneath the floor, its treads withered and yellowed with age. Something that looked like a white fungus or moss crept over the top step.

"Hang on," Lucy said. "We don't know what's down there, or how tight a squeeze it might be, so maybe it isn't such a good idea for everyone to go piling down there at once."

"She's right," agreed Old Rolly.

"Yeah, it might be like a mummy's curse, or something," protested Izzy, evidently having an emotional relapse. "We should send one person down as a guinea pig. See if they survive."

"So who's the lucky lab rat?" Machen asked, thereby making it publicly known that he had no intention whatsoever of doing the honours.

"I'll go," said Dale. "I can probably move faster than any of you, anyway." He let out a nervous laugh, but the laugh died in his throat before it gathered much pace.

Then he hesitated. "Wait a minute. Look at all these locks and chains. What if the idea was to keep something inside the cellar, rather than keep something out. And by opening the door, we've just let it loose?"

"If that's the case," Lucy said. "It's too late now. The door's open."

Chapter 32:

Tunnels

As Dale tentatively descended down the rickety wooden ladder into the bowels of the house, the cold, damp air closed in around his limbs and torso like icy fingers. He used only one hand to grip the rungs, holding the precious oil lantern in the other. The going was slow, but the last thing he wanted to do was fall and break his neck. When he reached the ground, he breathed a sigh of relief as he stepped off the ladder onto the floor.

Thank God!

Almost immediately, the lamp's encased flame flickered as if being attacked by a gust of wind. He held his breath until the flame righted itself.

"Dale?" Lucy called from above. "Everything okay?"

"Yeah, think so," he replied, surveying his surroundings. Even with the lamp, picking out detail was difficult. At first he thought the cellar had a carpeted floor. It felt so soft underfoot. Then he stooped to examine it more closely and found the stone floor was simply thick with dust. It must be a quarter-inch deep.

As he inspected the floor near his feet he noticed something, and held the lamp over the spot. It was an impression in the dust. A clear outline of a footprint. A large work boot, by the looks. It looked so fresh it could have been made just minutes earlier.

The missing builder?

Dale peered into the gloom as far as the light would reach, and confirmed he was alone. The flickering light revealed another impression in the dust, just in front of the first. And then another.

Now his eyes were becoming accustomed to the gloom, he could see what looked like a line of footprints leading toward the far wall and disappearing into a cluster of shadows too stubborn to be dissipated by the lamp.

Part of him felt compelled to follow the tracks, but another part was hesitant. Something was wrong.

He studied the scene, turning full circle a couple of times, and looked up to see silhouettes of Lucy, Machen, Rolly, Ruth and Izzy all bathed in candlelight and framed in the rectangle cut into the ceiling.

Then it came to him.

There was only one set of footprints.

As far as he could tell, the rest of the floor was untouched, the dust unmolested.

But that was impossible. There should at be at least one more set of prints returning to the door, otherwise how did the builder get out of the room? Assuming the prints were his, of course. He could have back-tracked, placing his feet carefully where previous footprints lay, but why would he bother?

Unless he didn't get out.

An icy shiver ran through Dale's body. It was cold in the cellar. Colder than upstairs. But it was more than that. The exposed skin on his face and neck crawled as if covered in cobwebs.

"Dale? What are you doing?" Lucy called.

"There's some footprints down here."

"Where do they go?"

"I can't tell. But I think there's only one set. Should I follow them?"

Even as the words left his mouth, Dale was reminded of the story of Hansel and Gretel, who almost followed a trail of breadcrumbs to their doom.

There was a brief murmur of conversation above, then Lucy said, "Wait for us, we're coming down."

Moments later she was standing on one side of Dale and Rolly was on the other, the three of them standing in a semi circle around the first footprint. After a quick discussion, they all drew the same conclusion. There was only one set of tracks.

"So what's over there?" asked Lucy, pointing in the direction the prints led.

"Let's go see," Dale replied, trying to sound calmer than he felt.

The tracks terminated against the far wall. Here there were multiple prints and the dust severely disturbed as if somebody had stopped here and shuffled back and forth a few times, or even got on their hands and knees and had a good old play in the dirt. Dale took a step back and scratched his head.

What the hell? Where did the footprints go?

He placed a hand on the wall to verify its existence, finding only a damp, solid stone surface. Moving his hand along the surface, he cringed as his skin slid through a slimy film covering the wall. Despite his probing, there didn't seem to be any tell-tale knobs or door handles anywhere.

"What now?" said Lucy.

"I don't know. Any advice or suggestions would be more than welcome."

"Well, whoever made these footprints couldn't have walked straight through a concrete wall," Lucy said.

"Maybe the fairies spirited them away, eh, Rolly?" Dale meant it as a joke to alleviate the growing tension, but the moment ve voiced the words he regretted it. They could be just a little too close to the truth.

Then he became aware of a draught around his lower legs. Bending over, he lowered the oil lamp to illuminate the area immediately in front of them and saw what looked like a small opening just above ground level. Fresh air tainted with the acrid smell of the sea and a cold breeze drifted through it.

"Is that a passage?" Old Rolly asked.

"Seems that way," Dale replied. "How far underground are we?"

"Let's see," said the old man. "Right now we are in the cellar, probably eight or ten feet below ground level. From here it depends which trajectory that tunnel takes. It could stay on the same course or it could lead even further down."

"Well lets find out, shall we?" Lucy stooped to look through the gap.

"Not so fast," Rolly said, we don't know what's in there."

"You think this could be the vortex thingy?" Dale asked.

"Possibly," the old man admitted. "Or this could merely be the path leading to the vortex."

"What's a vortex?" asked Lucy puzzled.

"We think there may be some kind of doorway between worlds around here somewhere which could be causing of all the paranormal phenomena. Isn't that right, Rolly?"

"Something like that. If you open up a portal between dimensions that enables the spirit world to interact with ours, wouldn't you want to keep it from prying eyes? Especially the way things were around the time it was built. Anybody who didn't conform to the accepted religion was only ever one step away from being executed. It's possible the renegade monks who first built this place excavated a network of tunnels as a means of avoiding detection by the authorities. And maybe it was down in those tunnels a few of them began dabbling in things they shouldn't have."

"That's probably why Sker House and the surrounding area has a dark cloud hanging over it," elaborated Dale. "All the tragedy and everything else that happens here could be linked to that vortex, or portal."

"Could that even explain things like the Mumbles Lifeboat Disaster?"

"Quite possibly," Dale agreed.

"So, we can close it and restore harmony to the universe?" Lucy seemed to be taking it all very well, almost as if she battled supernatural forces on a daily basis.

"That's the theory," said Rolly. "If we can find the thing, maybe then we can figure out how to close it."

"What a fabulous way to spend a weekend," Lucy spat. "You certainly know how to show a girl a good time, Dale Morgan. Just wait until I tell the girls at uni about this. This will definitely put the time Dannii Braithwaite is supposed to have sucked off the entire five-aside football team at a house party into perspective."

Rolly and Dale looked at each other. Any other time that statement would be enough to spark a dozen debates, but tonight there were more important things on the agenda.

With a shrug the old man knelt on the floor and examined the area around the opening, holding the candle between his face and the wall. Apparently satisfied, he stood and stepped back.

"It's a tunnel alright. There are probably dozens of them underneath Sker, all criss-crossing and bisecting each other. Most were hiding places or escape routes, but some were dead ends intended to trap intruders. It was built like an underground maze. On top of that, there were store rooms and, word has it, sacrificial chambers."

"Excuse me?" Lucy exclaimed.

"Oh, the rogue monks didn't practice human sacrifice. At least, not that I'm aware of. It was just animals."

"Oh, that's okay then," Lucy said in a could-this-really-get-any-worse tone. "So that's what we are looking for now? A sacrificial chamber in an underground maze?"

"I'm not entirely sure," Rolly admitted. "But now we've come this far, I think we'll know what we're looking for when we find it. All tunnels have to lead somewhere."

"Very helpful," said Lucy.

Dale noted that even in times of extreme stress she couldn't keep that brutal sarcastic streak under control. To his credit Rolly either didn't pick up on he remark or was so used to the acerbic verbal lashings of the fairer sex that he had built up a tolerance.

Dale dropped to his knees and held the oil lamp at the opening. By its light they could see the sides of the tunnel had been painstakingly carved out of the earth with what appeared to be consummate skill and craftsmanship. "Maybe Machen should have called in whoever made these tunnels to carry out the refurbishments here."

"Sadly, I suspect whoever fashioned these tunnels passed into the Great Beyond long ago," said Rolly. "Certainly appears to be some high-quality work, though."

"I guess now we know what those monks did with their time when they weren't busy praying and stuff," Lucy said. "Do you think its safe?"

There was a considered pause. Finally, Rolly said, "Taking into account how long these tunnels have been here, you'd have to be damn unlucky if one collapsed on you in the comparatively short time we'd be in there. Keep in mind though that we don't have any phones or electricity to call for help, so if anything does happen, whoever happens to be in there will be on their own."

Dale suspected that some small overlooked part of his brain was aware of the possibility that something may go wrong, but the rest of him chose not to acknowledge it. There really wasn't much option. Somebody had to go exploring and once again, he was the most eligible candidate. The tunnel didn't exactly look inviting. It would be cold, dark, damp and probably crawling with vermin and insects, but it could have been a hell of a lot worse. Unless the width diminished, it looked easily big enough to crawl through. Quickly, if he needed to. And the oil-lamp would provide more than enough light. "Well," he said. "I suppose I'd better get going."

But Lucy threw an arm across his chest. "Wait," she said. "What if this whole tunnel system is one big booby trap? And that's why the builder never came out?"

Dale hadn't thought of that. And he was glad. "Why would someone go to all that trouble?"

"Because they were pissed off monks with a lot to hide."

"You know, it wouldn't surprise me if they utilized the close proximity of the sea in their defences," Old Rolly said. "Resourceful chaps, those monks. Maybe the reason the smell of salt water is so strong around here is because some of these tunnels flood with the tide. You'd have to know which tunnels would be safe at any given time." He whistled through his teeth in what sounded like deep admiration. "They were in hiding, remember. Hunted. Persecuted by the state. They weren't just fighting for their lives, but for their faith, their history, everything."

"This is beginning to turn into an Indiana Jones movie," said Lucy, who seemed increasingly unimpressed with all the problem-solving.

"In that case, I hope it doesn't turn into the Last Crusade," said Dale.

"Why? Does the hero die in that one? I haven't seen it," said Lucy, feigning interest.

"No. Nobody died. Except some bad guys. It was just shit."

Chapter 33:

Underground

As he crawled through the tunnel holding the oil lamp awkwardly out in front of him, Dale's elbows and knees sank into the sodden earth where narrow furrows had been worn. The tunnel must have transported a lot of human traffic over the years. From the era of the monks through Isaac Williams and his wreckers, and now to the present day.

He paused to take a breather, trying to ignore the moisture seeping into his clothes, and tested the wall with a hand. The sides of the cavity, damp with condensation, were uniform and fashioned almost smooth, the earth compacted so much that it was almost stone-like. Wooden support splints had been placed every few metres, making the tunnel look like a miniature mine shaft. It wasn't difficult to imagine hordes of elves scuttling back and forth mining gold.

A few metres in, Dale encountered the first junction where the tunnel split into two paths of roughly equal dimensions.

Which way?

They had anticipated such an eventuality, and decided on a course of action before Dale had entered the passageway. Nobody wanted Dale to get lost, least of all him. There were concerns that the vibrations made by too much verbal communication could cause a cave-in, so a length of string they found discarded in the sub-cellar was tied around Dale's right ankle and now trailed behind him. That way, if anything did happen, Lucy and Rolly would at least be able to find him. It was agreed that if Dale made a turn he would tug sharply on the string once for left and twice for right, and if he ran into any kind of trouble he would tug repeatedly.

Lucy was in charge of holding the spool, paying out the string and waiting for signals so she should map out Dale's progress in her mind. When the length of string was running out, she was to tug on it. That would be Dale's cue to come back. This was, after all, just a reconnaissance exercise.

He paused to think. He didn't think he'd travelled very far. Twenty or thirty feet, maybe? That meant he was probably still somewhere beneath the house. He couldn't be certain but judging by his assumed position, the left path would lead to the sea and the right in the direction of the fields. He remembered reading somewhere that when confronted with this kind of dilemma, most of the time right-handed people chose the right-handed option and vice versa, simply because the dominant part of their brain overruled the other.

Dale didn't want to be governed by anything, not even his own brain, so he checked the string was still secure around his ankle and gave a single sharp tug before continuing down the left tunnel.

It wasn't until later that he realised the significance of taking the left path.

No sooner had he negotiated the turn, a sudden wave of claustrophobia hit him, robbing him of his breath, his orientation and his composure in one fell swoop. He stopped and rolled on to his side, breathing hard and fighting to regain control of his senses.

It felt like he was suffocating.

Drowning.

He remembered the dream he'd had, and became convinced it was a premonition. The greasy walls appeared to be closing in around him.

Then he became aware of sounds. Grunts, voices, faraway moans. They seemed to fade in and out of clarity and rise and fall in volume.

He held his breath to listen.

It doesn't mean anything, the logical part of Dale's brain protested. You're in a tunnel, sound carries. What you can hear is probably coming from two miles away.

No.

Something had changed.

He felt different.

Nervously, he contorted his body and shone the oil-lamp behind him.

As far as the limited light would enable him to see, he was still alone.

As he turned back, his arm dragged against the wall and dislodged a chunk of mud which dropped to the floor with a soft thud forcing his heart to skip a beat.

It's falling apart!

He stared at the patch wall the chunk of mud had fallen from, and something caught his eye. Where the layered mud was flaking off, a smooth surface was visible beneath. Contorting his body in the cramped sspace to generate more flexibility, he brushed some more dried mud away with his hand.

Was that wooden panelling? Some kind of structural support?

He tapped at the wood with a knuckle. It sounded hollow. There must be a cavity behind.   Another tunnel?

Surely not. What purpose would that possibly serve?

He would need to prise off the cover and take a look, and wondered how much string was left on the spool Lucy was holding. It couldn't be much. Luckily, there appeared to be some kind of through-draft, so ventilation wasn't a problem.

Carefully removing the wooden covering, he leaned it against the sloping wall of the tunnel and shone the oil-lamp into the newly-created hole. A thick mass of musty air rushed out to meet him, making him gag. Evidently, this was one section of the elaborate subterranean excavation that hadn't been exposed to the open air for some time.

The light of the oil lamp revealed a stone-lined floor, walls, and a low, but neatly rendered ceiling. It was a tiny enclosed space, hidden deep underground and accessible only via the secret passageway.

Dale gave a few excited tugs on the line attached to his ankle to let the others know he had found something, and crawled through the opening into the secret room beyond.

It was easily big enough to stand up in, and he took full advantage after spending so long crouching by treating himself to a luxurious stretch. The oil lamp sent the massed shadows scurrying away to regroup in forgotten corners.

It was then, as he held the lamp above his head, that he noticed the markings that adorned every surface of the room. In some areas there was such a concentration that they interconnected or overlapped, new markings all-but obscuring the old. Most of them appeared to be painted or chalked, while others seemed to be etched deep into the stone with some kind of tool.

As he peered at them more closely, Dale realized that the cryptic writings were similar in nature to those that had been scrawled in his notebook. Some figures could be construed as letters, while others were clearly defined symbols. There were also jagged crosses and a few things that looked like hieroglyphs or

Oriental characters. Some looked familiar, one being a large five-pointed pentagram painted high on one wall.

"Jesus, this is like a Motley Crue video," he muttered.

The hidden room was bigger than it appeared from the outside, measuring at around three metres from wall to wall and a little over two metres from floor to sloping ceiling. The dimensions seemed somewhat out of whack to him, like he'd stepped through the looking glass, and the whole room had a decidedly odd, unbalanced feel. It was completely empty, except for what looked like an old blacksmith's anvil in one corner. Dale cautiously went over for a closer look, and saw that the object wasn't an anvil at all, but a large altar fashioned out of what appeared to be opaque marble with iron ringlets embedded into each side. He was no expert, but to him it looked as though those iron ringlets were designed to support ropes or chains. What kind of activity would require such restraints?

The kind involving an unwilling participant.

Just then, he heard another noise. Earth being dislodged. Then a scurrying, and the strain of muffled voices getting closer. His eyes fixed on the narrow opening in the wall that, he now realized, represented the only means of escape. To all intents and purposes, he had trapped himself.   Staring nervously at the marble altar that now seemed to fill half the room, he fleetingly imagined himself fastened there, struggling to free himself, all the while knowing it was futile.

Something out in the darkness whispered his name.

Dale took a step back into the room, away from the opening. Then he felt something on his ankle, fingers? He rammed a fist into his mouth to cover a scream, and looked down to see the string tied around his ankle being pulled taught. The other end reached out of the opening into the passage beyond where some unseen force was tugging on it.

"Dale?"

His name again. The voice sounded strange and distant, yet familiar.

He began to swoon.

This was it.

Whatever they had disturbed here at Sker, whatever supernatural entity they had angered, was about to exact its terrible revenge.

There was movement directly outside now, mere feet away. His back was against the far wall and he was glad of it, otherwise he was pretty sure he would slump to the floor in a dead faint. He scanned the room for a weapon of some kind, anything he could use to defend himself. But there was nothing except the altar itself, which looked far too heavy to lift. Even if it hadn't been, the thought of touching it with his bare skin filled him with revulsion.

Out of options, he braced himself for attack, determined that if he was going to die he at least wanted to face his assailant head on.

Suddenly the string went limp, and a face appeared framed in the mini-doorway.

Lucy!

"Ah, there you are!" she said. "You had us worried there for a minute."

She clambered through the opening bum-first, once inside looking around the room wide-eyes. Rolly was immediately behind her, though he took considerably longer to squeeze his withered frame through the entrance than his nubile young predecessor.

When he regained his feet he looked around in wonder, mouth hanging open, then finally exclaimed, "The markings! This is it, the vortex! We found it!"

"How can you be sure?" Dale asked.

"Look at the ceiling."

Dale did so. The same array of weird symbols covering the walls and ceiling also covered the ceiling, but there the symbols seemed to be arranged in concentric patterns creating a weird spiral effect.

"This room itself must be the portal. The epicentre. And look there..." Old Rolly nodded at the altar.

"That must be where the sacrifices took place."

Lucy gazed around at the walls. "Damn it. Man, I should have brought my camera. This is some pretty cool stuff. Would have made a great double-page montage."

"The flash wouldn't work," Dale reminded her. "All the power got drained, remember?" Turning to Rolly, he said, "So what do we do now? If this is the vortex, how do we close it?"

"Just because I know what's happening, it doesn't mean I know how to deal with it," the old man shrugged. "I have as much idea about this as you do."

Lucy bit her lip while while Dale stayed in the corner doing his level best not to exasperate the situation. Finally she said, "Why don't we just paint over everything. Obliterate it. Make it all go away. Maybe the symbols are what makes the vortex work. No symbols, no vortex. Right? The workmen left tonnes of paint behind, and its not like anybody is going to complain about the colour scheme, is it?"

Dale wasn't convinced. "But the symbols would still be there, underneath the paint. It can't be that simple, surely?"

As all eyes turned to Old Rolly, he shrugged. "Why on earth not? It's certainly worth a try."

Chapter 34:

Facing Evil

Lucy remembered where she'd seen some discarded tins of paint on the fourth floor and went back to tell Machen, Ruth and Izzy to go and get them. They must be getting anxious by now anyway, this would allow her to update them and give them something to do. Machen wasn't overjoyed with being asked to go to the fourth floor for the second time that evening, but didn't protest too much.

On her return she, Dale and Old Rolly endured an anxious wait of their own as the instructions were carried out. Deep in the inner sanctum of Sker House, the din of thunder and lightning outside was little more than a constant muffled drone. A breeze blew through the cellar from the exposed tunnel entrance.

"Where do you think the other part of that tunnel goes?" Lucy asked. "I thought I could smell the sea."

Dale didn't surprise her often, but right then he did. "You wanna go on a little excursion and see if we can find out?"

Anything was better than standing here feeling awkward, so she flashed her most wicked smile and said, "Sure, let's go."

"Wait a minute you two, are you sure its a good idea to split up like this?" Old Rolly protested. "Haven't either of you ever seen a horror film? All the young, good-looking, stupid people peel off by themselves, usually to go off and have sex somewhere, then get horribly slaughtered one-by-one."

"Who's going to slaughter us?" Dale said, genuinely mystified.

Lucy, on the other hand, didn't know which sleight to be more angry about, the assumption that she would have sex with Dale in a tunnel or being called stupid. Luckily for him, Rolly had also managed to drop something in there about being young and good-looking too, so she figured it was about even.

She was the first back into the tunnel, plucking the oil-lamp out of Dale's grasp as she passed. Dale was close behind, and she heard Old Rolly call after them, "I'll stay here and keep and eye on things then, shall I?"

"I'm sure it'll be fine," Dale said. "You're the custodian here, after all. This room's been undisturbed for hundreds of years. Just keep that candle lit."

"Oh, that I will. You be careful, lad. And you keep that string tied to your foot, just in case."

275

"Don't worry," Dale said. "We'll be back before you know it."

Dale and Lucy climbed up through the chamber opening and began crawling steadily through the tunnel, periodically tapping the walls around them in search of other hidden chambers.

They tried not to talk too much. The tunnel was well ventilated, but that situation could change. Plus, it didn't matter how well ventilated the tunnel was there were still psychological hurdles to overcome. At times the tunnel grew so narrow it seemed to be trying to form an earth-clad cocoon around them.

After a while, Dale surprised Lucy for the second time in minutes by exposing his sensitive side. Something he usually only did when he was drunk.

"You know," he said, "Even though I've been away for so long I still miss Wales. Sometimes, I hear the Hiraeth."

"You hear the what?"

"Hiraeth. There's no direct English translation, but it means something like 'the Calling'. It's like homesickness I guess, but a bit different. It's more intense, kinda like a longing, or a yearning for some other place or time."

"I thought you didn't speak Welsh."

"I don't. I speak Wenglish. Welsh English. Mostly English, but spoken in a funny accent and with a few Welsh words thrown in."

"Like what?"

"Like cwtch? For example."

"Cwtch? What does that mean?"

"Hug."

"Oh. That's kinda cute," Lucy said as she found herself moving faster, her feet kicking up clods of loose earth in her wake. The tunnel seemed to go on forever. She hoped Dale could keep up.

Suddenly, she encountered something that forced her to stop. It was an almost physical wall of darkness so dense that not even the light from the oil-lamp could penetrate it.

"What's up?" said Dale from somewhere behind her. "Why have we stopped?"

"There's something here. Blocking the way."

"Maybe whoever was digging this thing didn't finish it, and this was as far as they got," Dale suggested, reasonably enough. "Either that, or the tunnel's caved in."

Lucy wanted to tell Dale that he was wrong. This blockage was nothing as solid as soil. But the mere mention of the words 'cave-in' struck fear into her. Tentatively, she reached out into the blackness.

There was no resistance.

Instead, her hand disappeared, swallowed by the darkness. The sensation was like holding your hand under a running tap. The numbing cold seeped through her skin, chilling her to the bone.

With a sharp cry she pulled her hand back and wiped it on her t-shirt. It was dry, but there was a sense of repulsion, like she was somehow tainted. She'd never wanted a hot shower more at any time in her life.

She scooted back a few inches to put some distance between her and the dark mass, which was now undulating like a cloud. As she watched, it appeared to be solidifying before her eyes. She could make out the blurred contours of a flailing arm, then shoulders and a head. The head had two protrusions sprouting out of it. Like horns.

Oh God.

She wanted to scream, but was frozen in place, transfixed.

"Lucy? What's going on?"

"It's moving," she whimpered. "Dale, it's moving."

"What is?" Behind her, Dale's breathless voice rose a few octaves.

Don't panic, Lucy told herself. Not now, not here. With Dale behind and that thing in front, there was nowhere to go. She would die down here, gasping for air and heart beating out of her chest.

The seething mass was now twisting and swirling before her, billowing like black smoke. As she watched, a face took shape and loomed out at her making her squeal and recoil.

It was the face of a man, bearded, with thin, sharp features and deep-set eyes with a dull red hue. It was like the embodiment of evil.

Isaac Williams.

Lucy didn't know how she could be so certain it was Elizabeth Maid of Sker's father. The knowledge was just there, implanted in her brain.

Upon seeing the face, Lucy wasn't scared anymore. In a flash, her fear was gone and replaced with a blind rage. Inexplicable, unreasonable, all-consuming fury, coursing through her veins like caustic acid. She didn't know why she was angry, or where she should direct it, just that she had to release it somehow. She wanted to destroy, kill, inflict pain on anything and everything around her.

She wanted revenge.

She lashed out with all her limbs at once but while her fists found nothing but the cold pocket of air, one of her feet connected with something more solid.

"Ow!" Dale cried out. "Lucy, what the hell are you doing?"

As suddenly as it had descended, the rage left her and the swirling black mass evaporated. The face had disappeared. "I... I don't know," she stammered.

"What do you see?"

"Nothing. It's gone."

"Do you want to go back?"

"No. I want to get the hell out of this tunnel."

She ploughed forward with a renewed sense of urgency as fresh air rushed into the cavity and the sounds of wind and rain grew louder. Mixed in so effectively that it all merged together into the same white noise were the unmistakeable sounds of crashing waves and churning breakwater. The sounds now represented freedom.

A few metres on, the tunnel opened out onto a narrow ledge cut into the cliff-face. Lucy cautiously crawled out, bracing herself against the wind as it tried to blow her from her perch.

Far below, tumultuous white-tipped waves churned and smashed against jagged spikes of rock, and a thick bank of mist rolled inexorably toward the shoreline.

"What was that?" Dale asked, crawling out to join her. "You kicked me in the face!"

Lucy saw his nose was bleeding. The blood, cascading down the front of his hoody, looked black. Guilt washed over her. "Sorry about that. For a moment I... I couldn't control myself."

278

Dale's injury was apparently forgotten as he surveyed their surroundings. "Wow. Check this out. So the tunnel does lead to the sea. This was probably an escape route for the monks, and later must have been repurposed by Isaac Williams and his men in the wrecking days. It could explain the mysterious disappearance of the builder. He must have come out this way and legged it. But why would he do that?"

"Something happened to him in the tunnel," Lucy said, certainty weighing down her voice. "And after that he didn't want anything more to do with the house. Didn't even want to go back to pick up his tools, or tell his colleagues he was leaving."

Dale looked pensive. "Yeah, maybe. Anyway, let's report this back to the others."

"Okay. But I'm not going back in that tunnel."

"I agree. Which leaves... this ledge. There must be a way down the cliffs."

The ledge was cut into the rock face at a jagged angle. At this point it was around two feet wide, but the far edge was gradually crumbling into the sea and it wouldn't be totally unexpected if the width diminished further along. It was precarious, but compared with going back in the tunnel, the ledge posed an acceptable risk.

Lucy pushed her back against the slippery wet stone and edged her way along as the slippery ledge morphed into a steep, winding path leading down the cliff face at an acute angle.

"Try not to look down," Dale said from behind her.

"Thanks for the advice," Lucy replied. "That's only been in every film ever made where people are on top of something high. I thought you would've come up with something better than that."

"Sorry to disappoint."

"And you know what?"

"What?"

"They always look down." Lucy realised that it was easier to move when they talked. It took their minds off the perilous descent. She searched for something else to say. "So... Are you glad you came back to Wales or what?"

"It doesn't get any less weird," Dale answered wryly.

"Hey, have you read 'You Can't Go Home Again' by Thomas Wolfe?"

"Can't say I have. Beyond Catcher in the Rye, I'm not really into the American classics. Why? Am I missing something?"

"It's a story about an author who writes a book exposing the dirty secrets in his home town. The book makes him famous but when the townsfolk find out about it they start sending him death threats and generally making his life a misery. The subtext is that once you leave home, everything is different. The actual place, the people, your home, might not change, but you will. So... you can never go home again. Definitely not after you talk ashit about everyone."

"Who says you can't go home?"

"Thomas W... Hey, are you quoting Bon Jovi at me?"

Dale didn't answer.

Lucy, focused on maintaining her balance against the buffering wind and rain, continued forward, edging tentatively around a large boulder that lay in the middle of the path.

"Dale?" she pressed, risking a glance behind. For one terrible second she thought she was alone on the path, that her friend had tumbled off the cliff into the thrashing sea. Then she began to make out the shape of his body, pressed flat and unmoving against the sleek dark rock. "Dale? What's up?"

"Look!" he shouted. He was staring down into the churning black water below.

Lucy followed his gaze. There was something in the mist, trying to force its way through. She could distinguish right angles and a dark mass. The shape seemed to be solidifying before her very eyes as tendrils of sea mist wrapped themselves around it, the mist which now appeared to be concentrated just beyond what the locals called Sker Point and its deadly rocks.

"What's that?" Lucy said, raising her voice to be heard against the tumultuous waves and barrage of wind and rain.

As they both watched, mesmerized, something broke through the ranks of mist, protruding from its core, and pointing towards shore. The object looked familiar to Lucy, yet at the same time undeniably out of place. It rose and fell on the swell of a gigantic wave, and on the downturn more of its bulk was revealed.

It was an old-fashioned sailing ship, hopelessly out of control, and being dragged ever closer to the vicious banks of rocks guarding Sker beach.

Lucy glanced at Dale.

His lips were moving. He seemed to be speaking.

Lucy moved a few steps closer in an attempt to hear what he was saying. He was repeating the same sentence, over and over again.

"I know that ship, I know that ship, I know that ship."

"How? How do you know that ship?" Lucy almost shouted. "It's going to crash into the rocks!"

At the sound of her voice, Dale stopped talking and his head snapped toward her. His eyes were wide and his jaw hung open to aid his panicked breathing. Satisfied that her friend was in no immediate danger, Lucy fixed her attention back on the ship just in time to see more of its massive bulk lurch out into view.

As she watched, it was jolted mercilessly as yet another huge wave struck it side on. Even above the roar of the wind and waves, the groaning sound of timber under duress was plainly audible. Despite the size of the ship, it was like watching a child's toy being tossed around in a bathtub.

"Look over there!" shouted Dale, prying his fingers off the sheet rock onto which he clung just long enough to point at Sker beach.

Lucy did, and saw lights littering the beach. "What's that?" she asked in wonderment.

"I think it's the Wreckers," replied Dale. "Or... the ghosts of the Wreckers. Using lamps to lure the ship onto the rocks."

Rain beat against Lucy's face as she watched the ship tilt sickeningly to one side. Disaster was imminent. Suddenly, the ship shimmered and lost a little of its solidity, wavering in and out of focus, as if being viewed through a lens that was being manipulated. "Dale, what's happening?"

"Looks as if it's... going."

Lucy craned her neck to stare at the stretch of coastline which moments before had been illuminated with rows of disembodied lights. The lights were still visible, but seemed to be losing their intensity. Most were now just dull specks of orange.

Whatever strange phenomena they were witnessing seemed to be ebbing away.

"Lucy was dumbfounded. "What the heck did we just see?"

"I think we just saw a ghost ship," Dale said, voice wavering. "And some ghost lights. Wrecker's lights. What we saw was probably a replay of some earlier event."

"But... why now?"

"Maybe it's a sign that the forces, or whatever they are, are getting stronger. More powerful. I've seen that ship before. In a dream."

"What happened?"

"I was on it."

"And then?"

"It hit the rocks."

"Come on, Dale. We should get back to the house. Poor Rolly will probably be worried sick about us by now."

"Yeah, no shit," replied Dale. He took a few tentative steps along the path toward Lucy, which was enough to get her own limbs moving again.

As she moved off, Lucy risked a last look down. Below them the waves still crashed against the jagged spikes of Sker Point and the sea mist still rolled in wispy clouds, but there was no sign of the ship. The lights had also completely vanished, leaving her free to concentrate on putting one foot in front of the other and getting back to the relative safety of Sker House.

Chapter 35:

The Plan

Machen stood with Old Rolly and Champ in the bar, which had evidently been recommissioned as Base Camp. They were hovering over a grand total of nine tins of assorted paint, all they could find, while Ruth and Izzy loitered on the fringes. Machen was pretty sure there were a lot more tins lying around. But as much as he tried, he couldn't remember where and hunting around Sker House in the dark wouldn't be a good idea. Not tonight. Anyway, he thought they'd managed a pretty good haul under the circumstances. Ruth and Izzy were even able to source a handful of used brushes. Now all that remained was to get the supplies to their required destination.

"What d'they want all this stuff for?" he said.

He was pretty sure he'd asked Old Rolly that very same question before, maybe more than once, but though he couldn't remember the exact answer Old Rolly gave, he knew it hadn't made much sense and therefore didn't stick in his head.

"We're going to do a spot of decorating, Mach. Let's just leave it at that, shall we? It's for your own good. And the good of your precious business," the sharpness in Old Rolly's voice belied a growing sense of urgency. Then his tone softened slightly. "Look, I think the quickest and easiest way of doing this would be for Ruth to go first with a couple of candles in case one decides to go out, then you and I will follow. A couple of sprightly young fellows like ourselves should be able to carry most of these tins in one go."

Machen felt himself nod.

"Ruth and Izzy can carry any leftovers, the brushes, and some more light. When we get all the stuff over to the beer cellar, we'll pass them down the trapdoor into the sub-cellar one by one, and take it from there. Agreed?"

There was more a lack of obvious disagreement than any enthusiastic agreement. Nobody was sure of what to do, but knew they had to do something.

Personally, Machen would love to pop up and win the day with a better idea. An idea so great it would put Rolly's recently-revealed master-plan to shame. But he wasn't thinking clearly just lately, and good ideas were at a premium. He was spurred into action when he realized Rolly had already started seeing how many tins of paint he could load into his skinny, tweed-clad arms. No way was he going to be upstaged by that old fart.

He'd just managed to ram the last remaining tin into the space between his arm and his side, when there was a sudden loud rap at the front door. There were several gasps, and the last tin of paint tumbled back to the floor as Machen's arm involuntarily spasmed. Champ leapt to his feet and into a defensive stance, barking, growling and advancing toward the reception area with his paws splayed on the floor and his ears flattened to his head.

"Steady, boy," Machen said. "It's probably just a new guest."

"A new guest, at this time of night?" piped up Ruth, always interfering, that one. Always had to have her say.

Machen glared at her. "Sssh! We know it's not a bloody customer but Champ doesn't! Or he didn't before you opened your trap, like. What do you think he's gonna do now he knows the truth? He might go bloody mental and rip somebody's throat out."

Champ stopped barking and tilted his head up at Machen as if to say, 'who, me?'

"Get the door Iz, it's probably just your young guests returning," said Old Rolly. Izzy picked up a candle and head for the front door.

"Guests? Returning?" was all Machen could manage. There were other things he should say, he should know what was going on, really. He was the landlord of this establishment so he should be the first to know... well, everything.

But right then he couldn't decide what he wanted to know most. He had the feeling that one question would lead to another, and that would just confuse him. The kids were inside, they went outside for whatever reason, and now they want to come back inside. That was all he needed to know. Anything else would be superfudge.

Superfluous?

The gatecrashers were indeed Dave and Betty.

Was that their names?

Old Rolly went to meet them, and Machen's heart sank a notch when he realized that even Champ was invited to the little town meeting they had going on over there. He sat on the floor looking up at whoever was talking, head flicking from speaker to speaker. That was loyalty for you.   The girl was gibbering on and on about something.

What's she saying?

Machen could only make out the occasional word or part of a sentence, but she seemed to be talking about tunnels, ships and lights. Now Rolly was going on about his plan again. Who put him in charge, anyway? How did that happen? If anyone should be calling the shots around here it should be him, he was the bloody landlord!

Wait, he was supposed to be thinking about something else right now, wasn't he? Something more important.

Concentrate.

What...

That's right! They were painting stuff!

Now he remembered.

But the details were lost.

What were they painting, and why?

Damn it, these were things he used to know, but now he wasn't sure. The parts of his brain that used to be occupied by answers now contained only holes. More than holes. Dark bottomless pits. When things fell into them, they rarely came back out. And when they did, they came back changed.

He was about to go and break up the meeting when all the attendees suddenly dispersed. There was a sense of purpose in their collective stride as the group passed him and busied themselves going about their delegated tasks.

Unsure of what else to do, Machen joined in.

Chapter 36:

The Darkness Fights Back

Getting all the tins of paint and other materials to the beer cellar proved to be the easy part, because the next stage was to lower the supplies through the trapdoor and manoeuvre them through the tunnel to the hidden room.

As Dale prepared to go down the ladder into the waiting blackness for the second time, it occurred to him that he or Lucy should have brought a rucksack. That would have made things infinitely easier. Hindsight was a wonderful thing. Instead he gritted his teeth and, holding the oil-lamp in one hand, carefully made the descent.

When he reached the bottom of the ladder, he placed the lamp carefully on the floor, and held his hands up to the hole in the ceiling. Lucy and Rolly knew what to do. The first tin of paint, medium sized and half-empty judging by its weight, dropped out of the sky into his hands. Dale caught it, set it down next to the lamp, and held up his hands for more.

Soon, there was a miniature mound of paint tins shaped like a supermarket display. Before Dale even had time to admire his artistic skills there were sounds of movement above, and one of Lucy's feet appeared on top of the ladder. "Ready or not, here I come!"

Minutes later they were joined by Rolly, and a special guest in the form of Machen, who presumably came along to make sure nobody stole anything. He didn't seem quite 'with it.' His speech was slurred and he was always half a step behind everyone else. The more Dale thought about it, the more he came to believe that the landlord's condition was down to the cumulative effect of living at Sker House for so long.

An anguished whine came from above. Champ also wanted in, but he'd been compromised by those cursed canine legs of his that wouldn't allow him to use a ladder. He would have to hold the fort with Ruth and Izzy.

Dale wondered if Machen had ever set foot inside this part of the house before, and seriously doubted it judging by the way the landlord kept looking around in wonder. He watched for a tell-tale glance in the direction of the tunnel in the far wall, but there was none.

"Let's get a move on," Rolly said. The light from the oil lamp illuminated an arc as the four of them formed a human chain and passed the tins and brushes down the line hand-to-hand. Dale was at the head of the formation, and re-stacked all the paint just outside the tunnel opening for the sake of convenience.

So far so good.

When the final tin arrived he didn't bother stacking it, but kept it in his hand and asked for the oil lamp.

Machen was nearest. He held the out the lamp, but at the last second jerked back as if reconsidering his decision. It was enough to throw Dale off, and he missed his grab. As if in slow-motion, the lamp tottered and fell to the floor where it's glass casing smashed. The light momentarily went out, the stench of paraffin filled the air, and darkness swarmed over them.

There was a growing sense of panic as everyone rushed to find candles and cigarette lighters, but they needn't have worried. The first flames that sprung up around their feet hungrily devouring the spilled accelerant was enough to make the shadows retreat. However, this was the equivalent of a tactical withdrawal, and the shadows conceded ground only to await another chance to advance.

Lucy shrieked and put her hands to her mouth as Dale quickly moved to stamp out the flames. A fire this deep in the building would surely mean the end of Sker House. Maybe that wouldn't be a bad thing, he thought, and he imagined he wasn't the only one. They should all get out while they still could, and let nature take it's course.

But they couldn't leave yet. Their work wasn't finished.

For one horrifying moment, Dale's shoe caught fire, the flames lapping against his the bottom of his jeans, and he hurriedly beat them out before they could take hold. Later, he would realize how lucky they had been that there was nothing more flammable in the vicinity than a battered old pair of trainers.

The fire safely extinguished, Dale leaned against the wall to catch his breath, taking the opportunity to light a candle for the next leg of the journey. Fumbling in his pockets he found a Sker House-branded lighter, struck the wheel, and lit the wick. The candle blazed into life, then immediately died. He lit it again, but with the same result.

Strange, he couldn't detect a draft.

He turned to face the other direction. Shielding the candle with his hand, he tried once more.   Again, the flame failed to take hold.

Must be a damp candle, he thought as he threw it to the ground in frustration and fished another out of his back pocket. He checked his supply. One more after this. He hoped it would be enough.

But that candle wouldn't stay lit, either. Dale then realized that everyone else was having the same problem. All around him there were little bursts of light like tiny explosions accompanied by mutters of frustration.

"Where's the bloody draft coming from?" asked Lucy.

"I don't think there is one," replied Rolly. "This must be where the resistance begins. If, as we suspect, that room in there has been acting like an open door to the spirit world, then all manner of things may have come through. And they don't want to go back."

"Can't we wait until morning?" Lucy asked. "We can come back and do it then, when we can all see what the hell we are doing."

"It has to be now. Tonight," replied Rolly. "Don't you get the feeling that we are standing on the brink of something? It's a race against time. I know you sense it, my dear. You have the sight. I knew that the moment I saw you. Can you feel all the energy buzzing about the place right now? The activity is building. Something's coming. Something big. Unless we can stop it."

The darkness was all around them now. It didn't have a uniform quality, instead it seemed more concentrated in some places than others like splotches of ink, or bloodsplatter at a crime scene.

Giving up on the luxury of a candle, Dale resorted to repeatedly striking his cigarette lighter. Even then, it was useless. No sooner as his thumb struck the wheel and the flame burst into life, it withered and died. Unperturbed, he sank to his knees and peered into the yawning cavity carved out of the earth. The cold clamminess of the tunnel didn't phase him as much as the first time. The fear of the unknown was gone. He knew what lay ahead, and he knew what had to be done. He would just have to do it in the dark.

Stuffing a brush into his back pocket, Dale grabbed the biggest tin of paint he could get his hands on. Then, he pushed his head through the opening and commanded his body to propel itself through the narrow stretch of tunnel toward the hidden room. As the blackness engulfed him he felt his stomach churn, as if he were crawling through a sewer overflowing with filth and excrement. He coughed, and a mouthful of hot bile rose up his throat into his mouth. Grimacing, he swallowed it back down.

Immediately behind him, he heard voices, raised in panic rather than anger.

"Get away from me!" shouted Machen, his tone shrill. "Who's doing that?"

"There's nobody near you. Get a grip, man," scolded Rolly. "Concentrate on getting some light."

"But someone touched me!"

Now there were sounds of shuffling.

Dale had company in the tunnel.

He hoped it was Lucy, but didn't stop to make sure.

Soon, he arrived at the entrance to the hidden room, what Old Rolly had called the epicentre, and stopped.

Taking out his lighter, he struck the wheel again. Sparks flew from the flint and died on the floor, but still the flame wouldn't catch. The micro-seconds of illumination from the falling sparks made him wince, but it was enough to enable him to get his bearings.

More shuffling behind, closer now. And with it the sounds of breathing.

Dale manoeuvred himself around and squeezed his shoulders through the opening, using his splayed fingers to claw his way through.

Suddenly, a hand closed around his trailing leg, holding him in place. Dale jumped, and instinctively tried to kick the hand away. The hand seemed to caress his flesh through his layers of clothing. The grip was gentle yet firm, and seemed to be pulsing, applying pressure then relaxing. The sensation would not have been unpleasant in the right circumstances, but unfortunately these were anything but.

"Lucy? Is that you?" Dale said into the darkness behind him, making another doomed attempt to ignite the cigarette lighter. "Let go of me."

Using all the strength he could muster, he shook his leg free and felt the grip fall away. Snatching his leg back he pulled it through the opening into the little secret room where he sat on the floor, panting. "Lucy?"

There were scuffles, sounds of movement, but much further away than before.

From a distance somebody said, "Dale? Is everything okay in there? Hold on, we're on our way through."

It was Lucy. Her voice was distinctive. Evidently the rest of the group was only just preparing to join him in the room.

So who had grabbed his foot?

Who or what had been in the tunnel with him?

He didn't want to think about that just now, but knew it was the kind of thing that would haunt his nightmares later. In the pitch black void the hidden room had become, Dale prised the lid of the tin of paint he had carried with him and dropped it to the floor. It landed with a metallic clang, and the confined space began to fill with the noxious aroma of chemical-laden paint. He reached into his back pocket for the brush.

It was gone.

Shit!

It must have worked itself loose and fallen from his pocket somewhere in the tunnel. There was no way he was going back to look for it. He would have to improvise.

Think, think, think.

He could just throw the paint over the wall. But then most of it would go to waste, and he'd have to go and get more paint. Not likely. Laying the tin back on the floor, Dale tugged on the sleeve of his hoody as hard as he could. After a couple of good pulls the stitching broke and the sleeve came away. It wasn't a great look, but he doubted anyone would care. He quickly rolled the material into a ball and dunked it into the paint, using it to smear the thick, sticky substance over the walls.

The noises were at the door now; scrambling, grunting, puffing and panting. "Who's there?"

"It's me. Who did you think it was?"

Dale had never been so glad to hear Lucy's high-pitched, south coast burr in all his life. His task momentarily forgotten he held out his arms until they brushed against Lucy's in the dark, then they embraced like long lost lovers.

"Is this your cwtch?"

"It is," Dale answered, feeling the warmth of Lucy's breath on his cheek.

He didn't want to let her go, he wanted to stay there locked together forever. He felt a rush of heat in his loins, and could have sworn Lucy felt something similar, but then he pushed her away. "Come on," he said. "Get painting. Time's running out."

Chapter 37:

The Battle

Lucy didn't even bother trying to light a candle. She'd grown tired of all the wasted effort. Instead, she quickly yanked the lid off the tin she was carrying, thrust her brush inside, and eagerly began defacing the nearest surface. She felt empowered and invigorated, yet it was a tainted kind of enthusiasm. Almost as if she were getting kicks from doing something she knew was wrong.

She remembered experiencing a similar feeling as a teenager when she'd spray-painted her name on the back of West Gate Shopping Centre in town. On that occasion, however, the euphoria was cut short when the police showed up and arrested her at school. How embarrassing. She'd made the elementary mistake of spraying her own name instead of using a tag, and may as well have supplied her home address and phone number along with a note saying available for arrest at the following location.

In a perverse way, on that occasion her own boundless stupidity had actually saved her from a life of crime. The police knew no experienced vandal would be so dim-witted and were very lenient.

There were more sounds of struggle at the entrance to the room as Old Rolly and Machen scrambled their way into the tiny dark chamber one after the other, each identifiable by the various expletives that accompanied them.

"What's this?" Machen asked as he finally squeezed through the gap. "Are you kids in here? Dave? Erm, Betty?"

"It's Dale and Lucy, and yes we're here."

"How did you find this place?"

"It's a long story," Lucy said. "No time to explain. Later. Right now, grab a brush and start painting!"

"Painting what, like?"

"Anything!"

Muttering to himself, Machen made several unsuccessful attempts to spark his cigarette lighter before also giving up.

Lucy continued with her task. In the darkness, there was a lot of guesswork involved. She employed her sense of touch as she worked her way around the immediate vicinity, and could hear the others using whatever means they could to open the tins and transfer the contents onto the walls.   At one point, there was a solid thunk and Machen swore loudly. Lucy guessed he must have found the altar with some part of his anatomy. Probably his hip.

Suddenly there was a loud whoosh like a massive displacement of air and a strong breeze rippled around the enclosed space, riddling Lucy's arms and neck with goose bumps.

Rolly grunted loudly as if he'd been punched in the stomach. There was a clatter against the far wall, and the old man shouted, "My brush just got ripped out of my hand! Somebody hit me and stole my bloody brush! Who did that? WHO DID THAT?"

"You don't need a brush," came Dale's voice from the other side of the tiny room. "Use your hands, use anything!"

Something was trying to stop them. Using all the force it could muster, and utilizing every dirty trick in the book.

Lucy continued frantically throwing paint at the walls and sensed others around her doing the same. "It must be working!" she shouted.

"Something's gotten them tetchy," wheezed Rolly, sounding as if he was still reeling from the physical attack he had just endured.

Just then, a meaty slap echoed around the tiny chamber and Machen let out a startled grunt. The slap was followed by what sounded like a bag of cement being dropped from a great height onto a concrete floor, the noise amplified in the cramped space.

Something unseen brushed past Lucy's elbow in a downward motion. She flinched away before realizing it was just the landlord, who until that moment had been standing next to her.

Apparently, he was now pole-axed on the floor. "Mach? What happened?"

Through strangled gasps of air the landlord managed to say, "Something... something pushed me over."

He sounded on the verge of a panic attack.

Lucy reached down a hand to console him, or help him up, whichever would benefit him the most, but in the darkness she couldn't pinpont where he was. Her out-stretched hand made contact with something that felt like a silk sheet, then she suddenly felt tired and woozy. Her arms felt weightless, and the sounds around her decreased in volume as the surrounding darkness enveloped her. Whatever had seemed so important just minutes ago now sank into oblivion. She could hear a voice in some far off place, the thick syllables dancing through what felt like musical notes in a dream, but the words made no sense to her.

It was all going to shit. Was anyone else still painting?

There were sounds of a commotion all around, everyone seemed to be fighting their own battles.

Dale continued rubbing paint over the wall with the torn sleeve of his hoody, but couldn't shake the feeling that he was just going over the same ground. That was the problem with painting in the dark. He decided to stop and try to use the lighter again. It was the only way they would be able to tell which parts of the room still needed attention.

He struck the wheel. There was a flash, but it didn't last long enough for his eyes to drink in anything of value. He thumbed the wheel again and again, not allowing the smallest detectable break in the mini-shower of sparks cascading to the ground. A stray spark leapt onto the back of his hand and stuck there for a second, searing the flesh, before he could brush it away.

Then, suddenly and unexpectedly, the flame caught and for a few stolen moments he could see. It was like opening his eyes for the first time. The first thing his brain registered was Machen sitting on the floor, a look of dumb confusion on his face. Dale shouted at him to get up. They'd all agreed that under no circumstances should anyone raise their voice, but he figured he was allowed one transgression. Rolly was still hard at it on the far wall, working with the vigour of a man half his age. To his delight, Dale's quick evaluation concluded that they were almost done obscuring all the symbols.

Then his eyes settled on Lucy, standing motionless in the centre of the room with her head bowed. Bizarrely, she seemed a few inches taller than normal. The top of her head was usually level with Dale's shoulder, but now she could rest her chin there if she wanted. He thought she must be standing on something, or perhaps the uneven floor in this place was higher on one side of the room than the other. But when he looked down, he saw that her feet were off the ground. She was hovering. Levitating. Then, she started talking.

"Hurry! They're here, waiting. I cannot keep them away much longer."

"Who's here?"

"The evil ones." It wasn't Lucy's voice. Her mouth was moving, but the voice coming out was softer than hers, more timid. Furthermore, this voice spoke in a flawless local accent, the words rising and falling in pitch.

"You're not Lucy," Dale said, his voice quivering. "Who are you?"

"You already know who I am," said the thing that wasn't Lucy. "My name is Elizabeth."

"What are you doing to my friend?"

"Protecting her."

"From what?"

"The others. They want to possess this shell. Yours, too. All of you."

"Why do they want to possess her... us?"

"They... They wish that you can take them away from this place. They have been bound here so long."

"Where do they want to go?"

"Anywhere but here."

"They want to use us as vehicles?"

"Like ships..." The thing that wasn't Lucy appeared to be having great difficulty forming words, her voice now breathless and rasping. "Hurry, finish your work. Trap them here."

"We're trying. What else can we do?"

"Ceiling."

"She's right," said Machen from his position on the floor. "Everything's covered up now, like. Except the ceiling. That's all still full of scribbles."

The lighter died again, and Dale threw it to the floor in frustration. He stretched, but the ceiling was just out of his reach. The distance could be made up if he jumped but that wouldn't be a very effective method of painting. Plus, he was unsure what would happen if somebody his size started jumping up and down in a subterranean chamber. He might cause a collapse.

Then he had an idea.

He felt about with his hands until he located the altar, and climbed on top of it, holding his hands out at his sides to help get his balance.

"Pass me some paint and a brush!" he shouted.

Someone thrust a paint brush at his stomach. Dale grabbed it, then flailed around until he felt a tin of paint someone was holding up. "Rolly, Machen, keep trying to make those lighters work!"

In the harsh light of the sparks, Dale dipped the brush in the tin then immediately threw his arm over his head. For one surreal moment, he felt like a rock star pumping a fist into the air on a stage before thousands of salivating fans. Then he sent his arm slashing in a diagonal motion. The action must have been like a strike to the heart of the beast, as there was an almost audible groan from the massed ranks of shadows lurking all around them and the house itself seemed to sigh deeply.

He dipped the brush again, adjusted his position slightly, then attacked a different part of the ceiling. If the strings of letters and symbols were a physical representation of an incantation of some kind, the most effective way of breaking the spell would be to disrupt the continuity.

Dale began to move his arm in huge, all-encompassing strokes. Up and down, left and right. His shoulder ached and white hot bolts of pain shot through his back and neck from the effort. More than once, he felt something touch him, something of very little physical substance. Whatever it was made his skin crawl.

When the tin of paint he was using was empty, he dropped it to the floor and asked for another. Somebody immediately pushed a plastic handle into his hand. Dale could tell by its weight the second tin was almost empty. Also, it was smaller than the last, making it difficult to force the head of the brush into the sticky liquid near the bottom. When he raised his arm to start painting again, he just had to hope there was some paint on the brush.

While he worked, Rolly and Machen frantically strummed at their lighters and did a quick inventory, counting off the empty tins which were clattered noisily against a wall.

One, two, three, four, five, six, seven, eight...

That must mean...

"Is this the last tin?"

"We think so."

"Let's see where we are at, shall we?" Dale stopped painting, stepped off the altar and rested his hands on his knees. He was exhausted. He had an idea he might have actually ran out of paint a while ago, and since then had simply been rubbing a dry brush against the ceiling.

To his, and probably everyone else's surprise, Machen finally succeeded in lighting a candle and the tiny room was suddenly filled with a pale yellow glow.

Dale looked up hopefully. Apart from a few scattered spots where fragments of symbols were still visible, the ceiling was now covered in a hideous collage of colour.

He realised he hadn't heard a peep out of Lucy since her last outburst, which to him it felt like hours though it could have been no more than a few minutes. To his relief she was still standing in the centre of the room, and thankfully had seemed to have stopped levitating. "Lucy?"

"What?"

"Is that you?"

"Of course its me, stupe. Who d'ya think it is?"

The old Lucy was back! Which was just as well because if he took her back to Southampton with a Welsh accent, her family would kill him.

Rolly lit another candle. "And then there was light!" he said, with a somewhat belated theatrical flourish.

"Which makes it all the more impressive that he did everything else in the dark," snapped Lucy, proving she was indeed back to her old self and firing on all cylinders again.

As Dale examined their handiwork he saw that despite functioning blind and much of the time in a state of near-terror, as a group they'd performed admirably. The once-uniform stone grey walls were now adorned with garish streaks of paint. Red, white, green, blue. In places, two or more colours ran together or had been daubed over each to form a pleasant apricot colour. The entire room looked like a blown-up child's painting. The work wouldn't win any awards for artistic merit, though it could be an outside bet for some weird abstract piece. The important thing was, virtually no weird symbols were visible any more.

The fumes from the paint were dizzyingly strong in the confined space. All four of them were standing around the altar, which still took pride of place in the centre of the room, and all four suddenly realized this at the same time and retreated a few awkward steps back.

Rolly passed his candle to Machen and began rummaging through his plethora of pockets. He eventually pulled out Dale's notebook and began leafing through it. Then, apparently finding what he was looking for, he stooped to pick up one of the paint brushes that littered the floor.

"What are you doing now?" asked Dale, bewildered.

"Looking for some space," Rolly replied. Then, apparently finding one, began painting new symbols on an unbroken diagonal streak of white smeared on a wall, which was already beginning to dry.

"What are you doing? Stop!" Machen said, and made a movement toward the older man.

"Relax," Rolly said. "It's what they call a closing spell. A very powerful one, or so I am led to believe. As long as it stays here, it renders any other spell carried out on the grounds obsolete. Think of it as a kind of insurance policy."

"Where did you find it?" Lucy asked. "Has it been handed down through generations of custodians?"

"Not exactly," Rolly said with a wink. "I looked it up on the internet before the power went out."

Lucy looked at Dale, then back at Rolly. "Well, I guess that would be okay."

The old man smirked, "Thank you for allowing me to indulge myself, miss."

"Don't mention it," said Lucy. She then abruptly turned and without another word began scooting backwards through the tunnel. After her graceful exit, the others followed suit and began filing out of the tiny subterranean hovel.

Dale was the last to leave.

Chapter 38:

Epilogue

Five months after their first eventful stay at Sker House, Dale and Lucy returned unannounced one unseasonably sunny Saturday afternoon. At first glance, nothing much seemed to have changed. The building was just as large and imposing as ever, except there wasn't enough room to put the car in the car park any more. "Business must have picked up!" Dale said as he carefully manoeuvred into a tight space on the road outside.

"That's nice," Lucy giggled from the passenger seat. As she opened the door a ray of sunlight caught the diamond encrusted in the ring on her finger, making Dale's heart swell with pride. They walked hand-in-hand down the drive to the foyer, the front door of which stood open invitingly. The soft buzz of conversation came from inside. They had purposely arrived just before dinner so they could have one of Ruth's home-cooked meals, and were surprised to find the place already so lively.

To Dale's relief, the bar area was still intact. The only new addition to the décor seemed to be the framed magazine article hanging up behind the bar in such a position that it would attract the most attention. The two-page spread was blown up so big that even from some distance, the title and byline were plainly visible, superimposed over a breathtaking colour photo of Sker House set against a dramatic skyline filled with angry, bloated grey clouds:

Secrets of Sker, by Dale Morgan.

Original images and additional research by Lucy Kerr.

In the top left corner were two pictures of the authors.

The minute the issue of Solent News containing their article was published, Dale had sent down a couple of copies as a courtesy, and was glad to see that Machen approved. The published feature focused mainly on the macabre history of Sker rather than the 'other business.' Neither Dale nor Lucy had any great desire to recount any of the more recent bizarre happenings they were involved in, many of which Lucy took incredibly personally and would take a hell of a lot of explaining, anyway.

The couple weren't surprised to find Old Rolly sitting in his usual place reading a newspaper alone at a table in the corner. He had spotted them when they came in and watched them expectantly from a distance, the beginnings of a smile tugging on the corners of a mouth still mostly obscured by a tangled mass of white facial hair.

Lucy did a little squeal and rushed over to greet him, while Dale went to get the pre-dinner drinks. He planned to enjoy his only alcoholic beverage as much as he could. At the bar, he was surprised to find a sharp-featured but pleasant-looking middle-aged woman polishing glasses. "Yes, my lovely?" she said. "What can I get you?"

"Erm, a pint of lager and a large orange juice, please." As the woman turned away to get the order he added, "I was just wondering, where's Mr Machen, the landlord?"

"Mr Machen? Oh, you mean Mach. Don't call him mister, he says that's just for the..."

"Tax man," Dale finished. "We know."

The woman grinned. "Yes, that's right. You must be an old customer. He's just off seeing to something. Is there anything I can help you with? I'm his wife, Sandra."

Dale smiled.

At last! Irrefutable proof that the lady of the house is alive and well. There were more than a few moments when he and Lucy had imagined Machen had murdered her and buried her somewhere in the grounds.

"It's okay. I'm sure we'll catch up with him later."

As Sandra Machen handed over the drinks, she pressed a painted fingernail against her lower lip and said, "I recognise you from somewhere. Are you the journalists who wrote that article about us?"

Dale grinned. Did somebody just call him a journalist?

"You mean that one?" he asked, motioning at the framed picture. "If so, I guess we are."

"Then the drinks are on us. You know, after you published that article a couple of local newspapers picked up the story. Made quite a splash. We have copies ready for framing, but haven't got around to doing it yet. Things have been so busy lately, we haven't had time! A film crew from the Travel Channel is coming in next week to make a programme. Your article set the ball rolling, we can't thank you enough!"

"It was a pleasure," Dale said with his best 'aw shucks' shrug. "We're just glad more people have started coming here. You and your husband deserve it."

"Why, thank you for saying so," said Sandra, with a polite little curtsey.

"Thanks for the drinks."

Just then, Machen himself appeared. "Well, if it isn't our friendly journalists!" he said. Clean-shaven and sporting a new designer polo shirt, he looked a few pounds lighter and at least ten years younger. When he gave Dale a brief, brutal bear hug he noticed the landlord now smelled of aftershave rather than Jack Daniels. "I see you've met the missus, then!"

"Yes, I have," confirmed Dale.

Behind Machen trotted Champ the dog, who also seemed to be new and improved. There was a spring in his step and a sparkle in his eye that hadn't been there before. Tail beating at the air excitedly, he trotted over and rubbed his damp snout against Dale's hand. There was another squeal of delight from Rolly's table, and the dog scampered off to greet Lucy.

The whole atmosphere of Sker House seemed to have changed. The dark cloud that had previously settled over the property had lifted. Late autumn sunshine streamed through the windows, and Rolly was no longer drinking alone in the bar. A group of four men sat in a corner drinking beer and talking about sea fishing, a reserved-looking middle-aged couple were at the bar studying the menu, while a younger couple tried desperately to control their giggling, romper-suited toddler who seemed intent on climbing over as many tables and chairs as possible.

"Do Ruth and Izzy still work here?" Dale was eager to catch up with them on his visit. Although they hadn't been such an integral part of events as Old Rolly and Machen, he and Lucy both felt a strong bond with the mother-and-daughter team.

"Ruth does," Machen replied. "She's in the kitchen cooking as we speak. A bit busy, she is. We just pulled up some nice looking onions from the veg garden. I'm sure she'll get a move on with your dinner when she knows it's you two, like."

"Good to hear, but we don't mind waiting our turn. And Izzy?"

"Izzy's, gone," Machen said stiffly. "Worked here all over summer, saved up enough money to pass her driving test and buy a car, then went away to college, she did. Chepstow, I think. Just like that, like."

He didn't want to show the landlord whose displeasure was obvious, but Dale was secretly happy for the girl. It was difficult for the older generation to understand the calling of the young. He sometimes wondered if it was borne out of a kind of latent envy, a result of wishing they themselves could somehow have another chance. If he did have another shot at life in the modern technological age, maybe Machen himself would choose to move away and spend some time in a different part of the world. For a young girl like Izzy, growing up in a tiny, isolated place like Nottage couldn't be much fun.

"So will you be wanting a room, like? Or is it just dinner you're after?"

"Just dinner, I'm afraid," replied Dale. "We're on our way down to visit my parents for the weekend, then back to Southampton tomorrow night. Lucy's doing a post-grad course at uni, and I just started writing for a magazine in London. I love the job, but it's a long commute."

"Sorry to hear that. About the commute, I mean. But congratulations on the job. I would suggest having a little celebration, like. But I'm officially on the wagon now, as they say."

The landlord and his wife exchanged a look, leaving Dale in no doubt as to the origin of this drastic lifestyle change.

"Good for you," Dale said. "I couldn't, anyway. I'm driving."

"Well, another time." The regret was evident, but the man seemed a lot more composed now. Not to mention confident and controlled. The nervous ticks and awful habit of tripping over his words seemed to have vanished.

"Hey listen, while we have a minute..." Dale began, and then stopped. He had no idea how to proceed. He didn't want to bring buried memories to the surface and jeopardize this friendly reunion, but he had to know...

"What?" The landlord's eyes searched his.

"It seems more relaxed here. Lucy and I were both kinda wondering how things are now. I mean, has all that... stuff stopped happening?"

Machen looked perplexed. "What stuff?"

"The.... you know... noises? The Shadow People, the noises, the moods, the rest of the activity."

"Oh, that! Nah, nothing untoward has happened 'ere since the night of the storm and that bloody power cut. No complaints from the customers, either, and there's been a few. You know, the more I think about it, the more I wonder how much of that was all down to the boozing, see. Wasn't myself back then, I wasn't. You can ask anybody."

Dale didn't need to ask anybody. He was there. The landlord could be right, maybe spending all his time at Sker a long way from sobriety made his experience different, more intense. His being drunk wouldn't begin to explain the vast array of phenomena the rest of them experienced, but if that was how he justified it to himself, and it helped him reconcile certain things, so be it. Maybe he was trying to blame the demon booze for every negative in his life. And why not? At least it would help him stay away from it.

"Anyway," Machen said dismissively, "We had that trapdoor in the beer cellar blocked up. No need for anyone to go down there again. When we get around to it, we'll have them tunnels filled in, too. Permanently. They might lead to subsidence or something. Cost me a bloody fortune to put right, that would. Right now we're concentrating on getting that fourth floor finished. Get us up to full capacity, see. Looks like we're gonna need the extra rooms."

"Yeah," Dale agreed. "Sounds like a good idea. Your wife and I were just talking about how busy the place is. Its nice to see her back, by the way."

"It is, indeed. It was almost as if she knew when the... when things changed for the better. Like she sensed it. That was when she came back. Not two or three days after you left. Just turned up one afternoon with all her things in suitcases, she did."

"Women are more spiritual than us," Dale reasoned. "They just know stuff. Intuition, and all that."

"True enough. You know, looking back, I really can't remember much from the night of the storm. It's all a bit of a blur."

"Probably just as well."

307

The landlord chuckled, "True enough. Sometimes it's better not to know everything."

"Certainly is," Dale said as he picked up the drinks and started off toward the table Lucy had commandeered.

Later, when he thought about what Machen had said, he decided he was right. Sometimes, it's better not to know everything.

Sker House:

The Fact & the Fiction

The characters may be fictional, but many of the events described in this story are matters of historical record. Sker House and Sker beach are both very much real. I visited the place with my parents many times as a child, and remember being wowed by all the tales of ghosts and spooky occurrences. I first became aware of the Maid of Sker legend when I read about it in a book I picked up in a gift shop.

Wrecking was a grisly but all-too common practice along the treacherous Welsh coast (and elsewhere in the British Isles) and the tragic loss of the steamship S.S. Samtampa and the Mumbles lifeboat remains one of the worst disasters in British maritime history. The ghostly lights along the seafront, the phantom ship often spotted on the Black Rocks, the persecuted monks, and the myth of Kenfig pool, are all popular local legends. Skirrid Mountain Inn is another real location.

Everything else, I made up. Well, almost everything.

What follows is a revised version of an article I originally wrote for a now-defunct travel website. I hope it serves to help distinguish the fact from the fiction, adds another dimension to what you've just read, and highlights some key events in Welsh history we would do well to remember.

*

Croeso y Cymru, the sign says. Welcome to Wales, the lush green mountainous region in the south-west corner of the UK often referred to as God's Country on account of its staggering natural beauty. A mysterious land steeped in myth and legend, Wales is a land of magic, superstition, dragon slayers and fairy-lore, and consequently has more than its fair share of paranormal activity. There are regular sightings of ghosts, lake monsters, spectral black dogs (collectively known as the cwm annwn) and a steady stream of UFO sightings. Naturally, there are numerous supposedly haunted castles and houses.

Arguably one of the most infamous of these is the aptly-named Sker House, situated in Kenfig (or Cynffig to give it its Welsh spelling) on the rugged south coast near the town of Bridgend, Glamorgan. The Grade 1 listed building is widely regarded one of the most important historical sites in the country.

The main structure, now radically altered from its original form, is a huge detached rectangular building fashioned from local limestone and built on a north/south axis overlooking the beach. In its construction the building is unique in many ways, one of its most peculiar features being that until comparatively recently it had no main entrance. Instead, the front of the house was fitted with two symmetrical towers through which visitors could gain access, making it reminiscent of other, more gothic or arcane structures elsewhere in Europe.

The history of Sker House dates back almost a thousand years to when it was first built as a monastic grange to support Margam Abbey by monks of the Cistercian order, who made a living farming the surrounding land. After the dissolution of the monasteries, ownership of the estate changed hands several times in quick succession whilst remaining a refuge for renegade monks. In 1597, then-owner Jenkin Turberville, a staunch Roman Catholic, was allegedly tortured to death after being accused of promoting the 'Old Religion' in Glamorgan and in 1679, Saint Philip Evans was hung, drawn and quartered in Cardiff after being arrested at Sker House. Many dignitaries and prominent historical figures have spent time there, and visitors once travelled from far and wide to marvel at its spectral beauty.

Over the years, witnesses have reported seeing shadowy cloaked figures on the grounds and hearing high-pitched screams and wails, and it's not unusual for visitors to experience feelings of crushing dread upon entering the residence. There have also been reports of poltergeist activity.

As time marched relentlessly on, the estate passed through numerous different owners. Although in a prime location surrounded by vast swathes of arable land, Sker House seemed forever blighted by misfortune. As much as each successive new owner tried, they simply couldn't make a success of things. In the 18th century, it fell into the possession of its most famous landlord, Isaac Williams (1727-1766), whose daughter, Elizabeth, swiftly passed into legend as the original Maid of Sker. How much truth is in the tale will always be a matter of conjecture, but popular local folklore maintains that a young and beautiful Elizabeth fell in love with a local harpist called Thomas Evans. Isaac strictly forbade the prospective match and imprisoned his daughter in the house until she reluctantly agreed to marry a wealthy local man by the name of Thomas Kirkhouse instead.

It was a marriage of convenience, with both families hoping to benefit financially from the union. However, Elizabeth pined for her true love, so much so that she fell ill and died at a tragically young age. Some versions of the story claim that she died of a broken heart, others that she starved herself to death. It has also been suggested that she was murdered by either her father or husband, who then concocted a ghost story to frighten locals into not asking too many questions. It is said that her ghost can still be seen gazing forlornly out of an upstairs window of Sker House, waiting in vain for her true love. At one time, the sightings were so frequent that many locals refused to believe that Elizabeth was even dead. For his part, the spurned Thomas Evans is credited with writing a folk song in Elizabeth's honour called Y Perch or Sker.

His role in the creation of the Maid of Sker legend was not the only contribution Isaac Williams made to the long, tragic history of Sker House. During the Industrial Revolution, the Bristol Channel, the stretch of water it overlooked, was one of the busiest waterways in the world carrying a steady stream of vessels between Britain and the Continent. It was also one of the most perilous. As well as the strong currents and ever-shifting hidden sandbanks, just off the coast lies what is known locally as Sker point (otherwise known as the Black Rocks) submerged ranks of sharp rocks jutting up from the seabed that can literally tear ships to pieces. At that time, smuggling and looting were considered legitimate enterprises, and shipwrecks were so common in the area that they were seldom investigated in detail.

Local landowners routinely claimed 'Right of the wreck', whereby they were legally free to salvage whatever 'lost' cargo washed up on their property. Some less scrupulous locals were said to engage in the sinister practice of wrecking – deliberately luring ships to their doom. Traditionally, this was done at night by tying lanterns to cattle or grazing sheep and leading them along the seafront. From a distance, especially to unfamiliar eyes in bad weather, the lights would look like those of ships lying safely at anchor. A cautionary tale often told is that of the Welsh wrecker who helped lure a passing ship onto rocks, killing everyone on board. While he busied himself looting the ship's cargo, the bodies of the unfortunate passengers and crew were brought ashore for burial. Only then did the wrecker see the body of his own son who was returning home unexpectedly after a long voyage.

A pivotal event not just in the history of Sker, but in the practice of wrecking as a whole, occurred on December 17th 1753, when the French merchant ship Le Vainqueur was en route from Portugal when she struck Sker Point. It is generally held that Isaac Williams and his cohorts were responsible for the wrecking. No sooner had the ship hit the rocks, impoverished locals and respected nobility alike descended on the wreck and plundered it for all it was worth, stealing her cargo of fruit, rifling the bodies of dead sailors, and even setting fire to what was left of the ship in order to recover the iron nails that had once held it together. The Orangery at nearby Margam Abbey was supposedly built to house orange trees recovered from the doomed ship.

Due to the delicate diplomatic relations between Britain and France at the time, the fate of Le Vainqueur was treated as a serious international incident. In the aftermath, no less than 17 people were arrested, including Isaac Williams himself, who was then an influential local magistrate. When questioned, he claimed to have placed goods from the wreck found in the cellar of Sker House there for safekeeping. Remarkably, he never went to trial, but his reputation was tainted forever and he died a ruined man. Of those who did go to trial, one man wasn't so lucky and was hanged by the Crown to set an example to others and reiterate new government guidelines proclaiming that, 'Looting wrecks was punishable by death.'

In the years since wrecking was abolished, countless witnesses claim to have seen ghostly ships out at sea off Sker. Also frequently spotted are orb-like anomalies flickering on the barren sandbanks and hillsides of the area and a single, solitary light hovering over Sker Point. Locally, this is taken to be a prelude to bad weather, but is eerily reminiscent of the much-feared Canwyll Corph, or Corpse Candle, prominent elsewhere in Welsh folklore. The Corpse Candles were disembodied lights appearing in the vicinity of someone who faced imminent death, the size and brightness of the light directly proportionate to the age of the victim. Sometimes, one could see a grinning skull in the soft glow, and several tales exist whereby terrified witnesses saw their own faces, or those of loved ones. When seen on open ground, the Canwyll Corph are said to follow the exact route of the victim's funeral procession, which intriguingly ties in neatly with yet another popular legend of Sker.

One night early in the 19th century, a local man was returning home from work. His path took him along the beach, where out on the Black Rocks he saw the shimmering wreck of a huge ship. As he watched, a small group of translucent figures waded out to the vessel and carried something ashore. The man couldn't see what the object was, but guessed from its size and shape that it was a coffin. Fascinated, he followed the ghostly procession into town where, to his horror, it stopped outside his own house and vanished. A week later, a vessel was wrecked off the coast of Sker and among the dead was the man's brother. When his body was recovered and taken back to the family home, the funeral procession took exactly the same route as the ghostly one he had witnessed.

Though the fate of the Le Vainqueur effectively put an end to the grisly practice of wrecking around Sker, the tragedies kept on coming. In 1947 the 7,200-tone US Liberty Ship Samtampa, constructed in Portland, Maine during WWII and carrying a cargo of crude oil, ran aground on Sker Point during a storm with the loss of all 39 passengers and crew. A lifeboat, Edward, Prince of Wales, was dispatched from nearby Mumbles, but the conditions and sheer amount of oil leaking from the wreck made rescue impossible. Witnesses later said the sea around Sker Point was black like molten tar. The lifeboat was also smashed against the rocks, killing all eight volunteers. The crews of both vessels were buried at nearby Nottage cemetery, and hardened lumps of black tar were still being washed up on the beach at Sker half a century later.

By this time, Sker House had been abandoned for many years and lay derelict. It was officially declared an unsafe building in the late 1970's. Twenty years later, an expansive refurbishment project was undertaken to restore the house to something approaching its former glory. It is still standing today, a living testament to its own macabre past. Since 2003 it has been privately owned, but its current owners rarely welcome curious visitors.

However, much of the surrounding land remains public property, and a footpath runs alongside the house down to the dunes which line the beach. It is there that if you are very lucky, you may catch a glimpse of the ghostly wrecker's lights, or even a passing ghost ship.

Many thanks for reading.

Please consider leaving a review on Amazon or Goodreads!

Also by C.M. Saunders:

Novels / Novellas:

Devil's Island (Rainstorm Press)
Out of Time (DeadPixel Publications)
Sker House (DeadPixel Publications)
No Man's Land: Horror in the Trenches (Deviant Dolls Publications)
Apartment 14F: An Oriental Ghost Story - Uncut (Deviant Dolls Publications)
Human Waste (Deviant Dolls Publications)
Dead of Night – Uncut (Deviant Dolls Publications)
Tethered (Terror Tract Publishing)

Collections:

X: A Collection of Horror (DeadPixel Publications)
X2: Another Collection of Horror (DeadPixel Publications)
X SAMPLE (Deviant Dolls Publications)
X3 (Deviant Dolls Publications)
X: Omnibus

Feel free to connect on Twitter:

@CMSaunders01

Facebook:

https://www.facebook.com/CMSaunders01/

Or visit my website:

https://cmsaunders.wordpress.com/

Tethered

Out now on Terror Tract Publishing!

Craig, a journalism graduate trying desperately to get a foothold in a fading industry, is going nowhere fast. While searching for a project to occupy himself, he stumbles across a blog written by a girl called Kami about internet rituals - challenges undertaken by those seeking to make contact with ghosts or other supernatural entities.

Craig becomes obsessed, and when Kami suddenly disappears he goes in search of her. From there he is powerless to prevent his life spiralling out of control as he is drawn deeper and deeper into a dark, dangerous world where nothing is quite what it seems, a world populated not just by urban myths and hearsay, but by real-life killers.

He thinks he is in control, but nothing can be further from the truth.

Coming Soon…

BACK FROM THE DEAD

A Collection of Zombie Fiction

By C.M. Saunders

Including the previously-unpublished novellette

'The Plague Pit.'

Printed in Great Britain
by Amazon

13218496R00183

ATi Book Club 1/23